CW00506117

The Room Within the Wall

L. J. Hutton

ISBN 9781792915932

Published by Wylfheort Books 2014

Acknowledgements

Once again I have to thank my two *beta* readers, Karen Murray and Teresa Fairhurst (now an author herself writing as M. T. Fairhurst) for their continued support, and invaluable suggestions and criticisms. Every author needs to know where they've slipped up as well as getting encouragement, and without them this book would have been the poorer.

I would also like to thank other friends and collegaues who have read parts or the whole book, and who have put up with me talking about it at length. And of course I have to credit my husband with putting up with my long absences from the real world whilst glued to the keyboard.

My lovely lurchers have again kept me company – Minnie and Blue, and our new addition Belle, who came towards the end of the process when our lovely deerhound lurcher Raffles passed on. Evesham Greyhound and Lurcher Rescue have my eternal gratitude for saving such wonderful dogs, and letting them come to live with us.

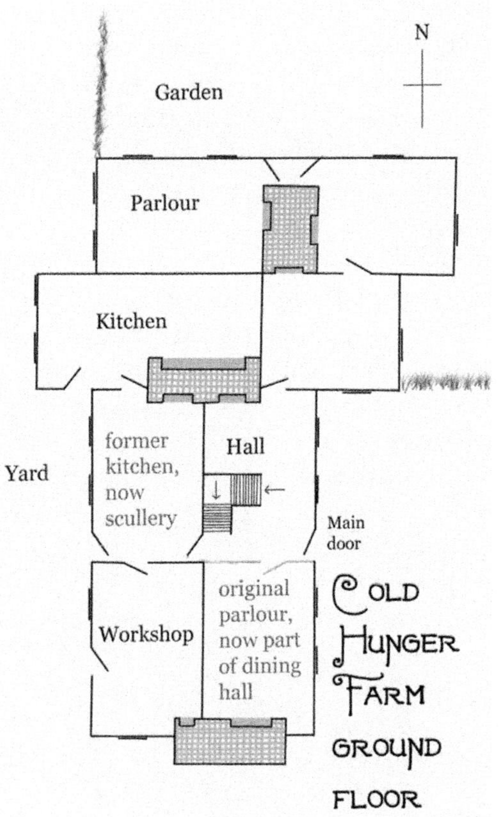
N
Garden
Parlour
Kitchen
Yard
former kitchen, now scullery
Hall
Main door
Workshop
original parlour, now part of dining hall
COLD HUNGER FARM
GROUND FLOOR

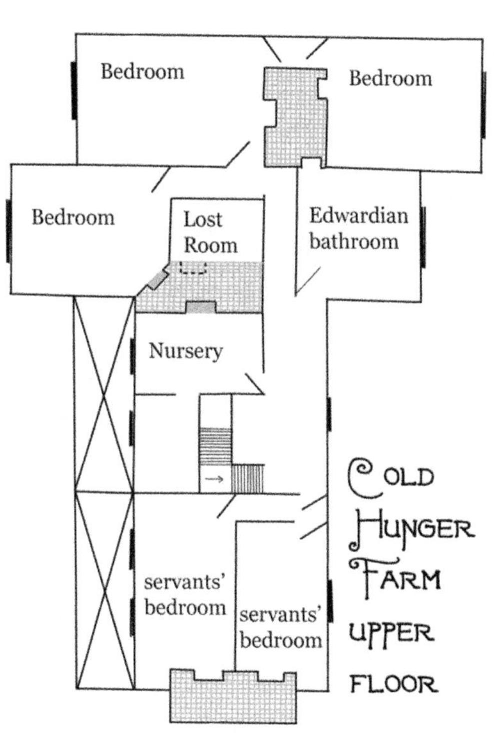
Bedroom
Bedroom
Bedroom
Lost
Room
Edwardian
bathroom
Nursery
servants'
bedroom
servants'
bedroom
Cold
Hunger
Farm
upper
floor

Prologue

Near Talavera, central Spain: July 1809

As the army camped amongst the cork groves by the Alberche River, Major Young signalled Sergeant MacDonald over to him.

"I'm assigning Lieutenant Clifford to you." Technically it would be the new lieutenant who would be in charge, but both Young and MacDonald, and the men under them, knew that the veteran sergeant was the man holding things together in practice. Clifford was as raw as it was possible to get, since he and the other new lieutenant had been hurried forward to catch up with the Huntingdonshire regiment, having come straight off the ship at Lisbon from England.

MacDonald looked down from his considerable height at the diminutive major and grimaced. They'd been fighting alongside one another for long enough now for the sergeant to have considerable leeway with his senior officer when it came to speaking his mind. Now, for all that he'd not said a word, Major Young knew MacDonald was unhappy with the situation. Dropping his voice so that others wouldn't hear, Young became less formal.

"I know George, I know, but I've got to put them *somewhere.*" He turned his gaze to the two newest additions to the officers' ranks, where they sat by a camp fire being addressed by Captain Knowles. The first was a lad of medium height with dark hair and the kind of good looks which would lead him astray – if they hadn't already. He was chattering happily to the captain, whereas the second young man was silent and solemn. Young sighed but turned back to his friend. "Wellesley is planning a dawn attack tomorrow, but on the bright side, we outnumber the French, so as battles go this is probably as good as it's ever going to get to have a useless pair like that with us."

MacDonald sniffed. "Aye. I ken that that right enough. But could I no' have the other laddie?"

"You want Green?" Young was surprised. "Why?"

"Well I'd no' go as far as to say 'want'," MacDonald clarified, "but o' the two I'd rather the tall gangly lad. I mean, look at him. Aye he's scared to death at the thought of a proper fight – look at the way his leg canna keep still – but mebbe that just shows he has some brains. And he's listening to the captain like his life depends on it – which it very well might! Whereas his pal is all mouth and no ears!"

"His pal?" How MacDonald came by such information in such a short space of time was an endless mystery to Young, but time and again the sergeant's information proved to be correct.

Now MacDonald was nodding sagely. "Oh aye. I understand that they didn'a just join up at the same time. They knew one another afore then. Both lads from the Midlands over by the Welsh borders, I'm told. Young Clifford is the son of a minor son, of a minor son, of one o' they big families over there. He's no-one in particular, you understand, but he wants to think he is!"

"And Green? What's his family?"

"Och, he's the second son of a poor parson. Only got the commission 'cause a maternal uncle wanted to be able to say he had someone fighting the French, and poor wee Green was the one lad they had spare to send. Anyways, those two met at school in Worcester I'm told – Green being there on account of his father being in the kirk, and on what you might call charity." MacDonald paused and scratched his nose as he looked again at the two lieutenants. "I'll tell you what, though, ...young Green might not have two ha'pennies to rub together, but he's been right sensible with what he's been paid so far. Whereas that spoilt wee brat Clifford has already gone through what his father sent him out with, and is already trying to borrow money wherever he can."

Young sighed. He could see why MacDonald would want Green now, and not just because of his Scottish sensibilities when it came to money. The young man might just turn out to be a good soldier if he was here because it was the only chance he would ever have to make something of his life.

"But that means I'll have to put Clifford with Sergeant Hobspawn." He hadn't realised he'd said the last thought out loud until MacDonald replied,

"Aye, but think on it this way. Hobspawn's unlikely to ruin young Clifford since he's most of the way there already. Whereas it would be a shame to have him corrupt Green or teach him bad ways."

Hobspawn was the kind of sergeant who got the army a bad name. Bent as a butcher's hook, there wasn't a scheme or dirty deal he didn't have a hand in, and worse, he was a bully. The young gentlemen who came within the orbit of his twisted power inevitably seemed to come to rely on him to run the platoon, never quite seeing that he was also gaining power over them too. The sensible ones came to fear him and moved on as fast as they could. The others got drawn into his blackmailing schemes and petty thefts until they no longer knew wrong from right. However, the depths of his minor crimes seemed forever to be obscured from the sight of those with enough power to do something to stop him. Even Major Young's hands were tied, since he only knew about things via Sergeant

MacDonald, and that brought it down to one sergeant's word against another. And with Hobspawn having a malevolent hold over at least three senior officers in the regiment that Young and MacDonald knew of for certain, if it came to an official enquiry they both knew they would lose.

So Young nodded. "Yes, I see what you mean. The least we can do is deny Hobspawn the better of the two. Thank you, George. I'll go and tell them now."

"In which case I'll come and get young Green and introduce him to the men. He's no' one for drinking the evening away with the other young gentlemen, I'm told, so it's mebbe better if he doesn't just slink off to his tent leaving them laughing at him behind his back."

Four days later MacDonald was glad he'd made his choice. Harry Green might not have experience but he was steady, and as events on the bank of the Alberche River all went to hell in a handcart, Green stuck by MacDonald and his men, and did as good a job as any novice officer could be expected to do at leading by example. By mid afternoon on the 27th the Huntingdons were amongst the men under General Mackenzie's command covering the retreat of General Cuesta and his Spanish troops; yet the French came on hard and fast before Mackenzie's battalions could withdraw themselves. The fighting was as hard as any Major Young had seen – so much for an easy fight to blood the young officers with! And although the retreat back to Talavera was orderly, his men were taking an awful beating. Hard pressed to see what was happening at first amongst the trees, and with the smoke from the guns shrouding everything, Young had only spotted MacDonald and his men as they'd emerged onto the plain. MacDonald and

Green made a good pair, both head and shoulders taller than many of the rank and file, and they were easily picked out by that despite the chaos. The sergeant and young lieutenant's men were working in two ranks, the first firing and then retreating as the second fired, and then were themselves covered by the first firing again. Only when they had at last reached Talavera did Young discover that young Clifford and the dreadful Hobspawn had survived too.

As the battered survivors of the Huntingdons regrouped at Talavera, excluded from the greater battle being fought outside of the town on the following day on account of their casualties, MacDonald and Young at last had a chance to speak alone once more.

"Green looked as though he was doing well," Young observed, as MacDonald collected together the belongings of those who had died.

"Aye, the lad's no' wanting for courage. And no' of the idiot kind either!" Neither of them had much time for the fools who sauntered into battle too stupid to be scared stiff. Then MacDonald sniffed and glanced about him to make sure his next words weren't about to be overheard. "And I'm right glad I had Harry Green wi' me, because that wee bastard Hobspawn was the first to get to the back of our ranks."

"He fled?" Young had seen no sign of that, but then that wasn't surprising in the confusion. However to flee from the enemy was a grave accusation to make against any man.

MacDonald gave another derisive sniff. "Och, I'm no' saying the little shit ran – although God knows I wish he had and been seen doing it! No, he's too canny for that. But he did make sure he and his stayed right at the very back of our ranks all the way back to Talavera. Never once did I see him at the fore and facing the enemy. And I'll tell ye' something else. For all that wee rat Clifford was spouting off about not being able to wait for his chance to fight the enemy, Dougie MacLean says that he was egging Hobspawn on to get them out of there."

Dougie was another friend of MacDonald's and a fellow sergeant, but with the 88th Foot who had been fighting alongside the Huntingdons.

"Did Dougie hear this himself?"

"Aye, but like me he canna accuse Hobspawn since none but him and his men heard anything. But you watch out for yon Clifford – he's hungry for the trappings of victory, but if I'm any judge of character he's a coward and he's crafty! As sure as I'm a Scotsman, he'll be quick to shift any blame that's owing to anywhere but on him. I can keep an eye on Green for as long as I'm spared, but you need to watch for Clifford ingratiating himself with some of the other young gentlemen – especially not of our regiment."

Young knew what he was implying. It would do the regiment no good if one of their own was caught up in some scandal. Not that the young gentlemen of any regiment could be described as being of a saintly persuasion, but there was a difference between the inevitable gambling debts and the like, and something worse like blackmail or active accusations of cowardice in the face of the enemy. Edward Clifford had only been with them less than a month and already he was starting to look like trouble. And once again MacDonald had been right. Putting Harry Green with him instead of the dreadful Hobspawn, and letting Edward Clifford show his true colours this early on meant that now Young had his worst troublemakers in one platoon.

Over in another part of the camp Edward was making his own case to Harry.

"Come on, old man, just lend me the money won't you?"

Harry sighed and wondered for the umpteenth time how Edward could not understand that he had none. "Edward, I don't *have* any money," he told him emphatically. "My father didn't send me out with any funds, as you know full well. Don't you remember how when we got to London I couldn't come out on the town with you before we sailed? You were quick enough to taunt me about my lack of cash then, as I recall."

But Edward wasn't even listening now. "But your benefactor must have given you *something*!" he protested. "Come on Harry, give it up, there's a good chap!"

"I can't give you what I haven't got," Harry replied firmly. "And anyway, instead of getting into another card game you can't afford to lose, what about writing to Amy?"

"What?" Edward had suddenly spied a young lieutenant in the 88th whom they'd travelled out with, and was wondering if he could be strong-armed into parting with some cash.

"Amy! Have you written to her?"

"Oh for God's sake, Harry! We just survived being slaughtered by the French and you want me to start penning verses to a simpering girl?"

Harry ground his teeth. "Except she's not just some simpering girl you met once or twice, is she, Edward? She's the girl you're going to marry! The girl you took me to meet, telling me she was the finest girl in all of Worcestershire. The sweetest, prettiest girl you'd ever known, that's what you said."

Edward waved an airy hand of dismissal over Amy. "Yes, well, that was before I'd seen a bit more of the world."

"That's as maybe," Harry snapped, "but are you going

to write to your father and tell him that you're breaking off the engagement he was so keen for you to make?" That normally brought Edward to heel. Any thought that might lead to his father cutting back on the money he sent, or God forbid, stopping it altogether, was usually a way to get Edward's attention. "How do you think he will feel if Amy's father tells him she's read the accounts of this battle in the newspapers and yet hasn't heard if you're dead or alive? Come to that, what if *he* presumes you're dead?" That really was pushing Edward hard, but to Harry's amazement Edward's mind was still flitting so wildly between the shock of how bloody a battle could get, and his craving for more money to go out drinking and whoring with, that the words barely sank in.

"Oh very well, I shall write to them tonight. Now be a good fellow and leave me be. I must go and have a word with young Lieutenant Crawford."

As Edward strode away Harry knew his words had already been forgotten. Sighing, he turned for the tent where his things were stowed and braced himself for the task of writing the letters that Edward wouldn't. Mr Clifford was a crabby old bastard who wouldn't mourn the passing of his son, only the lost business opportunities, and the chance to tie Amy Vaughan's father financially deeper via her into the industrial empire he was building in the counties along the Welsh Borders. But Amy herself merited a good deal more consideration, Harry thought. She had turned out to be everything the then smitten Edward had said she was, and Harry had found himself feeling deeply envious of his friend for the first time in his life.

He would still lie awake at night wishing that it was him Amy looked to with such devotion and adoration, but in comparison with the handsome and elegant Edward, Harry knew he was as plain and gawky as any eighteen year old could possibly be. If Edward seemed older than his years, and could fake a sophistication he was working on acquiring for real, Harry knew that in social situations he had two left feet when it came to dancing, and became tongue-tied and incoherent whenever a girl came near. Yet the one thing he could do for the object of what would probably be his eternally unrequited love was to write that letter. The one which would allay her fears that Edward lay dead on the battlefield. But he mustn't write a word of criticism of Edward. That might smack of envy in Amy's eyes, for she was bound to think that Edward was being successful over here. How could he not be, she would believe? And so Harry gritted his teeth once more and forced himself to make the written excuse that Edward was already being singled out for more duties, and had begged him to write on his behalf.

Chapter 1

Monday and Tuesday, modern day Worcestershire.

"Where on earth is this place?" Nick, the driver, muttered impatiently.

The minibus full of archaeologists was wending its way down cramped lanes, seemingly getting nowhere fast. Pip turned the map around and squinted at it as best she could as the minibus lurched drunkenly over yet another pothole.

"When you come to the T-junction go right and then immediately left," she told him.

Nick sniffed. "Are you sure?"

"You want Phil to take over navigating again?"

With the map in Phil's hands they'd been back into Clifton-upon-Teme three times already, and given that Tim as the only other male on board had admitted he could get lost outside his own front door, male egos had given way and Pip had moved into the front seat and taken charge of the map.

"Yes I am sure," she riposted with mock exasperation and a theatrical rolling of her eyes to the other female archaeologists in the back. "If you do that then slow down, the driveway should be somewhere on your right after we've gone over a tiny bridge. There'll be a thin strip of trees to our right by the bridge, but then the house we're looking for is by the bigger plantation of trees after them."

"Over the bridge and then right," muttered Nick, flipping a finger at the driver of a sleek BMW which came tearing round the corner at them in the middle of the road, just as they were about to pull out at the T-junction. "Bloody hell! How much more of the road does he want?"

"Hey! There's the ruined church we were told to look out for!" called Chloe from the back. "It's over in the field on our left!"

"Go left!" Gemma chimed in, female solidarity right behind Pip for showing she knew what she was doing.

"I *am* going bloody left!" grumbled Nick, but with a hint of a grateful grin flashed briefly in Pip's direction.

The road narrowed to a single carriageway again after the crossroad and the banks alongside it began to rise.

"Wow!" Tim breathed. "A real medieval holloway! Cool!" It was certainly atmospheric even on a fairly bright day like today, making those on board feel as though they were going deeper into the earth than the road would have suggested. At the bottom, trees virtually encased the road.

"Bridge!" Gemma yelped, as they passed a pretty white cottage set just back from the road. "I saw it! There was a tiny bridge where those railings were!"

"That's the one!" Pip confirmed.

The minibus' engine began protesting again as the climb up from the stream got steeper, and Nick asked, "Nearly there yet?"

"Just at the top of this rise," Pip answered confidently as the gloom of the overhanging holloway disappeared.

The driveway appeared suddenly as little more than a hole in the hedgerow, and Nick struggled to get the minibus to make the turn.

"Well the first thing I'm doing is pulling out those two rotten gateposts!" he declared. "They're doing bugger all, and did you see the size of those nails sticking out of them? We'll have all sorts of medals down the sides of the bus by the time the dig's done if we leave them there!"

The minibus bumped along a roughly made track, which looked for all the world as though the stones grubbed out of various fields had simply been dumped on it by the resident farmers, and then ground in by the weight of tractors passing over them. Not that you could have got a modern machine down here. This had been built with carts in mind and never widened. Passing alongside the wood Pip had mentioned, they crested the small rise, and then as the land suddenly fell away on the far side, the track jigged back to the right into the wood. As they began to go downhill again towards the way they'd come from, suddenly they found themselves emerging into an open space which turned out to be the yard in front of Cold Hunger Farm.

"Jesus! What a gloomy old hole!" Gemma exclaimed. "Who on earth would want to live here?"

"It's no wonder no-one knew it was here," agreed Tim. "Blimey, you can forgive the county planners for missing this one when they put some of the other buildings round here on the listed buildings schedule."

In comparison to several other cherished old buildings in the vicinity, Cold Hunger Farm was neglected and uninhabited. It had only been brought to the county council's attention by a wealthy business man, who had spotted it as he flew over it and now wanted to buy it. However, since any existing current owners could not be traced, it had offered up a prime chance for a team of archaeologists to go in and make a full investigation of the place, and to the council's delight the rich industrialist had been only to happy to fund the team. No doubt it was a pittance in comparison to what he intended to spend on the place, and there was always the potential of having something interesting turn up for him to show his guests at a later date.

"Why would this rich bloke want to live here?" Chloe wondered. "Surely he could have some swanky new-build if he wanted it?"

"Oh you're not thinking creatively, hon'," Pip teased. "Those trees at the back will come down and be replaced by a patio and a jacuzzi, with uninterrupted views back down into the valley. This high up I bet he'll be almost able to see Wolferlow Court up the valley if he prunes enough back – and you know how pretty that is!" The court was a tourist board's dream of a place even if it was privately owned, half-timbered and even with the nicety of its own oast house in the farm yard. A perfect view of one of the best building Herefordshire could offer was not to be lightly dismissed! "They'll probably even have a summer house built that's nearly the size of the house! And don't forget the industrial sized barbecue on the lawn for all those 'nice' parties."

"Silly me!" snorted Chloe derisively, "how could I have forgotten!"

"Oh how the other half live!" Gemma sighed, looking down at her battered Doc Marten boots which were in desperate need of replacement, and on what they were being paid for this venture would have to do a bit longer too. Funding didn't run to paying the archaeologists much, and Chloe, Tim, and the three other members of the team who would be coming tomorrow, were volunteers on summer vacation from university archaeology courses.

"Right, let's get the gear out and have a mooch round," Nick declared, although officially Phil was the one in charge as the representative of the county archaeologist. But in these straitened times he had several projects on the go, and on the ground it would be Nick who would be running things. For that Pip was heartily grateful. She'd worked with both men before, and for all his grumbling, found Nick by far the easier to be around. Phil stood on his dignity a bit too much to be a comfortable colleague, but was also as prickly as a hedgehog around Nick, seeing Nick's greater experience and expertise as an archaeologist as some kind of personal affront.

"I shall go and open up," Phil declared haughtily, disembarking first, earning himself some black looks at his departing back for shirking his part in the lugging of shovels and buckets, and all the other bits and pieces which went with a dig.

"Place hardly needs opening up," Tim muttered darkly. "The bloody front door looks like it doesn't know what a Yale lock is!"

"Now, now!" Pip chuckled. "You know he'll strain his back if he has to carry the finds bags in!" Then throwing the light pack of tiny plastic bags out of the back of the bus to him.

As she walked towards the front door with a pile of plastic trays into which any finds would be placed, Pip could see how damp the overhanging trees made the path. Moss and lichens grew on many of the flagstones making them slippery, and there was a musty air about the place. She looked up to the roof tiles and noted that many of them were moss encrusted too.

"It's amazing that this place hasn't fallen down," she thought aloud, and heard Chloe behind her say,

"I bet it's as damp as hell inside."

"The chimneys look pretty sturdy, though," Tim observed optimistically as he strode past on his long legs.

"Well there's no shortage of wood for fires," Pip added. "I reckon we could get fires going in a couple of the grates. That would make it a bit more pleasant to work in – especially if it starts raining again and we need to have somewhere to dry out." It had been a thoroughly soggy summer so far. "Just don't suggest it until Phil's gone! If you do he'll assume we're going to sit around the damned thing all day toasting crumpets instead of working."

"What is it with that man that he always assumes the worst," sighed Gemma, who like Pip, knew Phil of old.

"I don't know," Pip confessed, "but I'm afraid I don't have the energy or inclination to tackle him over it. What I know of Phil is as much as I ever wish to know. Let's just try not to wind him up for the rest of today, and then he'll go away happy and leave us to get on with things."

Walking in through the front door, she had to peer even harder in the gloom to see where she was going. She was in what must have once been the main entrance hall, with a dining area off to her left and the main stairs to her right. The stairs looked interesting, she noted, or at least in this light they might be. What they'd turn out to be when she got a better look with a flashlight was still in doubt.

"In here," Nick's voice called from the room ahead of her, and shouldering her way in past the next door, Pip found herself in a surprisingly pleasant old kitchen, although centuries of spiders had left their webs dangling from every possible angle. "No running water by the looks of things, though. Seems we might be using that!" And he gestured out through the window to the other end of the yard where an antiquated pump stood in isolated splendour.

Pip went and peered out of the rippled old glass. "You know, that might even be safe to use. The OS map says there's a natural spring here. I wonder if that's what feeds the pump?"

"I think we'll still boil the water to be on the safe side," Gemma said firmly. "I've no wish to get sick and then find I've been drinking diluted sheep shit!"

"You're such a cynic!" Pip sighed but with a laugh.

However, it turned out that this was merely a huge scullery, and the room to the right of it was a more recent kitchen – not that it could have been called modern by anyone's standards. Here there was not only running water, but also the means of heating it by an antiquated range with a boiler at its side.

"I'd guess that other room was the original kitchen when the first house was built," mused Nick. "Then when the extension was built – or was even done in two phases – then the old kitchen got relegated to a kind of glorified boot room. The place where the farm workers with their muddy boots would come in to speak to whoever was in charge, and where any grubby work was done."

"I bet a few lambs have been nursed by that old grate, too," Pip added thoughtfully. "It's just the right sort of place for that."

They weren't about to start lighting either fire just yet, though, but the water was crisp and clear when the stop-tap had been found and turned back on and allowed to run through for a bit, and with a brew-up on the primus stove they'd brought with them, it made a good cup of tea. Both the kitchen and scullery looked westwards across the flagstone yard and it was quickly agreed that the kitchen would become their incident room. Even without a fire it would be reasonably warm, and whoever had lived here last had usefully left behind a huge oak table in the centre of the room.

"That looks really old," Tim observed. "I wonder why they left it?"

"Take a look at the doorways, wonder-boy," Nick sniffed. "How the hell would you get this monster out through that? It was probably built right here by some local carpenter."

He had a point. The table was wider than even the substantial width of the old doorway to the backyard, and its great length would have made any turning to the angle of the door utterly impossible even if it could have gone through. Nor would it have gone through turned up on its end – it would probably have destroyed the ceiling first! As Phil pontificated to Nick about the restrictions of the dig, telling him what he knew already, the three girls clustered together at the far end of the table, ostensibly sorting out things like bundles of labels and the finds trays, although in truth there was little sorting to do yet.

"When he's gone, how about we go and have an explore upstairs?" Pip whispered to the other two. "If they left this lovely table there might be some other bits and pieces left up there too." She didn't need to elaborate. The new owner wouldn't be needing old stuff like this – locally made items which didn't have the cachet of a maker known to every good antique dealer – and any such bits and pieces would end up on the builders' skip. The girls, on the other hand, were all desperately short of cash, and any smaller item which might be of use would be gratefully retrieved and cherished. It was hardly stealing when no-one had been known to live here in over forty years.

"Arthur Wormesley will be coming on Friday to take samples for the dendro' dating," Phil was saying loudly to everyone now, "so please have some beams accessible for him – and preferably dusted off! He's doing this for us in between other jobs as it's come up in such a rush, so let's be nice to him."

Pip gave Gemma and Chloe a furtive thumbs up and a wink at that. A perfect excuse to go rummaging! Not that Pip minded doing the preparation for Arthur. He was a sweet soul who was never anything less than polite, and wouldn't mind any number of spider's leavings if it got him to an interesting bit of wood. She'd learned an awful lot from tagging along with Arthur on a couple of previous occasions. With any luck he'd be only too happy to give the students a crash course in dendrochronology as they worked with him this time as well. No, Arthur would be no trouble – he might even be able to date the table for them. So the instructions were just another way for Phil to pretend he would be in charge for the coming weeks.

"Right, everyone outside!" Phil now declared. "Let me show you where you're going to be digging."

"Christ, we can read the bloody map!" Tim muttered. "It's not like we're digging a site the size of Petra!" His last summer had included a month with an American university team out in Jordan, not that he rubbed anyone else's nose in it over his good fortune. It was a measure of how much Phil was already annoying him that he said anything now, but his indignation brought on a fit of giggles from Chloe and Gemma, earning them black looks from Phil.

"Shhh!" Pip hissed trying to sound severe, but barely managing to stop from joining in the giggles as well when Phil turned and glared specifically at her this time.

Having walked round to the front of the house, Phil gestured to the slight rise to the east of it. "The surviving nineteenth-century map we have of this land shows some sort of building up there. It's not named and quite small – hardly of much consequence. I want you to put a trench in there, but don't waste too much time on it. Just go down enough to prove that it was probably an old barn sitting on a timber plate with nothing beneath. Your main focus should be this garden area to the north-east of the house. You can't see it for the trees now, but this would have looked across the valley to the site of the Roman fortlet we already have mapped up by the main road. So you're checking for any signs of Roman use, but primarily you're looking for the usual things which would give us a timeline for occupation on this site."

He turned and gestured to the two ends of the building. "On the south end there, that single storey wreck under the catslide roof was an old workshop, or possibly a dairy, so the floor can come up inside. It's not of any great importance, and the new owner intends to completely remodel it, so see what you can find beneath it. You may also investigate the yard at the back and those two kitchen rooms you've already seen, since they too will be completely refitted." He sniffed haughtily. "I can't see that there'll be anything worth listing in this place to prevent the new owner doing that."

He now drew himself to his full five-foot-six and did his best to peer down his nose at them, despite the fact that only Pip and Gemma were shorter than him. "*If*... I repeat *if* ...you have a solid and fully documentable reason for doing so, you may extend your investigations into the main ground floor rooms. *But* ...only to lift those flagstones as are absolutely necessary to complete your assessment." He stared at each of them in turn, reserving a particular glare for Pip and Nick. "Have I made myself perfectly clear?"

"Does he think we're so dumb as to try digging the first floor?" Gemma grumbled softly, but it was Pip who openly challenged Phil.

"Yes sir, perfectly clear sir," Pip said, while rubbing her one boot on the back of her combat trousers in a mockery of a school girl. "Do we get the cane if we fuck up, sir? Or should we expect bottom smacking?"

For a second everyone expected Phil to explode. Instead he went a strange shade of puce, then turned on his heels and stomped off inside once more.

"Wow!" Tim breathed, looking at Pip in astonishment. "That was brave!"

Pip sniffed. "No it wasn't. Phil and I have what you might call history." However, she didn't expand on her comment and instead went the long way around the house to the minibus.

"History? Pip and Phil?" Tim gulped, turning to Nick for an explanation.

Nick shook his head. "Not the sort you're thinking, my lad. Someone they once had in common. And that's all I'm saying on the matter. If Pip wants you to know, she'll tell you. But let's just say that I'm glad she's along on this one, because Phil tries it on every time I've worked with him, whereas with Pip he can only push so far and then she reminds him that she knows some things about him all too well."

They could do little more that day, and Phil was itching to be gone to get back to his pile of paperwork now that he'd seen the place for himself, and mentally dismissed it as a rich man's folly. The following morning, however, there was a much more jovial atmosphere in the bus as Kirsty, James and Will joined the party and they arrived early enough to get some real work done.

"It's a pity we haven't got the resources to get a geo-phys' team in here," Nick declared to the company as he sipped from a huge enamelled mug filled with the first tea of the day.

"Why's that?" James asked, lumbering past with an armful of spades.

Nick squinted at the long shadows the early sun was casting across the eastern side of the garden. "Well I'm not convinced dear Phyllis has the right of it that there's nothing to find here." Behind his back Phil was frequently referred to as Phyllis for his old-womanish fussing and pomposity. "Architecturally I agree it's not in the same class as some of the other houses around here. But it is old, and it's not been messed about with."

Gemma came to stand by him and then turned to look back at the house. "Yes, but that's brick in-fill between the timbers, not wattle and daub. So it's not much earlier than the seventeenth century, surely?"

Pip joined them. "No, you're right about the house as we see it. But it's that mound that's got your cat's whiskers twitching, isn't it Nick?"

He nodded as the younger members of the team looked bemused.

"It's because it's to the east," Pip elaborated. "Sometimes with these old places you get a manorial chapel in that sort of spot."

"Bloody hell!" Tim gulped. "You mean Phyllis' 'destroyed barn' might actually be something worth digging?"

"That it might," Nick grinned, "that it might!"

"So who's digging what?" Gemma asked him, bringing the conversation to the practical.

Nick gestured with his mug at the mound. "Well I'm going to put a trench in up there with Kirsty, James and Will. Can you and Chloe start doing some test pits in the garden, Gem? And Pip, would you and Tim start having a go at the yard area around the pump and the old workshop? See if there's any pipe-work around the pump which might give us a date for when it was installed?"

Pip nodded and tapped Tim on the arm to follow her. She and Gemma not only already had their degrees but had several years' worth of digs to their credit too, and if they weren't full-time archaeologists, they did have enough experience to be able to supervise the students. As they went to retrieve a couple of picks in case they needed to lift flagstones, Tim sighed,

"I know Nick is trying to give the others a chance at finding something interesting since this is their first proper dig, but I can't help thinking we've been given the short straw going looking for some piece of engineering while they get to look for a lost chapel."

Pip smiled. "Know what you mean! But think on this. Our chunk of Victorian pride, with a name and date stamp, will be much easier to give to Phyllis for his confirmation of dates than anything they're likely to find. And Phil is so very much into his industrial archaeology when he's not chasing Romans, so that will keep him quiet and out of Nick's hair." Then added thoughtfully, "But also, I think Nick wants you to experience what it's like on most ordinary digs. You've been dead lucky, Tim. You've had the chance to go on digs where there's been a lot of funding, and so you've seen stuff that's a bit closer to TV archaeology, where money is splashed around far more liberally than normal."

"I know that!" Tim protested. "Good grief, Pip, I'm not daft!"

"No, I know you're not, and Nick doesn't think that either. But I think he wants you to actually experience the dreary end of things as well – for your own sake, not out of some grudge he holds against you. You're a really good archaeologist, Tim, and with the references you've already got you're more likely than most to get a job in the field."

"So that's why he wants me to see what most of the jobs I'd be likely to work on will be like?"

"You've got it. Now let's scrape back that bit of garden earth on the side, up by the wall, and see if we can find any clues as to which way we're going to dig!"

By the time everyone assembled in the kitchen for lunch, Pip and Tim had very little to be able to tell Nick.

"There is some pipe-work," Pip confirmed. "But it's certainly older than Victorian. It looks like clay pipe and possibly locally made pipe at that."

"And cracked pipe!" Nick grinned, looking at Pip's muddied combats and top. Her boots were outside the door with Tim's, too mud-caked to bring inside, even to the tatty floor of the scullery. Everyone else's were bone dry. However Pip shook her head, revealing that some of the mud had made it into her tangle of brown curls too.

"No not cracked. Pretty sound, actually. The water seems to be coming from a natural spring they tapped into. And of course with the rain we've had this year the water table is ridiculously high just now, as well. But I don't think this is just that we're sinking into ground water here in the yard. It's running down to us, not rising up. We're tracing it back right now, because the line of both the pipe and the water would suggest it's heading for your mound."

"Is it, now?" Nick was intrigued.

Pip took in his grin and sighed. "Oh come on, Nick, don't make me work for the good news, there's a good soul. I thought only Phil and my family played those sorts of head games with me."

"Sorry, Pip." Nick had forgotten that sometimes Pip could be a bit fragile on account of her past. A family who had all but dismissed her had left hidden scars, along with the ex-fiancé who'd been the common link with Phil. With Phil she'd meet him head on letting her still simmering anger have vent, but with Nick, whom she trusted far more, she would be more open over the hurt which went with the anger. He drew her over to the table where Chloe had just bagged up something she'd been carefully washing and drying.

"Take a look at this," he said, picking the plastic bag up and placing it in her hand.

"Wow! A pilgrim's badge." It was an almost complete scallop shell badge. "Someone went to Santiago de Compostela, then. And wasn't the shell something to do with the Palmer's Gild at Ludlow? That's not exactly the other end of the country from here, is it?"

"Nice, eh? And found right inside the area at the top of the mound."

"Date?"

Nick shrugged. "Can't be sure, but I'd be surprised if it's later than the sixteenth century."

Now Pip's grin broadened. "So older than the house! Oh that's nice! That's very nice! And on the first morning too!"

It didn't entirely make up for the fact that by the end of the day Pip and Tim were soaked through, with little to show for their drenching except a deepening trench which was threatening to make a mini moat around that end of the house. However Nick took her up to the other trench as the others stowed away the equipment in the house. Pointing down into the trench he just stood grinning.

"Bloody hell! Is that herringbone stonework?" Pip gasped, dying to get down into the trench to look, but unable to on account of knowing she would be dripping all over precious archaeology.

"I think so. We'll know more tomorrow when we can get it properly cleaned up and down a bit further. But it looks to me like a chunk of collapsed wall."

Pip turned to Nick with shining eyes. "Anglo-Saxon? You think we might have an Anglo-Saxon chapel here?" Everyone had their favourite periods in history, and if Phil's was the Romans, for Pip it was the Anglo-Saxons.

"I do hope so," was Nick's fervent wish. "Maybe only a tiny place. Might even be only some hermit's cell, but the Saxon church at Edvin Loach can't be more than half-a-mile to a mile away over the fields, so it's possible it's some kind of outlier of that."

Pip was speechless. It was her dream come true to find something like this. Then something occurred to her. "It could even be Celtic," she mused. "Something even older, maybe. I'm thinking Conversion era, here, Nick. Sixth or seventh century. Our spring is definitely starting somewhere up here. Maybe it was the spring which was the original pagan sacred site – like with so many of those other tiny churches along the Welsh border? Very small but very local. Somewhere which was already being overtaken by the outside world by the time the first records were being written. That would be cool! A tiny chapel built on a sacred site before there was even a farm here, and so it just faded away while the church over the hill got to become a proper parish church." She stared at the stonework, lost in her reverie.

Someone hooted the minibus horn, signalling the others' impatience.

"Come on," Nick said cheerfully, "I think we're keeping the rest from their beer! But you'll be digging that spring a bit harder tomorrow, won't you!"

"My God! Yes!" As they walked back down to the yard where Tim had pulled the minibus to the head of the drive, Pip couldn't resist a backwards glance to the mound. There was a definite atmosphere up here, but also down in the house, as if it was resisting the disruption. Almost as though nature was hanging a 'do not disturb' sign up which they were ignoring.

Chapter 2

Worcestershire, June 1814

Captain Harry Green shook out his clothes and hung them up in his room in the Old Talbot Hotel, then looked out of the window onto the busy Worcester street. These days he felt almost like a foreigner in this town, despite having spent many years at school here. After five years of almost constant fighting he'd forgotten what it was like to be footloose and fancy free, and the sight of young gentlemen of means walking about the city with not a care in the world only served to remind him of how out of place he felt. He also knew that in part his feelings of dislocation came from knowing that sooner or later he was going to have to face Amy.

The last time he'd been home had been almost three years ago in the autumn of 1811, and that had been to accompany Edward and stand beside him as he married Amy. He recalled standing here at this very window with Edward, and the conversation which had gone with it.

"God damn it, I'll be an old married man by this time tomorrow," Edward had said gloomily, sitting on one of the dainty chairs and resting his elbows on the window ledge, cupping his chin in his hands. It was a pose Harry knew of old from their school days, always signalling that Edward was about to get bored and do something foolish. Now it looked incongruous on a fully grown young man. It made Harry want to grab him by the collar and shake him. He might even have done it if he'd thought it would work. Unfortunately even back then – let alone now – he, if not

Edward, had done a lot of growing up in those two years since leaving home. Enough to know that Edward would probably never change now.

Indeed Harry had been amazed that Edward had asked him to be his best man given how much they'd drifted apart of late. It had only been as they were leaving the rest of the regiment – who were recuperating from another bloody battle, this time at Albuera in the May of 1811 – that it occurred to him that, while he was wished well for the journey by several men, not one spoke to Edward. Looking back now from the distance of the additional three years, Harry knew that was when he first realised how thoroughly disliked Edward was, which bizarrely came as a shock given that he'd always thought of Edward as the popular one of the two of them.

The main problem was that Edward hadn't the money or the breeding to back up his assumed airs and graces, and everyone but him knew it. The truly high born looked down on him as an upstart, and having a father in trade who ferried coal along the Wye wasn't impressive enough for the sons of industrial magnates among the officers either. Even that wouldn't have been a problem, though, if he'd kept his head down like Harry had. Having made no pretence that he was anything better than he was, Harry had at least found acceptance amongst the professional soldiers for his abilities in the field. But Edward had been tarred with an even worse brush than 'upstart'. Some were already openly saying 'coward' even in 1811, a mere two years after they'd arrived in the regiment. For a man could be the biggest ass in creation as long as he showed valour in the field, but few wanted to serve with a man who couldn't be trusted to at least do his duty if nothing more noteworthy.

So when Edward had begun bemoaning his fate in the

Worcester hotel room for having to marry Amy, Harry had been unable to stop himself.

"By God, Edward, you never know when you're well off," he remembered his younger self saying with barely disguised anger as he stood by the bedroom's fireplace, well away from Edward just in case he forgot himself and hit him. "It can hardly be the worst chore in the world to marry a dear girl like Amy!"

"Oh for pity's sake, Harry! Me? With hoards of tiny copies of her squalling around my ankles? Me? Sitting by the fireside on some dreary winter's night with no-one to play cards with? And where would a man go out for some fun in a place like this, hmm?" Clearly escaping out of a school window to go out in Worcester town had been exhilarating for Edward the schoolboy, but had long since lost its charm for Edward the man.

Harry couldn't stop himself. "Well you aren't exactly enamoured of the real side of fighting are you?" he demanded with heavy sarcasm. "Not exactly out there looking after your men. You leave all of that to Hobspawn! So why don't you come back here and take whatever your father offers you – no doubt it will be a controlling interest in one of his industries, a mine or ships or something. Then you can turn up at the office a couple of days a week and spend the rest of it spending your money. You don't even have to stay in whatever house you have with Amy! You'd be able to afford a decent horse or two and go out riding with the county gents."

Edward had risen with a sneer on his face. "Lord, that shows how little you know of this county or any other! I've been rubbing shoulders with young men of *real* breeding in the regiment. Do you really think I would be content to go plodding round some soggy fields with the sons of farmers? All right for you! Son of a country rector. That's about your station – mixing with farmers – but not for me! I'm used to better things now. And I want a wife who will show up well in the kind of circles I intent to mix in when I leave the army. And Amy won't do! By God, sir, she won't!"

"Then why are you marrying her tomorrow?" Harry had asked, suddenly saddened by the thought of what was about to take place in the old church across the river. "Why didn't you break it off months ago? Back when everyone started making arrangements for when you could next come home on leave?"

"Because the old man is still so for it, you dolt!" Edward had snapped back bitterly. "Until I can make my own way a bit further he still controls the purse strings, and I can't do without him."

"You could try living off your pay," Harry suggested acidly. "I have to!"

"Off my pay?" Edward was horrified. "It's nothing!"

"It's sufficient," Harry riposted dryly. "Sufficient if you don't gamble every night and go out whoring and drinking."

Edward looked down his handsome nose a him. "You know, I don't know why *you* don't leave the army and go into the church like your father. You're sanctimonious enough!"

At that Harry had given up any attempt to hold a conversation, and to this day he could still recall the bitterness he'd felt towards the supposed friend, who'd so forgotten his circumstances as to not remember that Harry's brother had already taken the church route. Two sons going into the church was more than their father could have managed to influence. Had there ever been a time, the twenty-year-old Harry had belatedly wondered, when Edward had seen him as anything but his toady? The hanger on whom he could use? It was a souring thought, and one which had stayed with him through the night as Edward had paced the room moodily, and Harry had struggled not to hit him hard enough to knock him out in order to at least get some sleep after the long journey.

Therefore there had been a strained atmosphere between them on into the next day as they had stood in the old church of St John in Bedwardine, and watched Amy, pale but radiant, walking up the aisle on her father's arm towards them. To give Edward some credit, Harry had to concede that had he not known how Edward truly felt, he would never have guessed it from the way he acted. He flattered Amy and charmed the guests at the Vaughan's gentleman's villa down the road afterwards, whereas Harry had felt as though he was walking around with a lead weight in his stomach.

The point when it all got too much, and he'd had excused himself to go and take a walk along the river bank, was when Amy introduced her friend, Miss Natalie Walker. Harry's first thought was 'this one's trouble'. Then to his horror saw the smitten look on Edward's face. Oh Miss Walker was a stunner, there was no doubt about that! Piles of dark hair cascaded about her pert face in glossy ringlets, but there was a knowingness about her which disconcerted Harry. Yet in a flash he also knew that Edward was thinking that here was a woman to make an entrance with. A woman who would get noticed no matter what the social circle, and beside whom Amy looked pale and girlish.

Had Edward's covetous looks been all there was, Harry might still have managed to hold himself in check, but it wasn't. On Miss Walker's finger was a pretty ring which Harry recognised a once.

"You must be a very special friend for Miss Vaughan – or Mrs Clifford, I should say now – to be lending out her jewellery to you," he said with strained pleasantry.

Amy had been simpering at being called Mrs Clifford, then realised what Harry had said and looked to her friend perplexed. Natalie Walker, however, went the faintest shade pinker but recovered and waved the ring at Amy while pulling a very studied pout.

"Oh dearest Amy, don't be cross, I just borrowed it for today. I so wanted to look pretty for your special day, and you know I have nothing of my own."

"Of course," Amy replied sweetly, but her expression was more telling since she was unable to conceal her surprise at seeing the ring on her friend's finger.

"And very fine it looks on you, Miss Walker!" Edward had gushed, making Harry squirm in his dress coat.

"Oh well, if you don't mind either, my dear," had been Amy's wan response.

"Mind? Why should I mind?"

Harry was wishing that the floor would open up and swallow him now. How could Edward be so bloody tactless? Surely he should know that Amy would have no jewellery other than what he'd bought her?

Before Harry could try and rescue the situation, though, Amy had said, "Why because you bought it for me, dearest! Do you not recall?"

Too late Edward realised the trap he'd set for himself. "Ah yes! Well you know we men are hopeless at recalling those sort of things!" he bluffed heartily.

"Oh come, Edward," Harry heard himself saying, as if some inner demon had taken sudden control over his tongue and was ignoring his better self. "Don't you remember? You got it from that goldsmiths by the little white church in Lisbon!"

Harry could have described the very street, and the diminutive Jewish goldsmith to whom he'd described what he wanted, and who had made it to order.

"It was the same place you got the pearl necklace made up," the inner demon added mischievously, rubbing salt into Edward's wound. And why not, since it had also been Harry's money which had bought the damned things? It had been Harry who had checked on the letters Amy had written back. Harry who had realised that it was Amy's birthday in a couple of months, and Harry who had prodded Edward into thinking of buying a present for her. Yet even then, Edward had made excuse after excuse and done nothing until Harry had acted, and posted the present which he'd bought months ago in a moment of optimism that he might get to give it to Amy face to face.

Now, back here in England and facing her, Harry's better side was praying that Amy would wake up and wonder how come Harry could remember such things when Edward was standing looking utterly vacant. *Ask him*, Harry was screaming silently inside, *ask him*! Yet all the adoring Amy did was smile indulgently up at her beloved.

"Oh Eddie, you are a silly goose for forgetting," she cooed, "but Harry's told me how busy you are and how the regiment couldn't possible cope without you."

"Did you? Jolly decent of you, old chap!"

However Edward wasn't half as surprised as Harry. He'd never thought his own words would come back to haunt him so badly. Had he laid it on that thickly? Or was it that she was construing that from the fact that every time he'd written he'd said that Edward was too busy, somewhere else, or in the company of senior officers? Inwardly Harry was mortified. How bloody stupid had he been? He'd played right into Edward's hands, and now he could hardly speak up and put things right on the very day Amy had married this pathetic excuse for a soldier.

That was when he'd made his own excuses and left, and now, three years on and standing in this same hotel room as before, Harry could see the whole day being played out again before his inner eye as if it was happening again right now. Rousing himself he forced himself to go out and walk along the same quays he'd paced three years ago, which lined the banks of the River Severn. Beside the great medieval cathedral he watched the swans go gliding by and wondered what on earth he was going to say to Amy when he saw her this time. So much had changed and yet in a strange way had not. He'd continued to play the letter game, perhaps even more so given what he knew was going on with Edward behind Amy's back, once they were back in Spain. But then there had been the fateful battle at Orthes in February of this year and Edward had been killed, and Harry had felt compelled to send a letter with all speed, even knowing that an official one would follow.

He straightened his shoulders and took a deep breath. Nothing for it, he would hire a horse ready for tomorrow and ride out to see her. It would be torture, he knew. To see Amy and not be able to say the truth even now. For how could he? How could he drag Edward's name down into the dirt where it belonged when Amy's grief would still be so fresh? She would be thinking that the battle at Orthes had finally seen Edward off to a heroic death, and whatever the truth of that situation, it was still only late April now. Both his letter and any official missive could have arrived here only weeks ago, and he had no doubts that she would have taken the news hard. He sighed. What to say, what to do?

Then another thought presented itself. The one visit he could make before then was to Edward's father. That at least shouldn't be too exhausting emotionally. In fact it was purely a courtesy call as far as he was concerned – a obligation to someone who was an important man in the county community, and who could make things awkward for his own father and brother if he chose. So better to mollify the old curmudgeon first. And he could do that while still staying here in Worcester before he rode on to visit Amy. Get himself into practice, so to speak, for the greater ordeal to come, for with Edward's father he could no more speak the truth than with Amy, but at least this time there would be fewer questions.

The following morning, wearing his best uniform, Harry presented himself at the fine house set just back from the cathedral close in Worcester – not the very best of addresses in the city, but not far off. It hadn't been the Clifford's home when he and Edward had been at school together. Then the family had been over the river in St John in Bedwardine close to the Vaughans, but in the intervening years old man Clifford had invested in, and then got control of, one of the city's largest glove factories and business was booming. A suitably unctuous servant opened the door to Harry and he was ushered into a smart hall to wait.

He fully expected to be kicking his heels there for the best part of the morning, and was amazed to be taken through to a room overlooking the river within minutes. Rarely had he seen such a transformation as the one he now saw in Roderick Clifford. The man he remembered as being so bombastic and impatient now sat dwarfed by his huge armchair, a withered husk of a man. Only when he stood to greet Harry did he realise that in part the illusion was created by the lack of vigour in Sir Roderick, in stark contrast to his former permanent restlessness.

"Good of you to come," Sir Roderick growled, although with very little sincerity. The old man scanned Harry up and down, taking in the details of the uniform. "When did you make captain?" It came out like an accusation rather than any compliment. As though it was almost an affront to the late Edward that a mere clergyman's son should achieve the same rank as his son, beloved or otherwise.

"At the Battle of Nive, storming the heights of St Pierre in December," Harry lied. How could he tell the old man that actually it was Edward, not him, who had only made captain in the field at that recent battle, and only because better men had already died? Dare he tell him that Edward's commission hadn't even been made permanent? No doubt he would hear that soon enough from official sources. Oh well, if pressed during some unlikely later encounter, Harry could always say that at this time he had thought the commission was permanent when at this present meeting.

What he really couldn't bring himself to say was that he had made his own name at the Battle of Albuera, way back in May of 1811, and had been waiting for a permanent captaincy to become vacant even when he and Edward had been over here in England for the wedding that same autumn. True he'd had to wait a long time to get the position, and had been overtaken a couple of times by men with the money to buy a captaincy, but he'd been a full captain back at the Battle of Vittoria in June of 1813, a full six months before Edward had even been considered. No, he could never tell Sir Roderick that he had overleapt his son!

"Were you with him at the end?" Sir Roderick interrupted Harry's thoughts. "Did you see him? Did he make a good end?"

Blast and bother! The old man wanted a hero's death for Edward! He should have expected as much given Sir Roderick's ego, but he'd put too much weight on the old man's former disdain of his posturing only son. So how to try and make the best of this without getting himself into a veritable hornet's nest of deceits? Harry thought frantically as he said,

"No, Sir Roderick, I wasn't there. We were in different parts of the battalion by then. And on the battle field it's hard enough to see the men right by you. All the smoke from the guns, don't you see? And the noise. Worse than in a workshop full of smiths!"

"No doubt my boy was with the higher officers," Sir Roderick growled more to himself than addressing Harry.

There was no response to that. How could Harry say that at the actual battle Edward had been near soiling his britches at being right at the fore for once? That he'd been on the far edge of the battalion because he wasn't trusted to stand his ground in the centre where Harry had been. Or of how he'd heard Major Young speaking with their colonel and saying, "You can trust Green to stand, sir. Go through the fires of hell, that one would, but don't put Clifford anywhere except where he's expendable." What a bloody reputation to die with!

"Will he have a grave here?" the old man was asking now.

"No sir," Harry lied again, and thinking fast. "Not possible you see, sir. Cannon shot. Did the most awful damage. Identified him by his belongings."

He felt an utter rat for that when Sir Roderick slumped back into the chair and covered his face with his hands. Harry hadn't expected genuine grief. If he had, he might have been even more subtle. As it was he'd told the truth, if adjusted. Edward really had been identified by his belongings, but not because he'd been struck down in battle. That – to everyone's surprise including his own – Edward had survived. The fatal moment had come afterwards when the men had been celebrating. That he'd been found lying face down in the latrine pit behind the tents which the whores used, with his throat cut and his face kicked beyond recognition, wasn't something Sir Roderick should have to hear, however much of an old bully he'd been to both Harry and Edward in the past.

"I have some of his things here with me now," Harry said gently. He'd picked out items he'd known Edward's father had given him and brought them back to England with him. "I'll put them over on the table," he added, and placing the small package on the elaborately veneered side table, let himself out.

Only as the door closed did he hear an almost feral howl of grief from back inside the room. He stood rooted to the spot for a moment, wondering whether he should go back in again. But what could he say that would soften the blow for the old man?

"He always thought Edward would come home covered in glory and then follow him into business. That if nothing else, war would make Edward grow up," a cold, flat voice said quietly from the shadows, and Edward's sister appeared. "Silly old fool! He never saw him for what he was!"

Harry turned to face Beatrice Clifford, as he still thought of her, although she had been married long before he and Edward had joined up, and had been widowed in the time that he'd been away. She'd never been a beauty, nor even girlishly pretty like Amy, but now there was a sour, disapproving air about her, as though the world was a continuous string of disappointments. Without thinking he asked in surprise,

"You don't mourn your brother?"

Beatrice sniffed. "Why should I? I was the elder by six years and yet all that old man ever saw in me was the means to marry into some other family who would help him get even richer. Never mind what sort of husband I might be saddled with."

Inwardly Harry cringed. That sounded as though her husband might have been a brute, but she was carrying on.

"It was always Edward this, and Edward that! All he wanted was his son. Well he spoiled him rotten and now he's paying for it! If he'd forced Edward to behave and knuckle down to working alongside him, then Edward would still be here. Oh don't think I don't know what sort of man my brother had become! The one thing my late and unlamented husband never stinted on was telling me what news he had of my feckless brother. How he had huge debts to some fine families because of the endless gambling. How he spent his last night here in England with that whore of a friend of his wife's."

Again Harry was shocked. He'd always known that on their last night in Worcester, after the wedding and preparing to return to Spain, Edward had left Amy at her parent's house in order to stay in a hotel again under the pretext of needing to leave very early. But Harry had never thought that anyone but himself had known of the wild night Edward had spent with Natalie Walker. He'd found out when he'd gone to Edward's room to wake him, only to walk in on a scene of wild passion.

Harry was no prude, and he'd seen the inside of enough whorehouses when hauling others out to know what men and women could get up to. But what had taken his breath away was to see Natalie astride Edward – who was, God help him, happily tied up to the bedstead – riding him for all she was worth as if she were at the hunt, wild curls tossing and utterly naked. And Natalie was quite a sight naked! Slim to the point of almost boyish athleticism, and full bosomed, she was unlike any woman Harry knew or had experienced. And the knowing grin she had flashed at him as he'd backed out of the door haunted his dreams for many a night afterwards, as did her sexual prowess. That he'd dreamed of Amy doing such things to him had shamed him on waking, but nothing had drawn his blushes the way the thought did that Beatrice knew about Edward's exploits.

"Oh yes, I knew," Beatrice said with almost malevolent enjoyment as she took in Harry's scarlet cheeks. "And we heard how she followed him to France. I told Father, you know, but he wouldn't believe me." Now Harry was writhing inside as well. Good grief, was there anything left of Edward's reputation to be saved? Not for his sake but for Amy's. Oh God, there was another thought! Had Beatrice said anything of this to Amy? And dare he ask?

"Well it's all worked out in the end," Beatrice told him with a smirk. "Now my to boys will inherit all of this! And I shall make sure they don't make the same mistakes or come to the same end."

"Not your sons alone, surely?" Harry protested. "Amy has a son by Edward! He's Sir Roderick's grandson too!"

"Oh Father has nothing to do with her," Beatrice sniffed disdainfully, making Harry almost physically reel with shock.

"Good God! Why not?"

"Oh didn't you hear? There was a fire at the mine her father bought. The mine couldn't be saved. The family were already in debt because her father borrowed to buy it – borrowed some of it from Father, too! Father won't have anything to do with them now they're not in society. You'll have to ride out to Lower Sapey if you want to visit her. They don't live in town anymore. Goodbye Captain Green."

And with that she held open the front door, effectively dismissing Harry from the household. As he stepped out into the spring sunshine his head was reeling. So that's why Amy had sent letters from a new address! The implication had always been that she was living quietly because Edward had to use what money he had for his army expenses. But Harry had always thought that her own family had provided her with a separate house of her own. Now, though, it seemed that it might be the whole Vaughan family who had moved out!

"Oh God!" Harry sighed, looking up in supplication towards the cathedral tower. "What on earth am I going to find when I meet her?"

Chapter 3

Wednesday and Thursday, modern day

The next day the drizzle which had plagued the summer was back with a vengeance, making Pip and Tim's section of the dig even soggier. Down in the yard the pump end was soon declared of limited interest, but some sherds of Roman pot which had probably been washed down by the spring encouraged them to dig on, working their way uphill towards Nick's main excavation. The elevation of the spring wasn't quite as high as Pip had at first thought, and as she and Tim progressed, they found their trench cutting deeper and deeper into the small mound on which Nick and the others were working.

By lunchtime they were thoroughly drenched and very glad that Gemma, before continuing with the test pits in the garden with Chloe, had lit the range in the kitchen with a bag of coal they'd picked up from a petrol station on the way in.

"Jeez! It's bloody freezing for June!" Tim muttered through chattering teeth as he all but sat on the range, trying to dry out the seat of his pants so that he could at least sit down to eat the doorstep ham and mustard sandwiches Kirsty and Chloe were making up.

"Oh the joys of an English summer!" agreed James as he brewed up yet another large pot of tea. "Somehow I can't see me going back to uni' with a tan to show for being outside for a month or more!"

"Hmm, you might be orange from all this rotten

bloody clay, though," Will ribbed him, although he clearly feared the same fate for himself. The gelatinous earth had a habit of clinging to every surface which came into contact with it. Already the archaeologists were beginning to worry what their clothes would do to the washing machines on the campsite where they were staying. On their next trip into Worcester the girls were suggesting they pick up some cheap buckets, into which they could dunk the worst affected garments and soak them before washing.

"I hate to be the prophet of doom, but get used to it if you want to be an archaeologist," Nick said wryly. "It's sod's law that just when you start a dig the weather will take a turn for the worse – not every time, I grant you, but I've been wet far more often than I've been sunburned."

Trudging back out into the fine drizzle, which still managed to seep into every possible opening, Pip could feel Tim's enthusiasm for his chosen career taking a downturn.

"Are we actually going to find anything, do you think?" he asked Pip in subdued tones as he went to wheel the barrow-load of more excavated, sodden clay away from the edge of the trench.

She looked up from where she was in the bottom of the trench, nearly up to the top of her brightly patterned wellies in water. "Like what? We've found some pottery."

"Tiny sherds!"

"Tim this is the arse end of nowhere. We're not digging where there were great big Roman villas or forts. Nothing much happened round here from one century's end to the other. The most exciting thing you can say for this place is that it's right at the junction of three parishes and near the Worcester-Hereford border. A liminal space on the boundaries of just about everything. That's it! So bring your expectations down to that level. And don't think that just finding the head of this spring isn't interesting. It is!"

"How come?" asked a voice from up above her from where James was working. "I don't get the interest in the spring at all."

About to make a cutting remark, Pip had to remember that James was the youngest of all the students, and had only just finished his first year at university. Standing up to ease her back, she peered up over the lip of her trench to where he was working.

"Ah! Is that a bank that Nick's got you uncovering by any chance?"

"Yes." James sounded as unenthusiastic as Tim. From what Nick had said, James was going to make a good industrial archaeologist, and at the slightest chance he would talk with endless enthusiasm about places like the Ironbridge Gorge Museum. However, Nick had also said that James' tutor had apparently been saying that he needed to show a bit more interest in earlier history if he was going to get through this degree, and make it into the job in heritage conservation that he dreamed of.

Pushing a dripping strand of hair back off her face, Pip clambered up to him. "What do you remember reading of the early Anglo-Saxon period, James?"

"Not much. I think I tried to avoid that for the essay in that part of the term."

"Right then! Here's your starter!" and further up the trench Nick smothered a smile. It would do James good to be on the end of someone else's enthusiasm for a change!

"Look at where the bank is in relationship to where our potential chapel is," Pip was instructing James. "Now even with what you've uncovered of this bank so far – which has been subsequently covered with more soil over the intervening centuries – I can see that it's curving. That's good!"

"It is?"

"Oh yes! You see, early churches or chapels are often identified by the circular enclosures about them. If you want to see a cracking example of one still standing, there's a lovely church up at Escombe in County Durham. So although *you* don't think this bank is anything in particular, it shows that this little place we're digging could be a very early Christian site."

By now Tim had returned with the wheelbarrow and was also standing listening as Pip got into full flow.

"Now since you clearly didn't do much reading on the period for an essay, let me tell you that unlike the industrial archaeology you love so much, James, we have very few records surviving for pre-1066. So we can't just go and look up whether or not there was a church here. There's something called the Book of Llandaff, which all on its own has generated many PhD theses, which supposedly tells of a whole string of Welsh churches a bit south and west of here. If you take it at its face value, these churches predate St Augustine's mission to convert the pagan Anglo-Saxons – and the best source even for something as important as *that* is primarily in the Venerable Bede's writing, so we're not exactly overwhelmed there, either!

"And the problem with the Book of Llandaff is dating it. It could be a later medieval forgery you see, to claim parishes for the Welsh Church in the face of a very acquisitive Norman Church from England. It's the classic case of 'academic opinion is divided'! Anyway, these churches were *reputedly* founded by the Welsh Church before the Anglo-Saxons came – the Welsh Church having hung on to Christianity after the Romans left. A little corner of remaining Christianity in Britain, you see, which elsewhere went back to pagan practices until Augustine and his monks from Gaul, – i.e. what's now modern France – appeared to reconvert them."

James wasn't quite raring to go yet, but Tim had perked up. "Oh right! Yes I remember now. Augustine's appearance is the start of the various Anglo-Saxon Kingdoms converting to Christianity, isn't it. But didn't some of them take two or three goes to become fully Christian?"

Pip nodded. "And the thing is, we know from Bede that Augustine was specifically told by Pope Gregory to consecrate places like pagan springs and holy trees, and build places of Christian worship on, or by, or over, them. A very crafty way of getting the locals to keep coming, you see? And also, if they'd left the pagan springs and trees separate, they would have remained alternative places of worship..."

"...Whereas this way they were overwritten right on the spot!" Tim finished. "So that's why the spring's so important!"

"Exactly!" Pip said with a triumphant grin. "A tiny church with a circular enclosure by a spring stands a very good chance of being really early eighth century, or possibly even seventh. And Worcester is a very early diocese too, so it's not beyond the bounds of possibility that someone came westwards from there. Of course we'll need a lot more evidence than what we have now to prove something like that. And be warned – we'll probably never find it! In fact it would cause massive excitement if we did, such things are so rare! But this is a good start. And even if we can't get any further than that in proving there was an Anglo-Saxon chapel here, quite often having a small chapel on the site would indicate that any evidence we find of a house here would mean it was fairly important. Manorial chapels are of interest all by themselves, even if they never become parish churches. So in our brief to establish some kind of time line for this place, it really is all relevant."

"Okay, you've sold me!" Tim said with a laugh. "Let's get back in the mud bath and see if this bloody spring turns out to be close to the bank or, heaven help us, inside it."

Yet having prepared the two lads for not finding anything more than water, when they got to the point where the spring bubbled up through the subsoil, Pip spotted three small grey areas in the mud.

"Hold on, Tim, let me have a look at this," she said, putting a restraining hand on his arm, and washing the mud off her trowel before beginning a much more gentle scraping. With great care she teased around the objects until she could ease them out into her hand. Even just holding them under the running water of the spring for a moment washed more of the clay off, and showed them to be a dull grey. One was crumpled up, but the other two seemed to be flattish once the clay was off. "Shit! ...Nick! Come here!" she called out.

Moments later Nick appeared at the lip of the trench, something in Pip's voice alerting him to the fact that she'd found something more than a piece of un-datable pot.

"What do you make of these?" she said, handing them up to him. "Am I imagining it, or are they lead?"

Nick peered hard at them. "Yep, definitely lead." He looked harder. "Bloody hell, Pip! I think these are Roman curse tablets!"

"What? Like the one they found at Bath?"

Nick nodded. "And of course that was found at a spring, albeit a hot one! We should get these cleaned up properly. A reference to Sulis, like there was at Bath, would really put this on the map as a Roman site!"

"Nice one, Pip," Tim complimented her as Nick hurried away with the precious pieces of lead. "I'd never have spotted them in these conditions, even with them being grey in all this red clay. I don't know why, but I'd have expected curse tablets to be bigger than those were."

"Well they're probably only fragments," Pip admitted, "but they're hardly going to have an essay on them, are they? Just something like, 'a hex on Guilia for stealing my house boy'!" and even James laughed with them.

However, before Nick could tell them more on the tablets, there was another revelation. Pip and Tim thought they were just widening the trench around the spring to make sure there was nothing else, and that they'd be in the main trench from tomorrow onwards, when Tim's trowel clunked on something more solid. Scrapping back some more of the clay, which at least was more solid now that they were out of the water's flow, he revealed something which looked suspiciously like worked stone.

"What on earth have we got here?" fretted Pip, joining him in exposing the stone, and which turned out to have another stone butting up to it.

By the time they'd got to the end of the day, it became clear that the first stone Tim had found was sitting on the natural subsoil with nothing beneath it. However the next stone had every appearance of having been a threshold stone, going by the way it was worn.

"I wonder if they robbed this building to make the first house?" Kirsty said as she joined the others in inspecting the stones before they packed up.

"But the house isn't in stone," Chloe pointed out to her friend, "it's brick, and those aren't Roman bricks in the in-fill, are they, Gemma?"

Gemma stared hard at the house's exterior but shook her head. "Not that I can see. Of course, if there were Roman bricks around here then they could have been reused, but when this house was built they'd already have been over a thousand years old and probably pretty rotten, and I doubt there'll be any of them round here anyway. Roman bricks would go with some kind of pretty permanent settlement, which this isn't as far as we know at the moment."

"I'm more bothered by why they didn't build the church in stone if there was stone here in an old building which they could recycle," Nick said thoughtfully. "And we're not seeing any big slabs of this kind of size in the old church. The herringbone-work is of pieces which are a much smaller size and a totally different colour."

"Maybe they thought it was contaminated?" Kirsty wondered as they all piled into the minibus and got scoffed at for her superstition.

By the time they got back the next morning, Nick had had a chance to look harder at the small and bent sheets of lead. One was too worn to make anything out on it, apart from faint depressions where once there might have been writing. The second had better markings, but was so crumpled Nick wouldn't try to straighten it to read it. On the third, though, was quite clearly written 'Deae M...' ('[to] Goddess M...').

"I thought you were expecting a dedication to Sulis," Kirsty said as they clustered around the farmhouse table to look at it.

"I was," he said, "but you do get Sulis-Minerva at Bath. I'm not going to quibble if here they were specifically asking Minerva for help instead of Sulis – and anyway, the two seem to have got a bit blurred in the Romano-British minds!"

"What's the rest of it say?" Will asked since, as the tallest, he was also at the back of the group and couldn't see it so closely.

Nick wrinkled his nose. "Well it's a bit of a guess since not all of it's survived and it needs better cleaning than I can do here, but it seems to be a curse on those who 'disturb this sacred space'.

"Euw!" Kirsty squeaked, "I hope that doesn't include us!" She had made it clear that she was an ardent churchgoer, and as such was more inclined than the rest to take against anything ancient and pagan intruding into the present.

"Oh give it a rest, girl!" Chloe said with a roll of her eyes. "I think any curse will have run its course in the thick end of two thousand years, don't you?"

"I'm more curious as to why we've found no other offerings," Gemma said. "As I remember, at Bath, where the other lead curse tablet I know of was found, it was in with lots of other votive offerings. I can understand that maybe here anything which would rot down is long gone, but you'd think we might find at least one or two coins, or maybe a trinket like a decorative bead."

Nick was nodding his agreement with her. "Yes, if this was a place of regular supplication you'd expect to find all manner of offerings to Minerva, or whoever else was commemorated here. Maybe more will turn up today?"

However, when Pip and Tim, with Nick's help, lifted the stone which they thought was the doorstep into whatever the place had been, they made a grisly discovery. Buried beneath the stone was a baby's headless skeleton.

"Oh that's gross!" Chloe objected, even her earthy sensibilities drawing the line at assumed child sacrifice.

"Don't be so quick to judge," Nick reprimanded her. "We have no way of knowing if this was a child deliberately sacrificed to be put under this threshold, or if a child died of natural causes and was then used here. There's a big difference! This little one may have been well loved in life and given a burial here out of a kind of respect, however odd that seems to us now." He carefully scraped around the small bones as he continued saying, "What it does imply, though, is that this might be something like a small shrine, or at least somewhere of importance. You wouldn't expect to find a burial like this with an ordinary home, I don't think."

"Could we have found a temple?" Tim asked with obvious excitement, but was quickly quashed by Pip.

"Oh I doubt it. We're too far away from any big settlement for it to be a full temple – and they're bloody rare finds in England even then! A wayside shrine, on the other hand is much more in keeping with this kind of location. Mind you, we're not exactly on one of the main Roman roads, either, which would be a more normal location for a permanent shrine. It's a puzzle as to why it should be here."

They worked on with care, and at last found a couple of badly worn coins which would only give up their secrets of which emperor's head they wore in the conservation lab. Then, when Nick had gone to check on the main chapel site, Pip's trowel once again struck metal.

"Bloody hell, Pip, have you got a hidden metal detector in that trowel?" Tim teased, then looked harder at what was appearing. "What on earth is *that*?"

Pip was uncovering a piece of metal which looked to be about a foot long with small decorative heads along the upper edge of it. One end was curved like half of the head of a pair of modern pliers, and at its tip was a female head. Altogether there seemed to have been about four or five heads along the upper edge of the metal, although two at least had broken off, and what might be a bull or lion's head at the end which might have been a handle.

"I've never seen anything like that before," Tim breathed. "Not even out in the east. ...Pip? Are you all right?" She seemed to have gone very pale.

"No." Then she took a ragged breath. "Sorry, Tim, but I think I know what this is, and it brings back some very odd memories of something in my past. Be a love and go and get Nick, would you?"

As Tim scrambled up out of the trench and hurried towards Nick, Pip hung her head and offered up a curse of her own. Damn it! Would she never be free of the ghost of Dave? Dave and his fetish for bondage, and the strange *ménage à trois* he had enjoyed with Phil and Natalie from before he'd met her and tried to go 'straight', as he'd put it later.

"Pip? What's up?" Nick jumped down into the trench beside her and put a comforting arm around her shoulders.

She gestured with the trowel. "That thing! Please tell me I'm wrong and that it's not half of a castration clamp to do with the cult of Attis and Cybele!"

Nick's jaw dropped then turned from her to the find. With quick and deft scrapes he finished the work Pip had started and lifted the item. Once he had it in his hands he careful inspected it. "I have to bow to your knowledge, Pip, but I can see nothing which would say it *isn't*."

"I thought you were an Anglo-Saxon specialist, Pip?" Tim asked solicitously as he helped Pip out of the trench.

"I am," she replied, then became aware of the others, now clustered around the trench edge, all looking at her worriedly. God rot, Dave! She would have to explain now, there was no getting out of it. "Okay, you might as well know the whole rotten story. Up until four years ago I was engaged to another archaeologist called Dave. We'd met on a dig and it was all pretty normal until I moved in with him. Then I found out he'd had a friend called Natalie at university. I don't know what it was with her. I never actually met her, but I reckon she was more than a bit unstable. What I do know is that she was really preoccupied with some of what you might call the gorier ancient cults. She was also heavily into what might politely be called rough sex! That and bondage. For the first year with me, Dave managed to hold things together and give the appearance of having a normal relationship.

"Then he lost his job and so he got very stressed and his past all started coming out. One of the first clues I got that he was into some very odd stuff was when he dug out some drawings of some seriously strange items, including one of a pair of castration clamps which were found in the Thames in London. The drawings had been done by Natalie. Well you can imagine I got pretty upset by that! I love my history, but I draw the line at having to wake up in the morning looking at pictures of things used for self-mutilation, but also probably created my fella's one-time sex partner, if not actually his ex in the sense of a relationship like I thought I currently had with him!"

"Woah! Hang on a tick!" Will interrupted. "*Self*-mutilation?"

Pip sighed. "Oh yes. Even the Romans didn't like the cult of Cybele and Attis! Cybele is often called the Magna Mater – the Great Mother. Attis was supposedly her lover, but their cult – or rather Cybele's – involved her male priests dedicating themselves to her by castrating themselves. You'd have to be pretty devoted to inflict that kind of pain on yourself without the aid of an anaesthetic!"

"Fucking hell!" James and Will muttered in appalled unison.

"Well, from what I finally got out of Dave, Natalie really got off on the idea that she was another 'Great Mother' – not through actually having children, but by having men self-harm to prove their virility to her." She took a deep breath. Now for the killer information. "Phil – as in Phil, our pedantic man from the county offices – was another in that weird S&M group. He was another of Natalie's groupies."

"You are fucking joking!" Tim hooted. "Lady Phyllis gets his rocks off on having them crushed? Oh that's rich!" The others were laughing outright too.

"Bloody hell, of all the things I thought of him I'd never have guessed that!" Gemma gasped in mirth.

"But you can never let on that you know this!" Nick told them sternly. "If you do he will assume that it's Pip who told you, and that will make a lot of trouble for her, because Phil gets very nasty if he thinks his dirty secrets are out. I know! I made the mistake of hinting at it when Pip told me years ago. The end result was that he got Pip chucked off the university archaeology team. How I don't know. He has some high-up contacts there, and his dad was some pretty important professor years ago, although not at our uni'. Somehow Phil, too, was conveniently shunted off to the county archaeology services out here, because after he thought his errm... 'personal tastes' ...had become common knowledge, he said he couldn't continue working with the rest of the uni' team – even though it was a pretty big department then, and I swore I'd not said a word to anyone but him. So please, everyone, if you can't look him in the eye without howling with laughter, make yourselves scarce if he turns up again! For Pip's sake."

He looked at Pip and smiled. The rest didn't need to know that once Dave had had his breakdown he'd returned to Natalie's group. Nor that he'd concealed his ongoing infidelity from Pip until the day when she'd discovered she had an infection. Nick couldn't begin to imagine how Pip had coped with that. Bad enough to find that your partner was sleeping around, but how on earth did you come to terms with the fact that he'd abandoned you for someone who chained him to a wall and hurt him for pleasure? On one night when Pip had had a few drinks too many he'd heard her tearful confession that she'd threatened to leave when she'd challenged Dave over the STD, and then seen the marks on him that night when she'd forced her way into the bathroom as he'd been showering. They'd been in separate bedrooms for a while by then, and Pip had been away for a few weeks at that point, which was how she'd not seen them before. Given the ultimatum to stop or lose her, Dave had turned on her and said he would never have had his breakdown if he hadn't been trying to force himself into denying what he truly was for her sake.

That Dave had left their house there and then, and had gone to Phil's, was another reason why Nick loathed Phil. It had virtually made Pip homeless overnight, since she couldn't afford the rent alone, and that, Nick thought had been pretty selfish. Dave could have waited until Pip had found somewhere else to go, not disappear the week the rent was due. What Dave did for fun was up to him, however strange Nick thought it, but Phil had taken Dave in and helped him make Pip's life even more wretched than it need have been at that point. Coupled with the way Phil had taken Pip's chances of a career away from her, Nick was still of the opinion that if he got the chance sometime on dark night, he would give Phil a beating he'd never forget – not because of his fetishes, but for being such a bloody miserable specimen of a human being!

Now Pip was smiling weakly at him in thanks for giving the others the warning. "Thanks Nick," and to the others, "so you see I can push my luck with Phil only so far. If I ever get to the stage of being able to prove officially that he's bullied me in front of others who have no knowledge of our past, he knows he'd be on rocky ground. Because in any subsequent hearing our past history would come out, and not only would he be provably in the wrong this time, but what he fears most would happen – which is that his past would become public knowledge again. I don't know if Phil still goes to clandestine meetings with others who like that sort of thing anymore. I don't think so, but you never can tell."

Tim was now handling the find from the trench. "So you know about this from the pictures this Natalie woman drew. Where's she now?"

He was surprised that Nick and Pip suddenly looked to one another in horror.

"What? What did I say?"

"Not you, Tim," Nick answered weakly. "Bloody hell, I can't believe we forgot!"

"Forgot what?" Gemma demanded. "Come on you two, tell us for God's sake! We're dying of suspense here!"

"Over tea!" Nick insisted, and led them into the farmhouse. Only when he and Pip had had a few gulps of the hot, strong tea would Nick be persuaded to continue the tale.

"Well again it was only around four years ago, immediately before Pip and Dave spilt up – in fact, it was to be the other trigger for that, although Pip wasn't to know it when she was challenging Dave that night. You see Natalie was on an evaluating dig just across on the other ridge from here at the Roman marching camp site, as was Pip's now-ex, Dave – although as I said, Pip and Dave were still together at that point. Then one day Natalie disappeared! And I mean really disappeared! The police were involved and everything!"

"Wow!" Kirsty breathed. "That's some story!"

"Oh it gets better," Nick told them grimly. "Neither Pip nor I were involved on that dig, so we were well out of it, thank God. And we were provably up in the wilds of Scotland out on a dig on Orkney with a whole bunch of other people who could swear we were there, and with no way of getting back and forth overnight."

"Shit! Why did you have to have alibis?" Will asked in awe. He'd never known anyone who'd had to do that before.

"Oh not me," Nick said with a more relaxed wave of his hand. "But Pip did! It was because other people said that they thought there was something between Natalie and Dave, and they'd been heard arguing the night she vanished. Well of course the police started looking into Dave and found that he was engaged to Pip,..."

"...And if ever there was a motive, then the fiancée who was bring lied to was a pretty good one!" Gemma gasped in understanding. "God Almighty, Pip, you really were put through the mill weren't you!"

Pip sighed. "Yes I was. That was how so much of it came out, you see. The police were interviewing me up on Orkney, and I was wondering why the hell they were looking at Dave so hard? And then I got back and found out! Dave had been asked to leave the dig, not just because of the scandal but because he was acting really weirdly, almost as though he knew Natalie was dead or something. That's when he cracked up for the last time, and our relationship went into melt down because suddenly he was always with his old friends again – people I hardly knew at all." She wasn't going to say that she'd discovered the STD while up on that dig on Orkney with Nick, and had already been wondering what the hell was going on with Dave, even before the police arrived – and of course under the strain of everything she'd blurted that bit of personal information out as well, which had made the police more curious than ever about her. That row on the evening she'd got home had been the worst night of her life!

"Did they ever find the body?" James asked, earning a frown from Nick for his tactlessness.

However Pip wasn't upset by the question. In a tone of almost relief she said, "No. That in the end was what closed the investigation. Natalie was a grown woman, and if she was thought a bit weird, she still wasn't thought to be what the police would classify as a vulnerable adult. And come on folks, you must have seen all the adverts in the *Big Issue* of people trying to find vulnerable adults who've been missing for years! The police are overwhelmed with missing persons. And despite all the investigations, with no hint that anything untoward had happened to Natalie, they had to let it be. But she's never been seen since, and both Dave – who I also haven't seen in nearly that long – and Phil even now, get very upset when you mention her."

"But you can see how it's pretty weird for us to find something which reminds us of Natalie right up the road from where she disappeared," Nick added. "And I tell you something else I've just realised, that curse written on the lead isn't likely to be calling on Minerva! That's why the second letter looked a bit weird to me, because it's not an 'i' as in Minerva but an 'a' as in Mater. It's a curse on anyone who disturbs the site dedicated to the Magna Mater! And if ever there was a cult which would want to be out of the way it was that one!"

Pip nodded. "I reluctantly looked the bloody thing up when I was trying to put things right with Dave just before I went to Orkney. It was pretty vilified by the other Romans, whether in Rome or the provinces, because even they – who were pretty broadminded over most things – drew the line at deliberate self-harming. One of the other things I learned about it was that these crackpot eunuchs were known to the Romans as 'Galli', after the location further east where the cult was supposedly begun, and that the name became one of derision – a 'Gaul' apparently coming to be a colloquial name for a eunuch or 'half-man'. It was something the Romans used when they got to France to make a taunting pun of with the Gaulish people."

"Oh the joys of discovering the Roman version of calling someone a wanker!" Will muttered in disbelief.

Pip seemed to be pulling herself together a bit more now and managed a laugh with the others at that. "Oh they were a right lot, were the Galli. They mutilated themselves in other ways as well. Arm slashing was another choice habit, but you wouldn't want them too close for other reasons. Apparently they were a rowdy lot, blowing trumpets and creating a right old racket, if I remember correctly – and as you can imagine, I've tried rather hard *not* to remember! But it might also account for why no-one wanted to reuse any stone from even a small shrine. You were unwittingly closer to the truth than we allowed for when you said the place was contaminated, Kirsty. If this place was the site of such an unsavoury cult, and one bad enough to have a lingering local memory of it even a couple of hundred years later, then the locals might have welcomed with open arms some travelling Christian priest offering to cleanse the offending site and make it 'safe' again. Not every conversion was done under duress, even back then."

Tim was scratching his chin and looking thoughtful. "Hmmm, and what do you think Natalie's reaction would have been if she'd found a shrine to her favourite Roman weirdo had been re-consecrated as a Christian place? Because we've only found half of this disgusting contraption, haven't we. Could the spring have washed the other half down its course, is what I'm thinking, you see? And if this Natalie was a bit off her rocker to start with, could that have been what tipped her over the edge?"

Both Nick and Pip looked at him in surprise, Nick being the first to recover. "God, that's a thought, isn't it! And would the police have thought to look here? It's pretty remote, and I don't think the search for Natalie was so urgent or so extensive that they brought helicopters in to look from above. It might have been missed."

All the archaeologists went silent, but they were all thinking the same – this dig could get very gruesome if they suddenly stumbled on Natalie's body!

Chapter 4

Worcestershire, June 1814

When he got to Clifton-upon-Teme, Harry realised he was going to have to ask directions, and that raised a whole new spectre from the past. At the point when he'd planned this visit, he'd hoped to ride in, see Amy, and leave – indeed he'd hoped he would be seeing Amy at her parent's old house near Worcester, and he'd not even have to come out here at all. Then things had got so bloody complicated with Beatrice Clifford's news, and he'd been forced to adjust his plans beyond all recognition. Not least because of the knowledge that he could hardly ride the dozen miles from Worcester to Lower Sapey, spend time with Amy, and then make it back to Worcester that same night. Now it was never going to be the short but tortuous visit he'd originally expected.

So he'd reluctantly moved on to Bromyard and taken a room, and now had made this ride out from there on yet another day – already doubling the length of time he'd intended to be in the shire. Yet today Cold Hunger Farm was proving ridiculously hard to find, and with a sinking heart he'd been forced to recognise that either he would have to retreat to Bromyard (and in his head this whole trip was becoming like some dreadful miniature campaign of his own, with its peculiar retreats and advances), ask for directions and then return on yet another day, or ride on to Clifton.

Yet there'd been a good reason why he'd not wanted to go to Clifton in the first place, and it wasn't because he had anything against the inn at Clifton. The Red Lion was a perfectly acceptable hostelry, and one where he was sure of a warm welcome. No, his reason was that folk there would have thought it strange for him to be stopping at the inn when he had family in the village. And although Harry had not lived here long enough himself to be instantly recognised, he knew his name would automatically incite the question,

"Are you the Reverend's son, then?"

After all, if someone so lacking in outward paternal feelings as Sir Roderick Clifford had sought word of his son from business associates, it was unlikely that his own father would never have said a word about him, even in this new incumbency. And Harry had to acknowledge that the bitter awkwardness between his father and himself had been generated by his uncle, and not through any act on his own behalf. Therefore he had no wish to bring embarrassment on his father by giving the village something to gossip about – and in any country village, gossip was always rife!

So now he rode up to the rectory, tethered the hired horse to a nearby stout wooden fence, and walked up to the door. Taking a calming deep breath, he grasped the large iron knocker and rapped it hard on the wood twice. Part of him desperately wanted to see his father after all these years, and the other part was praying that he'd be away from the house visiting some sick parishioner, thus giving Harry every reason to ask at the inn.

When the door opened, though, it was to reveal the one person he really didn't want to see.

"Yes?"

Harry recognised his brother in an instant, but clearly the changes he had gone through since Robert had last seen him made him unrecognisable, and of course here he was in a white-trimmed red coat and blue breeches, with his captain's shako sporting its red and white cockade under his arm, hardly the boy who'd left. What to do? Act the stranger and take a risk? But then how could he ask after Father if he did?

"Hello Robert," he said gravely and held out his hand.

For a moment Robert was puzzled, then recognition flittered across his face to be instantly replaced by a disapproving frown.

"So you came!" He gave a bitter bark of what might have been meant as a sarcastic laugh. "Well you're too late!"

Harry was taken aback. Of all the responses at their meeting again, he'd never imagined this one. "Too late? Too late for what?" And as he tried to fathom what his brother was talking about asked, "Is Father in?"

Yet Robert reeled back as if Harry had struck him. "What kind of sick joke is that? How dare you ride up here and ask that!"

Now Harry was getting worried. "Robert? What's wrong? What's happened?"

"Oh don't play games with me! You can't pretend you don't know after all of the letters I wrote to you. And not once did you write back!"

"Letters? Robert I swear to you I received no letters. Not from you nor from father." Now Harry was starting to feel more than a little aggrieved. "Indeed I stopped writing to you because I never got any answers."

"What arrant nonsense! Of course Father wrote back!"

An old man pushing a handcart with a squeaky wheel was passing, and it belatedly occurred to Harry that they were giving the village plenty to talk about by standing arguing on the doorstep. But he was unprepared to hear the old farmer say,

"Mornin' Reverend," and doff his cap as he doddered on by.

"Reverend? Here?" Harry felt a dreadful nausea creeping up on him. "Oh God, Robert, what's happened? Is Father dead?"

It must have finally dawned on Robert that Harry couldn't be feigning his sudden pallor, and similarly, that they were making something of a spectacle of themselves out here.

"I suppose you'd better come in," he said brusquely, and turned his back to lead the way down the hall to the parlour, leaving Harry to follow, shutting the heavy old front door behind him.

Standing either side of the fireplace, currently as empty and cold as the brotherly relationship, Harry felt as though they'd suddenly stepped back ten years. How many times had he and Robert stood in confrontation in one parlour or another during the years they'd been growing up? Robert wore the same tight-lipped expression of disapproval which so often had provoked an angry reaction from Harry, and he knew that if things weren't to disintegrate fast, he had to make the first move.

"Please Robert, tell me what's happened?" he asked humbly. "I swear that if," no he mustn't question his prickly brother! There could be no 'if'. "...that your letters never reached me."

Mercifully Robert must have been thinking along similar lines, because he seemed about to make a cutting remark, then took a deep breath and turned away to walk a few paces before turning to face Harry and say,

"Father died last May."

"*May*?" Harry was aghast. "Nearly a whole year ago? No, over a year! Dear Lord, he wasn't yet fifty! Why...?" He stopped himself from the instinctive reaction of demanding to know why no-one had written to tell him. If Robert was telling the truth – and whatever faults Harry could have laid at his brother's door, lying hadn't been one of them – then he had tried. He turned, spotted a familiar old chair and slumped into it, the smell of the pipe his father had so loved smoking wafting up at him as the upholstery gave under his weight. Shaking his head in unwillingness to accept the fact he asked, "How? Was he ill? Was it some accident? He wasn't old enough to die of age!"

Robert sniffed. "I suppose I have to believe that, however unlikely I find it, you didn't know."

"Oh for pity's sake, Robert! If you can't take my word for it, work this out for yourself – when Father died we were on the march. From July through August my regiment was fighting in the Pyrenees. Then by the autumn we were marching up and through France in hot pursuit of 'Boney'! Only in April, after we helped take Toulouse and had marched to Bordeaux, were we sent back here to England." The memory of the ragged remains of his Light Company, battered and wounded, still marching with pride behind him for the last time as they'd landed in England, threatened to choke him if he thought on it too hard, and he fought the memory back. "Can you not concede that in all of that, your letters might have gone astray?"

Robert's expression softened a little. Clearly he hadn't thought about the particulars of what his brother had been doing. However, he wasn't about to admit total defeat yet. "But we addressed the letters most carefully. Lieutenant Harold Green of the Huntingdons. Father found out from the bishop that that was the 33rd Foot and so that's what he wrote, ...what *we* wrote too. He took the letters with him in to Worcester to make sure that they were sent off to the army."

Harry was stunned. "I don't serve with those Huntingdons, Robert. And that's the 33rd's old name! Now they're the First Yorkshire! I serve with the Huntingdon*shire* Regiment. The 2nd/31st Foot!"

Now Robert had the grace to look dismayed. "But the bishop said that the Huntingdons were raised in Gloucester!"

Burying his head in his head for a moment to cover his grief at how little his family had cared to find out about their son's fate – for how much effort would it really have taken to trace him if they'd cared a jot? – Harry finally managed to answer him. "The Huntingdons he was talking about were raised by one of the earls of Huntingdon, I think, and I suppose that might even have been around Gloucester, but that was over a *century* ago. *Now* they recruit from Yorkshire." He was finding it hard beyond belief not to show how hurt he was by all of this. "But that's not *my* regiment!" He tapped the silver badge on his uniform where the regiment's name lay beneath the rearing stag. "See? Huntingdon*shire*! Why on earth did you not simply ask Uncle William where he'd purchased my commission?"

Then the answer came to him. "Oh God, it was that same old argument, wasn't it? Why did Uncle William spend the money on me, when Father was struggling to get you put through your education to follow him into the church? Damn it, Robert! Why could you both never see that all Uncle wanted was to have a relative fighting with Wellesley – as the duke was then? I didn't ask for preferential treatment! If you must know I didn't want to go at all! I was scared stiff! But the Cliffords were sending Edward, and Uncle William never could stand being outdone by them. By some upstart family in trade, as you know only too well that he called them. If I hadn't gone, he would have found some other way to get what he wanted, even though I was the only spare male on either side of his family. And that's what I was, Robert. The spare one. The one you could all afford to lose. He wouldn't risk his own son! For pity's sake, did you not hear enough of the arguments with our grandparents to realise that they saw Mother marrying a poor parson as a comedown of such social magnitude as to never be forgiven?"

Now Robert was the one to hang his head. "Yes. Yes, I remember the arguments." He took a deep breath and finally managed to look Harry in the eye. "I remember Mother telling me that I had a choice when I finished school. That I could either disappoint Father or her family, but that I'd never please both. That there was a job for me in one of the family glove factories under Uncle William if I wished, but that Father would feel betrayed. Or I could follow Father into the Church, but that I would never see a penny of her family's money – not now or in the future." He gave a rueful half-smile. "Since I wanted the Church for myself it wasn't a hard choice."

Harry couldn't refrain from adding, "And in the process you condemned me."

Robert blinked in surprise. "Me? Condemn you? How? Don't be dramatic, Harry! It doesn't suit a man of your age."

"Oh I'm not being dramatic just for the effect," Harry told him bitterly. "I went to Worcester and begged Uncle William for a job. Even an apprentice's job. But he told me he wouldn't have one of the family on the factory floor. It wouldn't be right, he said. And he wouldn't give me a job higher up unless you joined me. He wanted the factories to stay in the family, you see, but he feared that if he employed me, then I would be handing out money to you for the rest of my life. And even in a second-hand way, Uncle William wouldn't support a cleric in the family after Mother's fall from grace, especially having seen how poorly we lived in the early days. And I tried to talk to you, Robert, but all you could do was keep on about me finding some way to make Uncle William pay for me to follow you into the Church, and how it wouldn't cost him much. You condemned me to finding something else, Brother. To take what I could or starve, because Father could hardly have kept another grown man on what he had coming in. You know this! You know now firsthand what a parson has to live on."

As he'd spoken Robert's face had been a picture of changing emotions. He'd clearly not thought much on that period of their childhood, but now that he did he could see the truth of what Harry was saying. "I'm sorry, Harry, truly I am. I didn't see it like that at the time. Did you really not want to enlist?"

"No I didn't! I don't know what I would have done given the choice. And that was part of the problem, don't you see? Father expected me to have the same calling as you and him, but I didn't, and even worse I couldn't tell him what I did have a calling for, because I didn't know myself! Therefore when Uncle William offered me the commission, I felt I had to take it because it was the only option I had. And just in case you think he's been keeping me in wine and tobacco and fine horses, let me tell you that he bought only what he needed to! Ever since then I've had to live on what I get paid!" Perhaps now wasn't the time to let on about the spoils of war which had increased his financial situation for the better. Anyway, they weren't relevant, since they'd only come in the last year or so after far too many of scrimping and saving.

"Has it been very hard?" Robert asked gruffly. If some brotherly love was finally creeping back he was still not keen to show it, and somehow that made Harry angry.

"Hard? Bugger me, Robert! What do you think it's like marching for days on end in the freezing cold or the baking sun? With the soles coming off your boots because some thieving quartermaster has turned a quick profit and sold the spares? Horses don't come cheap on a captain's pay! – So I certainly wasn't riding! – And what it's like getting drenched in the high mountains where there aren't even any trees to make a fire in the evening to dry out by, and then to find men dead in the morning from the cold? To eat biscuit made out of flour full of weevils? Or to see men blown apart by cannon mere feet away from you? Splattered into pieces you can't even recognise? I've had friends mashed into one another and never been able to tell who was who!"

He took in the way Robert was wincing but couldn't stop himself because the feelings were so raw.

"I got to Portugal when I was shoved off the boat from here, and no sooner had I joined the regiment then we were in an absolute catastrophe of an engagement at the Alberche river by Talavera. The bastard Spanish let us down, useless buggers! Nothing new in that, I was to learn later. So there I was, barely eighteen years old and as green as the grass, facing what seemed like a never ending stream of Frenchmen coming at me, all wanting to kill me, and me expected to set an example to the ordinary men because, God help me, I was an officer! Don't pretend you can even begin to understand how hard that was, Robert, because you can't. The only thing I can remember about that first bloody fight was the unnaturally scarred trees – because I discovered it was in a cork grove, and you can see where they take the bark off every so many years – and the dreadful acrid-smelling smoke from the guns stinging my eyes, and the biggest Scotsman I'd ever seen, shouting orders I couldn't understand, to men who pretended I didn't exist, because they didn't trust me not to get them killed!

"That Scotsman has since become one of the best friends I shall ever have, even if Uncle William would turn his nose up at having him to dine. He at least saw the promise in me when all Father could do was upbraid me for disappointing him so badly. That hurt, Robert, that really hurt me. I felt as though I were some dreadful criminal after the way I was sent away from here. And when other men talked of home with longing, I never knew what to say. Because what did I have? The place I thought of as home was the old vicarage on the other side of Worcester. We'd not been here a year when Father packed my bags and told me not to come back if I was going to be Uncle William's lapdog. The army has become my home, and yet you may believe me or not, but had I known Father was dying I would still have come, because despite all of that I still loved him."

By now Robert was looking at his younger brother in appalled shock. "I didn't know Father had said that to you," he said softly. "For that I'm truly sorry. You didn't deserve that. He did talk of you with affection, you know. He just didn't understand."

"Didn't he?" Harry was in no mood to cede ground. "If it was just understanding, why didn't he get in touch with me?"

"He tried!"

"Bollocks!"

That made Robert blanch. It wasn't the kind of language most of his parishioners used to him. "Harry!"

"Well it is!" Harry couldn't sit still any longer and began pacing the small parlour like a caged lion. "What did I do so very wrong, Robert? Because I cannot grasp why, when if – as you say – you had no reply from me to your letters, you or Father didn't try to find out if the letters had reached me? I wrote when I got chance, but there were precious few of those moments in the first few weeks. Did he not look at where they'd come from when my letters did finally arrive? So why did he not question where I was?"

"I told you, he went to the bishop!"

"Why? What in the name of Heaven would the bishop know about the army? Christ, Robert, you would think it pretty strange if I had wanted to trace you through the Church and had gone to one of my lord Wellington's aides to find out, wouldn't you?"

"Put like that, yes, I suppose so."

"It *is* so! So I can only assume that you wrote me off as the black sheep of the family. Is my name still in the family bible, or has it been struck out? Because if you really didn't want to go to Uncle William, then if you'd cared at all, you could always have got in touch with Horseguards in London. ...But you didn't, did you! Just how long did Father give me before he gave up? Weeks? Months? A year? Not long, I bet!"

Robert ruefully answered, "After the sixth letter went unanswered."

"And how long was that?"

"Probably about two or three months."

Harry's anger suddenly vaporised leaving him feeling drained and weary. "Bloody hell, my own first letter to you would barely have reached you by then! Did he not wonder at why I wasn't responding to what he said?"

"I think by the time they must have arrived he was so angry he wouldn't have read them."

"Angry? Good God, over what? My confessions that I was scared half out of my skin most of the time? Did he think I was a coward to add to my sins? That I would shame you all by deserting? Or was it him being put out that I hadn't responded instantly? Surely he realised how long it would take for post to catch up with me?" He took in Robert's expression of dawning horror. "Oh, so that would be 'no', then! And of course, since I never did get his letters, he would have put every scrap of blame on me, never wondering if he'd been sending them to the right bloody regiment! Well, they would barely have got to me in his unreasonable version of time even if you *had* been sending them to the right place!" He could now see why his uncle had become so exasperated with his father. However much he had loved the old man, he could now see that his father's view of the world had been as parochial as the area he served. Beyond Worcestershire it was all one and the same to him. Probably the only time he would have counted Napoleon as any kind of threat would have been if he'd appeared in a flotilla of ships up the River Severn! And was his brother any more worldly? Was there any point in trying to explain further, or should he sever all connections with his family right now?

As if reading Harry's mind, Robert said, "I'm sorry. Of course they would. Even with me away in Oxford, letters sometimes took longer than expected to reach me. I'm ashamed, Harry. He never showed me your letters or told me of them, but I should have seen where the flaw lay in his expectation of a response – I know how he was impatient with me just writing from the next county! I should have stood up for you and told him to be more patient."

"It wouldn't have done you much good," Harry added bleakly. "If you were sending them off to the 33rd Foot they've been in the West Indies for the last ten years! Or so we heard just before I sailed back here. Those letters you sent have probably just got out there and are being shipped all the way back!"

The sheer insanity of the situation made Robert laugh, but at least it broke the tension in the room, and now

Robert had got off his high horse he could see Harry the man, not the boy, and sympathise more. "Harry, I'm now so sorry I was curt with you when you arrived. This must have come as such a shock to you."

Well that was certainly a step in the right direction, Harry thought, and if Robert was going to make some effort to mend things then he wasn't going to metaphorically spit in his eye. "So how did Father die?"

Robert sighed. "Oh things had been all right while Mrs Jones was coming in to keep house for him, but then her husband died, and she went to live with her brother further into Wales. At that point I think it dawned on me how little notice Father had been taking of the world. I think it started when Mother died, just before we moved here – maybe I should have been more alert to his grieving given that the first thing he did after the funeral was request a move of parish. I don't think he could ever deal with the reality of her loss, and he'd been in a slow decline since then, but it was a couple of years after you left that it got noticeable. Luckily I was working directly for the bishop by then, so I could come over from Worcester whenever possible, not having a parish of my own to deal with. I managed to get another local woman to come in in the mornings, and it was she who told me that in the winter she would come in and the fire would have been stone cold. He didn't even think to put coal on, Harry, he was just lost in his own world with his books. He just faded away. He wasn't ill. He didn't have anything like a fall. He just gave up on living."

"So how come you're here? If Father died a whole year ago you can't be here still sorting his things out, and that man called you 'Reverend' just now."

Robert nodded. "The last year, maybe a year and a half, he started neglecting his duties with the church. He had a head full of theology but he forgot his parishioners, and of course someone eventually complained to the bishop. We agreed it was easiest if I simply took over as the incumbent – after all I was already ordained and in the diocese. Then he could carry on living here and I could watch over him. But in a rural parish like this it takes time to get around to see people, and to do the rest of the job properly takes even more time. So I didn't have more than a few hours a day with him, and he became more and more withdrawn."

"That can't have done your career any good, though," Harry sympathised. If Robert had been working that closely to the bishop he'd probably been singled out as someone with potential for a higher office than a mere parish priest. He was expecting Robert to complain about that, so he was quite surprised when his brother gave a half-hearted shrug and smiled.

"What?" Harry was puzzled.

Robert seemed to be gathering himself together as if to make a confession, and when it came it was the last thing Harry had expected.

"It wasn't so hard to do. You see I'd decided that ...well the truth is, I'd had something of a crisis of faith."

"You?" Harry was astounded. If anything he'd thought his brother more devout than even their father had been. "But you wanted so much to go into the Church!"

"I did. But once I got there I found it wasn't what I'd expected. It was all the politics which finished me, Harry. The backbiting and manoeuvring, the squabbling for the tiniest degree of seniority. The men I was working with could have been in the House of Commons or on the local town council, they were no more Christian in their ways. And before you say why didn't you leave..."

"...you couldn't because, like me, you have nowhere

else to go. Oh I understand that! You see I'm in a bit of a limbo myself."

"Really?" Robert was sounding relieved that at last he'd found someone who understood, so in response he could now sympathise with his brother as never before.

"We've taken terrible casualties in the last year. Several major encounters in a matter of months. It takes its toll. And Huntingdonshire isn't the biggest place to recruit from. So there's talk of us in the 2nd Battalion being absorbed into the 1st. Of the 31st becoming a regiment of just one battalion instead of two. The second battalion's colours are probably to be laid up at Wrotham Park. But that will mean there are too many officers even despite our losses, because it's the men we're missing most. I've been to Horseguards to put my case, Robert, but I hope to God I get a post, because if not I shall have to find the means to change to another regiment – if I can! Because I've not been a captain long enough to make me someone another regiment will want to snap up, you see. Also I've been with the Light Company, and they are only ever one of ten in any battalion, so I'm not the most useful of officers in many commanders' eyes. And coming out of the army isn't an option at the moment for the very reasons you're staying in the church."

"Captain? You made captain? Well done! I wish we'd known."

"It would have made the papers in the sections on the war," Harry said, unable to resist making the point. "We don't exactly get the *Berrow's Journal* out in Spain to read of local events, but you could have read about me if you'd kept up with what was going on in the war."

Robert grimaced. "Father wouldn't have it spoken about in the house, and I'm afraid I took little interest."

"You may find you'll wish you had when the war is over and you have soldiers returning home and looking for work," Harry told him wryly. "They won't be the obedient lads they were when they went away."

"Very much like you, then!" Robert said with a small smile, but there was real warmth there now.

"Yes, very much! So do you have a secure position here? And can you cope if you don't have your faith anymore?"

"I do. And I find it much easier out here. A lot of what I do as the rector is about helping people with their everyday lives. In a way, that's helped me regain some of my faith. It's just the all-too-earthly Church I have trouble with sometimes, now. And there's a part of me that quite enjoys finding the more obscure passages of the bible to quote to help the ordinary folk feel better about God, rather than eternally striking fear and damnation into their hearts."

"You rebel!" Harry laughed.

Then a thought struck Robert. "But if you didn't know about Father, were you just coming here to visit us or what?"

"Ah, well that's another story," and Harry explained about wanting to find Amy and the rest of the Vaughan family. He had to edge around him coming back with Edward three years ago, but covered it by saying, quite truthfully, that they'd only been back for a few short days, and that when he'd written to say he was coming and their father hadn't replied, he'd assumed he wasn't welcome. He also got some approval from Robert when he said he'd feared old man Clifford would have made thing difficult for Father if he'd refused to stand beside Edward. Maybe Robert really was starting to believe him?

"Good Heavens!" Robert sighed when he got to the end. "Well I can't say I'm surprised about Edward. I didn't know him and his family as well as you did, since as children they had no-one of my age to play with as you did Edward, but I always did think he was trouble. I can't think who that young woman he went off with was, though. I have no memory of seeing her about Worcester. Maybe she wasn't here for long. But poor Amy! And her family. I knew Cold Hunger had been let out to someone but that they were keeping themselves to themselves, so I hadn't taken a lot of notice. I certainly haven't seen them at church here, but then although Lower Sapey is in our diocese, Upper Sapey is nearer and that's over the border in Hereford's, so I suppose I thought they must be going there."

"Can you show me the way there?"

"Certainly, but why don't we go over to the inn and have some lunch first?"

Harry agreed, and not only because the morning had already disappeared and his stomach was reminding him of the fact. If half of what he'd heard of the Vaughans' fall from grace was true, then they might be in very straightened circumstances, and he had no wish to embarrass them by placing them in the situation of having to ask him to dine, when there might be little they could offer him.

While he waited for Robert to get his coat, Harry turned to the mirror to adjust the collar of his uniform. He was feeling more and more self-conscious in the uniform, not having realised how few men there would be around dressed this way over here. But he'd had almost no chance to purchase civilian clothes since returning to England, and those he'd left home with five years ago were long grown out of. As he worried the high collar into a more comfortable position again, he found himself yet again surprised at his own appearance. Lacking such luxuries as mirrors for the last few year – or at least ones good enough to see detail in – he'd not realised how he'd changed in five years. As children, Robert had been the angelic looking one, with a shock of fair hair and grey eyes verging on blue. He, on the other hand, had been the mischievous one, with hints of red in the brown hair and a heavy smattering of freckles across his nose. Now the freckles had become lost in the tan, and his face had lost the boyish roundness and was suitable battered for a soldier. No major scars as yet, but more than a few tiny white lines marking close calls with blades and bullets. There was also a steely glint in the green eyes which hadn't been there before. Robert had already been able to give disapproving looks by the time his voice had broken, but Harry had always been more inclined to laughter. Five years of war had changed that.

When Robert appeared beside him to straighten his own collar, Harry reflected on how well his brother looked the part of his chosen role. His classical features were, if anything, even more Grecian than their father's had been, and Harry could now see why their mother had been so taken by the handsome young man who had courted her. Robert also effortlessly managed an air of gravitas, of substantial learning coupled with stern inflexibility when it came to right and wrong – in other words, if an artist had wanted to paint the epitome of a good parson he would have come up with Robert. He would also have cut a fine figure in bishop's robes, had he wanted to press his career that way.

Therefore, stood side by side, no-one would have taken them for being even related, let alone brothers, when the only thing they had in common was their height. Yet for the first time in his life Harry felt equal to Robert rather than in his shadow. He'd been tested and tempered by far harsher events than any his brother could have encountered, and he'd done more than survive, he'd excelled. Now at twenty-four he wasn't the black sheep compared to the perfect son anymore. Was it hurt pride which made him feel anger that his father wasn't here to see the man he'd become? No, he didn't think so. The anger was over the wasted time between them, but for his own part he wouldn't want to come back here to live now, even if the old man had been alive. Maybe in becoming a soldier he had found his vocation after all?

Chapter 5

Friday & Saturday, modern day

The following day, Nick gave the team a day off. He needed to get the skeleton of the baby dealt with officially, since any human bones had to be confirmed as being too ancient to warrant police involvement, and anyway the heavens had opened up and the rain was coming down in torrents. The team had spread tarpaulins over the trenches the previous night in preparation, but there was no way they could continue working in them with such a deluge coming down. So with most of the team deciding to escape into the warmth of the cinema in Worcester, Pip volunteered to go back to the house alone to prepare for the arrival of Arthur Wormesley, the dendrochronologist, who had deferred his visit until Saturday morning. She didn't mind this. Being in old buildings alone had never worried her, and after the emotional revelations of yesterday she was quite welcoming some time away from the team's scrutiny.

Pulling the minibus as close to the back door as possible, she scuttled in fast lugging another bag of coal, and set to getting the range going in the kitchen again. With the chimney of the kitchen being the nearest to being a central chimney stack, she knew from long-past visits to her grandparent's old farmhouse that if she could get it warm, then it would take the chill off much of the rest of the house. For all that it was ancient, the old range soon lit, making Pip observe,

"Someone knew how to build a chimney which would draw properly, didn't they!" as she gave the old cooker an affectionate pat. It had been her dream for most of her life to live in an old place like this. "Damn, I could do with that lottery win!" she muttered as she put the kettle on. Nothing short of that was going to give her the kind of money she'd need, even to buy a place as dilapidated as Cold Hunger, but she could still dream. Why, she inwardly fumed, was it always some tasteless prat who got their hands on lovely old houses like this? People who then proceeded to sanitise them to the point of destroying all of their charm?

While she waited for the hot-plate to get warm enough to heat the kettle, Pip kept her coat on and went exploring. It was barely nine in the morning, for Pip had come early, and yet the thick, dark rain clouds made the summer's day feel more like a chilly late autumn afternoon. Luckily Pip had brought with her two big torches and spare batteries, because in the gloom she was needing them even before she started looking for fine details. So like someone creeping round in a badly made horror film, she went though into the old scullery, where the gusty wind was making the decrepit window frame whistle and rattle, and opened the door into the workshop opposite the kitchen.

"Bloody hell!" she squealed, as an unexpected gust of wind ripped the door from her hand and slammed it behind her; then realised why it was so cold in here. The two windows were nothing more than barred openings, with no glass in them and no evidence that they had ever been glazed. Once upon a time there had no doubt been shutters on the outside to fend off the worst of any winter weather, but none were visible now.

Not wanting to linger, Pip flashed the torch around the room and swiftly decided that there was little worth investigating here. If something outside warranted extending a trench inside then there wouldn't be any problem, because as far as Pip could see the floor was only beaten earth, but the room had little to offer itself. Retreating to the comparative shelter of the house proper, Pip went into the hall. Nothing exceptional here either. Her only thoughts were that it was no wonder they had to have a fireplace at either end of the long, thin room. With it facing east it must have been a frightful room to try and keep heated in the winter, especially with the front door coming straight into it from the outside. If Arthur wanted to take a look at the staircase, then that was up to him, but there were no promising beams for him to work with here. Someone had plastered over them all, no doubt in a vain attempt to make the place look a bit more modern sometime in the nineteenth century.

The room backing onto the kitchen had the remains of an old Victorian office in it – a bookcase with pigeonholes as well as shelves, and a big old desk which looked as though it was so rotten with damp that it would fall apart the minute it was touched. Going on through into the next room, it was clear that this was definitely a later extension. The ceilings were higher and had some semblance of decorative plaster coving. The fireplace was also a much grander thing altogether, and from studying the outside, Pip knew that this was the third and end chimney stack, and probably the newest.

"The dining room, no doubt," she breathed, imagining the late-Georgian farmers who had lived here using this as a much more congenial room for family gatherings than the draughty old hall. It certainly had no other function screaming at her, whereas when she went into the final room on the ground floor there were two very dilapidated and mouse-eaten old sofas lingering in faded glory, proclaiming that this had been the parlour. Looking out of the two side windows, Pip could see why the room had been chosen too. Despite them facing north, the land sloped upwards slightly to the woods beyond, and on a nice day the view would have been of the garden bathed in sunlight. Even in such a soggy summer, some ancient delphiniums, honeysuckles and roses were doing their best to put on a show.

If there had been another door in the room it would have led straight back into the kitchen, but for some reason this had never been made, so Pip had to go back round the loop of rooms to check on the range. Making herself a good sized mug of tea, she then went up the stairs, sipping as she went. She'd always expected to be doing most of her searching for beams upstairs, and almost immediately she was rewarded. The two rooms to the right of where the stairs emerged onto the landing had maybe once been main bedrooms, but had fallen from favour very early on, not least because with the workshop being beneath one, they were bitterly cold. Even as she looked approvingly at the nice beams in the second bedroom where the roof sloped downwards, Pip felt sorry for whoever had had to sleep in here.

"Some poor lass of a maid, no doubt!" she muttered darkly, tapping at the sloping ceiling and realising that there was very little between the plaster and the actual backing for the roof tiles. Even the fireplaces in these two rooms looked pathetically small. Most nineteenth century bedroom grates were smaller than those downstairs, but these were barely brazier size. "Brrrr! It must have been terrible in here in January! I bet there were icicles on the inside of the windows!"

It made the house feel even gloomier than the dim light did already, and she found herself humming the old folk tune 'Bitter Withy' as she went into the next rooms (the ones across the stairs from the main landing), which looked as though they might have been a nursery. A song about Jesus as a child getting punished for drowning the sons of the local nobles seemed fittingly bleak in this setting. An apology of Victorian wallpaper hung in damp tatters off the sloping ceiling in the first room. In its decline its faded attempt at looking cheerful only achieved the reverse, yet at least this room had a fireplace which was more than the room off it did.

"Good grief, the poor little buggers would have frozen in here!" Pip sighed. "Even when the old scullery below here was the kitchen, it couldn't have given off that much heat! I wonder if this was the play-room? Surely no mother would let her children sleep in a room without a fire if there was a choice?"

Looking out of the right-hand window of the room with the fireplace in it, Pip was surprised to see that the current kitchen's great chimney stack must be forming almost all of that side's wall in this room. Maybe the pair had been one big L-shaped room originally? That would explain why there was only the one fireplace between them. Perhaps the subdivision had been to create a storage room later on? Pip tapped on the separating wall and was gratified to hear it echo thinly.

"Hmmm, shoddy workmanship! Yes, this is probably quite a late change. Wonder how the bedrooms were laid out when there was only this bit as the original house?"

There was only the one grate centrally located on the chimney breast, so there hadn't been a second bedroom taking advantage of the big chimney – or at least not on this west side. She laid her hand on the chimney wall and was sure she could feel that it was less cold then the one at the end of the house. The range hadn't been going for long enough to really make its presence felt, but it surely would in time.

"Hmmm. The master bedroom back then, maybe?"

She wandered back out onto the landing and stood back to look at the walls. Yes, if she squinted hard she could see a line in the plaster over the stairs which might indicate that once there had been another, different doorway into what was now the unheated room beyond, and that it had been reached by there being more of a floor over the stairwell. However, Pip and Nick both reckoned that the first extension which had made the house T-shaped had come quite quickly after the original building. The bricks were just too good a match for it not to have been, and they had weathered to the same degree. Not that the final addition could have been much later than about 1750, but the first two sections of the house were almost certainly pre-1700 and probably pre-1650 if Nick's guess was right. And there, as if on cue, she found the beam she was hoping to find for Arthur – a nice fat, load-bearing piece of oak carrying the ceiling out and over the staircase, but easily accessible from the landing.

"Great!" Pip couldn't help enthusing out loud. "Oh that's good, that's very good! And no need to go chipping through too much plaster either!" She hated going into old plaster, and not only because there was always the remote chance of finding something more important to preserve in it, like an old wall painting. Old plaster was also a nightmare because especially in ceilings it was usually thick with dust. Pip had choked on enough examples to not want to repeat the experience, but here a small leak in the roof had done the job for her, and a good chunk of the ceiling had already descended into a filthy heap on the landing. A quick going over with a broom so that they didn't fall over the bits, and this timber was ready to be got at.

"Now if I could just find one like this in the other two sections..." Pip mused, scouring the ceilings with the torch. However, despite the room on her right in the second phase having been made into a bathroom sometime in the early twentieth century, no such wear and tear had taken place. It was a surprisingly comfortable-looking room, Pip thought, and for their age the various bits of bathroom-wear were in remarkably good condition. "Reckon they'll be restorable," Pip said to the enormous spider sitting on the wall, "so you'll have to find another home, pal!"

She was rather more surprised, therefore, when she came out of the bathroom and turn sharply right to walk along the other side of its wall, to find herself in a narrow corridor. She was expecting some partitioning, because while the earlier inhabitants would have found nothing odd in walking through one bedroom to get to another, by the time the bathroom was made privacy was rather more expected. Where it confused her was in the way this corridor kinked to the left to skirt the new chimney stack. The access doorway into the newest extension was much as she expected, but there seemed to be too much wall on her left to get to the second room of the middle phase.

"This can't be right," she muttered, "or maybe there's a dressing room behind there?"

Passing on the puzzle temporarily, she went into the end of the building and found two suitably nice bedrooms built over the dining room and parlour. The ceilings of the rooms themselves were too good to hack into, but there was a small connecting corridor alongside the end chimney stack, and Pip reckoned they would find a good enough beam to be datable in there in its low ceiling or wall. She went back downstairs and got steps and some tools and happily set to work. Only when her stomach reminded her that it was lunchtime did she halt, gratified to have found another good beam for Arthur to work on.

Retreating back downstairs, she happily pottered around in the kitchen, heating up some soup and cooking-on an already part-baked baguette in the oven to go with it. Only when she sat down to eat did she realise that she'd been singing along with the faint sound of someone else singing 'Over The Hills And Far Away'. She stopped and let her spoon slip back into the large enamelled mug she was using.

"Who's there?"

She stood up and went to the kitchen door. Outside the rain had actually stopped, and a weak sun was picking up the droplets still falling off the trees every time a gust of wind shook them, but there was no sign of any other person out there. Just to be sure she called out, "Hello? ...Hello? ...Anybody there?" It was pretty unlikely that any of the team would have come out now, not least because she had the bus, but maybe some ardent walker had wandered by? Yet there was no sound of anyone at all out in the yard.

Closing the door and going back to her seat, Pip had just picked up the baguette and was breaking off a piece when she heard it again. It was definitely a man's voice and he was singing the same tune, but now she came to listen harder it was most peculiar. It was as if he was a very long way off but still inside. Could he be upstairs? That gave Pip momentary shivers! Shit, had she been up there with some weirdo squatter behind her all the time? Then reason took over. No of course not! For a start off, hers had been the only footprints going through all that old plaster, and you couldn't get far from the top of the stairs without going through it either way, because it must have come down with a right old thump and spread itself about all over the landing. But the voice was still there, singing away quite cheerily, then it stopped.

"Hmmm, some passing vehicle on the road," Pip told herself sternly. "They'd just lost the radio signal or something when you went outside. Probably some workmen parked in the driveway eating their sandwiches."

Then to her horror she heard voices. This time it was talking, as though someone had gone to the front door and let a second person in and then come back – not that she could make out what was being said, but it was clear enough for her to know it was two men.

"Who's there?" she called sharply, and the voices suddenly stopped. Then shockingly one of the distant voices in return called faintly, "Who is that?"

In shock Pip grabbed her mug of soup and the baguette and legged it out to the minibus to finish her lunch.

"Bloody hell, I'm going crackers there!" she said to the stuffed mascot on the dashboard. The small Scooby Doo gave her his lopsided grin but mercifully said nothing back. "Good boy! You stay that way!" Pip said, some of her normal humour returning. With the radio on, and the usual inane chatter of the presenter in-between the music, she stopped feeling so jittery, and an hour later when the rain came on again she felt more like tackling the house again.

"Right!" she said decisively to the stuffed Scooby Doo. "Time to go and find a beam in the middle bit of the house!"

She took the torches up stairs with her after checking round the ground floor, which she felt more than a little foolish for doing, but it meant she knew for certain that there was no-one there. No-one to creep up behind her and do something dreadful. Upstairs she checked the small bedrooms once more, but there really wasn't anywhere anyone could hide in the original house when all four rooms came out onto the same section of landing above the stairs.

"Oh come on, you idiot!" Pip scolded herself. "This is getting daft! Just get on with the job or you'll be here all night!"

She poked and prodded about in the bathroom for a second time, but decided that when the bathroom had been fitted some fairly extensive restoration must have taken place. That meant that the only other place to look was the lone bedroom in this section – the L-shaped corridor being too cramped to start bringing down chunks of plaster ceiling in, and the internal walls were almost certainly lightweight with no useful beams in them. She was avoiding using the walls between this phase and the first phase, and also it and the third phase, because it would be hard to tell which section of the building they belonged to, so it had to be something firmly within this middle section.

Passing the door into the north-end wing, Pip pushed open the door into the bedroom and looked about her. To her surprise the room was somewhat smaller than the two others at this end of the house. She turned so that her back was to the window and scrutinised the back wall. Something there was strange – a bit out of kilter – and kept tweaking at her instincts. The fireplace was at an angle in the corner of the room. Of itself that wasn't so terribly odd, since Pip could see that this must once have been on the shoulder of the chimney when this had been the outside wall of the original house. If the chimney had narrowed in its climb then it would have been easier to just alter it rather than build a whole new side to the stack. But what perplexed Pip was why they hadn't used the rest of the chimney? Down below the same great brick stack served both the scullery and hall in the original build, and still had the big range in the kitchen on its other side. Granted, the kitchen's range would have needed a pretty big outlet, and there were places on either side of it where hams would have been hung to cure once upon a time. But there was still room for another flue up on this floor when this bedroom and the nursery's were so small. So why wouldn't they use more of the existing chimney?

Going back out and round to the corridor close to the bathroom, Pip tapped all along the wall and shone the torch over it almost inch by inch. By such careful scrutiny she found what must once have been another small fireplace at an angle, not in the wall, but with the remnants of the grate floor tiles still being visible beneath the tatters of carpet. Clearly some of the brickwork had been changed when the third phase of building had taken place, removing a small fireplace here – where it could never have been convenient – and replacing it with one in the new stack. That answered Pip's unspoken question of how (before the corridor and the bathroom had been created out of it) the original second bedroom of this phase had been heated.

She checked the wall over again, becoming more and more convinced that the wall which ran from the nursery door, across the chimney breast and on for nearly the same length on its other side, was all one construction. A wall which had been created when the house had been first extended, and a new way had had to be found to give access to the extension up here. Pip sketched the house out on the old diary she used as a notepad, doing a second sketch of the original house only, in which the stairs now had a gallery, and there were two bedrooms on the north side of them as well as those still surviving on the south side. Yes, she thought, tapping the pad, that would have been how it had worked. A bedroom which had been turned into a corridor. But that wouldn't be a problem when you were going to gain at least two more bedrooms.

She sighed. This was a real puzzle, but it wasn't getting her anywhere with finding another beam for Arthur to take a sample from. Back in the bedroom, after another fruitless search, she decided that her best bet for this wing would actually be for Arthur to look at the beams down in the kitchen, not up here. Then with the still stormy sky making the house ever darker, she gave up for the day, but not before she'd had another strange encounter.

With thunder now rattling around overhead, and the house being unnaturally lit up by lightning at increasing intervals, Pip was just checking she'd picked everything up when it happened again.

"What a storm!" a faint male voice said, and without thinking she'd answered,

"Yes it is, isn't it," before starting in shock. "Oh God!" she gulped as the pleasant voice replied rather shakily,

"Are you a ghost?"

"No. Are you?"

"No." He sounded as confused and worried as she was.

"Where are you?" Pip called out. "I'm standing in a place called Cold Hunger Farm."

"So am I."

Shit! This was beyond bizarre! What on earth was happening? "When?" she called.

"When?"

"What year? I'm in two thousand and... Hello? ...Hey, are you still there?"

But as the skies above went silent so did the disembodied voice. "Hello? ...Hello? ...Are you there anymore?" Pip stood listening for a bit longer, but the voice never came back.

Picking up her bag again, Pip went and started up the bus, but as she trundled carefully along the narrow track she decided that she would definitely not be telling the others about this! They probably thought her more than a bit odd already. With the confidence of youth, all but Gemma and Nick would be wondering how you could live with someone and not know that they had some strange tastes in sex. It was a question which had plagued her to near distraction after she and Dave had split up, and it had only been when she'd gone and talked to a councillor, at a friend's suggestion, that she'd started to come to terms with it all. That the problem had lain with Dave's determination to give the appearance of what most people would regard as normality. A determination so strong that for a while he'd actually succeeded in convincing not only her, but himself as well.

"If he actually believed it himself. Believed it in his heart of hearts. Then you can hardly blame yourself if you didn't think to question him," the councillor had told her gently. "I see many people who find things out about their partners they'd never suspected – sometimes after many years of marriage too. So the fact that you remained in ignorance after only a year of living together, and a year when – by your own admission – you had periods apart with your work, is not something you should berate yourself for."

Yet for all the sense those words had made, Pip still knew that there were few people as understanding as Nick. Certainly the police who had come to talk to her when Natalie had disappeared had already thought there was something odd about Dave, even if she hadn't known then. So how had they spotted he was covering something up when she couldn't?

She turned out onto the main road and picked up speed, saying to the Scooby toy, "No way, mate! I'm not painting another target on my chest by telling them I heard voices in the house! I had enough of that kind of trouble four years ago, I'm not starting again! And they're not going to forget my story in a hurry with us finding that sodding half a clamp here – why couldn't it have been some nice anonymous amphora, for God's sake? Or something to do with Minerva? Someone nice and mainstream! Why did it have to be a bloody *perverted* Roman goddess?" She smacked her one hand hard against the steering wheel in frustration. "Damn you, Dave Marston! What did I do to deserve you keep on creeping out of the woodwork and buggering up my life just when I don't expect it?" She could almost feel the tears starting to well up at the injustice. She'd done nothing except be a bystander to his strange affairs with Natalie, yet both of them had disappeared and she was left with the wreckage. How unfair was that?

Come the morning she was feeling calmer, to her own relief, and she spent the morning with Arthur and the rest of the team, drilling neat holes in the beams to take samples for Arthur to date. As ever, Arthur was kindly and expansive on his subject, willingly sharing his expertise with the students, and making the whole thing enjoyable. He left in his battered and ancient Subaru, the four-wheel drive coping with the drive far better than the minibus did despite the car being far older, and with the promise that he'd process the samples as fast as possible. Phil had apparently already been on to Arthur about the need for speed, so Nick was quick to reassure Arthur that they would still be digging for a good couple of weeks, during which time the proposed buyer wouldn't be getting anywhere near the place, so it wasn't so very urgent, whatever Phil was saying.

"He's such a nice man," Pip sighed as they came back inside from waving Arthur off. "Phil's such a wanker for pressuring him like that."

Gemma sniffed derisively. "Phil is asking to get his ankles kicked by someone a lot more important than us, if you ask me. If Arthur lets it slip how he's been spoken to there'll be all hell to pay, because," she wagged a knowing finger at the students, "Arthur is very highly thought of in some very elevated academic circles! If one of his professor friends gets wind of this, I'd bet strong words will be passed down the line, and Phil will be in deep shit!"

"Can't come a day too soon!" Nick agreed. "But, hey, he's not here today, so let's not ruin a nice day talking about him."

"Then have you got time to do a bit of building sleuthing?" Pip asked, and explained about the bedroom upstairs. "It's a lovely room," she concluded, "but it doesn't go back far enough to connect with the corridor by the bathroom. By all my estimates there's a space the size of another small room somewhere in that 'wall' space. It might even have its own fireplace, because the north side of the kitchen chimney is in that space too. See?" And she pulled out the old diary notepad and showed them the sketch she'd made.

"Ooh, that looks interesting!" Kirsty enthused. "I love a mystery!"

"Wow, that's a bit Agatha Christie!" agreed Chloe, and in the face of the students' enthusiasm, Nick threw up his hands in mock surrender.

"Okay, okay! We'll go and investigate! Someone get the tape measures. If we're going to do this then we'll do it properly – all measured out and recorded."

Once they were upstairs it didn't take long for everyone to agree that Pip was right, there was a space the size of a small room behind the walls.

"Do we knock them down?" James asked, eying up a sledgehammer with relish.

"Down boy!" Gemma said with a playful slap on the hand which was reaching for the hammer. "Don't be such a hooligan! We look to see if we can find where the door once was and go in that way – not that I've ever done anything quite like this before."

"I agree with Pip that the wall on the bathroom side is part of the first rebuild, so we shall definitely preserve that," Nick said firmly. "I don't want to damage that wall in any way." He rubbed his chin thoughtfully, walked into the bedroom and then out again, went back and knocked on the wall in several places and seemed to come to a decision. "Because of the fireplace, I'm inclined to think that the bedroom back wall might be original too – or at least a goodly part of it may well be – so that means that it's this stretch of wall opposite the final build which is the oddity. Let's get this paper off it. It's only relatively modern and it's wrecked with damp anyway."

It took all of twenty minutes to get the paper completely off the wall, including a couple of layers under the top one, all of them barely hanging on at all. As Tim and Kirsty dragged several bin-bags full of the paper downstairs, Nick, Gemma and Pip made a further inspection of the wall.

"This is bloody weird!" Nick muttered. "There's no sign of any door in the plaster at all! It has to be on one of the other walls, then."

"Nick, don't you think the current bedroom doorway looks out of place now you look closely at it?" Pip said thoughtfully. With today being much brighter it was easier to see it now. "Like it's not the right size to match the others up here?"

Nick grabbed a tape and measured both it and the bathroom door. "Hey, you're right Pip! It's a smaller door!"

"So if this isn't the original door out of the bedroom, maybe the doorway was further along the wall?" wondered Chloe, hurrying into the bedroom and turning round and round looking at its walls. "Oh hang on a minute, we haven't looked behind this mirror," and pointed to the full length, old and badly foxed mirror against the wall.

As Will got hold of it on one side, with Nick on the other, it moved easily.

"Bloody hell, that's a bit dangerous!" Nick observed. "They're normally screwed to the wall when they're this big. If that fell over it could do one of us a serious damage! Lean it against the fireplace, Will."

Now, they could see that a door frame had been taken away, visible as an outline through the wallpaper.

"Hey, hang on a minute!" Will suddenly gasped. "Look at that paper!"

"What about it?" Chloe asked.

"It's come from off the window wall!" Will exclaimed. "Look at either side of the window! Where the curtains would have covered it! Two long drops are missing!" As the one who'd been facing the window for longer his eyes had adjusted and had spotted what the others hadn't.

"Oh! And this paper's only attached at the top!" Gemma breathed softly as her fingers gently brushed it. She lifted up the loose wallpaper. "Oh this gets stranger and stranger! This has bits of the plaster surface still attached, but not from this wall – this plaster underneath is too modern by far for that going by the colour. Mind you it's an awful job! You couldn't paper over that properly even if you wanted to! It's as rough as a bear's arse! I reckon you're right, Will. Someone's hung this paper recently to hide the fact that the door's been covered over."

"But why would someone do that?" James wondered.

"Only one way to find out," Nick said grimly. "Phil will no doubt have me over the coals for this, but I think this constitutes sufficient a problem as to require investigation. Archaeology it may not be, but if this is modern then we might find a clue as to who really owns the farm." He didn't need to add that whoever that might be could well prevent the industrialist from inflicting his idea of country house chic on the poor old building, nor that he disapproved of the house's impending fate. "James! You wanted to use the sledgehammer? Well knock me a hole in that modern plaster!"

Chapter 6

June 1814.

"I think you may have to introduce me," Harry said with a smile to Robert as they shared reflections in the hall mirror. "I doubt anyone will assume I'm your brother."

The way Robert's face uneasily assumed the smile back made Harry wonder if he'd done much smiling at all in these intervening years. Even in the hell of fighting, he at least had shared jokes with the men – albeit often of the blackest kind of humour – and had shared moments of hilarity with the small number of close friends he'd made. Did Robert even have any friends, he belatedly wondered? And why had he not married? Being older than Harry, Robert was now a man of twenty-eight – old enough to have found someone by now, surely? Maybe not someone as locally as in this village, but there would be plenty of young women who must have noticed a man as good-looking as Robert when he'd been in Worcester. Or was Robert still so uncertain of his role in life as to be wary of adding a wife and family to his burdens? Yet somehow Harry couldn't bring himself to ask. Or at least not yet. The truce between them felt rather too new and too fragile for him to want to test it at the moment.

Instead, as he walked across to the inn with his brother, having rescued his horse before it cropped the verge to nothing, he asked tentatively,

"If the Vaughans are keeping so apart from the world, could it be that they are close to poverty? Would the local shop keepers know them for instance?"

Robert nodded. "I could ask Thomas the butcher, certainly."

"Would you? They would probably answer more openly to you than to me. They might not know the Vaughans, but I remember village life well enough to know that they'd resent someone they saw as a stranger prying into village affairs, whoever I was asking after."

"Oh yes! That they would!"

"Only, if there are any debts," it was a delicate subject, but Harry wanted to tackle it, "I would like to settle them. I feel I owe Amy that, you see. I feel rather guilty that I might have led her to believe that Edward's situation was ...well, better than it was. That his captaincy had been confirmed when it wasn't. And now I've found out that she's unlikely to have got any help at all from her father-in-law, I fear if I don't help them then no-one will." Robert gave him a strange glance. "What? You didn't expect me to care?"

Robert gave that unaccustomed strained smile again and shook his head. "No, I'm just coming to realise that maybe I never really knew you before. I was off playing with my own friends by the time you were old enough to do things with, and I'm sadly realising that I took Father's disapproval of you as the truth and without question. But now hearing about how you came back with Edward for the wedding, even though you weren't really friends anymore but for the sake of all of the families – including ours – and now why you're here, well, it makes me rethink a lot of things." He seemed embarrassed and struggling over whether to say the next thing or not, but took a deep breath and said, "Do you think we can be brothers as grown men in a way we never were as boys?"

"Oh I do hope so!" Harry replied instantly and from the heart. "I never wanted that coldness between Father, you and I – especially after Mother died."

Now Robert really smiled. "I'm glad! I would have felt awful if you'd said that the wounds went too deep for you to be able to forgive me."

Harry shook his head. "The wounds weren't yours to give. All you did in my eyes was love Father rather too well so that you believed him at every turn, and given how you cared for him at the last, I can't fault you for that." It wasn't the whole truth. There had been cause enough, if he cared to dwell on it, for him to thoroughly loathe Robert for himself and his pompous attitudes as a young man, but now wasn't the time for that, particularly as he wasn't likely to be stopping for long. If he didn't get a commission in the reduced Huntingdonshire regiment he would have to look further afield, and that might mean one of the colonies. So he had no desire to leave here with a whole new batch of bad feelings between him and Robert, who was saying,

"Then I shall gladly help you find the Vaughans and do what we can for them!"

At the Red Lion, once the innkeeper knew who Harry was, nothing was too much trouble for them. Yet once again Harry was delayed, and half the afternoon was gone by the time a succession of Robert's parishioners had come forward to be introduced. The only good which came out of the lengthy introductions being Harry paying the Vaughan's butcher's bill and others, and leaving more money with the trustworthy grocer to be used by them on account.

"You'll stay with me now," Robert declared. "In the morning we'll send a cart to Bromyard to lead the horse back and bring your baggage here." Then as Harry made to protest, albeit half-heartedly, "No, I insist! We shall find these friends of yours by hook or by crook! Together!"

Returning to Robert's house, Harry was dreading a whole evening in his brother's company, recalling long evenings at the old parsonage filled with theological debates between Robert and their father as their mother lay in bed upstairs, slowly succumbing to consumption, leaving Harry to the torture of no other conversation down below. However Robert had either mellowed substantially or he was making a real effort – and Harry suspected it was in equal measure – because he encouraged Harry to talk of his life in the army. So to his surprise Harry found himself regaling Robert with some of the tales of the last five years. Of the men whom he served either under or over, and the sometimes weird and wonderful things which happened in battle which someone who hadn't been there would hardly credit.

"It's true, I swear!" Harry found himself laughing with Robert, as he told of one man blown clean out of his clothes by a close explosion but otherwise unharmed. "Poor bugger was stood stark bollock naked in the snow with not a stitch on him!"

"You won't settle easily back here after all of that," Robert observed as he showed Harry to the spare bedroom.

"I doubt I shall ever be back here permanently," Harry admitted. "What would I do here? Unless I'm lucky enough to earn money sufficient to retire upon I shall have to work at something, and I don't see me going into Uncle William's factories after this. And that's not just the thought of having to go cap in hand to him again which makes me say that. If I saw men I once served with being treated the way Uncle treats his workers I couldn't stand by now, Robert, I really couldn't. I should have to do something to help them. So if you have any prayers spare, pray for me to find another commission, because if not it could well be the colonies and something like the East India Company for me."

Robert's face was one of utter shock. He clearly hadn't thought of Harry's lack of choices in quite that way. "But that's near the other side of the world! We'd likely not ever see one another again!"

"No," Harry said gently as he entered the room which had once been his, "I doubt we would."

Robert said no more as he turned away to his own room, but Harry could see that the thought that they might be separated for good hadn't really sunk in before now, or that Harry might not have lived to see today. In Robert's neat and ordered world the idea that his younger brother would not outlive him was a shocking intrusion, and one Harry suspected he was wholly unprepared for.

Maybe because of that, Robert was all for helping when they met over breakfast the following day.

"We shall walk over to Lower Sapey," he declared. "It's not too far for you I hope?"

Harry rolled his eyes. "Heaven's Robert, I've marched damned near the length of Spain, and twice over at that! I think a mile or two down an English road is unlikely to do me in! I'm not some newly trained parson you're breaking in to walking the parish!"

Robert shook his head in bafflement. "I keep forgetting. I see you dressed like some of the older gents of the county who are reliving their military years over and over, and forget that for you it's been very different."

"Militia, for many of them, no doubt?" Harry guessed and got a nod of confirmation.

However, once on the road on a pleasant summer's day, the mischievous side of Harry's nature couldn't refrain from showing Robert the pace of the Light Companies. He didn't press him too hard or too far, but was secretly amused at how quickly his brother became breathless.

"You kept this up for how long?" wheezed Robert as Harry stopped to let him catch his breath.

"Oh an hour or so. Then we'd stop for a short break and start over again," Harry told him, all innocence on the outside, but chortling underneath.

"Lord be merciful!" Robert gasped.

"Well I wasn't planning on going at that pace all the way to Cold Hunger Farm," Harry said with a twinkle in his eye. "It's a grand pace for catching the French, but you do work up a sweat in this kind of weather, and I don't want to be arriving at the Vaughan's in that kind of state! It's a bit unsavoury for the ladies, if you get my meaning!" and both of them laughed – another bond made, which felt both strange and good at the same time.

With Robert to guide him, Harry now discovered why he'd missed the track the day before. It was narrow and looked for all the world as though it was no more than the track to a farmhouse down in the small valley off to one side. That it continued down to the tiny river, snaked alongside it for a stretch, and then climbed up again, was a revelation. A rather less happy discovery was coming up out of the cold overhanging shadow of the trees in the river's cutting and finding Cold Hunger Farm. It wasn't what anyone would have called a prepossessing place.

"What a gloomy hole!" Harry breathed softly to Robert. "Oh dear, this is worse than I expected! Amy always loved pretty things, but there's not much pretty about this place, is there? It isn't even what you might call ruggedly picturesque."

Robert too was looking at the shadowed farm yard and the way the trees loomed close to the house. "There's something unsavoury about this," he said with a shiver, and that wasn't just from the chill of coming out of the warm sunshine.

"Oh well, we're here now," Harry sighed, half to himself. This was looking worse with every step, and however much he'd braced himself for meeting Amy face to face, being here was going to make it even harder. He squared his shoulders, then marched up to the front door. There didn't even seem to be a bell or a knocker, so he rapped hard on the wood of the door and then stood back so that he was out of the shadows for anyone opening the door to see. To his horror it was no maid who opened the door but Mrs Vaughan herself. How far had the family sunk that they had no maid?

"Good morning, Mrs Vaughan," Harry said politely and in his gentlest of tones, "I hope we're not disturbing you calling unannounced like this? I would have sent word but I'm only newly come to England myself and I came here with all haste."

"Captain Green!" she exclaimed with real warmth. "Oh this is a pleasant surprise! Please, come in! Come in!"

"This is my brother, Robert," Harry said, standing to one side and waving him forward. "He's now the rector over at Clifton, as you no doubt recall my father was before him." He had a pretty shrewd idea that Mrs Vaughan would have no such recollection, which was why he'd been so specific in his introduction. He had no wish to get Robert inside and then subject them to the embarrassment of not knowing who the rector was from just over the hill.

"Oh yes, of course, I didn't recognise you there for a moment, Rector," Mrs Vaughan recovered neatly, making Harry think he'd guessed correctly. "Do come in. You're both very welcome, but you must excuse us, we're not set up to receive visitors these days. We live very simply," and Harry could hear the worry in her voice, as it belatedly occurred to her that she was no longer inviting him into the pleasant villa they'd left behind in St John's.

She turned right as they came inside, and they passed through what once had been a goodly hall a few centuries back. But it had never been updated, and now was in dire need of at least some fresh paint. They passed through two more rooms which contained bits of furniture which Harry vaguely recognised from the old house, and then came into a pleasant parlour, which faced onto the back yard and the garden to the side of the house.

Sat in a large wing chair and almost dwarfed by it was Mr Vaughan, who didn't even look up when they came in.

"Horace, my dear, we have visitors," Mrs Vaughan said with forced brightness. "See? It's dear Captain Green come to see us all the way from the war." When the old man simply looked up and blinked, she began to blush, making Harry feel desperately sorry for her. However it was Robert who immediately rescued the situation. He came forward and gently took Mrs Vaughan's hands in his saying,

"Ah, I see now why I've not seen you about much. Our father was just like this after our mother died."

Then he stepped round her and went to the big chair, sitting down on the padded fender around the fire. "Hello Mr Vaughan," he said in the voice which Harry guessed he must regularly use to his sick parishioners, and began to draw the old man out of his reverie, leaving Harry to speak to Mrs Vaughan.

"Mrs Vaughan, I was so sorry to hear of your misfortune," Harry began. "Unfortunately I had no idea until I got to Worcester of how things had... had..." How on earth could he say this without causing offence?

Mrs Vaughan placed her hand on his sleeve, biting her lip and with tears in her eyes. "No doubt you would have visited Sir Roderick," she said thickly.

"I felt I had to go to give him my condolences," Harry explained. "He and Edward weren't close, but as I was coming here I felt I couldn't pass his door and not speak. And I had one or two items which he'd given to Edward which I thought he would wish to have back."

Mrs Vaughan bobbed her head. "You were always a kind man, Captain, and whatever else he is, I dare say Sir Roderick at least deserved that much. He has, after all lost his son, although in the losing of him he has managed to somehow hold us in part to blame for it, I fear. Not that we were seeing much of him after Edward and Amy married."

Harry was in a terrible quandary. Should he ask what exactly had happened to Mr Vaughan? As if seeing the confusion in his face, Mrs Vaughan said brightly, "May I offer you gentlemen some tea?" And as Robert thanked her, she tapped Harry on the arm to draw him out of the room. "We have no maid so I shall have to go to the kitchen myself," she added, "but if you would wait in the old office..."

"My dear Mrs Vaughan, I've been on campaign and on many an occasion have made my own tea," Harry told her with a smile. "Humble lieutenants don't get waited on hand and foot, even if someone generally makes it for me now I'm a captain. I shall come and help, if you don't find the thought..."

"Not at all!" she agreed readily, finding it much easier to deal with this dreadful situation than she'd feared thanks to Harry's easy manner.

Leading the way back through the hall and through the scullery into the kitchen, she put a kettle onto the range and then explained, "We have a girl from the next farm who comes in three times a week to clean for us, and her sister comes and cooks us a luncheon daily, but we make do for ourselves for breakfast and supper. She'll be here soon."

"How has it come to this, though?" Harry asked softly. "May I hazard a guess that your husband's state of mind comes from your current circumstance?"

She nodded. "Oh, Captain! He gets so distressed to even mention it! That's why I couldn't speak of it in the parlour." She bit her lip again, unsure of how to proceed.

"I can assure you that anything you tell me will not be repeated except to my brother, and he's the soul of discretion."

Harry was already thinking that Robert would be coming to visit often now, whether Harry asked him to or not, and therefore he deserved to know what had happened to this family.

Another bob of her head. "It was Sir Roderick's doing," she said bitterly. "He told Horace that if our Amy was to marry his son, we must not rest with what we had and should invest our money further. Amy was so in love with Edward, Horace couldn't refuse. So he bought into one of Sir Roderick's mines in the Forest of Dean. Or at least that's what Horace thought he was doing – buying a portion to show willing to someone who was now sort of family, even if he wasn't the most likeable of men. Only later did we realise that Sir Roderick had sold it to us in its entirety because the production was already slowing down! The old devil! It wasn't making enough for his liking, so he wanted a quick sale, and he took advantage of us! Well it was only a year or so later that there was a terrible fire at the mine. Now it's completely shut down. But Horace had borrowed the money to buy the mine from Sir Roderick, and now that dreadful man wanted every penny back, and straight away!"

"Oh my God!" Harry was appalled. He'd known old Clifford was a miser, but he hadn't thought he would sink so low in his love of money as to ruin someone who had once been a friend. "How could he expect you to find the money with none coming in? You'd have been hard pressed to pay the loan at the original rate on what your glove factory brought you in, and still have enough to live on to a gentleman's standards, let alone in a lump sum!"

"He took us to court for debts!" Mrs Vaughan said bitterly, making Harry want to sweep her into his arms and hug this poor motherly lady in the way he would have done his own mother in such circumstances. "The shame of it destroyed Horace. To have to stand in that courtroom in Worcester with people we had known all of our lives looking on... To tell the truth, Captain Green, I don't know how he got through it. I used to sit up all night watching him for fear that in his shame he might do something terrible to himself. I followed him one night to Worcester Bridge. He was like a man walking in his sleep. I had to pull him back..." She hiccupped back a sob. "That was after he discovered that the interest Sir Roderick was claiming on the loan would mean that not only did he have the right..."

She had to stop to wipe her eyes and blow her nose, and to save both her embarrassment and his, Harry went and made the tea. When she'd recovered a little, she came and set a tray out on the table onto which he put the teapot ready to carry through to the parlour.

"Since we owed him so much, Sir Roderick took over our small glove factory," she said angrily. "He took it all. It never went to a proper sale, and he talked the judge into believing that its value was less than it really was."

"The bast...!" Harry just about remembered where he was. He was beginning to wish he'd throttled Sir Roderick when he'd been alone with him.

"Yes! So with there still being money outstanding after the factory was gone, we had to sell the house too. At least Sir Roderick couldn't grab that without a sale, but we were so beset we had to accept the first offer we had, and I'm sure Sir Roderick set one of his cronies up to make an offer below the true price of that too! Once our beloved house had been sold, I realised that for the sake of what remained of his sanity, we had to get Horace away from Worcester. And for Amy and little Eddie! He's not yet of an age to go to school, but I couldn't bear the thought of him having his grandfather's name being thrown at him all the time when the time comes."

"And what of Mrs Clifford?" Harry found himself near choking on her name. "Of Amy?"

He'd know from her letters that she'd had Edward's son – a wedding night gift from Edward that was likely to be the only one she would ever have now.

Mrs Vaughan sighed. "My poor innocent girl. She went to see Sir Roderick. She couldn't believe, you see, that her beloved Edward's father would do such a thing to her own. To this day, Captain, she won't tell me what he said to her. All I know is that she was in floods of tears when she arrived back and didn't eat a thing for days, she was so distressed. But then the day after her visit we also had a letter from Sir Roderick, telling us that if his son continued to support her then that was all she would get from his family. Sir Roderick wanted nothing to do with his daughter-in-law and would communicate only with his son. For all that little Eddie is his grandson, he wants nothing to do with him."

"But what did he think would happen when Edward came home?" Harry wondered. "Was he planning to cut him off too?"

Mrs Vaughan's head dropped in shame. "It's my belief that the miserable old goat was planning on getting Edward to set Amy aside. That he was intending to find some reason ...some way ...of getting a divorce, even if he had to fabricate the evidence needed." Then she looked up at him urgently, "But please! Not a word of this when you see Amy! Please, Captain! She still believes that Edward would come home and stand up for us, and that everything would be all right once more."

"Oh Lord!"

"Well I didn't have the heart to tell her it was all a fairy tale in her head. I thought the truth would come soon enough. And we all needed some time in peace to recover before the next batch of ills best us. But then the letter came saying Edward was dead and she's been inconsolable ever since. For two weeks she wouldn't even rise from her bed!"

"But what of her son? Surely for his sake...?"

"That's what finally got her up, but I'm ashamed to say that I had to be harsh with her."

"No not harsh," Harry said comfortingly. "You were quite right. The poor child isn't old enough to understand what's happened. Where are they now?"

"Oh I've persuaded Amy that it's good for both of them to take a morning walk in the woods when it's nice like today. They should be back soon."

They would have to go back into the parlour soon before the tea got cold, but Harry could now see that Mrs Vaughan was the one who was holding the family together. If help was to be offered then he should be talking to her and not Amy.

"I know this is a delicate matter, Mrs Vaughan, but out of concern I would know if there is anything I can do to help. The rent on this farm, for instance. Is it ...is it all in order?" It was the most tactful way he could think of to ask if they were going to be able to keep the roof over their heads, even out here where rents were cheaper. Mercifully

Mrs Vaughan took no offence and instead her face broke into a weak smile.

"Oh that's such a kind thought, Captain, but we are provided for by our son."

Belatedly Harry recalled that there was a son. It was easy to forget because he was so much older than Amy. If Amy was a couple of years younger than Edward had been, and therefore of Harry also, her brother was several years older than Robert, making him a good ten years older than Amy.

"Ah! Where is...?" For the life of him Harry couldn't remember the brother's name.

"Augustus."

"Ah yes, Augustus." It didn't sound familiar, but then Mrs Vaughan added,

"Gus has been most concerned for us. He would be here, but he works for the East India Company in India, you see. He gets a very good wage and so he undertook to pay for the house and sends some extra for ...provisions."

In a flash of understanding Harry also grasped that if Gus had been in India for a good many years he would have little idea of what it cost to hire a servant, and what food and other commodities would cost over here these days. No doubt he would be thinking he'd provided more than enough, and Mrs Vaughan would have sufficient pride not to want to ask him for more.

"He writes to his father, you see," Mrs Vaughan said as she led the way back to the parlour with Harry carrying the tray behind her.

"And Mr Vaughan is somewhat vague as to the, erm ...realities of life these days?"

Mrs Vaughan gave him a grateful smile as she gestured him to a small table with the tray.

"Have you written to Gus of the loss of Edward?" Harry asked her softly after she came back from taking a cup each to Mr Vaughan and Robert.

"Only briefly," Mrs Vaughan answered. "We were all too upset when the news came, and of course we knew very little of the circumstances so there wasn't much to tell."

"Then if you would furnish me with his address I would very much like to write to him myself," Harry told her gravely. "There are certain matters regarding Edward's death which are not seemly for me to pass on to you or Mrs Clifford. I had hoped to speak to Mr Vaughan about them, but in the current circumstances I would not wish to distress him. To Gus I can write man to man. One day young Eddie may wish to know, and living the soldier's life as I do, I cannot guarantee that I shall be..." Lord he dare not say dead! "I may have to take service overseas myself," he said hurriedly, seeing Mrs Vaughan going pale.

"Oh I see!" she said with relief. "Yes! Gus has said that he will be coming home in a few years time, maybe only one or two. The heat out in India has taken its toll on his health, he tells us, and he's just waiting on a position to become available in London for him."

They passed a few more minutes in polite conversation about the colonies, trying to draw Mr Vaughan into it without success, then the door burst open and a robust little boy bounded in and threw himself at his grandmother.

"Look, Grandma! An eagle's feather!" It was probably from one of the huge red kites which circled these ridges and fields rather than any eagle, Harry thought, but he could understand the youngster's enthusiasm. But before he could say anything Amy walked into the room. For a moment Harry could barely get his breath. She was as pale as a ghost, and girlish prettiness had turned into a fragile loveliness which might have fallen well short of conventional beauty, but did nothing to detract from her in Harry's eyes. He was so taken with the sight of her he didn't see his brother's gaze suddenly sharpen or the hint of a smile which came to Mrs Vaughan's face as she watched Harry's reaction.

"Mrs Clifford," Harry said gruffly, rising to his feet and going to her.

"Oh Captain Green!" Amy gasped. "Oh! You came!"

Harry wasn't quite sure whether she was glad about that or not.

"Of course I came," Harry answered, somewhat taken aback. "My first thought when we found Edward was that I must make sure you were taken care of."

"Oh my darling Eddie!" she wailed, and the tears immediately began to flow leaving poor Harry nonplussed. What was he to do in the face of such passionate grieving? Luckily Mrs Vaughan bustled up to her daughter and all but shoved her to a seat on the other side of the fire from Mr Vaughan.

"Come, come, Amy!" she said firmly. "Captain Green has come through war and heaven knows what trials to come and see you. He doesn't need to see your tears. He knows you miss Edward without such a show! Now dry your eyes and talk to him. And this is his brother who, would you believe it, is rector just down the road in Clifton. So we have friends here after all!"

God bless her, Harry thought. How often had Mrs Vaughan been beset with these troubles? Her husband and her daughter leaning on her for support. He'd seen enough women in widowhood from those who travelled with the army to know that some coped better than others. Somehow, though, he'd always imagined Amy being one of those who would be pale but calm. He was unprepared for this kind of wailing. He'd also seen enough of capable women to recognise it in Mrs Vaughan. Here was the real strength of the Vaughan household, not the husk of a man still sitting blankly in the fireside chair.

Mercifully Amy calmed quite quickly, and young Eddie was fascinated to learn that Captain Green was a real soldier and promptly began asking all sorts of questions, taking some of the focus away from Amy for a while. When Harry got to speak to her as they walked out into the garden, to allow Eddie to run around some more, he found himself embarrassingly not knowing what to say to her. For the time being, though, he was enchanted by having her delicate hand resting on his arm for support. She looked like some little wraith by his side, the black of her cheap mourning dress draining even more colour from her face than another colour might have. And it was a cheap dress, he realised. He was no expert in ladies dress materials, but he knew this kind of cheap serge from uniforms. But how to get her to accept him buying her a better dress?

"For propriety's sake you must have bought this dress in a great hurry," he observed gently, "but having got it and now with more time in hand, would you accept an offer of me paying for another cut more to your figure? Out of respect for Edward? Only I feel it would be what he would want. You wouldn't have to go into Worcester to get it made. You could go to Hereford or Leominster. Maybe one for everyday and one you could wear to church on Sunday?"

For a moment he thought she would refuse or burst into tears again. There was a definite wobble to her lower lip, but then she caught her mother's eye and instead said, "Thank you, Captain Green, that's most gracious of you."

It wasn't quite the effusive thanks he'd been hoping for, but he must remember that she wasn't that long widowed to welcome another man's intrusion into her life.

They didn't get to talk of much else, and soon the cook was calling to say that the lunch was ready. Harry and Robert had already declined an offer to eat with them and so they left, but not before agreeing to come and visit in the afternoon the following day.

Despite all he'd found out, Harry felt as though he was walking on air on the way home, not realising how wrapped in his own thoughts he was until Robert said,

"So how long have you been in love with young Mrs Clifford?"

Without thinking Harry answered, "Long before she was Mrs Clifford."

"Ah!"

"Ah?"

Robert grinned at his brother. "Yes, ah! Now I see why you were so anxious to find them."

Harry feared his brother was about to chastise him for wanting to see the Vaughans out of some selfish motive – the old Robert he'd known would have done so without hesitation. Instead Robert flummoxed him by saying,

"Dear me, we are a pretty pair."

Harry stopped in the middle of the road and turned to him. "A pair? How do you mean?"

Robert sighed. "You loving a girl who's already married to a worthless wretch."

Suddenly the penny dropped for Harry. "Is that why you've not married? There was someone but she wasn't yours to have?"

He got only a nod from Robert, who walked on a little until they had got inside the house. Clearly not wanting to say a word until he could be sure no-one was listening, Robert now revealed,

"She was the wife of the dean."

"Bloody hell, Robert! The dean? Christ man, no wonder you had a crisis! Did it ever come to anything? I mean, clearly you left in no small measure because you couldn't stay, but did she ever give you any sign of... of..."

"Liking me? Yes, that was the worst of it. Georgiana had been married off to him when she was scarcely old enough to know what she was letting herself in for. It began one Easter in the cathedral. She'd dropped her glove and I went to retrieve it for her. Oh I had noticed her long before that, but it was the first time she noticed me. Soon we were meeting at every opportunity, at first just to speak, but then speaking wasn't enough. That's when I realised I was as fallible as any other man. My high principles meant nothing in the face of my desire, my most desperate need to see her and touch her."

"Touch her? Oh Robert! How far did it go?"

All he got back was a baleful look but it confirmed Harry's worst fears. Strangely it wasn't the thought of his straight-laced brother making love to a woman which bothered Harry, but the danger he had been in from losing everything he had formerly held so dear.

"Did the dean ever suspect?"

"Not at first. Oh Harry, it was all so romantic in those first months. But after a while we could scarcely be in the same room as one another for fear of giving ourselves away, and then in the summer the bishop went visiting and for reasons I can no longer remember the dean went with him." Robert turned and gazed wistfully out of the window, but Harry knew he saw nothing of the street outside. "We met on a walk down by the river the day after her husband had left. It was a hot summer day like today." He sighed deeply. "We lost all restraint down there on the cathedral meadows. The four happiest days of my life followed – and I like to think they were of hers too – but then her husband came back and for her sake I knew what I had to do. It was a strange blessing to have Father take ill just at that point. It would have been different if we'd had family money, and I could have left the Church and taken her to live far away. Somewhere like Italy."

"But that wasn't an option for you," Harry sighed. "Oh Robert, I'm so sorry. That's as bad as having a young wife and losing her with the first child – and God knows I saw that a few times during the war amongst the women who marched with their husbands. At least there's now some hope for me. Oh it won't be for a couple of years, I've no doubt, but Amy as a widow is a more hopeful situation than Amy wedded to Edward for the rest of all our lives. Given time, I shall be able to press my suit with her, and if I have to go abroad for a while now, then at least I shall not be tempted to do or say something too soon, and which might jeopardise my chances."

They talked well into the night, and come the following afternoon both of them went once more to the Vaughans'. Then, and again the following day, and the day after, and yet Harry could never seem to manage to speak a word of the truth of how Edward had died. To his horror Amy seemed to have made Edward's death into something out of Greek or Roman heroic legend. His dissolute former friend was now elevated to a modern day Caesar or Achilles, fêted by his men and fellow officers alike.

"I shall make sure Eddie knows what his papa was like," Amy gushed to Harry as they once more walked the circuit of the small garden. "What a brave soldier he was," then a pout came on her face, "And how the army has robbed us after his death!"

"Robbed you?" Oh dear, Harry thought, here it comes, the reality that he wasn't a captain, but what she said shook him even more.

"They say he was a mere lieutenant! He, who was a major!"

"A *major*?" Harry was aghast. "My dear A... Mrs Clifford, whatever gives you the idea that he was a *major*?"

"Why he wrote me so!" she riposted indignantly.

"Really?" Harry hadn't thought Edward had sent even one letter!

"I still have it!" Amy declared triumphantly. "I mean to go to London one day, when Gus is back and can come with me. We shall go and challenge those old men who dare say my Eddie wasn't the man I know him to have been!"

God help us! Harry thought, his imagination filling in the image of Amy at Horseguards.

"Would you allow me to read this letter?" he asked fearfully. What kind of dreadful shit had Edward written? He must squash this as soon as possible!

"You don't believe me, do you?" Amy said huffily, "Well I shall fetch the letter and then you shall!"

It took her no time to bring the letter down – a single sheet much crumpled and tearstained but still legible.

> *Dearest Amy*, it began, *You must prepare yourself. I now habitually keep the company of some fine gentlemen, and I do not intend to stoop lower when I return home. I therefore wish you to look at yourself and make such changes as are need for you to be associating with the wives of majors and other high-ranking officers.*
>
> *Also, I have spoken with my fellow officers, Major Howard and Major Hughes, to whom I am much indebted. They and I have plans for when we return home, but you my dear must play your part and visit my father, for I fear he does not understand the*

financial calls upon a gentleman of my rank. You must pursued him to send me the funds I have requested already in several letters, for I know he will not be able to resist your sweet requests.

Your loving husband,

Edward.

"Now do you see?" Amy demanded, then took in Harry's expression of horror.

"I know these men of whom he writes," Harry said cautiously, glad that Mrs Vaughan must have spotted the dreadful letter and had come in hot pursuit of her daughter accompanied by Robert. "I fear you have misread this."

Amy bridled. "In what way?"

"My dear Mrs Clifford, nowhere does Edward say he was a major,"

"He was!"

"No, he was not, and I know for a fact he was not."

"Listen to Captain Green, my dear!" Mrs Vaughan interjected. "For pity's sake, my dearest, Captain Green was your Edward's closest friend. He would not malign him!"

"No I wouldn't," Harry confirmed sternly, and inwardly sighing with relief as Amy's anger seemed to lessen. "These majors he speaks of, ...they are not the kind of officers you no doubt imagine them to be. Major Howard was a quartermaster, and a very corrupt one at that! Since you received this letter he has been court-martialled, and shot upon the express orders of Lord Wellington himself for thieving off the Spanish. He was a thoroughly disreputable man! And Major Hughes is little better. He has been discharged dishonourably from the army, but only because those investigating him have been unable to find such solid evidence as they found against Major Howard. Neither were honourable men fighting with the main force, and they certainly weren't serving alongside Edward and myself in our regiment!"

Amy's lip was quivering again. "You mean these dreadful men tricked my dearest Eddie?"

Harry thought that was hardly the way he'd have put it! Edward had been right in the thick of it with those two thieves, and had he not been dead he too would have come under investigation. Indeed the net had been closing around him even as he'd fallen foul of one of those he'd no doubt been trying to swindle out of something or other. But if Amy wished to think of it that way, Harry wasn't about to argue as long as it stopped this foolish nonsense of going to Horseguards to protest.

"Oh dear, Captain Green," she gulped as the reality sank in.

"Harry. Please call me Harry. Edward did."

She blushed prettily at the offered familiarity. "Harry. ...You must think me a foolish little goose for not understanding."

"I could never think that of you."

"Could you not? You're so kind to me to take such an interest."

Behind them Robert felt himself cringing. How could Harry be so blind? The girl was an utter nightmare with not a sensible thought in her head! And if Harry should ever marry her, the chances were she would never take to the life of a soldier's wife. That would take far more engagement with the realities of life than she was capable of!

Then a wholly different train of horrors entered his head. If he and Harry could be so alike as to make the same mistake, then had Georgiana been as desperately unsuitable too? And him too blind to see it? God help him! It was a ghastly thought. And he certainly should be wary of taking the moral high ground over Harry when his own behaviour might be even worse – Harry at least had never made love to Amy! Maybe it was no bad thing that he'd never seen Georgiana again, after all. In a strange way he would rather keep the thought of the ideal he'd once thought he'd possessed, than see a living parody of it. It so unsettled him that he resolved there and then to do all he could to help Harry, for the lack of hope Harry had so genuinely commiserated with him over now looked like a boon. The better of the two options by far. Harry's misguided hope was no hope at all!

Chapter 7

Saturday, modern day.

No sooner had James lifted the sledgehammer and whacked the centre of the roughly laid plaster then there was a rumble and a thump, and a big chunk fell in.

"Jeez!" Tim said in awe looking at the hole. "There was hardly anything holding that up! Look! It's a rough bit of frame and cloth with the plaster just thrown on it! I could do better!"

With no natural light coming into the lost room from anywhere else it was just a black cavern, mysterious and musty.

"Phwar! It honks a bit in there!" said Chloe with a wrinkling of her nose as she wafted a rather unpleasant smell away.

"Probably a few dead pigeons in there," Tim added wisely. "My mum and dad have an old place with open fires, and every summer some daft bird falls down the bloody chimneys and has to be rescued. The other year it was two wood-pigeons which fell into my old room while I was away, and so no-one noticed until mum went in to air the place for me coming back in the vac', and found two maggoty corpses and shit everywhere where they'd panicked when they couldn't get out."

"Euw!" Kirsty cringed. "Gross!"

Pip shrugged, "But a reality of life without central heating, like when this was built."

Nick had picked up a torch and now shone it into the hole. "Well there's one mystery solved!" he said triumphantly, as the beam picked up the outline of another door frame on the bathroom side. "You were right, Pip. This must have been an anteroom for this bedroom all along. But when it was first built it was probably accessed from that way. There'd have been no corridor until the third phase was built, after which there'd have been too much coming and going to have it all going through a bedroom. Oh! And there's a heap of something over in the corner by the fireplace. Looks like old rags or something. It's probably that which stinks so bad, it looks rotten."

"Ah! The fireplace! Thought there'd be one!" Pip was triumphant.

"Very small but perfectly serviceable from what I can see," Nick agreed. "Okay, folks, let's get this hole widened back to the original frame and make sure it's not going to drop anything on us, and then we can go in and have a look."

Expanding the hole was easy, just being a matter of pulling away the plaster-clogged cloth and the two bits of wood supporting it. The original lintel over the door was still in place, and quite sound, so Nick led them inside. By the fireplace they could now see that the bundle was a rolled up old carpet, but in bundling it up, whoever had done it had exposed another intriguing clue in the floorboards.

"Oh look!" Gemma breathed excitedly. "That looks like there was a second staircase!"

"Now that makes more sense," Pip agreed. "I bet it went out of what's now that old office room downstairs that's behind the kitchen. Probably a servants' stair, so not as grand as the main one, or maybe even one which just served the two new bedrooms in this middle wing when it was first built. That would make this not a room but a second and separate landing before it was linked to the original one. That's not unknown in some of these old farmhouses – two stairs, two landings and each to their own set of bedrooms. And that would mean that doorway we're seeing opposite us was the original access to a larger room, which has since been made into the corridor *and* the bathroom. Yes that's much more logical, because it would have been a nice big room looking onto the front. Quite the master bedroom in its time! Only when the third phase got built did this whole section get downgraded."

"So what would they have done?" Chloe asked. "Taken the staircase itself out at some point and then just blocked over the floor to make it safe?"

"Pretty much," Nick replied.

"Shall we get that grotty old rug out of the way?" Will suggested, with Tim coming forward and saying,

"I'll give you a hand."

"Yes, but put some of the plastic gloves on," Nick cautioned. "If there are dead birds around it could be full of fleas. If you get bitten you'll be itching for days!"

As the two students hoisted the rug up, Tim was just saying, "Good God, what did they make this out of? It's bloody heavy!" when something went thump on the floor and then Kirsty screamed.

"Euw! It's an arm!" she shrieked, backing off and pointing in horror.

Chloe too looked and screamed, the two lads dropping the rug in shock and backing off fast.

"All you girls out, *now*!" Nick ordered. "Gemma, Pip, get Kirsty and Chloe downstairs!"

He was insistent even though he too had gone white with shock.

"There's chivalrous," James said shakily. "Get the girls out! Never mind us!"

"Stop it!" Nick snapped. "You're going too, but I want you to move the minibus to the far end of the yard so that the police can get vehicles in here. Then I want you to go to the end of the track and watch for them. I doubt they'll be long in getting here! Take one of the girls, if they want to go." He threw the bus keys to James who, mollified, left without further argument as Nick was dialling on his mobile.

"Police, please," Tim and Will heard him say. "Hello. I'm the leading archaeologist on the dig at Cold Hunger Farm near Clifton-upon-Teme and I want to report that we've found a body, and it's not an old one. Very recent in fact. ...yes. No, I don't think it's accidental or suicide because someone rolled the body up in an old carpet to disguise it. ...No, no-one's disturbed it beyond the first discovery, and luckily they were wearing gloves. ...Yes, we'll wait. ...My name is Dr Nick Robbins. ...Yes, this is my phone. ...Thank you."

He put the phone back in his pocket and then waved Tim and Will out of the room and into the bedroom.

"I feel a bit sick," Will confessed.

"Not as sick as I do," Nick said, shoving the old window open so that he could get some air. "I know who that is."

"What?" both almost yelled, stunned.

"You *know* the body?" Tim gulped. "Fuck!"

"Shhh!" Nick hissed urgently. "Not so loud!"

Tim and Will were now utterly baffled. "Why?"

Nick took several deep breaths before answering. "Because it's Pip's ex, Dave."

"Oh bollocks!" Tim groaned, Will adding, "Oh fuck, no! Oh that's not fair! Poor Pip!"

"Precisely!" Nick said firmly, getting more control of himself again. "The first thing I saw was the bloody signet ring he took to wearing. I've never seen another one like it. And right then I thought, 'Oh God, Pip mustn't see that!' And not just because it would upset her terribly. You see it instantly struck me that the police need to be watching her when she's told the news. They need to see her shock."

"Christ! You don't think they'd think she did him in, do you?" Will asked, appalled.

But Tim was already catching up with Nick's thinking. "Maybe not, but if they could question her when that Natalie woman went missing, how much more of a suspect will she look now? Oh crap, Nick, what are we going to do?"

"Well for a start off, neither of us three will let on to her that it's Dave in there. When the police get here I'll tell whoever is in charge who I think the body is and why. If they're some officious wanker, then they can go and break the news downstairs themselves and see the reaction. That's bloody hard on Pip now, but I'd rather that than have her a suspect. If it's a decent bloke I might be able to explain more of what went on in the past. But whatever happens I'm doing my best to protect her."

"That's why you sent all of the girls out," said Tim, catching his train of thought. "That way you weren't giving Pip a clue but got her out of the way."

"And James nearly mucked it up," sighed Will. "God, I wish he'd grow up a bit! He's a terrible kid at times."

Nick nodded. "So when the police get here, would one of you go downstairs and bring them up? I don't think I can face Pip at the moment in case she asks me something I daren't answer, and unfortunately she knows me all too well.."

"I'll do it," Tim volunteered. "I can play dumb for Pip's sake."

Although it seemed forever, it wasn't long before the

sound of sirens were heard and then of cars coming up the drive. As the cars doors began to open and shut, Tim went downstairs and emerged a moment or two later with a burly plain-clothed officer and a slimmer one following him.

"DCI Bill Scathlock and DI Danny Sawaski," the bigger man introduced themselves as.

"I'm Dr Nick Robbins," Nick said coming forward to shake hands. "I called you."

The slimmer detective just gave him a cold stare, but DCI Scathlock took his hand, and then gestured to the hole in the wall. "Is this it?"

"Yes, we realised that the internal measurements of the house were all to pot, and that there was a room-sized space behind this wall. To be honest we'd normally just record the fact and then see if the owners wanted us to go in and investigate."

"So why didn't you do that?" challenged DI Sawaski. Clearly he was going to be the one who would give them trouble, and Nick was suddenly glad that he wasn't going to be the senior officer here. He sighed,

"Because ownership has been impossible to establish. The house had become lost down here in the woods, the local farmers keeping the track open to get to the fields but not going beyond the field gates. We got involved because some industrialist bloke saw it from his helicopter, got his minions to hack their way in past the saplings and undergrowth, and then got on to the county council to try and buy it. That's all above board and legal, officer! As senior archaeologist on this dig, although we've been focusing on the outside of the house, I made the decision to go into this space on the off-chance that we might get a clue about who owns it. It hasn't been lived in for over forty years as far as anyone knows, and some local old boys told one of the planning officers that before then it had been rented out for as long as anyone in his family could remember, and that was a fair old time. It would make things a lot easier for the county archaeologist if he could contact an owner, and the same goes for the planning officers. That's all we were trying to do."

DI Sawaski sniffed sceptically, earning him a glare off his DCI.

"Right, why don't you show us the body," DCI Scathlock said calmly. "Have you touched anything?"

"Only Tim and me," Will said shakily. "We thought we were just moving an old ratty rug out of the way."

"We'll need your prints and..." DI Sawaski began to say when Nick snapped,

"They were wearing the plastic gloves we use to handle finds with. I told them to put them on because I thought they might get flea bites."

"Well that's even better," Bill Scathlock said soothingly, then turned to Danny Sawaski. "Why don't you go and get the SOCOs up here, eh?"

As the disgruntled DI stomped off downstairs, Scathlock turned apologetically to Nick. "Sorry about him. He's just been passed over for promotion, so he's trying to prove everyone wrong. Don't worry, I made a call to your boss on the way over here. I know you're just the unlucky sods who've found this."

Nick felt the tension flood out of him. Thank God for that, he thought! Then as Sawaski disappeared down the stairs he stood in front of Scathlock at the hole in the wall and said, "But I'm afraid I do have a confession to make. I think I know who the body is."

DCI Scathlock stopped in his tracks. He certainly hadn't been expecting this! "Really?" he said in his most noncommittal voice. "Who?"

Nick suddenly felt very wobbly all over again. "Well

when Tim and Will lifted up the rug a hand fell out – well an arm really – but I saw a ring. It's a very distinctive ring. Not one you'd mistake easily, although I grant I could be wrong, but the ring I knew belonged to another archaeologist called Dave Marston."

"I know that name from somewhere," said Bill, racking his memory for where.

"Four years ago there was another archaeologist who went missing not far from here," Nick continued, praying this wouldn't all blow up in their faces despite his best efforts. "Her name was Natalie Walker."

To his side DI Sawaski had reappeared with several people in white coveralls, and glowered at Nick until Bill Scathlock said triumphantly,

"That's where I remember the name from! I was on that case. Young woman. Went missing. No body ever came to light. In the end we decided she'd gone off of her own accord. Wasn't she diagnosed as borderline schizophrenic or something?"

"I believe so," Nick agreed, "although I never knew her personally. She was a friend of Dave's, that's how I heard about her."

"He was one of our suspects, I recall," Scathlock added pensively. "Hmm, so you think it's him in there?"

Nick nodded. "But I'm afraid it gets worse. You see the lass who was engaged to Dave at the time Natalie disappeared is downstairs."

"Is she!" Sawaski said with worrying enthusiasm, making Nick say hurriedly,

"But she doesn't know that I think it's Dave up here! You see she wasn't in the room when the arm fell out of the fold of the rug. She was still in this bedroom here behind Kirsty and Chloe. She saw nothing. So I got her to take the other girls downstairs. They and James don't know either. Only Tim, Will and me, and we haven't said anything."

"Why not?" Sawaski demanded belligerently. "Why wouldn't you prepare her for such a shock?"

Nick's already frayed nerves snapped. "Because you bastards gave her such a God-awful time when Natalie disappeared, that's why! She was in fucking *Orkney* at the time! But that didn't stop her from being treated like she was a prime suspect. So this time you can have the shitty job of telling her and see her honest reaction. Then maybe you'll believe her this time!"

"Woah! Steady now!" Bill Scathlock said soothingly. "Calm down, Dr Robbins, I remember the young lady. I thought I recognised her face vaguely when I came in. I was on that case – one of the more memorable ones I've had to deal with, not least because all along we thought that Mr Marston was hiding something. We never did figure out what. I also remember that we were trying to work out whether he'd told his fiancée, and in the end decided that she knew nothing. Remind me, what's her name?"

"Philippa Devenish, but she's Pip to all of us." Nick scrubbed his hands over his face. "Sorry. I was a bit sharp there. This hasn't been the best day of my life. I know I dig up a lot bones all the time, but it's a hell of a difference to find someone you think you know. And the consequences went on for Pip long after you'd finished with her. Because of some of the scandal of what went on between Dave, Natalie and a couple of other men – one of whom was, and still is, very well connected – poor Pip had to give up on the doctorate she was hoping to do, and she's never got a proper job in archaeology since. She has to earn her living working at a local plant nursery and just coming on digs in her holidays."

"You feel very strongly about that," Sawaski observed less aggressively than before but still very coolly, as if he was far from convinced of Nick's tale.

Nick met his eye frankly. "Yes I do! Pip and I have been friends right from back when we were at university."

"Friends? You sure that's all?" Sawaski challenged him. "No question of you wanting to take her bloke's place?"

"No. I'm gay!" snapped Nick. "As my long-term partner Richard will testify! He's a friend of Pip's too, and no, we don't go in for weird threesomes in case your mucky mind was inventing that kind of relationship!"

Bill Scathlock's looks at Sawaski would have turned a lesser man to stone. "Maybe we should get on and have a look at this body, then?" he said through gritted teeth, hissing at his partner as they followed Nick through the hole, "For fuck's sake get a grip! If he wanted this kept quiet all he had to do was cover the damned hole up and walk away and wait for the builders to find the body. Or better still not come in here at all! Use your fucking brains, Danny, or piss off downstairs and start taking statements from the lads. And don't you dare say anything in front of Miss Devenish! I want to do that myself, and I'll have your balls on a plate if I find you've gone ahead regardless!"

However Sawaski followed him in silently if sullenly. The SOCOs were already working away inside and had some portable bright lights rigged up to illuminate their work. By the stark white light the rug was now revealed as a once multicoloured and patterned carpet, now faded to more muted hues. The arm which the girls had seen was lying across the open edge of the roll just as it had fallen out, with the heavy silver signet ring in clear view. DCI Scathlock bent over, and with a now gloved hand, carefully lifted the mouldering hand.

"Hmm, like you say, not a ring you'd forget easily. What is it?" he added, peering at the head on the ring.

"It's from a Roman cult he and Natalie were very taken with," Nick sighed. "He bragged about getting it specially made up in the jewellery quarter in Birmingham. I doubt you'll have any trouble tracking down the maker. Dave and Natalie, and possibly Paul and Phil, all had one made and I remember at the time thinking they were giving the poor jeweller a tough time over getting the detail right."

"I thought you said you'd only seen a ring on Mr Marston? Yet you're saying that there's at least one, or maybe three, more in existence." Bill Scathlock asked cunningly.

"Look, like I said, I didn't *know* Natalie. I just heard of the other rings from Dave. I've worked with Dave on several digs in the past," then a brighter thought came to him as to who should be sharing in this grief and added, "and I also know Phil. Phil Wilkinson. In fact he's with the county archaeologist's department here. He and I were working on documenting a dig just before the whole thing with Natalie happened. He wouldn't shut up about these bloody rings! Me and another archaeologist called Clive threatened to gag him he banged on about it so much, and then he brought Dave's in to show us. Said his would be just the same! Clive said it was the ugliest thing he'd seen in ages, and finally Phil got the message, so we never did see his, and in truth I've not seen him wearing one, but after Natalie disappeared he went rather quiet on the subject of cults. I only know of Paul by name. In fact I don't think I *ever* knew his surname, just that for a while he and Dave and Phil were big buddies."

DCI Scathlock nodded, satisfied that Nick's story so far was consistent. He was as suspicious as his DI over the repeat coincidence of these archaeologists being involved in a second disappearance, and this time with a body to work on, but he was also experienced enough to know that going at them like a pit-bull would get nowhere. The disgruntled DI was now looming over the SOCOs, watching their every move.

"Can we unroll him?" Sawaski asked one of the white-coats and got a nod.

"You don't have to stop for this," DCI Scathlock told Nick kindly. "It won't be a pretty sight going by what we've seen already."

Nick nodded. "I know, but I think I ought to. And anyway, if I can identify him now it will save me or anyone else having to do it later on." That he was thinking of Pip went unsaid, but was understood by all.

Two of the SOCOs came forward and carefully unrolled the carpet until the body lay revealed. Mercifully it lay face down, sparing Nick the grimmer sight, but even so the tangle of what had once been Dave's long hair was encrusted with stuff Nick deliberately didn't think about. The jacket, though, was very familiar.

Nick sighed sadly. "That's Dave's jacket, all right. He bought it years ago and added those patches every time he went somewhere. I can't imagine there would be too many people who'd been on digs in that same combination of places."

Sawaski stuffed a mint into his mouth before saying, "Bit well travelled for one of you lot, wasn't he? Thought there was no money in your business?"

"There isn't!" Nick riposted. "Like I *said*, they were *digs*. He didn't get paid for going, but by the same token he got his bed and board, and all he had to find was the means to get there. And Dave's folks weren't short of a bob or two."

"Are they alive?" Scathlock asked, wondering who he'd be breaking the news to, but Nick shook his head.

"No. They died even before he met Pip. A head-on collision in a car one icy night, apparently, while he was still a student. He got their house and some money. Didn't take him long to spend it either! By the time Pip knew him he was as broke as the rest of us. After they split up it came to light how much he'd been left, and I think that made it even worse, because Pip – who's always had to stand on her own two feet – couldn't understand how he could have frittered away that much cash and then borrowed money off her. Money she sadly came to realise she would never see again."

"Does Miss Devenish have debts, do you know?" was Sawaski's next question.

Nick scowled at him. "I doubt Pip owes anyone a penny! She lives very frugally. In fact, after she nearly got saddled with Dave's debts when he upped and left without any word of where he'd gone, she's developed a morbid dread of being in debt. More than once, Richard and I have had her over for meals in the winter, because we've suspected that she's been having to choose between having the heating on the big bed-sit room she rents – which is a bloody fridge even in the summer – and having a decent meal. I'd be shocked beyond words if she had as much as an overdraft."

DI Sawaski looked as though he was about to ask more questions, but his boss cut him off by saying,

"Right, let's go and speak to Miss Devenish." and leading the way downstairs. "You go and start with the other students," he told Sawaski firmly before asking Nick, "Are there any other rooms we can safely use?"

Nick directed Sawaski to the old office and offered Scathlock the parlour. If Pip's questioning was going to be longer than the others, he didn't want Sawaski traipsing back and forth through the room at regular intervals. There was something about the disgruntled DI that Nick didn't trust, yet oddly he did trust Scathlock. "Can I sit with Pip while you talk to her?" he asked and got a 'yes' on the proviso that he didn't interrupt.

However, before that happened DCI Scathlock stood in the kitchen facing all of the archaeologists and broke the news of who was upstairs. At the mention of Dave's name Pip went white and then fainted. You couldn't fake that kind of reaction, Nick thought with grim satisfaction, and even Sawaski had the grace to look uncomfortable as Gemma and Chloe tried to bring her round. All of the others were shocked, but it didn't have quite the same impact since Dave had been a stranger to all of them. Pip, on the other hand had to sit sipping strong, sweet tea for the time it took Sawaski to interview James and Kirsty, before she allowed Nick to lead her around to the parlour with Scathlock following.

To give the big DCI his due, his questioning of Pip was thorough but never harsh, and he often gave her time to compose herself again when something upset her again. At last he leaned back carefully on the old sofa and said, "Well I think that's all pretty clear. Can I say, Pip, that you were never a suspect in our investigation into Miss Walker's disappearance, and I don't regard you as one now. However, Mr Marston was always high on our list the last time, so we have to consider that his death might be linked to Miss Walker's case."

"Yes, I can see that you would have to," Pip agreed weakly.

"I'll get a driver to take you home," Bill Scathlock said solicitously.

"No!" Nick said firmly. "I'm not having her going home to sit alone! She'll come home with me." He turned to her. "You're having the spare room for at least a week, no arguing!" Then to Scathlock, "Richard's a paramedic. Our house is the best possible place for her until the shock's worn off."

On shaky legs Pip walked with Nick back to the kitchen to wait for a car to take them back to Worcester. Neither she nor Nick had really needed to camp out for the dig, but it had seemed churlish to leave Gemma and the students roughing it while they went home to a bed and a bath every night. Now, though, Nick was on the phone arranging for the other six to be put up in a hotel for a couple of nights. After that he had a feeling they would be going home. While the police were crawling all over the house there wasn't much chance of the dig continuing. As Nick negotiated with the local Travelodge, Tim sidled up to Pip with another cup of tea.

"God, Pip, I'm so sorry," he said, concern heavy in his voice. Then slipped something onto her lap. "You dropped your notebook upstairs," he added softly. "It was lying on the floor. I didn't want any of those policemen thinking it was some kind of evidence – you know, after we found that revolting clamp thing, and that connecting to *her*." Even with no-one right by them he was reluctant to say Natalie's name.

Pip managed a smile. "Thanks Tim, you're a sweetheart." She couldn't find the words to express her relief, especially not here. What the police would think if that side of the story came out didn't bear thinking about.

"The big detective seems okay," was Tim's next comment, making the unspoken question as to whether Pip had been treated properly in her questioning.

"Yes, he was much nicer than I thought he was going to be," Pip reassured him. "He said they'll have to reconsider Natalie's case, because apparently Dave was always one of the prime suspects in her disappearance. I think he was trying to say that now, they're wondering whether Natalie is alive and well, and that *she* might have killed *Dave* because he knew too much about something. The trouble is they don't know what that was, and neither do I."

"Oh good. As long as they didn't bully you."

Pip now smiled properly. It was so sweet of him to be that worried. "Thanks for the concern Tim, but there's not much you could do even if they had."

"Oh yes there is!" Tim said forcefully. "Uncle Gerald is a barrister! And he's good at that sort of thing. He and I have always got on, so he'd do me a favour and take your case on if I asked."

Pip was stunned. She hadn't thought she'd made that much of an impression on him for that kind of favour. It was even more surprising when Tim scribbled a phone number on a tatty bit of paper and pressed it into her hand.

"If they do start coming down hard on you, ring me! The offer stands! That's Mum and Dad's number. If they shut the dig down and I go home you can reach me there."

"Gosh, Tim, thanks!"

"Yes well, I don't like that DI Sawaski. There's something about him I don't trust either. If DCI Scathlock ends up only overseeing the investigation, he might be the one actually running it, and that wouldn't be a good thing, I'm thinking."

However, the students were suddenly being ushered out to the minibus where a PC was waiting to drive them to the hotel and then take the minibus on to where it would be checked over. Apparently DI Sawaski wanted to eliminate it from enquiries right from the start, or so he said.

"See? Sawaski doesn't believe anyone!" Tim hissed as he hugged Pip before hurrying out.

Pip and Nick, meanwhile, found themselves being taken to Nick and Richard's house in a patrol car, and then left to themselves until Richard got in.

For the next couple of days Pip could only sit in the big armchair looking out on the pretty courtyard garden at the back of the house, too knocked sideways to think on anything much. However, she never had been the wilting type, and as the shock wore off she found herself getting irrationally angry at Dave. It was beyond a joke that even in death he was making trouble for her. The logical part of her brain was saying that he would hardly have got himself killed just to spite her, but her heart wasn't to be so easily put off.

On the fourth evening DCI Scathlock was back again, this time with a much more pleasant companion in the form of a female DC, who looked as though she should have auditioned for the part of a farmer's wife in a play or on TV. They needed Pip and Nick's movements for immediately after the investigation into Natalie, yet never seemed to be interested in their more recent activities.

"I'm sorry but I've got to ask you this," Pip finally blurted out. "Are you asking us all this because Dave's actually been dead for over three years?"

Bill Scathlock sighed and nodded. "We think that, bizarrely, the last person who might have seen him alive was actually the station sergeant in Worcester, when we had Marston in for the last time to answer some questions – well apart from anyone who saw him on a bus heading out towards Clifton."

"Shit!" Richard gasped from where he was sitting on the sofa by Nick.

Scathlock gave a wry smile. "Yeah! Ironic, eh? But the autopsy has narrowed it down – he's certainly been dead for years, going on the temperature in the room and humidity and the fact that the room was effectively sealed up, *et cetera*, you get the picture – and on top of that there were some bus tickets in his pocket which were still legible."

Suddenly Pip burst into tears making Nick rush over to her and hug her.

"Hey, steady on," he said gently, but Pip shook her head and sobbed,

"But all the time I was cursing him up hill and down dale for not answering my messages and phone calls he was dead! I feel so bloody awful about that now! The things I said to his boss over the phone when they told me he'd disappeared from his job too. I thought he was just being an arse and avoiding me. That it was all his crappy idea of ...of somehow paying me back because he was trying so hard to make the break-up all my fault. Mine for not understanding him."

An odd thought occurred to Nick. "Have you spoken to Phil Wilkinson?" he asked Scathlock. "Only as far as we all knew, Dave was stopping with him. What does he say?"

"Only that Dave was with him, but not for as long as you all seemed to think. He says that Dave had already talked about just packing his bags and going off hitching. Some daft idea of going to Italy. Mr Wilkinson says that until the day when he got home and found Mr Marston's things gone, he didn't really think he'd go through with it. I know you have some history with Mr Wilkinson, but he was at a conference up in Leeds at the university, actually giving a paper on the most important day, and he was chairing sessions on the ones either side of his paper. And we have the bus tickets in Mr Marston's pocket which track his movements from Mr Wilkinson's house into the city centre for his appointment at the main police station, and only then out to Clifton."

Pip blew her nose and then looked balefully up at Nick, perched on the arm of her chair. "I know we both think Phil's a petty little wanker, Nick, but even I don't think he's capable of murder."

"No, suppose not," Nick sighed regretfully, making Scathlock raise an eyebrow. "Oh it's just that sometimes it's like Phil's Teflon-coated," Nick explained wearily. "Nothing ever bloody sticks to him. He creates all sorts of shit for other people, but he never gets any back. It makes him damned hard to be around, let alone like."

"I've know someone like that," the DC sympathised. "They're their own worst enemies."

The conversation went on for a few minutes longer, but it seemed to be the end of the detectives' questions and they left soon after, but not before Scathlock had said that the dig would be on hold for a while, but that he couldn't see why they wouldn't be able to resume it in time. After that the two detectives thanked them and left.

Coming back from the door and pouring the three of them a large glass of red wine each, which they felt they'd earned, Nick couldn't help but bemoan, "But by the time they let us back up there we'll have lost the students and Gemma." Gemma, like Pip, had a wholly different regular job, and this had been part of her annual leave which couldn't be extended any longer.

"I'll come and lend a hand," Pip said with as much optimism as she could muster. "The plants won't be doing much through the autumn, so I'll just be doing my regular part-time hours." In the spring Pip worked incredibly long hours as everything needed potting on or planting out, but not at this end of the year until Christmas loomed, when she usually picked up extra work in restaurants, and so temporarily Pip had time to spare. "I really want to uncover that chapel."

However her first move was to get back to her own bed-sit. Much as she loved Nick and Richard, their concern was getting a bit overwhelming. She felt she needed some time on her own to come to terms with what had happened to Dave. So she went home, and with the weather picking up, spent the next week going on long, leisurely bike rides out into the countryside.

It was after she got back from a ride, with her legs aching but with a feeling of well-being from a having had a lovely day out, that she flopped into the chair and then thought to sort out her clothes from the dig which would need washing. The fair weather was set to continue, so she might as well get down to the laundrette tomorrow and get them washed and hung out. As she went through the bag of stuff which Nick had brought back for her from the camp, she found her notebook tucked in the waterproof jacket's pocket. Frowning, she held it up to the light perplexed. Surely Tim had given it back to her? She remembered stuffing it into the pocket of her fleece because it had been hard to get the small desk diary in past the pocket's zip. Come to think of it, now, she could actually remember leaving her waterproof on the seat of the minibus, and flicking open the book she saw her own writing and drawings, but if this was hers, whose was the other?

Going over to the ancient desk she had in the room's bay window, she picked up the other book. It was identical to hers – the same size, colour and brand. Then she looked at the date on it. Four years ago! Then this definitely wasn't hers even in the unlikely event of her picking up two of them. She was using up a batch of diaries which had been stocked over at the garden centre side of the business where she worked, but they'd been bought back in 2000, hadn't been sold, and had been discovered at the back of a storeroom only three years back. Since they were otherwise destined for the recycle bin, Pip had brought the box-load of them home on the bus, and just grabbed another out of it when she needed another notepad. But she knew she hadn't taken two with her on the dig.

She flicked the pages of the second book only to find a totally strange handwriting inside.

"Oh bugger!" she muttered as her good mood evaporated. If Tim had found this inside the room – and shit, why hadn't she remembered that she'd never actually got in there? – then... "Oh God! This could be the murderer's!"

She went and sat down heavily on the bed. Should she hand it over to Scathlock right now? Her head said of course she should. But something instinctive inside her said 'look inside it first'. Maybe she was still feeling a bit guilty about calling Dave all the names under the sun when he'd been lying dead, but a part of her also wanted to be the one who got some kind of justice for him. And after all, she could hardly take it down to the station before tomorrow morning now. Why not take a look? She'd already handled it, so whatever happened her prints were on it anyway.

Going back to the front cover, she carefully opened it up. There in the contact details was the name Natalie Walker, and a small sketch of a Roman-looking female with the name Magna Mater underneath it.

"Well I'm damned!" Pip breathed. "Of all the people! You cow! It was you who killed Dave!"

Chapter 8

Autumn, Bath, 1823

Harry looked in disbelief at the woman he had once thought the world revolved around, and felt all that fall away as if the soles of his boots had turned into drains. She stood in front of the ornate fireplace, doe-eyes filling with tears as they did on a regular basis.

"How could you?" she repeated. "Natalie has been deserted by her family, lost all she holds dear, and you dare to say I shouldn't invite her into my home."

"For heaven's sake, Amy," Harry remonstrated, "that's stretching the truth more than a bit! She wasn't deserted! She up and left if anything I've heard is going round is right. Left her husband – if that's truly what he was – and left her home. No-one dragged her off! And I'm not being cruel, I'm thinking of you. God Almighty, the woman's downright notorious! And what of your son? The teasing he will get at school and the taunts? Think of what having her as good as living here will mean for him, even if you think nothing for yourself."

Amy sniffed and the bottom lip began to wobble – a sure sign that the full waterworks were about to start. "Lies!" she declared in her best little girl voice. "It's just you men being nasty to her. She said *you'd* say things like that because she's pretty, and men just want to control her. To possess her."

"Possess her?" Harry gulped in astonishment. "Damnation..." he spluttered, desperately trying to remember where he was and not swear as he would have done in front of the troops. "Amy, what do you take me for? I wouldn't want to 'possess' *her* if the very Devil were at my heels! And if you won't think of yourself then, if I have any authority in this house, for all your sake's I shall have to put my foot down. She must not come here to stay!"

"How dare you!" Amy shrieked. "Authority? *You* are not my husband!"

And there it was, out in the open at last. The death knell for his once cherished dreams was sounded.

Harry took a deep breath before he spoke, for now he felt it deep in his soul that they had reached the make or break point as to whether they could ever even be friends. "No I'm not," he said far more calmly than he felt. "But you've been a widow now for over nine years. Nine years in which you've leaned on me at every turn. Oh, I was glad you did so! I cared for you even back when Edward was alive, and then afterwards I hoped that in time you would come to see me for myself. That you would, in time, consider marrying me."

"Marry *you*?" Amy's face was a picture of astonishment. She was so genuinely shocked she even forgot to cry for a second, then the tears began in earnest. "Oh how could you be so *cruel*, Harry? How could you remind me that my darling isn't here anymore? And how could I possibly *marry* you? My saintly Eddie is my husband, here and in heaven, and will be forever. I will never be untrue to him!"

Harry exhaled heavily, so that was it then! He had thought that if this moment ever came that it would come as a stab to the heart, a near mortal blow. That he would reel from it and suffer dreadful pain. The shock, however, was that the only sensation that he recognised he was feeling was one of relief. Had things in this last year come to such a state that he was already part the way to being over any hope?

"Really?" he heard himself saying with unnatural calm. "Saintly? Amy, if you think that then you really have deceived yourself, but I'll not argue with you over that, for there's clearly no point. However, I *will* have you hear me out *now*, for I shall say it only once and then I shall leave it be. ...I had hoped that your grief would take a more normal course. Most other women can pick up the threads of their lives in time, and look at the living without the dead constantly getting in the way. I never asked you to forget Edward. All I wanted was for you to see all that *I* did for you and little Eddie, and see some virtue in it."

Then something seemed to come unravelled inside of him, and he heard his words pouring out of him without any ability to stop them. "Now I can see how mistaken I was! A few of years of sporadic attention was what Edward gave you, that's all, a grudging couple of years. In comparison to that I've been faithful to you without wavering for over ten years. I've picked up the pieces Edward left behind – even when he was alive! I've given you time, I've given you the space to grieve, and I've never failed to shield you from the worst which might have come your way, whether it was physical or otherwise. And what have I asked for in return? Nothing! Nothing, because I hoped time after time that you valued what I did, even if you said nothing.

"But now I see that was all in vain. I was a fool to think that all those years of constancy and caring – of my deep and faithful love – could weigh against that pitiful thing you call love. Good God, Amy, that's not love! It's not love because you pick and choose what you look at, and what bits of a person you attach yourself to. You clearly never saw all of Edward! If you had, I might still have more sympathy for you, for then I could say to myself that you truly loved him, even despite all his many failings. But I see now that you couldn't have loved him any more than you can love me, because you only loved a cipher of your own making!"

"Get out!" Amy screamed. "Get out of my house now!"

"Oh I'm going," Harry said without emotion, his outburst spent. He walked to the door and then turned with his hand on the doorknob.

"Oh, and it's not *your* house! So you'd better get your brother to hurry up with finding a new place for you all, because *I've* been paying the rent on this place, and after next month I shall be instructing my bank not to make any further payments. Since I'm so expendable, so repugnant to you, you can make do without my army wages too!"

And with that he turned and strode out, grabbing his overcoat on the way, followed to the door by waves of hysterical wailing which he suspected were as much in temper as in grief.

The bite of the chill autumn air as he stepped out into the street came as a relief, even if it was tinged with the smoke of fires being lit against the colder nights of late. He walked without really seeing where he was going, just walking mechanically as his head churned with thoughts. After that first encounter with the newly widowed Amy back in 1814 he'd gone abroad for five years, most of them spent in Malta at the barracks at Floriana by Valletta. During those years he'd written to her regularly and had received letters back. Part of him wanted to go back to the rooms he had taken, rip open the package he'd kept every one of them in, and reread them all to see if he'd been a complete and utter fool. Had he missed some vital sign? Had the clues been there all along and him too foolish to be able to see them? He thought not. He sincerely hoped not! He'd come to pride himself on being a common-sense sort of man who faced life without foolish expectations, but in this instance he'd failed miserably.

Realising he'd walked completely out of the city, he found a farm gate, climbed up on it, and sat watching the stars appear. The trouble lay, he could now see, in that he'd not ever spent much time with Amy until he'd come home this time. Not the kind of time a young man might normally spend courting the woman he wanted to marry. Time spent in company at balls or country dances, maybe, depending on your station, and always well chaperoned for decency's sake. But time in which you might get some clue as to the temperament of the young lady in question. Letters, by contrast were so restrained. A letter written in the heat of the moment could be torn up before it was sent, or a hasty word scratched out so as to be illegible. It wasn't the same as talking to someone.

But during those years with his regiment at Floriana he'd done his best to keep in touch, and not only with Amy. As he'd promised, he'd written to Gus telling him of the true circumstances of Edward's death, and why he could never tell Amy even part of it, but that she should expect no help from the army as the widow of such a reprobate as Edward Clifford. And in due course Gus had written back. He had been many years serving the East India Company out in India, he told Harry, and was due to come home soon. Encouraged, Harry had written and elaborated more on what he'd found at the Vaughan household, and of Mr Vaughan's state of mind. A rapid exchange of letters had taken place after that, with Gus returning to England by the end of the next year.

However, all was not so settled as Harry had hoped, for Gus appeared to have talents the Company was loathed to part with, and for the next three years he had still gone on several long trips for them, even if he was now nominally based in England. Only when malaria had reoccurred and nearly claimed Gus' life had they allowed him to retire from their service. Then at the end of 1819, Harry too had come home with the last of the 31st Foot from Malta, and Christmas of that year had seemed like a whole new beginning, even if Harry had had to go to both Belfast and Dublin with the regiment for short periods after that.

Somewhere off to his right a vixen called out in the still night, bringing Harry out of his reverie. He knew he should start walking back. If he sat here much longer he would catch a chill, but he was enjoying the tranquillity. And therein lay another of his problems with Amy. Once he'd been back in England, he'd taken a more active part in her life. Between them, he and Gus had found a decent school for Eddie, and in order to distract the distraught Amy from the loss of her beloved baby, Harry had rented the modest house here in Bath, and brought her and her family to enjoy the summer season. It wasn't solely for the distraction either. Mrs Vaughan's health had finally broken under the strain of looking after everyone else, and Harry had received an anxious letter from Robert saying how much the poor soul needed a rest. So the house in Bath, which he paid for, and the staff which Gus paid for, had seemed such a good idea.

And for that year it had worked. Mrs Vaughan had rallied and Amy had enjoyed the society now that she could go out properly attired in dresses which had also come out of Harry's funds. But in the winter Mrs Vaughan had died, and then Mr Vaughan had followed her within months. Now Gus had really felt the strain of taking care of Amy, and had appealed to Harry to help him once more, and so one season at Bath had turned to two, and this year made three seasons. But Amy was a total butterfly, unable to settle at anything and needing constant entertaining or she became irritable and difficult. Having been used to almost exclusively male company for most of his adult years, Harry, by contrast, found the endless social whirl of a season at Bath grating to say the least. Hordes of people surrounding him, all twittering like demented caged birds over things of utter inconsequence, near drove him insane. Thank God he still had his regiment to attend to most of the year, and the season only ran from May to August!

Every night Amy had to be out in company somewhere. Even if they weren't asked out to dine – and often they weren't, since neither Harry nor Gus had those kinds of social contacts – they still had to go out to wander aimlessly amongst the crowds, so that Amy could gaze upon the beautiful dresses and fool herself that she was one of the social elite. Mercifully, with Harry now permanently in England, at least for a while, he could get away from his barracks to be with them in Bath. And Amy desperately needed escorting, not only out of propriety but because she was oblivious to pickpockets and other dangers, and she certainly had no other friends she could walk out with. So at first Harry and Gus had tried taking it in turns on alternate nights, but both of them soon found that they couldn't manage to suffer even a full night. Now they would arrange it that one would start the night, and then at an arranged time the other would come and find them – hopefully at some prearranged spot, but often drawn off by Amy's whims – and take over as escort. Since Gus' strength was still not good – and when the regiment demanded Harry's presence he shouldered the whole burden – it often fell to Harry to take the late shift, and when Amy would decide she'd had enough was wildly variable.

This too had begun to grate horrendously at Harry. He could cope with the late nights in terms of stamina. God alone knew he'd done enough fighting at night not to be that soft! But he bitterly resented going to bed so late that he lost great chunks of the following days. Used to being an active man, he hated sleeping on into the day. It was quite one thing for him to be strolling home to his bed now as the early September night fell – this was positively early in comparison to some of the nights he'd had of late – and another to be falling exhausted into bed with the summer dawn already breaking. Worse was the fact that with his regiment back in England there was comparatively very little for him to do in terms of duties, and therefore he felt unable to ignore Gus' pleas for help. Well, Gus would have to find some way of coping now, because Harry had had as much as he could take.

The next morning he sat eating his breakfast in the small hotel he'd been living at off and on for the season, and feeling most strange – for even with Gus there, he'd never stayed the night at the house when Amy was without other guests, such as a rare visit from a cousin. He'd been expecting another disturbed night after such a turbulent day, instead of which he'd gone to bed and slept like a log. Now sitting at the breakfast table he was perplexed by the sense of lightness and strange inner calm which came from the knowledge that today, at least, he had no need to brace himself for the daily visit to Amy. As he speared one of the last delicious mushrooms on his plate, he saw Gus walk into the hotel foyer beyond the dining room. The receptionist gestured to the table-filled room and Gus spotted Harry and hurried over. He looked really worried, poor chap, thought Harry, and gestured for another cup to be brought to the table along with a refill for the pot of coffee.

"Sit down, Gus," he said amiably, as the portly and smartly dressed man arrived at the table, twisting his hat in his hands and moon-shaped face a picture of misery. "Whatever Amy has told you, you and I have no quarrel with one another.

"What's to be done, Harry?" Gus asked miserably.

"Nothing," Harry said firmly, "if you mean will I change my mind?" Then felt very sorry for Gus. Now he was going to be left shouldering the burden of his younger sister all by himself, and what a burden that was going to be! "I'm sorry Gus, truly I am. I never meant it to come to this. Never thought for a moment that it *would* come to this! But I've taken as much of this life as I can cope with, and then yesterday Amy finally told me the truth, that she would never consider marrying me."

Gus' jaw dropped. "She refused you? Good God, Harry! ...I mean ...Good God! What is the gel thinkin' of?"

Gus had somehow adopted a strange speech affectation where girls and/or women became 'gels', and the 'g's at the end of his words got lost. Perhaps it was mixing for so many years with those who sought to aspire to a higher station in life while out in the colonies, or maybe to his ear that was how the upper classes really sounded. At first Harry had found it amusing, but Gus was such a sad little man he couldn't tease him about it, and by now he hardly noticed it for his own part, only realising how forced Gus' speech sometimes sounded when strangers reacted to it.

"Apparently I should never have dishonoured Edward's memory by even asking."

"Good God! Well I'm dashed!" To cover his discomposure Gus took a gulp of the coffee Harry had poured for him, only to splutter hard having not realised how hot it was. He dabbed frantically at the coffee splatters on his ornate cravat, then looked balefully up at Harry, who even sitting down towered over him. "Well I s'pose it's better that than her havin' set her eye on some unsuitable young buck here in town?" he said with almost wistful hope.

"No it isn't," Harry said firmly. "You didn't ever know Edward, did you?"

Gus blinked owlishly, "Well no, but I feel like I do, I've heard Amy talk so much about him."

"And that's the trouble!" Harry braced himself. The truth had to be told now in all its gory detail. There was no time for finesse anymore.

"Amy didn't know him either, Gus, and that's the truth. All she's told you is some foolish girl's wishes she's made into Edward's ghost, instead of the real man I served alongside. Do you remember what I wrote to you about the true circumstances of Edward's death?"

"Well, yes... But he was young and ...and ....well dash it, young men do make foolish mistakes!"

Harry leaned in and fixed Gus with a gimlet stare. "Gus, the time has come for you to know the truth. The whole truth! No excuses. No sparing the name of the dead. You have to know it because the source of my argument with Amy lies in the past, and its a past which has reared it's head again here and now in the form of Miss Walker."

"Oh Gawd!"

Harry signalled to the waiter. "I know it's rather early in the morning, but would you be so good as to bring Mr Vaughan a large brandy? I think he's going to need it!"

He pushed his plate and napkin aside and leaned towards Gus, never breaking eye contact and leaving poor Gus trapped like a stunned rabbit.

"Now let's get this straight once and for all. Edward was a rake and a wastrel. No! Don't interrupt or try to make excuse for him, Gus, you won't want to once you've heard all I have to tell! I repeat, he was a rake and a wastrel. No sooner had we joined the army then Edward was running up gambling debts. Now as you so rightly said, that was nothing unusual – there were many other young officers doing just the same. But Edward couldn't stop. He kept going even when he'd run out of his money, *and* the money he'd borrowed off other gentlemen and then couldn't pay back. So the only way out of it for him was to get deeper and deeper into the clutches of a truly evil sergeant named Hobspawn. Thank God a cannonball did for Hobspawn in the Pyrenees! He'd brought many a good man down to his wicked level, but in Edward he'd met someone with a soul as naturally twisted as his own!

"I say this not out of some strange pique because I wasn't able to keep up with the young gentlemen, Gus. I knew and liked some real rascals out there. Men who my brother would be horrified at meeting, but men who, when it came to the heat of battle, you'd be glad to have beside you, and who were as loyal as lions to their selected friends. Edward wasn't like that. All he ever thought of was himself and what was easiest for him. And the first time I really saw that clearly was when we came back for the wedding. He spent all of the night before the ceremony bemoaning his fate at having to marry your sister because his father was for it, and he wouldn't do without the money his father sent him. That was the *only* reason he married Amy, Gus. He was frightened of losing his allowance!"

Gus was shaking his head. "Oh Lord!"

"It's the truth. I swear that on my father's grave! And I was so angry Gus, because at that point I would have given everything I possessed to be standing in his place at that altar. And it was that day when I met Natalie Walker for the first time. She was wearing a ring of Amy's. A ring which to this day Amy thinks Edward bought for her. He didn't, ...I did. From a jeweller in Lisbon. You'll know the one. It has three pretty pink stones set alternately with three pink pearls. There's a matching necklace too. All paid for out of my money because Edward didn't even *care* that it was Amy's birthday. All he wanted was more money for whoring and gambling, not for buying Amy presents.

"But that's not the worst of it – and this you must now know. As your mother or father no doubt wrote to you, we were only home for a week – two days before the wedding, four after, and then travelling back to catch the ship once more. But on that last night of the four, instead of staying with Amy at your parents' old house, Edward insisted we go back to our hotel. Not to get the early start which was the excuse to Amy, but because he spent the night tupping that whore Miss Walker – Amy's supposed friend!"

"No! You cannot malign that lady so on mere gossip!" Gus spluttered.

"Gossip my foot!" snapped Harry. "I was in the room next door! I could hear the bloody bed going all night! And when I went in to drag the miserable sod off to catch the coach, there was Miss Walker, as naked as the day she was born, riding him like some Diana at the hunt!"

Gus went scarlet.

"Yes, I blushed too, Gus! I've seen some sights in my time, before then and since, but few as brazen. And she looked me straight in the eye and winked! So don't think I didn't see her face and made some mistake that way. I didn't! Only three days after taking Amy to the altar he left his wedding bed for Miss Walker's. That's how much he loved Amy, Gus. Well I got him back to the regiment and thought that was the end of it, but no. Damn me if the wretched Miss Walker didn't turn up in Spain! She'd only followed him! Thank God that she soon realised that

Edward wasn't going to keep her in a manner she was yet to become accustomed to. Some fool of a cavalry office soon took her eye and off she went, but I kept hearing about her because she always moved on, and always it was to someone who had more money. I doubt she ever does anything for love.

"And now we come to yesterday, Gus, because the damned woman is back and ingratiating herself with Amy once again. I've no idea why and I don't care to inquire, but I'd put money on it being that she's looking for a new mark, just like some card shark! I tried to put my foot down over Amy inviting her to stay in the house with her, because if anyone from the army sees her they'll know exactly who Miss Walker is, and *what* she is, and Amy's name will be tarnished by association. Now, though, Amy isn't listening to me anymore, so you must pack her up and take her back to Worcestershire with all speed! I doubt Miss Walker will follow you there! There aren't enough opportunities to meet rich men up there for her liking. I'm just glad Eddie is back at school! With any luck he'll never know what's going on. But Amy must leave Bath, Gus. I know you were going in a few weeks anyway, but now you must go immediately. As it happens I've been summoned back to the regiment anyway, so even if Amy and I hadn't quarrelled I would be leaving now, and for that I'm truly sorry because I wasn't intending to leave you in such a mess."

"It's all right, old chap," Gus said faintly. The truth had rattled him to his very boots, it was clear.

"You weren't taken with Miss Walker were you?" Harry asked with sudden worry.

"Well she was very flatterin', don't y'know, and gels don't often notice me. Don't cut the fine figure, in or out of uniform like you, y'see?"

"Oh Gus, I'm so sorry!" And Harry meant it. Gus was that rare thing, a thoroughly nice man. Too nice for his own good! And Harry knew from other conversations that Gus desperately wanted to settle down and marry and have a family of his own. Dotting on little Eddie, who wasn't so little anymore, still wasn't the same as having his own children in Gus' eyes – a sentiment Harry didn't quite understand for himself, but sympathised with. Yet Gus was never going to attract a young single woman in the kind of society which came for the season at Bath, and now Harry had another thought.

"And Gus? You need to separate yourself from Amy when you're back home too. Her fanciful airs and graces are stopping you from getting what you want. There are plenty of young women in Worcester or Hereford who would see you as a good catch. Women who will value a steady fellow like yourself with the means to keep a family in comfort. But every time one of them gets near you, Amy puts them off."

"I'm sure she don't intend to!"

"I'm damned sure she does! And for two reasons. Firstly Amy knows she depends on you for everything except the things I pay for. She may never acknowledge it – may never say thank you – but she knows! And it scares her that she may lose that to another woman."

"I'd never abandon her, Harry! Lord I never would! Surely she knows that?"

Harry sighed. "Oh she knows that, Gus. But what she doesn't want is to be *sharing* you! Amy wants to be cared for. To be looked after. But exclusively, not as the sister-in-law to some kindly farmer's daughter who would then be the real lady of the house! And if that weren't enough, have you not observed how other women look at Amy? She grates on their nerves with her girlish ways, Gus. I know

I'm not married myself, but when I'm with the regiment I do go to dine with other men and their wives, and Amy doesn't fit well with any of them. Amy is thirty-two, now, but it's hard to believe because she doesn't act her age. So to younger women she's not one of them, and they aren't comfortable in her company; while the women she *is* of an age with don't befriend her because she wants them to look after her all the time, instead of being one amongst equals. So please take this warning. If – or rather when – you meet a woman you want to marry, she won't want to have your wailing sister sitting in the corner of the parlour every evening with you!

"So take my advice. When you're back home, find her a small house in town – Hereford or Leominster if you fear your father's disgrace still lingers around Worcester thanks to the Cliffords' malice. But make it in a town where she can live alone without the need for you to drive her everywhere in the pony and trap. Then take yourself to whichever town she *isn't* in and make a home for yourself there! Somewhere where you will be taken for your own merits without Amy hanging like some albatross around your neck! Either that or find her a husband, and as the man of the household, march her up the damned aisle! Preferably some widower who is still in love with his late wife and just needs a woman in the house! That way you won't be making two people unhappy! Because she'll never be truly happy again Gus, because she doesn't want to be! It's far easier to play the weak and grieving widow, and having us two fools running around after her, than to pick up the pieces of her life and start living it again.

"She's close to driving Eddie away too, if you hadn't noticed. He goes to the homes of his school-friends, and now he's old enough to start comparing when he comes home, and Amy isn't standing up to the comparison with those other mothers. So set up a home of your own to offer the poor lad an alternative place to stay, or mark my words, as soon as he's finished school you won't see him again!"

"Oh dear!" Gus muttered, mopping his brow of the sweat which had begun to stand out on it.

"Have some more coffee," Harry said kindly, topping up Gus' cup and signalling the waiter for another brandy too.

He looked at Gus over the steam of his own coffee as he gratefully gulped it. That was the worst of it out of the way. Should he say more of Edward? Of how he'd planned to leave Amy for Natalie Walker at one stage? Or the other woman he definitely had been intending to run away from the army with just as he had been killed? No, there was no need. The Austrian countess with the shady past wasn't likely to ever appear here, unlike that bloody Walker woman, so he could let that lie. And he feared that the truth about Edward was proving so hard for Gus to swallow, that if he said more Gus might just think he was making it all up. No, better to be economical and stay believed.

"You've been a good son and brother, Gus," he said consolingly as he watched Gus sipping the brandy as fast as he could – Gus would never knock it back in one go! "You should have come back from your time in India to a quiet life, not taking over from your parents with a sister who's chosen to remain a child. Because I'm very much afraid that you're reaping the harvest of what they've sown with Amy."

"Mother and Father did always adore her. It was losing my brother and sister between having me and her, don't y'see?" Gus sighed.

Harry could see Gus starting to weaken already at the memory. "Now, now, Gus! I know you still think of her as the sweet little sister you left behind to go out to India. God knows it's taken me long enough to see her differently. I can still remember the adorable girl who had come home from school the day I first came to your house with Edward. She was lovely then!" He gazed out of the window wistfully. "Kind and shy, if not a stunning beauty in comparison to some of the girls we saw, but she had an inner glow which made up for that." He sighed heavily and shrugged. "I don't know when that went, but it's gone now. Maybe it was already waning when she married Edward. Maybe he saw her more truly than I did in those days. He said she'd never make a good wife. I thought all the fault was with him then. That he was being unreasonable in what he wanted from a wife – and maybe he was – but I suspect she wouldn't have made any man a *good* wife."

"Oh Lord" Gus gasped. "Oh Harry, has it been that bad? All these years? Did you stay in touch out of duty because I wasn't there to do mine?"

Now it was Harry's turn to be horrified. "Heavens no! Lord, Gus, you've misunderstood me if you think I'm brooding on some past resentment – that Amy married Edward and not me, or that ...that..." He stopped, unable to think of any circumstance which would fit. "No, that wasn't it at all! When I said I loved your sister, Gus, I meant it. I loved her devotedly for over ten years with every part of my heart! I really meant it ...It's just that things have changed."

He poured another coffee to give himself time to think, aware that soon he was going to have to stop or he'd be awash with the stuff.

"Look, I thought Edward was the luckiest man in the world to have her all but fall into his lap. To be virtually given a wife like her by both sets of parents' contrivance, and for her to be so smitten with him to boot. It was like a gift from heaven in my eyes. Then of course we went away, and all I knew of Amy was her letters to Edward. Letters I ended up replying to because Edward was always off in some whore's bed, or at the card tables. So you see, Gus, as often as not I was the messenger between her and Edward, picking up the pieces when he let her down, because I couldn't bear the thought of her disappointment. And then he died in that gutter, only one step away from being court-martialled and unfaithful to boot, and still I couldn't bring myself to tell her the truth that it was me, not him, who cared for her. Do you know, back then I would have exchanged my life for his to save her from that extreme grief.

"But life isn't like that, and life wasn't so bad for me in other ways. I hoped in time she'd come around to seeing me for the man I am, but I was still in the army and moving around a lot. So like you, it was dozens of letters which were the contact with her, and I loved writing back to her. It gave me something to think of outside of the army during those dreary nights as I penned my long replies back. So you see, up until we both came home more permanently, I was happy in my delusions! Only then did things change, and you were already here by then, so never think this is your fault, Gus because it isn't!"

"Oh! Dashed glad about that!"

"Truly, it isn't. It was dealing with Amy herself which changed my feelings. Because pleading letters were one thing. While I wasn't having her woes thrust upon me face to face I think I imagined them to be far worse than they were. And I confess it appealed to me to be the strong man in her life. That role was almost romantic, even chivalrous. I'll even accept that it flattered my vanity."

"You ain't a vain man, Harry! Never known a man less so!"

"Thank you, Gus, but I'm as fallible as the next man, as Robert will no doubt tell you! But I confess fault on my own part in this. It did flatter something within me. Yet once I was home – foolishly thinking that now was the time to press my courtship of her before we both get too old – I found that these woes, these great, insurmountable problems, were nothing more than a silly girl's *imagined* troubles. And worse, she appreciates nothing! Not the way you've kept a roof over her head, or the clothes I've bought her so that she never has to patch and mend, or make do. I didn't want effuse thanks, or for her to prostrate herself at my feet. All I wanted was for her to see that I loved her and that she was cherished in the way she fancied Edward had done. In other words, that even though she only imagined that caring on *his* part, that she could have it again for real with me. You know, one of my friends in the regiment has been in a similar position, and the widow he took care of and has now married adores him for his caring – and they've only known one another for a fraction of the time I've known Amy! Yet all I'm ever introduced as is her late-husband's friend. Not *her* friend! Edward's! Nothing more."

Gus hung his head miserably. "That's terrible Harry! I feel so bad that I never noticed that, but now you say it, she did that only last week, didn't she? Oh dear. Oh dear me, what's to be done Harry?"

"Do as I said, Gus. Get her a house or a husband – preferably both! There's a limit even to brotherly duty!"

"But what of you?"

"I'm staying in the regiment. I didn't say anything earlier Gus, because if Amy had said 'yes' I was going to resign my commission. You see the regiment is off to India."

"India! Oh my word, Harry! Are you sure? It's a terrible place, y'know! Nearly did for me!"

"I know. And yes, I am sure. You see, I've had few chances to further my career since the end of the war with France. Too many officers for too few posts. But there are a good many officers who enjoyed the high life while we were in Europe, but who now don't want to go to the far side of the world. Several have resigned already, and things aren't so wonderful out there anymore. When you went out there, a man could go out with the army or 'John Company', as you did, and make his fortune. Let's face it Gus, it's set you up nicely!"

"Oh yes! Upon my soul I don't know how I would have made ends meet if I'd stayed in this country. Not for m'self, you understand, but in these last couple of years. Would have been well and truly stuck if I hadn't had somethin' to fall back on."

"And that's what I need. Had I been due to wed, I would've had to look for something else in the way of employment, or live abroad for much of the year, but at least Italy or Malta wouldn't have been as bad for a wife as India. Now I must think of what's best for me, and I can see that a few years out in India could well set me up for life, not because I would gain a fortune, but because there's promotion to be had out there. Retirement as a major or a lieutenant colonel is a very different prospect to one as a mere captain. There's word coming back of unrest out there. Maybe even a hint of rebellion! And the heat and the fevers put men off, but for a man like me it's a chance, because for once merit, and the ability to simply survive, might well count for something. I shall only go for a few years, Gus, just enough to secure my prospects in old age, and it will do me good to get away from England again. Too far to come back in a hurry, as you know so well!"

"Oh I do, Harry, I do! I felt so wretched when it all went so wrong for the parents and I couldn't come and help."

"And you see for me, that might also be a very good thing, because I still don't fully trust myself."

"You don't?"

"No. You see if I were to see Amy, and she was to fall apart and break down in front of me – start pleading with me – I'd probably feel so awful I'd come back. But guilt isn't a reason to stay. And like you, Gus, I would like to have chance of life with a wife. Maybe with some nice widow whose children are already growing up and off to school or something. I *don't* want to be an old man who's bitter and twisted over a life spent tied to someone he didn't even like any more. God, that's bad enough when you're actually married. To be like that without ever having had the good side of it as well would be insupportable! So I shall stay away until I can trust myself not to be foolish."

Gus was wringing his hands. "You will write, though?"

"To you? Certainly! When I know where we shall be quartered, I shall write to Robert and let him know, and ask him to pass on the address to you. That way you can leave Cold Hunger Farm and still not lose touch. Just don't think of bringing Amy out to visit if I'm at one of the great ports!"

"Lord, I wouldn't do that! The journey alone would kill her!"

Harry stood up and stretched out his hand to Gus. "Now, I must go and pack, or Colonel Fearon and Major MacGregor will have my guts for garters if I leave all the organising to them!"

"So this it?"

"I'm afraid so. But cheer up! We shall no doubt meet

up in a few years time, and then we shall be able to swop stories of India!"

Gus stood up and picked up his hat from off the spare chair, then grasped Harry's hand. "Good luck, Harry! I mean that! You've been such a good friend, I'm just so sorry it's ended like this."

"So am I, Gus. But you and I will remain friends – just think on my words and act on them as the well-intended advice of one friend to another. I shall write as soon as I can!" And with that he turned on his heels and left without a backward glance.

Chapter 9

June, modern day

At first Pip wasn't sure whether Natalie had been using the diary just as a notebook, as she did with her own stash of old ones. Each page was filled with tightly packed writing, much closer spaced than the wide lines which had been pre-ruled on the pages, making it seem as though they were continuous blocks of script. However, on the first flick through she did find that there were some pages not fully filled, and then there was an end to the entries quite suddenly at the 30th of October. No other entries followed at all.

"Okay, what happened to you then?" muttered Pip, her curiosity piqued. She'd never thought she would ever care remotely what had really happened to Natalie after the chaos she'd brought to Pip's life, but after the events of the last week or so, Pip found that she very much wanted to be able to wave some kind of proof in the faces of the police and say 'See? I told you she was the problem, not Dave!' Not that it would get her anywhere, but the sense of satisfaction would be disproportionately high that she, a mere archaeologist in their eyes, could find what they had missed.

She went and poured herself a glass of the rather good red wine which Nick and Richard had sent her home armed with six bottles of. Heaven only knew why they thought she would have urgent need of that many, but it was far better than anything she would normally have bought for herself, so she was going to enjoy them and not dismiss good friends' kindly meant generosity.

As another thought occurred she said, "Why not?" out loud to the large ficus which loomed, triffid-like, to the one side of the bay window, and which Nick had on one wine-fuelled night christened Windy, in acknowledgement of the original triffid's creator, John Wyndham. "What do you think, Windy, eh? Bugger it, I'm a trained researcher for heaven's sake. Surely I can do as good a job as that nasty, pompous Sawaski bloke? That DCI Bill Scathlock seems like a decent type, but if he's expecting his sidekick to do much to help me he's fooling himself."

And too painful to say out loud even to the plant was the codicil of 'and when have you been able to lean on anyone but yourself in a real crisis?' Okay, Nick and Richard were being absolute stars, but they didn't have the time to be sleuthing on her behalf. They had a huge mortgage and so Nick needed to keep his job, which meant he couldn't go around upsetting the apple cart in the halls of the county archaeological services. And with bloody Phyllis throwing hissy fits here, there and everywhere, that would include even making the most innocent of inquiries about Dave and Natalie.

As for her family, that was just a joke. Her mum had been shoving her off to her father's parents at every opportunity ever since her dad had died, and now that they, too, were both dead there was no-one. Her mum was obsessed with the children she'd had with her new husband, although after all this time he wasn't that new anymore. What was clear was that Pip hardly ever crossed her mind these days. For the last two years there hadn't even been a birthday card, and her mum certainly had the right address because a Christmas card would turn up each year with some sickly sweet verse in, but written with no feeling. No, her mum wouldn't help whatever the problem, even though she was only as far away as Solihull.

And the folks at the nursery were lovely, but this wasn't the kind of thing they would understand. She worked with them, talked with them, but never got that close to them. Even her friends from the university had drifted away over these last four years, and who could blame them? The fallout from Phil's vitriol in the department had made it difficult for them to keep in regular contact, and that made her grow angry all over again when she thought of Natalie. Not only had the bloody woman robbed her of Dave, she'd put so many of her friends in such dreadfully difficult positions professionally, that she now only exchanged birthday and Christmas cards with some of those she'd once been incredibly close to.

"Screw you, Natalie!" she said forcefully, and gulped another mouthful with rather less respect than she'd intended for such nice wine. "Think you can keep your secrets and get away scot-free do you? Ha! Well think again! I'm coming after you, lady, and when I catch you the police will be the least of your worries!" She knew she wasn't in the right frame of mind to start tonight, but the following morning, after she'd taken her washing to the laundrette, and had it hanging out in her drying area at the back of the big old house her bed-sit was part of, she set to it. Taking a large mug of coffee out to the garden along with the diary, she sat down on a big cushion beneath a gnarled old apple tree which was covered in a rambling rose, and started to read.

I've have found it! she read on the first page for the first of January. *It took some time to realise what I was looking at and even now I can't quite believe it's true. It's like something out of Dr Who! A way to travel through time!*

"Oh fuck off, Natalie! Who were you kidding?" Pip scoffed. "Time travel, my arse!"

Then read, *Dr M says I must take the time to adjust to my new medication. She says there might be some side effect like hallucination, not that it happens with the vast majority of users.*

"No shit! You were really tripping there, girl!"

So I daren't tell anyone of what I've found. A way for me to go back to where I really belong! I don't feel like I belong in this time. It's not right for me. I'm not recognised for what I really am.

"No, we didn't see what a poisonous little wench you were! How daft were we in that, eh?" and Pip had to take a restorative swig of coffee before she could continue.

There were a few more pages of the same sort of thing, but then Pip came across several where there were what looked like some pretty serious mathematical calculations. She had no idea what they related to, but she did pick up on the fact that Natalie was watching phases of the moon. Then came the first break through.

I've been back to where I found the half of the clamp, Natalie wrote, *and I think I have to rethink the significance of the place. I'm sure the house has some of the spirit of the old shrine in it. That spring has virtually been running under it for centuries. It must have imbued it with some of its essence, surely? That's what the old grimoir said. To find a place which had been a sacred place for at least two thousand years. Therefore it has to be pre-Christian and Roman at the latest. I've tried looking at stone circles, but so many of them are so heavily visited these days there's no privacy. I must have privacy! So the house may well solve the problem. I can bring my lovely boys here and no-one will ever know. We can be all alone here and they will love me in freedom away from prying eyes. And the original shrine was to the Magna Mater – how cool is that?!?!*

"God, you were one sick person!" Pip shuddered, remembering Dave's last emotional confession to her before walking out, never to be seen by her again. How

Dave had talked of what they did with Natalie. Of two of them making love to her at the same time, or of her tying them up and then playing with them more like a cat playing with a mouse than a human lover. Then another horrible thought came to her. Where was Paul these days? She knew nothing of him except his name, not even what he looked like. What had Dave said? That Natalie would be furious if she knew he even had photographs of her? Pip felt sure she would recognise her, but Dave had never had any photos of the others in their group, and it was only by other means that she already knew who Phil was. She made a note on the A4 pad by her side to ask DCI Scathlock about Paul, because she had a nasty feeling that he might turn up as a body somewhere one day, if he hadn't already.

Ploughing on with Natalie's ramblings, she went through several weeks and then the tone changed.

I HAVE FOUND A PORTAL! Natalie wrote excitedly. *On a full moon the mirror upstairs in the farmhouse is now active! Bathing it in the spring and the blood of one of my men worked!*

"Christ, does that mean Paul really is dead?" Pip gulped, horror-stricken that her intuitive guess might have been right more than she would have dreamt. It was a ghastly thought indeed, and where had Natalie put the body in that case? Not anywhere they'd dug this summer, that was for certain, but then the answer was before her.

I tried sending Paul's body through. I thought it would be to Roman times once the mirror had someone in it, but it was to this house still. There's no way that this house can be that early, of course! Then I tried to reach out to him, because he was still bleeding and I didn't want to waste his blood, but I couldn't reach him without going through the mirror myself, and I don't want to do that and then not be able to get back. I must get a cat or a dog and send them through with a leash on.

Pip winced. What God-awful kind of experiments had she done on Paul and then on some poor animal? She really had been absolutely cracked!

I sent the cat through, came a few days later, *but the bloody thing slipped its lead and wouldn't come back to me.*

"Smart puss!" Pip muttered. "Best thing you could have done!"

I can't seem to get hold of a dog. The rescue centres still want money for them and they want to do home visits, which won't do at all.

"Thank God they do!" Pip said with relief. She'd been dreading what was coming next, then her fears were realised as Natalie wrote of getting hold of a large rabbit which she could attach a long lead to. *And it's not too heavy to pull back!* she wrote with glee. The next day she wrote of sending the rabbit through and getting it back successfully, but when she sent it through again the next day the rabbit died.

It was most disconcerting to see it turn to dust before my eyes, Natalie observed. *This is not good. It means that I shall only have one chance to go through and get back in one piece. Therefore I must get it right. I shall have to camp out here and see if any clues appear as to what time this mirror links me to. I've seen an elegant woman's glove dropped on the floor which then wasn't there the next day, but given the date when the house was built that tells me nothing.*

Then: *Damn, damn, damn! The bloody thing is only taking me back a couple of hundred years! I must research this place in the county archives. I need to know what the opportunities are! The Victorians were quite two-faced in their morality, so maybe I can find someone then who would serve me?*

"Oh in your dreams, sweetheart!" Pip scoffed. "I think the average Victorian gentleman would have quite strong ideas about who was serving who! Play Miss Whiplash with them, would you? I don't think so!"

Then maybe I can go back in hops of a couple of hundred years at a time?

God, she's obsessed, Pip thought. What on earth did she see that got her so hooked? And what did she think she was going to do if she actually got back to Roman Britain? Without the right money and social connections surely she would realise that she wouldn't be one of the social elite? Not that Pip believed for a second that Natalie really had found a portal – that was the stuff of fiction, not real life. But then with startling speed Natalie's objective seemed to change, confirming her mental instability to Pip as she wrote,

I've had a brilliant idea! I shall go back and find a man with money! Then I shall invest it in a bank which will survive into the modern times. If I put a condition on accessing the money, then when it's matured over years into a nice fortune, I can come back to now and live in luxury! But for today I must go to the doctors. Dave tells me he has an infection! I have spanked him resoundingly for cheating on me. He swears he hasn't, but how could he have got it otherwise?

"How indeed," Pip snarled. "But if you weren't the source of his Chlamydia, who was? Or had you just not noticed and it really was you who infected him?" That seemed more likely given Dave's confession that Natalie regularly had more than one sexual partner even in one evening. It was a small bright spot, though, to know that Natalie was as aggrieved over it as Pip had been. "Did he not tell you about me? Hmm, that must have been a nasty shock when you found out!"

It was.

He has a girlfriend! The dirty cheating rat! How dare he? He is mine! MINE! Not hers! I've told him he must give her up instantly, and the weak fool that he is, he asked to come and live with me. He says he would be strong then. I told him, no. I cannot have him underfoot. He came to me on his knees, so I had to forgive him, then I took him repeatedly to show him who was in charge. He does have his uses in that he can manage more sex than the others. Phil is particularly limited.

Pip guffawed at that. Oh well, that was something to relish, Phil being of limited use in bed – not that she ever intended to put him to the test!

I've told Dave I will not share him. He's going back tonight to tell her it's over.

Pip checked the date and sighed, it was right, exactly the date when he'd told her their relationship was over – not when he'd moved out, but when he'd first mentioned breaking up, not long before she'd gone to Orkney. She'd been desperately hoping the things she knew all about would be off by a few days, weeks, or wrong in some other way. That way she could put Natalie in the box marked 'completely bonkers' and just concentrate on finding if there was any confession of killing Dave. But if Natalie was lucid and correct on things like this, then what else was she telling at least half the truth about? It was a worrying thought. What strands of reality were in with the muddle of fantasies?

The subsequent entries were all about people in the past whom Natalie had checked up on, and Pip found herself making notes of the names too. There was nothing for it, she would have to go and trawl the local history archives, and probably the local newspaper archives too, and see if they matched up with what Natalie had said. If they were a total fiction, then in one way that would be a blessing, proving Natalie's state of mental decline. On the other hand, the more evidence she had that Natalie was telling the truth in this journal, the better things would be when she went to DCI Scathlock with it as evidence of Natalie's guilt – *if* she went to him. She still wasn't sure she was going to. There was still something a bit too flaky about this so far for Pip to be comfortable about presenting it to him as actual evidence.

She skipped to the end few entries and with a sinking heart read what she'd feared she'd find.

I've had it with Dave and his incompetence. Time and again I've told him he must leave that woman altogether.

"I wasn't 'that woman' at all," Pip snorted. "I might even have made him happy if you'd got you claws out of him." Not that she wholly believed that anymore.

I will go through tonight. I've checked the society pages of the newspapers and the records. The family will be back here and he will be with them – the man who will provide me with my fortune for the future! I will have it! I deserve it! Dave is watching my every move. I think he's scared I'll go and leave him behind. Little does he know! I've told him to come to the farmhouse tonight.

He'll fully open the portal for me and I shall make sure the room is sealed behind me. I don't want every Tom, Dick and Harry following me through! But for that to fully work no-one must come along and trip over Dave's body. Or at least not for a few decades, and with luck I shall be back by then, so he can be dumped through the portal once I've no further use for it. Paul's body has already been taken away on the other side, so I've no need to worry about that – I certainly won't be implicated in any wrong doing, which suits me! I may even destroy the mirror portal once I come back. I don't share my toys with anyone! And it's mine! All mine! I shall go and then come back a fabulously wealthy woman. Someone who can do as she wants in solitude on some nice island in the Med' I think. Reinvent the cult of Magna Mater, maybe?!? With some nice Greek boys, perhaps? I'm so excited!

The journal ended here, but Pip was already crying so hard she was having trouble not getting the tears on the page. Poor stupid Dave! Whatever the truth of the matter had been, this was the proof that Natalie had intended to kill him for some time before she'd actually gone through with it. It was premeditated, no accident. That settled her mind over what to do with the diary. She would take it to DCI Scathlock tomorrow. One day would make little difference one way or the other, but she still had time to get down to the library today and photocopy as much of this as possible for her own uses. She still intended to investigate these characters Natalie was talking about – if nothing else it would set Pip's mind at rest a little if she could say for certain that they were in the past, and not another unfortunate set of souls who'd had the misfortune of crossing Natalie's path in the present.

The next morning she went into the central police station in Worcester, the diary in a plastic freezer bag to appear to be showing willing over contaminating evidence, even though she was pretty sure that there would be little to find in the physical sense. The copious photocopies were back at her bed-sit. There was no way she would even risk having one sheet on her person when she went to give this in – no way she wanted to hint to the police that she was seriously doing her own investigations.

The man at the main desk turned out to be a small Welsh detective,

"Sorry, my dear," he said genially, as he scrabbled for the correct paperwork, "I'm a bit slow at this. We've got people dropping like flies with some stomach bug, so I'm covering on the desk today and I haven't done this side of the job for a fair few years." He smiled at her and there was something so genuine about it she couldn't resist smiling back.

"I'd really like to hand this to DCI Scathlock personally," she said to him. "Only I want to make sure he understands why I didn't bring this in sooner."

"Oh? Something complicated there?"

She sighed. "Well yes. You see, I was so thrown by the whole business I just picked this up and stuffed it into my pocket thinking it was my own. It was only when I got myself together and started washing the stuff I'd been wearing on the dig that I found this – or rather I found my own notebook, and then thought 'well what's this other one?', opened it and realised who it belonged to. I think DCI Scathlock will want to see it."

The cheerful Welshman nodded calmly. "Okay, but I should warn you, you might have a bit of a wait. Bill Scathlock's out at the moment and I don't know when he's likely to be back. Would you like to see DI Sawaski instead?"

"No!" Pip replied more forcefully than she'd intended. "I mean, no thank you." How was she to explain her antipathy to the DI, she wondered, but was saved any embarrassment by the sigh from the other side of the desk.

"Oh dear, Danny Sawaski been working his charm on you, too, has he? Oh well, he'll hopefully learn one of these days. In that case, if he'll recognise you by sight, if I were you I wouldn't wait around here, because he's somewhere in the building. Go and have a cuppa in town and come back around lunchtime. I've got your name. I'll tell Bill when he gets back you're coming."

Pip felt the smile of relief welling up from deep inside. "Oh thank you for that! Actually I'm only going to be working at the library down the road, so it's no problem to pop back in a bit."

"Right you are, then," the little man smiled just as a familiar, acerbic voice from within the building called,

"Owen? Has Bill called in yet?"

"No, not yet Danny," the little man called back while making shooing gestures to Pip with a wink.

She was just in time getting to the door, so that she was silhouetted by the bright light outside as DI Sawaski crashed a door open, and declared irritably,

"Well tell him I'm not waiting all day for him to reappear. I'm off to question that Wilkinson bloke again!"

Pip dived out of the door, and hurried away across the road which connected to where the police cars were parked. When she dared glance back over her shoulder it was to see Sawaski's back disappearing from view as he stomped round the corner to the cars. She blew her cheeks out and mouthed a silent 'thank you' to the heavens in relief, then hurried down to the newly built library and archive down the road, where Nick was waiting for her in the cafe.

"You look flushed," he observed teasingly.

Pip sniffed and gave him a squinty-eyed mock-glare. "I've just nearly walked into that bloody DI Sawaski up the road, that's why!"

"Ouch!"

"Precisely! Not someone I ever want to meet again! And especially with what I have to tell you!" Over a coffee Pip told him of finding Natalie's diary. "That's why I thought you might be interested to have a go at the archives today," she finished with. "Since Natalie has already done some of the groundwork for us, we could see if these people she mentioned really are attached to the house or not." She felt more than a little guilty over this, because she'd not told Nick about Natalie's weirder claims, nor that she intended to try and find Natalie herself. But she needed Nick to get her access into the archives without her booking a time-slot as just another member of the general public. That would take far too long given the waiting lists for computer terminal time, because for no reason she could explain, Pip felt time was of the essence.

"Right, let's go and have a rummage, shall we?" was Nick's cheerful response. "Richard's on duty until late tonight, so I was just going to hang around the place twiddling my thumbs and reading a pretty awful novel just to pass the time. This is much more fun!"

As Pip had guessed, Nick got them into the archives without any problem.

"What are these names, then?" he asked eagerly as they set themselves up.

"Well she seems to have been more than a bit obsessed with this family called Vaughan," Pip told him, pulling the single sheet of A4 from her pocket on which she'd written the names. "There's a Horace Vaughan, Augustus Vaughan, Matilda Vaughan, and Amy Vaughan. I'm not entirely sure what the relationships are, although I think that Amy is possibly Horace and Matilda's daughter, or maybe Augustus and Matilda's. And I'm pretty sure they have some connection to the farm in the nineteenth century. Natalie also made some reference to them owning a factory, so they aren't too low down the social scale to be untraceable."

Nick was nodding encouragingly. "Well I've got these references which I went in and pulled from the files at work on the way in here. These are the last references to Cold Hunger Farm the council has regarding occupants, so we might be able to trace them back via that route too."

They got so absorbed in their work it was only when Pip's stomach growled noisily that she looked at her watch. "Oh crap! It's two o'clock already! Would you grab me a sandwich downstairs, Nick, while I run this damned diary up to the police? He's going to kill me if he's been hanging around waiting for me!"

She jogged up the hill to the police station, but was

rewarded by the sight of DCI Scathlock's broad figure just coming into the building at the same time.

"Oh thank goodness!" Pip puffed.

"Looking for me?" Bill Scathlock enquired with a wry smile.

"Yes, actually I was. I called earlier but you weren't in, and I meant to come back over an hour ago to see if you were back, but then got engrossed in what I was doing in the library."

"Hmm, you'd better come in then," was all he said, not sounding in the least bothered that she hadn't dealt with Sawaski instead – and he must have known his DI had been in at least some of the morning, Pip thought. Was DI Sawaski such a known pain in the arse that people avoiding him was commonplace?

Up in DCI Scathlock's office Pip sat in the offered chair and then told him the story, handing over the diary. "I'm truly sorry I didn't spot it earlier," she told him, looking him in the eye, because she really was. That covered the fact that she hadn't found it last night but the night before. "If it had been a different make of diary I'd have spotted it straight away, but the colour's even the same as the one I was using on the dig. I just never gave it a thought when I scooped it up from the floor in the bedroom." She wasn't going to drag Tim into this. "It must have been in the hidden room originally, because it wasn't in the bedroom when we first went in there." Again looking him in the eye at that last, because the diary really hadn't been there.

"I can only think that it was shifted with some of the plaster we hauled out of the way to get in. But then everything else happened in such a flurry – Kirsty and Chloe were screaming their heads off, and Gemma and I were trying to get them downstairs, I was hardly thinking straight even before I found out it was Dave in there. I just remember being irritated at trying to get the bloody thing into the pocket of my fleece because it was a bit too big to go in. Normally I don't shove my notebook diaries in like that, because I don't want to break the pocket zips. But this time I'd got my hands full and it was... well it was just all weird! Then last night I got my waterproof out to brush the dried mud off and found my own book, went back and looked at this one and saw it was Natalie's."

"Did you read it?" Bill Scathlock asked neutrally.

"Of course I did!" Pip scoffed. "Blimey, I'm not inhuman! Suddenly finding that bloody woman's diary in my hands for the time she probably killed Dave – I'd have to be pretty strange not to want to look!"

He nodded with a smile. "And?"

"She was as cracked as some of those pottery sherds we found!" Pip declared vehemently. "Wait 'til you read it! Honestly, the woman was barking mad! But there's no doubt in my mind after reading that last page that she deliberately sacrificed Dave in some cockeyed rite, and that by the time he realised she was going to do for him it was too late." She took a deep breath, then said truthfully. "I must admit it's made me feel a bit better about the whole thing. Up until now I've still thought of Dave as being the one manipulating me, but reading that it's made me see how much he was being tied in knots by her. I just feel so sorry for him now."

"And her?" Scathlock was watching her carefully.

"I hope if you find her you lock her up and throw away the key!" Pip declared. "I know it will probably be some psychiatric ward in a secure unit. But in some ways that's even better than prison would be, to my mind, because she's never going to pass any test for sanity that I can imagine, and then get let out on an unsuspecting world again." She shook her head in despair. "I can even imagine a scenario where you find her and she has no idea what she's done in the sense of it being wrong. To her he was just some expendable sacrifice to get her barmy rite underway. In that diary you'll see that she's utterly obsessed with the Roman period and then just like that," she snapped her fingers, "she's ditched that altogether and is off on some weird trip about the Georgian period. It's like she got up the next morning and someone had rearranged her head overnight! Bloody scary!"

"Hmm, I know what you mean about that. The ones who do it, and haven't even got the mental faculties to know what they've done, are the ones who worry me the most too."

Pip nodded. "That's it with Natalie. I mean, I never knew her. Never met her face to face. So this diary is the first time I've seen inside her head and it's a bloody scary place, I can tell you. And to me what's almost as bad, is that I could see her doing it all over again at some point in the future. This taking people so for granted ...no, not even that! Being so emotionally cold that she doesn't see why she *shouldn't* take whatever she wants regardless of the cost to others."

He sat back and sighed, "But I should warn you, we might never catch up with her unless she *does* do something like this again. She's disappeared off the face of the earth as far as we're concerned. And I'm sorry to say this, but your ex has already been dead a long time, and these days we've come to recognise that the more time that elapses after the actual crime, the less chance we have of solving it."

Pip grimaced but nodded. "I know. I've heard other policemen say that. Well, on TV, that is. But at least you have this diary now, and maybe if the worst does happen, then at least you or some other policeman will look that bit harder at her if that time comes. Oh and by the way, if you can find out who the man called Paul was, I'm afraid he's dead too. She's confessed to killing him in the house too, but well before she did for Dave."

"Bloody hell!" Scathlock sighed wearily. "I can see why you're worried she might strike again. Hopefully DI Sawaski is talking to Mr Wilkinson about the identity of this bloke Paul."

"Well he'd better remember to call him *Doctor* Wilkinson," Pip said with a grin. "Most touchy about his title is Phyllis!"

Scathlock quirked an eyebrow, a mischievous twinkle in his eyes too. "Oh dear! Almost makes me sad to have missed that encounter, then!" and they both laughed.

After that it seemed that Scathlock was at least partially convinced of the truth of Pip's statements, because he got her to write it all down for him and then let her go without much in the way of further questioning. Hurrying back to Nick, she was just going to ask him what he'd found when she saw the broad grin on his face.

"What? What have you found? Oh don't keep me in suspense, Nick! My nerves are in shreds already! God, I'd never make a career criminal! It gives me the creeps just walking into that place!"

"Guilty conscience!" Nick teased, unwittingly coming closer to the truth than he knew.

"Piss off!" Pip riposted to cover her sudden inner quaking.

Nick grinned and gestured to the papers he had in front of him. "Well you were right, Natalie was here before us because she's signed to have access to some of these documents."

"Brilliant! Then we are on the right trail!"

"More than that. I've found your Vaughan family."

"Really?"

"Well my un-beloved colleagues in Planning were right, the trail regarding the house goes pretty cold in the early twentieth century, although I have found the nineteenth century owners. They seem to have owned a fair chunk of the village, though, so that tells us very little. There were mostly tenant farmers in the area in those days, and the tithe maps show that by the time the nineteenth century began, Cold Hunger was a very small farm indeed in terms of its acreage. So I think it's fair to say that the remaining few fields were probably let to other farmers, and then the house was let out as a separate unit."

"I can understand that. When we were there the land to the north and east didn't look particularly good."

"No, I thought that. In fact the woods we saw surrounding the house weren't as extensive back then, going by the tithe map again, so one or two of the original, small fields might have become part of the woods these days if they were only small to start with. So having drawn a bit of a blank in terms of any land ownership for the house, I remembered what you said Natalie had written, that the Vaughans were in trade, and would you know it, I found them as owning a glove factory here in Worcester."

"Great!"

"Yes, and it gets better. Because one year they're there and then the next year the factory is owned by another local family, the Cliffords. So I thought I'd have a look at the *Berrow's Journal* for 1812, and see if there's anything in there which might tell of any unusual happenings."

The two of them spent the rest of the evening going through the newspaper archives, but were gratified to find the reports of the bankruptcy proceedings for Horace Vaughan.

"Hey, it says here that Horace Vaughan's daughter

Amy was married to Edward Clifford, a lieutenant in the Huntingdonshire regiment," Pip said, frantically making notes. "Is that the son of the man who bought the glove factory, do you think?"

By the time they'd left they had found just when the Vaughan's had left St John's – their departure for Clifton had been sufficiently close to the scandal of the bankruptcy as to be news worthy – and Nick had arranged for Pip to come back and carry on digging on her own the following day. He'd decided that he might as well go into work and continue with the site report he'd started writing up at home.

Come the end of the week, Pip was gratified at what she'd found, but still had a list of questions. It meant that she was going to have to dig into her limited funds for a trip to London and the National Archives, because she had a nagging feeling that she needed to find Edward Clifford's army records. Something wasn't right here, but she couldn't quite put her finger on the specifics. Yet before that she got a call from Nick.

"Hi Pip! Is there any chance you could go and meet Arthur at the farm, please? He's quite excited about some of the beams and wants another sample, but we're going to have to provide official identification that he's with us, because Scathlock's had the SOCOs back in for some reason, and there's a copper going to meet you and Arthur before he can go in."

"Woops, that might be my fault," Pip confessed. "I told Scathlock that Natalie had written about killing that guy Paul who used to hang around with her, Dave and Phil."

"Jeez!" Nick gasped audibly, even over the phone. "Murderous little cow!"

"Isn't she! Shall I come into the office and pick up the paperwork?"

"Please. Arthur would like to do it tomorrow if possible."

The following morning Pip was back at Cold Hunger Farm in the minibus, which had been released as of no interest to the police. The pleasant female DC who had interviewed her with Scathlock turned up at the same time as Arthur, dealt with the identification, and after a plea for them to wear plastic gloves, left them to it.

"This is all rather thrilling, if you don't think it gory of me to say so," Arthur confided to Pip.

Clearly Nick hadn't elaborated on the fact that it was Pip's former fiancé whose body had been found. She didn't want to embarrass Arthur by making the point, though, and so made some bland remark about it having been quite upsetting at the time. "Why do you need more samples, then?" she then asked, to take the conversation away from bodies.

"Ah! Most peculiar!" Arthur enthused, suddenly becoming more animated than the mousy side most people saw of him. "The one beam in the ceiling of the oldest part of the house gave some very odd readings!"

"Really?"

"Oh yes! Far older than this house! That's why I want to double check it. It's good solid oak, and of course that keeps for hundreds of years in the right conditions, but even I was shocked at the date I found. I think it might be very late Roman, you see."

"Wow! That would tie in with the stones and the finds we got outside," Pip said, trying to sound enthusiastic too, but suffering more than a few qualms over such a strong link. And upstairs too! Just where Natalie had found her supposed portal. "So where do you want to start, Arthur?"

"Well I'd quite like to sample another beam in that section of roof – maybe right at the front of the house, though, this time. And if it's possible, one in that lost room you found, because that would be backing on to the original house. I'm wondering, you see, whether they just used one beam which happened to be lying around conveniently when some repairs needed doing – possibly at the time when the house was first extended. Or whether there were several of these beams which got collectively reused, because in that case Nick could reasonably argue for there having been a previous building on the site."

Getting to another beam in the ceiling of the landing was easy work once Pip had brought the stepladders up for them. They barely had to touch the old plaster before it was coming down in chunks. As Pip frantically opened windows to get rid of the clouds of dust, Arthur was already examining the wood and deciding which he would sample.

"I reckon we can get to a beam over the window in the nursery if you'd like," Pip offered, "then you can bracket your original sample with one from either side of it." So the two of them stripped the tatters of wallpaper and plaster off in the inhospitable nursery to take another sample.

"Do you actually want to go *into* the lost room?" she asked Arthur as they walked past the bathroom, quietly hoping that he wouldn't.

"I think so. I don't want to disturb this wall, and if you found the evidence of a second stairwell in there we might find something structural in there, you see?"

Pip nodded, but found herself surreptitiously taking some deep breaths to calm herself. It suddenly felt very strange to be going into the very room where Dave had died. Strange and more than a bit upsetting. Luckily, Arthur was eagerly walking ahead of her, and so he didn't notice her wiping her eyes before she followed him into the room. Once again the removal of more of the already loose Victorian wallpaper produced a surprise find.

"Oh that's nice!" Arthur exclaimed in pleasure, as a small cupboard built into the brickwork of the fireplace was revealed. The knob had been taken off the door, and there were marks as if it had originally been closed with only a wooden latch, but a claw hammer easily removed the four nails holding the door shut now.

"Oh yes!"

Arthur was instantly delighted when his torch picked up one of the structural timbers which hadn't been plastered over, on account of being hidden by the cupboard. However, Pip's interest was taken by the bundles of papers inside. Swiftly rescuing them out of Arthur's way, she put them temporarily into the tool bag, but felt that now she could share more of his excitement. Actually being here in the room wasn't as bad as she'd feared. There was nothing here which reminded her in any way of Dave. Not even the most ephemeral wisp of a spirit.

"Can we look at the fireplace in the bedroom?" Arthur asked, although now there was no way Pip was going to say no.

"You'll have to help me shift this mirror a bit towards over the doorway," Pip said, taking hold of the end of the long frame. She'd noticed that a mirror which had hung over the fireplace in the hidden room had disappeared, so presumably Scathlock had read Natalie's diary and come to the bit about bathing the mirror in Dave's blood. No doubt it was being subjected to all sorts of scientific scrutiny by now. That in itself was odd to her, because while Arthur had been sampling, she'd noticed holes in the original, blocked-up doorway of the hidden room, which made her think that the full-length mirror had been screwed to the wall there before its removal to the bedroom – possibly supported by the remaining door frame's stout timbers. Why have two big mirrors in such a small room?

Arthur willingly helped her slide the heavy mirror away from the fireplace and then began examining the wall. "Marvellous!" he exclaimed again as he found another cupboard to the right of the grate, which also gave access to another major beam. More astonished was Pip, who couldn't believe that there were more letters and some documents, albeit a much smaller pile this time. "What a treasure trove!" Arthur enthused, his voice echoing from where he was up to his shoulders in the cupboard.

"Isn't it just!" Pip breathed with equal excitement, for on the top envelope of the large bundle of letters she could read the addressee as being *Mrs Amy Clifford*, while the other letters were to someone called *Cpt. H. Green of the 31st Regiment*, and that, Pip knew, was the same regiment as Edward Clifford had been in.

Waving a thrilled Arthur off once more, Pip returned to the bedroom and found a seat on the floor in the warm sunshine which was streaming in. She was so excited she couldn't wait to get home to start reading these letters – she had to at least see what they were here and now.

She carefully opened the first of the letters to Captain Green. There, in a bold and legible hand was a letter signed by someone called Gus, and that could only be Augustus Vaughan since he was asking, *Dear Harry, What's to be done with Amy?*

"Bingo!" Pip breathed in triumph. The same Gus whom Natalie had been so fascinated with. The same Gus whom Natalie had gone to considerable trouble to find out the bank details of, Pip had discovered in the diary, for Mr Augustus Vaughan was a gentleman of no small means.

Chapter 10

On board the Kent, *March 1824*

Harry clung to the rope of the stairs as the *Kent* pitched down into yet another trough, flinging him hard against the bulkhead. He already had several spectacular bruises from similar encounters, and they hadn't yet crossed the Bay of Biscay. At this rate he would be black and blue all over by the time they reached India. However nothing in the turbulent passage so far had prepared him for the howling gale which was tossing the ship around like a toy at this moment. What he had taken for rough seas until now faded into insignificance in the light of the winds which had begun savaging them the previous night. At a guess they must be into the morning of the first of March by now, not that it was remotely possible to see what time of day it was. The sea and sky were inseparable, both churning and filled with white foam, the sea generating it in vast quantities and then tossing it aloft so that the air above the deck was filled with its yeasty strands of spume. Rigging and ropes were festooned with wreaths of the beaten waves, making the sleek East Indiaman look as though it was thick with snow. Indeed it might even have been snow in some places for all Harry knew, he was certainly cold enough for that to be the case.

He made it up onto deck without his arm being wrenched again and spotted young Lieutenant Dodgin. It wasn't really either of their watches, but in this dreadful storm the two officers who should have been on duty were heaving their guts up below, too sick to move, let alone carry out any duties.

"Captain Cobb says we must attach the men of our watch to the lifelines he has strung throughout the deck!" Harry bellowed in Dodgin's ear as the only way to be heard. The young lieutenant nodded, dashed as much salty spume from his face as he could, then gestured to Sergeant MacDonald to join him in passing the order. The men coming off watch would have a grim time going below, Harry thought. The ship was so heavily laden with all their gear it was wallowing something shocking, and down below the movement was much worse than up here. It wasn't surprising that many of the men were glad to at least get out into the blasting sea air, which even at its worst was some improvement on the cloying stench below.

"Looks like it's you and me up here, sir," Dodgin said with a watery attempt at a brave smile.

"Don't worry, lad," Harry said with more calm than he felt, as they both tied themselves to the lines. "Captain Cobb is an experienced master of his ship. This may look like the very gates of hell to us, but the sailors say that it's not so rare out here in the Bay."

"Glad I never joined the navy, sir!" Dodgin yelled back.

Me too! Harry thought. Even in the worst moments of battle he'd not been so damned terrified as he was now. There was something so primal, so feral, about this storm, and even praying seemed to leave him wondering if God would hear him over this dreadful din of rattling rigging, banging doors and hatches, and the thunderous crashes of the waves against the hull. Sometimes the ship seemed to be almost standing on one end or the other, with the great slate-coloured waves towering over them on all sides, giving the appearance of the ship diving for the depths of a watery hell each time it slide down the face of one into the trough below. A faint lightening of the sky eventually told him that it must be well into the morning by now, but there was no other hint that time was passing. For all he knew they could have already passed into some Dante-like, watery Purgatory outside of normal time, trapped in a terrifying limbo to await the Day of Judgement.

Then just when he thought things couldn't get any worse, he heard the thing even the sailors were terrified of,

"Fire!"

"Fire down below!"

"All hands to the pumps!"

"Get the buckets!"

"Fire!"

"Christ have mercy upon us!" Sergeant MacDonald prayed fervently, then all hell broke loose as panic-stricken soldiers and their wives began streaming up onto deck.

"Where *is* the fire?" Harry bellowed at Captain Bray as he finally recognised a face.

"Down in the hold," Bray yelled back over the still howling storm. "Of all the God-awful places for it to be, it's in amongst the rum casks!"

So this is where I shall die, Harry thought with a calm which surprised him. The rum casks for the voyage were still nearly full and would be highly flammable, and once they caught, God alone knew what else would go up. There were several hundred tons of shot and shell down there too, as Harry knew only too well, having helped the quartermaster, Mr Waters, to see it safely onto the ship, so that none of it could be slipped away to be resold for a quick profit. If they should ignite, their end would be swift and hopefully painless – undoubtedly a better fate than drowning, to Harry's mind. And here they were, two hundred miles from any shore, and already long separated from the *Scaleby Castle* which was transporting the other half of the regiment to India. The last time they'd seen the *Scaleby Castle* and their comrades, they'd still had the coast of England in sight, so there wouldn't be a rescue coming from them any time soon.

In the face of such danger, soon everyone seemed to be helping to hand buckets down to try to douse the fire – sailors, soldiers and wives all desperate to quench the deadly flames. Then young Ensign Tate came up to Harry and MacDonald, teeth chattering with fear more than cold.

"Major MacGregor says that Captain Cobb is going to scuttle the lower decks, and needs your help," he said, then puked pitifully in fear.

"Stay here, lad," Harry told him, tying him to the lines as he and MacDonald freed themselves and staggered towards the hatching to get below.

The scene below decks was hellish, with lurching dark shadows patchily illuminated in red against the smoke by frantically swinging lanterns. Just breathing was ferociously difficult, the ever thickening smoke having few ways out in the low-ceilinged deck, and Harry and the sergeant pulled their drenched neckerchiefs up over their noses. Meeting other officers more by collision than on purpose, it was hard to make out who was who, but by voice they recognised Major MacGregor and Captain Spence. The leader of the regiment, Lieutenant Colonel Fearon, wasn't there, but Harry guessed he already had his hands full in trying to calm the passengers and troops up above, not to mention keeping some semblance of order. On the way down he'd seen signs that some of the officers' baggage had already been riffled through. No doubt there were those aboard who'd risk stealing from just about anybody if they thought those they stole from might not survive the night. However, no-one who had served with Robert Fearon in his long years with the regiment would risk his wrath by openly stealing, and his presence alone would deter many opportunists. Duncan MacGregor was also a tried and tested leader, and Harry knew that he would be in this with them to the end, whatever course of action was decided upon.

"We're to open the lower ports to allow the sea in," the major told them. "Cobb is opening the sea-cocks below while we're to open these hatches. He says it's the only way, but we must shut them again as soon as we can or else we'll sink. The Colonel is with him." A statement which only increased Harry's respect for Fearon – if it was this bad up here, heaven alone knew what it was like a deck below and closer to the fire!

As Harry opened the porthole hatch beside him in concert with the other officers and mates of the ship, the sea exploded in, knocking him backwards and drenching him. Large chests were suddenly shifted and smashed around with the first forceful jets, as was anything else not bolted or strapped down, making regaining his feet a treacherous task. Twice he had one foot down, but then put the other on something which shot out from beneath him in the churning water. But then the force eased fractionally, the ship rolled and Harry managed to stand up, finding himself up to his knees in water beside Sergeant MacDonald on the one side and Captain Spence on the other, both dripping like him. Together they managed to shut the ports as the ship lifted them clear of the water on their side, and then opened them again after a second roll while those on the other managed to close theirs briefly. In this way there was a constant flow of water sliding below, but never without restraint, but how effective it was, or how long they could keep this up and not drown, was something no-one wanted to talk about. Below them they could hear sailors frantically working the pumps to the bilges, emptying the sea back out once it had sunk below the level of the fire, but would the pumps keep up with the flow?

"Damned if I ever saw myself going out of the world this way," Spence said shakily.

"Me neither," Harry replied. "Oh well, I suppose it was going to happen one way or the other. Not much we can do about it now, eh?"

"No," Spence agreed, just as MacDonald's soft highland brogue declared,

"Damn it, I always wanted to have a tree growing over me when I'd gone!"

It was such a ridiculous thing to worry over, they all found themselves laughing.

"Aye well at least you'll have some oak for a coffin," Lieutenant Campbell called from across the deck where he was hanging on to the cover of his port, earning more guffaws of laughter. It was strange, Harry thought, how once the moment of abject terror at the prospect of near certain death passed, men could laugh and joke at such times of crisis, but he'd known it happen in battles too. It was something he'd been unable to explain properly to Robert, and the thought of his brother brought a twinge of regret. He'd hoped that if he got promotion to major in India, or maybe even lieutenant colonel, he might be able to support both of them, allowing Robert to leave the Church if he wished. Now there wasn't much chance of that. He just hoped that these days Robert thought more kindly of him, and would remember him in a prayer or two.

"Close the hatches!" a disembodied voice in the chaos bellowed, relaying the Captain's order, and all the men wrestled to get the ports shut and barred again as the ship wallowed more deeply in the heavy sea.

"Was it enough?" Captain Spence called to Major MacGregor as the major came back into view.

"I don't know," MacGregor replied, sloshing over to them, "But Captain Cobb said that if we didn't close them now we'd sink for sure. He's seeing to the sealing of the deck."

To everyone's horror it hadn't been enough, and now Cobb ordered a hole to be cut in the main deck to try and draw the fire away from the spirit room. From out of the deck rose a black stream of smoke, visible even against the greys and tarnished whites of the storm.

"That's a desperate measure, I'm thinking," George MacDonald sighed. "And it means the powder room is going to be forward of the fire. Let's just hope that the water casks standing between the two are enough to stop that lot going up, or we'll all be having the angels' share of the grog!"

When they got back up on deck they were greeted with absolute pandemonium. Some folk were in a terrible state, families having been separated in the scramble to get up out of the way of the fire, and were now urgently seeking one another in the crush. Others were deep in prayer, and Harry could hear one of the young ladies calmly reciting the 46th Psalm, and others joining in with her. One batch of veteran soldiers even went and sat immediately above the powder magazine on the basis, they told Harry, that at least it would be a quick death when that went up. There was nothing like a bit of soldierly cynicism in the face of catastrophe! Indeed, for a moment Harry was halfway tempted to join them had his presence not been demanded elsewhere by the indomitable Major MacGregor.

The fire didn't take hold again so quickly or so fiercely in the drenched ship, but neither did it go out, and for a thoroughly wretched half day the whole company clustered on the cold, soaking, main deck, or in the few safe places on the one below, to await their fate. The sailors continued to do their best to fight the fire, desperately trying to keep it from reaching anything even more disastrously flammable like the magazine, but the first real ray of hope was when a man was sent aloft as the weather allowed just a glimmer of visibility, and spotted a sail. Suddenly there was urgent activity as the sails were braced to bring the ship around, flags were hoisted and the signal guns were fired.

"Shall we be saved, sir?" Ensign Tate asked Harry fearfully, as if he dared not hope they would.

"Maybe some of us," Harry reassured him, and resolved that if it was a choice between himself and the young lad, he would see Tate into safety first.

As the other ship finally drew closer Harry felt his heart sink. She was tiny! Barely a seventh of the size of the *Kent*! How would they all get on board her? Then, as Captain Cobb ordered the *Kent's* boats to be lowered, some of the sailors panicked, and the gig – the first to be swung out and the smallest of the boats – was overwhelmed with men and sank as it entered the water. In a heartbeat, Colonel Fearon, Major MacGregor and two other captains of the 31st had drawn their swords and went to stand guard at the next boat waiting to be swung out, and hot on their heels, Harry drew his sword and with Sergeant MacDonald and two of the young lieutenants, went to guard the next one.

At Colonel Fearon's order the cutter, being the largest of the ship's boats, was to take the women and children only for this first trip, but Harry saw little of that himself, since the only way for the fleeing families to get into the boat by now was through one of the windows at the quarter deck. Only when the seemingly tiny cutter was seen crabbing its way through the mountainous seas towards the brig trying to save them, could Harry see that it was crammed with women, the children being too small to see.

"God preserve them!" he found himself praying aloud, glad beyond words now that he had no family travelling with him. But would the cutter come back? Who would blame the crew if they refused to make the horrendously dangerous journey back to the *Kent*, knowing that they would then have to row another journey to the rescuing ship once more, all the time getting more and more exhausted? As best he could see, there did indeed seem to be an attempt by at least a few of the cutter's crew to climb the side of the other ship, but those lining the brig's rails were sending them back. Faced with rejection from the rescuing brig, the cutter's crew once more took to the oars and began the terrible pull back to the *Kent*.

Eventually there were six boats working between the two ships, but to Harry's eye it was all taking far too long, not through any fault of any of the men, but because of the nightmare of negotiating the huge seas. Just getting alongside either of the ships demanded extraordinary seamanship in conditions like these, and there was always the chance that the larger craft would smash against the boats and sink them. By night time only three boats remained, the other three having been swamped at various points during the afternoon, and even those still afloat were in a sad state from the pounding they had taken. Several times each of them had been dashed against the ships' sides, or had collided with the spars which by now were breaking from the *Kent's* rigging. With the women and almost all of the children evacuated, Harry felt a burning pride in the men, who had then lined up with fierce discipline to await their turn in the boats. Having faced the French and other dangers on land, the men of the 31st knew how to stand their ground in the face of death. There was no unseemly scramble to save themselves over their comrades here, and he prayed that they would all find safety, knowing that many wouldn't.

As the invisible sun sank low on the horizon behind the heavy clouds, taking the last of the poor light with it, Harry joined Major MacGregor in the last boat to leave, and to his sorrow there were still a few men on board. Men who had fortified themselves with liquid courage to be sure, many of whom were too drunk to climb the ropes, but he couldn't find it in himself to castigate them. Who wouldn't find their courage failing them in such hellish conditions? He'd only prayed he wouldn't break himself. What truly broke his heart, though, was the memory of seeing one of the men with three of his children roped to him still trying to save them all, then jump into the sea, all of them sinking like stones.

As hauntingly memorable were the brave souls who had tried to save others, yet had ended up being devoured by the ravenous sea, and he knew he would remember them for the rest of his days. His own arms were aching and shaking from trying to lower men down into the boats, and he had a terrifying plunge into the waves himself while getting off the *Kent*, only saved by a spar and by being close enough to the boat to reach out and grab its side. Now he was glad he'd ordered Sergeant MacDonald to go into the boat ahead of him, because the huge Scotsman had the remaining strength to pull Harry onto the boat even as another wave washed over them.

When they pulled up to the brig which he now knew to be the *Cambria*, the climb up its side nearly did for him he was so exhausted, but there was a strong hand reaching down to haul him over the side. Only when he had staggered to the weather deck with MacDonald, both of them soaked to the skin and heavily battered, did he discover that the ship had on board Cornish and Yorkshire miners, originally heading for South America, and who had manned the sides for all the long hours, pulling the survivors of the *Kent* aboard.

"Bloody heroes the lot of them," MacDonald croaked. "I'll never hear a bad word said against miners for as long as I live."

For the best part of two more agonising days, Harry and George MacDonald stood ankle deep in the constantly sloshing water. Captain Cook of the *Cambria* had recognised the only course open to him was to return to England and make the swiftest landfall, and that meant Cornwall. However the relief at seeing Falmouth harbour appearing out of the blackness of the night, as the third of March changed to the fourth, was beyond words for both refugees and the *Cambria's* crew. After two days and three nights of standing on the exposed weather deck, Harry could scarcely see straight, only held upright by the press of those around him, none of whom were in any better state, and at first he could scarcely believe that he was really seeing land. Everything had diminished into a haze, a blur in which he no longer knew what was real and what was just the wanderings of his fevered mind.

Somewhere in that night Harry would later be able to recall going ashore in one of the small packet boats, which normally plied their trade in and around the harbour, but on this night, along with every other boat which could be pressed into service, brought the survivors of the *Kent* ashore. Beyond that he had little memory of the night, only later waking up in the pleasant bedroom of a house in Falmouth where he discovered he was the guest of a chandler and his wife. The good folk of Falmouth had opened their homes to the ragged survivors, everyone being found somewhere to sleep and be fed, in a collective act of great generosity and compassion.

Having discovered that he'd been feverish and unconscious for two whole days, Harry's first thought was to write to Robert, especially when he was told by the generous chandler that news of the wreck of the *Kent* had made *The Times.* If Robert had read that, or had the information passed on to him, he would be worried sick, and Harry felt the least he could do was to let him know he still lived. His handwriting was so shaky it looked more like their father's, but at least he managed to pen a few words of reassurance. Those words were more than he felt. Although as a single man he was in a better position than those who had families, nonetheless he had very little left of any cash he could immediately put his hands upon. Like everyone else, he had invested in items to take out to India with him, and had had no small amount of cash stashed in the trunk which had held most of his worldly possessions – the same trunk which lay with the rest of the *Kent* at the bottom of the Bay of Biscay. For the time being Harry was penniless.

He managed to drag himself out of his bed the next day to attend the service of thanksgiving, organised by Major MacGregor at the church of King Charles the Martyr in Falmouth, but his recovery was short-lived. Whether it was simply a recurrence of the fever, or whether the emotional toll of the service coupled with being in the chill of the great church proved too much for his feeble strength, by the next day Harry was back in bed and insensible to the world. By the time he regained consciousness, those sufficiently able of the half-regiment from the *Kent* had marched once more for Chatham, albeit with much reduced numbers. Many of the enlisted men had had little choice but to march as long as they were fit enough. The Treasury was willing to re-equip them for service in India, his host recounted to him, but unless they agreed and took their lives in their hands and got on a ship once more, they would be destitute – and every soldier knew horror stories of brave soldiers reduced to begging when out of the service and back in England.

To his own shock and dismay, Harry learned from a letter that he had been put on half pay until such time as he could resume active service. However that service would be hard to come by now that the regiment was sailing to India on the second of April, and him at the other end of the south coast from them and in no fit state to travel. Not that he was alone in that. Even the valiant Major MacGregor had decided against instantly resuming his post when he'd so nearly lost all of his family in the disaster. And there were only eight of the original twenty officers who would be leaving Gravesend alongside the ragged survivors of the regular men.

Yet to Harry's mind there was one bright spot for his valiant men. To his utter astonishment he discovered that of the 344 men who had embarked on the *Kent*, only fifty-five had died, just one woman had died (and that while still on the *Kent* from the smoke), and fourteen children had perished – and given how many of them had been fragile babes in arms, Harry thought that nothing short of miraculous. Only seven of the *Kent's* crew had been lost, and Harry suspected they had gone down in the small boats which had been lost to the waves rather than from off the ship itself, or had been amongst the drunken handful left behind. For such an amazing preservation of life he vowed he would ask Robert to find him some suitable prayers to be said.

Harry also couldn't thank the chandler and his wife enough for their kindness, but was feeling terrible guilt at not being able to pay them anything towards his keep as yet. Therefore when he was well enough to read the letters which had come for him, he was only too grateful to accept Robert's offer of returning to Clifton to recover. It was some small mercy that Robert had clearly read in the papers of the financial hardship which had come hard on the heels of the physical one for the men of the 31st, and had sent him the money to pay for the coach to bring him home.

Even as he packed the odd assortment of donated clothing, which was all he possessed, he managed to pen a letter to the banker in London with whom he had deposited his spoils of war. It would take time to sell many of the items stored in the banker's strong-room, but Harry was insistent that the first money they raised should be sent to reimburse his kind hosts. The two had already said they wanted no such recompense, and so Harry thought that it would work in his favour to be far away when the money arrived. Somehow he couldn't bear to receive more charity than their innate kindness and care through his illness. For the sake of his own self-respect he had to reimburse them for what they'd spent on him, including the medications the doctor had prescribed.

He was shaking again by the time he'd made the arduous journey back up to Worcestershire, and he was never so thankful to stagger into the rectory and all but collapse in his father's old chair.

"Dear God, Harry, you look dreadful!" Robert fussed, hurrying to pour steaming water into a good-sized stone water bottle and place it under Harry's feet. A moment later a large woollen travelling rug was wrapped around his shoulders, and although Harry desperately wanted to tell Robert not to fuss, his eyes closed of their own accord before he could say another word. For another week Harry spent most of his time in bed in his old room, but by the end of that time he was able to get up and walk, albeit shakily, about the house.

To his surprise he then received a visitor.

"Gus has been desperate to come and see you," Robert told him with some amusement, and Harry could imagine the fussy, rotund little man collaring Robert at every opportunity to ask if Harry was up yet.

"I'll gladly see him," Harry declared, "but do prepare him that I won't be much company. I can't seem to find the energy or the will for light conversation."

That very afternoon there was a rap at the rectory door and when Harry had shuffled to the door, there stood Gus, wringing his hat in his hands just as he had in the hotel in Bath when Harry had last seen him.

"Oh my dear fellow! Oh my goodness!" Gus blurted in shock at Harry's haggard appearance. "Upon my soul, you look most dreadful set about!"

"Come in, Gus," Harry said, turning with a smile. Dear Gus, he never changed. A heart of gold but not one to deal with a crisis, however much of a genius he'd been in balancing accounts. "Do shut the door, and come into the parlour. I'm afraid I must sit down again. The slightest exertion still wears me out something shocking."

Behind him, Gus' feet pattered along to the parlour in his fussy walk, and Harry waved him to what was normally Robert's chair as he sank into the other.

"It's good to see you again, Gus. There was a point when I feared I might never see anyone again."

"I heard! I heard! Read it in *The Times*, don't you know! You're all being hailed as heroes, y'know. There's to be a commemorative medal struck too!" Harry groaned at that. It was far too much fuss for his liking. "Oh it is, I assure you! I told Amy, we must give thanks in church that you've been spared." Gus' spare chin wobbled with emotion. "I'm duced glad to see you again, old fellow. Duced glad!"

Harry managed to sit up a bit more straight to face Gus, but told him with as much firmness as he could manage, "I really can't talk about it yet, Gus. It's all too raw. Too fresh in my memory. It was... It was..." He faltered, embarrassed at how near to tears he was just at thinking about those awful days. "It was nothing like soldiering, you see," he finally managed to say.

"Oh, to be sure! To be sure!" Gus hastily agreed, biting his knuckles in distress at seeing Harry so affected. Ever since he'd got to know Harry he'd quietly hero-worshipped him, and to see him so battered and shaken only served to emphasis in his mind how spectacularly dreadful the event must have been.

"Do tell me, what's the news from around here," Harry asked him to steer him on to what he hoped would be safer ground.

Gus shuffled to the edge of his seat. "Oh my dear fellow! What news! I'm damned indebted to you."

"You are?"

"Oh yes, 'cos don't y'know, you put me on my guard with Miss Walker – well Miss Walker as was, don't quite know what she really is these days. All you said about her was quite right! I told Amy! I said 'you should have taken more notice of what Harry said. He's a man of the world. He knows these things.' But I don't think the silly miss believed me even then."

"Over what?"

"Well, no sooner had you left Bath, then there was a gentleman askin' all over town for a Mrs Natalie Parsons. Turned out it was our Miss Walker who was stayin' with Amy. The little minx moved in the very night you'd told Amy to send her packin'! I did a bit of askin' around, and,"

Gus leaned in confidentially, "it turned out this gentleman was a lawyer's man! He was tryin' to find her on behalf of her husband, no less! Well I managed to have a discreet word with him. Told him my sister is easily led and that I didn't want any scandal attached to us if at all possible.

"In return he told me that Miss Natalie had made off with jewellery which had been in her husband's family for generations. I told him that whatever she's made off with, she certainly hadn't got any piece that expensive with her now, but that she'd been into Bristol before comin' to Bath – or so she'd told Amy. He was most obliged to me, he said, and went off in search of the missin' jewellery, but not before he said it would go very badly for Miss or Mrs Natalie once he'd got the proof of her thievin'."

Gus wriggled himself back in the chair and folded his hands across his portly stomach. "Well I went back and told Amy that we should leave as soon as possible. Told her the rent had come to an end on the house to get her movin'. Upon my soul, Harry, I didn't know the gel knew such words as she called you then! I was quite taken aback!"

"I suspect Natalie whatever-her-name-is has expanded her vocabulary," Harry observed wryly.

Gus nodded with a sniffy look of distaste, which was almost comical on such a genial face. "But I'm glad you set me a'thinkin' about her having an eye on me, old chap. No sooner were we packin' our bags then she starts simperin' around me. Sayin' all sorts of guff like what a well set up kind of chap I am. Without your words I might have been drawn in, but you havin' warned me, and then discoverin' the lawyer chappie, I was much more on my guard. I got Amy back up here as fast as I could, I can tell you."

"Are you still at Cold Hunger Farm?" Harry asked, dreading that Amy might be so close.

"Only for another week," Gus told him with a very satisfied air. "Took your advice on that one too once I'd seen through Miss Natalie! Amy's to have a house near the cathedral in Hereford. Small but most commodious, so it will suit her nicely, and the neighbours are pleasant folk. I can afford for her to have a woman live in as a general servant and cook, and I've employed a chap to come three times a week to do the heavy work and the garden, so she'll not be lookin' too shabby by comparison. For the time bein' I'm taking' rooms there too – but not in the same street!" he added hastily. "I've been makin' enquiries and there's a man in cotton up in Manchester who wants a man with my talent with the books. I shall be movin' up there in two months time when the new mill has been finished."

"That's excellent news, Gus!" Harry said with relief, yet Gus suddenly went rather bashful. "And? ...There's something else, isn't there? I can tell by your face."

Gus went a bit pink, huffed a couple of times and then spluttered. "I heard you lost everythin', Harry! *The Times* said all of you lost not just your things but your funds as well." He picked up speed. "Now I've been a'thinkin' and I'm resolved to do this since you've been such a damned decent chap over Amy all these years. I've extended the rent on the farm for another six months and I want you to have it."

Harry was flabbergasted. "Me? The farm?"

Gus nodded, his face a picture of determination. "You'll need somewhere to stay while you recover, and this way you can be near your brother without livin' here in this house. I remembered, y'see, you sayin' that this was never a happy house on account of your father bein' a widower when he came here, and I thought, well, you might not want to stay here too long in that case. And it worried me, don't y'know, as to where you'd go? So I said to myself,

'Augustus, it's time for you to step up!' I have the money, that's not a problem, and I wouldn't have had it if not for you, 'cos that Natalie was tryin' her best in those last days in Bath to wring a proposal out of me. Well I ain't a man of the world of your calibre, but never let it be said that Gus Vaughan can't learn a lesson! So I told her I'd been warned of her tricks, and that it was no use her tryin' to embrangle me in her schemes. She weren't to please at that, I can tell you, but I was resolute, Harry, and I'm resolute now! You shall have time to recover, and I'm going to pay the bill. There! What do you say to that?"

"I'm overwhelmed," Harry said honestly. "Thank you, Gus, that's most gentlemanly of you."

"You'll accept?"

"Yes. Yes, I will. In fact, it's quite a relief, because I don't know Robert's financial situation and he won't tell me, so I don't know how long he can keep me here. I know he took over from Father, but there were complications there, and I've not been able to work out if he's getting the full allowance from the Church for a rector – especially as he has no family to look after which might have swayed the bishop into giving him more. So I'd been resigned to moving on as soon as possible but with nowhere in mind. Your kind offer settles all of that and without embarrassing Robert, so I'm most dreadfully grateful."

"Not at all, my dear fellow. It's me who's grateful – ever will be!"

Gus sat with such a gratified smile on his face Harry couldn't help smiling back, although he wondered whether Amy would be so happy when she heard who was taking over the house. She might see it as Gus shoving her out in favour of Harry, even though it was nothing of the kind.

A week later Harry sat on a borrowed horse in the shade of the trees watching Amy leave Cold Hunger Farm.

Going by the way she threw her purse onto the seat of the small trap beside Gus, she wasn't happy at all. So much for gratitude for all that he'd done for her in the past, or did she not know yet that he was the next tenant? As he let himself in by the back door he realised that in fact this was going to be far too big a place for him on his own, but with no other option he wasn't about to complain. He decided on using the bedroom over the kitchen as being the warmest of all, this after all being barely the start of the summer, and he would still be here for the beginning of the autumn, if no longer.

He'd brought some small amount of provisions with him, and was just setting to make some tea and toast when he thought he heard someone singing along with him. He shook his head. Some lingering effect of the fever, perhaps. He started 'Over The Hills And Far Away' again, but was then interrupted by a knock at the front door. To his delight it was Robert, here already with a trap in which there were some necessary oddments of utensils and provisions. Gus had generously left sufficient furniture for his use, saying that the small house Amy was going to would never accommodate all of their parents' things, and he himself was going to be in furnished rooms until he moved north.

"Can you help me pull the bed into the room over the kitchen?" Harry asked Robert as he led the way through the hall and back to where the kettle was now bubbling away on the range.

"I think that can come within a rector's remit," Robert teased and they both laughed.

It was comforting to Harry to find that he and Robert could now get along, and they companionably shunted a few pieces of furniture around so that Harry could virtually live in three rooms. It did amuse him that Robert was insisting that Harry should leave both armchairs in the parlour as well as the sofa in case anyone should call. Who on earth would be wanting to do that, Harry couldn't imagine! Who did he even know around here, much less be on visiting terms with? He himself had a far more realistic view of spending much of his time in the kitchen by the warm range, or at least until the dreadful remnants of the fever abated, and had thought to have an armchair in there. Never mind, once he was strong enough to do the moving alone he would rectify the matter, and by then he would be able to truthfully say that no-one had come calling to preserve the parlour for.

As the afternoon drew on, thick storm clouds began brewing up on the horizon.

"Will you be all right here on your own in a storm?" Robert asked worriedly. "It won't bring back nightmares of the ship?"

"It probably will," Harry admitted. "But a storm here on dry land is a very different beast, and I can't go through the rest of my life hiding under the stairs every time there's a thunder storm! I'll have to face it some time, and probably better sooner rather than later."

"You're sure you don't want me to stay?"

"And do what? Robert, you can't help me with this, and what if one of your parishioners needs you? As yet few know I'm here, so they won't know where to come to if you aren't at home. Please, go home. Go before you get a soaking! We can't have both of us jittering around with a fever!"

In truth Harry was more than a little apprehensive about the coming storm. Would he be a gibbering wreck by the time it passed? He didn't even dare speculate, but one thing he did know was that if he was going to end up sobbing like a child, he didn't want to do it in front of

Robert. This last year when they had met as equals had got rid of the bad taste he'd had lingering from their childhood, when Robert's limited caring for him had been far too stifling and dominating. No, he didn't want that kind of caring. It would have been different if it had been someone like George MacDonald. Someone who'd seen him face death in battle and knew his mettle. But where George was he didn't know – possibly already on the way to India.

A flash of lightning lit up the room from far away, but the rumble of thunder followed it quicker than he'd expected as the storm drew closer. Already the crackling in the air was making his stomach churn uncomfortably, but as it rolled in from over the Welsh border he forced himself to stand at the window and watch it.

"It's nothing like a storm at sea," he kept saying softly to himself over and over again. For a start, although the woods outside shook and groaned in the high wind, the ground itself wasn't moving and neither was the house. He'd stoked up the range early on, and now it was throwing out a comforting heat to the extent that he was actually starting to sweat a little – a far cry from the biting cold of being drenched to the skin for days! Pulling his jacket loose, he poured himself another mug of tea from the pot on the range, and then went and leaned on the draining board to stare out of the window.

"What a storm!" he breathed, as another huge lightning flash lit up the wood.

"Yes it is, isn't it," a female voice said distantly, making Harry jump even as she exclaimed, "Oh God!"

Harry almost dropped the mug of tea and scrubbed a hand across his forehead. Not fevered, but then where had that voice come from? Surely not outside in this weather.

"Are you a ghost?" he called, instantly feeling completely ridiculous until the voice replied,

"No. Are you?"

"No." God this was bizarre! He'd experienced some strange things on battlefields over the years, but nothing remotely like this!

"Where are you?" the unknown woman asked, at which point Harry realised that it sounded as though she was standing just beside him and yet a long way away at the same time, but certainly not outside. "I'm standing in a place called Cold Hunger Farm," she added.

"So am I," Harry answered, feeling a sweat of fear beginning.

"When?"

"When?" Harry echoed her, then realising what she was getting at even as the disembodied woman said,

"What year? I'm in tw..." but her voice disappeared as the storm rumbled off into the distance.

"Lord, I mustn't tell Robert about this," Harry said as he took a gulp of the rather too hot tea. "He'll be thinking I'm set for the madhouse!" Rather worse was the way his mind kept wandering back to the voice, even when he'd retired to bed. It had been a nice voice he thought, as sleep enveloped him. Not a posh voice, but not a coarse one either. The kind of woman's voice he could sit and listen to, not grating as Amy's forced girlishness had become. If she was a ghost she was a ghost he'd rather like to keep.

Chapter 11

June, modern day

With bated breath Pip turned the pages of the first letter and saw that it was dated 1814. It was clearly in response to a letter Gus Vaughan must have received from this new person, Harry Green, whom she gathered from some of the subtext of the letter, was waiting for his captaincy to be confirmed. At first she happily read the rather formal style with a vague kind of amusement. The writer must have been quite a particular little soul – and somehow she definitely imagined him as a little man, and possibly rather plump. A rather fussy bachelor type, she was thinking. He was confirming that he had wanted terribly to be home for the wedding of his little sister to the dashing Lieutenant Clifford some three years previously.

> *I wanted so much to be there to see dearest Amy be the blushing bride, but 'tis such a fearfully long way to travel from India, and Mama and Papa said that it was not possible to know a long way ahead when Edward would be granted leave. They wrote to me saying he would only know a short while in advance, and so I was resigned to my fate to miss the most important day in my dear sister's life. She wanted so much to marry Edward right from the day she first met him. I could scarce believe old Mr Clifford would allow the match, but then of course, that was before Papa's dreadful misfortune.*

Pip sniffed. "Misfortune my arse! Sounded to me like that Clifford bloke set your dad up for the fall right from the start!" Even with just what had appeared in the *Berrow's Journal*, it had sounded very much as if, despite the local paper reporting the fall of the Vaughans as something rather shocking, in the articles there was a more subtle expression of feeling that Clifford had acted with a certain lack of gentlemanly conduct. It was never explicit, but Pip had picked up immediately on the way the paper had expressed sympathy for the rest of the Vaughan family, even if it wasn't proper to say so about Mr Vaughan himself. By contrast, there seemed to be a distinct lack of pleasure in the reporting that Clifford had got his pound of flesh, with some rather curt sounding observations on him.

However, no such restraints were on Gus when it came to his brother-in-law's demise, and replying to letters from someone who seemed to have been a family friend.

> *I do not wish to imply any error or mistaken judgement on your part, Captain Green, but may I say how shocked I am to hear of the circumstances of Edward's death. When Mama wrote to tell me of his loss I confess I believed him to have fallen valiantly in battle. Yet you say he had amassed such gambling debts as would have driven him and Amy near into the poor house had he lived. This distresses me greatly. I know that out here many young gentlemen of means turn to cards as a diversion, without realising the danger it presents if gambling gets out of hand, but I have no personal contact with anyone for whom that has actually happened.*
>
> *I had long been in the belief that Edward was providing for Amy, and therefore that I was only supporting my dear parents. So to hear from you that they in turn have been supporting Amy all along, moreover her son as well and throughout the whole of her marriage, is an unpleasant surprise, for I believed*

better of him. I cannot understand why he would not wish to provide for his son, either, when I would give anything to have a dear boy of my own.

However, I am much obliged to you for taking the trouble to concern yourself with my family's welfare, and thank you for clarifying the matter. Indeed I believe I may well be indebted to you for more than you speak of, for I have had a letter from Mama arrive at the same time as yours, in which she writes that you have taken it upon yourself to make remuneration to various trades persons on Papa's behalf. I am not so insensible as to not comprehend what misfortune for my family lies behind such an act, and I therefore thank you most heartily and hope that one day I may be able to do you some service in repayment.

That gave Pip a welcome clue as to the character of this captain. "Must be a nice bloke if he cared enough to go around settling debts," she mused aloud. By the sound of it he couldn't have had a particularly high regard for Edward Clifford, so what had prompted him to be so generous? But then as she read on, she nearly dropped the letter in horror-stricken shock.

However, I fear I can provide you with no clue as to how my sister came to know this Miss Natalie Walker you wrote of.

"What the fuck!" Pip almost shrieked, dropping the letter as if it was about to burn her. "No! No, that can't be right! How did *she* get there?"

With trembling hands she picked the letter up again to read the next sentence, silently praying that this was all just some horrid coincidence of names.

Indeed, [Gus wrote], *I may safely say that I have heard nothing from Amy of any such friend before. I fear I took scant notice of the succession of little girls who came to play with Amy while I was still at home, and then when she went off to school I do believe there was a Violet and an Emilia, of whom she wrote, but no others. I am at a loss as to how Amy came to know this woman, nor can I tell you why she should be so accommodated as to be borrowing jewellery from Amy.*

It worries me greatly that you say the woman has been seen since in France and has gained an unpleasant reputation, but will do as you request and write to Amy to find out if she has heard from any of her old friends of late. I also appreciate your desire to make absolutely sure that this woman has not tried to take advantage of Amy in the years since the wedding and particularly since Edward's death. What I can tell you is that as a family we have had no connection with any family called Walker, nor can I think of any family of that name living nearby. She must be from much further away.

"Jeez, she was that all right!" Pip gulped. "About a hundred and eighty *years* further away!"

Suddenly wanting to open all the letters to find out more, she bundled them up again, hurried out to the minibus and drove back into Worcester. Luckily Nick wasn't around when she reported back that Arthur had taken his extra samples, and so she was able to get home fast and then start spreading the letters out on her table in the window. With a warm summer breeze occasionally ruffling Windy's leaves through the open window, Pip had to press all of her paperweights into service to stop sheets from disappearing under the desk all the time, but soon realised that the letters had probably been deposited by two totally separate people. The big bundle of letters from the lost room stretched over a much longer period of time, and had been written to Amy for the most part by Captain

Harry Green, although with a few additional ones from Edward Clifford. When the dust of ages was wiped off the outside of them it was clear to see that they'd been put into bundles with various pieces of pretty ribbon.

By contrast, the other letters had been tied together with string, and there was a note on the bottom of the pile which Pip had missed before, which said,

Harry, these are the letters you left with me for safe keeping at the rectory, Robert.

A quick glance at the research notes she'd made confirmed to Pip that the incumbent at Clifton rectory at around this time had first been a Robert Green senior, and then Robert Green junior. Then she looked at the dates again and decided this was a note from one brother to another. That made sense. If the Greens had been resident here for a while, then no wonder Harry had come here and discovered the Vaughans living in penury. And these letters and papers were quite varied. Some related to Harry's army career, the last of those concerning the regiment going to India in 1824, with instructions over the assembly of men and equipment in order to embark from Gravesend.

Turning to her laptop, Pip did a quick search and was rewarded by finding that the Huntingdonshire regiment had been involved in a famous disaster out in the Bay of Biscay in March of that year. It had clearly caught the popular imagination for the courageous actions of both the soldiers onboard and the miners on the ship which had made the rescue.

"Blimey! The fire on board the *Kent* was national news! Even Dickens wrote about it decades after the event!" Pip told her plant. "So there you have it, Windy! Quite the Victorian melodrama!" Except that the original event wasn't even Victorian. A quick check to refresh her memory revealed that it was during the reign of George IV.

"Was he the mad one, Windy? Or was that George III? I can't remember, but it would be pretty ironic if all these crazy events went on in his reign. But the popular view seems to be that there were no cowards on board those ships. Courage and fortitude of the highest kind, and stuff like that. Well, well, well, Windy, Captain Green is starting to look something of the quiet hero!"

As she carried on reading the various letters and documents, her opinion of Captain Green as an altogether good bloke was if anything reinforced. In the years which followed his first letter to Gus he must have sent many more, because the replies from Gus to him alluded to a vigorous correspondence, and always Amy was at the heart of things.

"Were you in love with Amy?" Pip mused as she returned to the desk with another large mug of decaff'. It was one of those exceedingly rare English summer evenings when it was warm enough to sit with the window open wide late on, and Pip was glad that her room was at the back of the house so that she looked onto the garden. On the front she would've had to close her window up more by now, to avoid the rush hour traffic fumes of the cars queuing to get out of the city along the main road beyond the narrow front garden. But here at the back, the ancient honeysuckle was wafting its old-fashioned scent in, creating an appropriate ambience to the place for reading the second lot of letters.

Almost immediately Pip picked up on the affection with which Harry was writing to Amy. It bemused her, though, that he continued to write to her in a style which retained a certain formality.

"Bloody hell, girl, why did you pick the waster?" she wondered, bemused. "This Harry is all but pouring his heart out to you here, and yet I don't reckon you saw it.

And why is he having to make all these excuses for your husband all the time? Are you not wondering why it's always Harry who writes? You must have been a right bimbo if you didn't question that even once!"

Utterly engrossed, Pip read on even after darkness fell and she had to put a table lamp on. With the odd moth fluttering in and out of the window on the soft night air, she was almost in this other world. One where the absolute rat Edward wrote such careless and self-absorbed notes, while all the time his fellow officer was writing such lovely letters at ten times the frequency. When she got to the last few letters, though, she began to sense a change, almost a desperation in what Harry was writing. He was returning to England and to Pip it was blindingly clear what he was hoping for.

"Heavens, Harry, you were a faithful one, weren't you," Pip sighed. "All those years, through shit, shell and shot you kept writing home in the hope that she'd marry you in the end. I bet she bloody didn't though!"

Then it occurred to her to check her notes. No, Amy had finally died a good many years on, according to the basic records she'd looked into, so no details of how, but still very much Mrs Clifford. Not a hint of her ever marrying again and becoming Mrs Green.

"Poor old Harry, you never did get the girl," Pip sympathised. Then something in her notes made her look back again. Yes, there it was, it was the year which had caught her eye on the list she'd made of the deaths of the various members of the Vaughan family. Gus Vaughan had died in 1824, the same year Harry Green had been nearly killed on the *Kent.* "Hmm, no wonder there's no more correspondence between them after that time," she muttered, then sat up sharply with a shiver. "Oh bugger!" How could she have forgotten? "Stupid, stupid me!" she chastised herself as she dived for another set of notes. There it was in black and white, all the details Natalie had taken down about Gus' financial situation! Yes, Gus had been Natalie's intended target!

That took all the sweetness out of the evening, and she shut the window up and hurriedly put the other lights on. Tomorrow she was definitely going back to the archives, because she wanted very much to see what she could find out about both Harry Green and Gus Vaughan in the last year of his life. If Gus was hit by a brewer's dray, or some other mundane but accidental death, then she would force herself to see sense, and write the whole coincidence with Natalie off as a freakish clash of names.

Yet Harry Green wasn't so quick to let go of either, and as she showered and then settled down in her bed, Pip couldn't help but wish she'd known him. The letters had shown her a very different kind of man to the needy person Dave had turned out to be. She turned over and pulled a pillow down to hug. Four years she'd been on her own and it was starting to feel like far too long. Yet somehow she just wasn't meeting the kind of men she would want to take a chance on again. So how bloody unfair was it that when she did find someone who caught her eye he was already dust in some Victorian churchyard? If she wasn't careful she was going to end up mourning the passing of someone she'd never even met! *Find the record of his death and then write the whole episode off*, she told herself sternly as sleep failed to come. *You can't go mooning around over someone who was dead before even your grandparents were born! That's bloody silly!* Then forced herself to admit that she'd been far more shaken by the discovery of Dave's body than she was prepared to allow. *You're all out of sorts,* she chastised herself. *You'd never consider such tosh as someone slipping through time if you weren't all at sixes and sevens to start off with! Go into the record office tomorrow and look for a Natalie Walker back then. There'll be some nice, logical explanation, you'll see!*

However, try as she might, Pip could not find a Natalie Walker living at the right time to disprove the possibility of the modern Natalie being there. In her desperation to prove her fears unfounded, she spent a whole day chasing every link she could think of, even using things like the genealogical index to search in other counties. But with her search focusing on a time before there was a legal requirement to register births, deaths and marriages, she knew there were huge holes in her search. Unless she wanted to spend the rest of her life hunting for this historical Natalie by going to parish churches in distant locations to check their records, she was never going to be able to be certain. It upset her more than she could credit to not be able to nail this whole thing down as a mad woman's imagination vented in a personal diary. So much so that she ended up going home, eating a ready meal she'd bought in the end-of-day reductions at Sainsbury's, and then putting her headphones on and listening to her favourite music as loud as she could tolerate. That was the trouble with living in a shared house. You always had to consider the person in the next room.

And suddenly she was heartily sick of her life. All of it! Of living in an apology for an independent life in this bed-sit, however large it was. Of having to do a job which was far beneath her capabilities, because someone as petty as Phil had put the poison down for her where she ought to have been. Of not having a decent relationship in her life, let alone a full-time partner. Where was the Pip of five years ago? The young woman who'd been looking to buy a house with the man she thought she would be with for years? Who had been looking eagerly forward to a career? Looking forward to life!

After she'd thrown herself onto the bed and howled her heart out for half an hour in a wave of self-pity, she sat up and realised she could pinpoint the moment when she had begun fire-fighting crisis after crisis instead of moving forward. It had been at the moment when the doctor had told her she had been infected with Chlamydia and that she would likely never have children. She'd been told already, after an unexpected couple of nasty ovarian abscesses, that she might have trouble conceiving, but up until that point she'd just thought it would be a matter of persevering, and that that wouldn't be such a hardship with a man she loved. But in that moment she'd had to face the harsh reality that because Dave had been unfaithful, her hopes for a family were gone. That alone would have been hard enough to deal with, but to lose the prospect of a career which might have helped to fill some of that gap – and at virtually the same time – had been the last straw, and Pip could look back and see how she had begun to withdraw into herself.

Yet that wasn't her, though. Not the real Pip, not the person she'd been before all this crap had descended on her. The real Pip was open and outgoing, had enjoyed social gatherings of all sorts, and had never been given to such moping about as she'd done on the last few years. It was time to change! She sat up and looked about her. There wasn't that much to leave behind here. Apart from the plant, which had rewarded her care by growing at a frantic rate, her belongings could fit into a couple of suitcases and several boxes of books. So why stay? The more she thought about it the more making a complete change seemed like a long overdue decision.

Why not move to somewhere completely fresh? Make a new start in every way? If she wasn't looking for work in archaeology then she wouldn't be dependent on Nick finding her places on random summer digs every year to keep her c.v. looking up to date – and in truth it was getting harder every year to get time off at work. How much better would it be to go and find a decent job instead of working herself into the ground every spring doing long, long hours watering and potting-on at the nursery, just to get a month off later on for digs? Granted it would most likely be work at something like a supermarket, but at least it would be a guaranteed wage. A regular one, month after month the same. One with a proper pay slip which she could take to a bank and think, in a few years, about getting a mortgage on a tiny starter home with. Maybe even a dinky house with enough of a garden that she could have a couple of dogs? Ever since she'd been child she'd wanted a dog, to such an extent that she'd tried walking at the local dog rescue centre until she'd admitted that it upset her too much not to be able to take them home with her. Yes, that would be better! A dinky house with a couple of dogs was way better than this, even if it wasn't the husband and family with kids and dogs she'd once dreamed of.

She got up the next morning with a new resolve. Until the police had safely drawn a line under this current investigation she could hardly disappear out of the county, but she could start making job searches to see what was out there. And in the meantime she could try to draw a personal line under this murky mystery which Natalie had sucked her into. A dive into the world of internet job applications on her laptop saw her through breakfast, and then she headed for the library and archives again. To hell with Natalie, she could be anywhere! Harry Green and Gus Vaughan, on the other hand, might be easier to bring to a close and she chose to start with the newspapers for the second half of 1824.

It didn't take her long to find. Splashed as a headline in the local papers was the news that Captain Harry Green was accused of murdering Mr Augustus Vaughan.

"No!" Pip gulped, aghast. This wasn't the Harry Green of the letters – but of course if the bloody letters were still in their hiding place in the twenty-first century, then no-one had found them back then! She found a pencil sketch of him done by a reporter and scrutinised the face. Not handsome, not even particularly remarkable. The sort of man you might pass by in the street and never notice. In that she was glad. She would have been strangely upset if he'd turned out to be some handsome rake of the day. Part of the initial appeal to her had been that he'd been overlooked by Amy because superficially he hadn't been able to compete with the handsome Edward Clifford.

Forcing herself to read on, she discovered that the alarm had been raised by Mr Vaughan's widowed sister, Mrs Amy Clifford. According to the paper, at least, Mr Vaughan had taken rooms in Hereford temporarily while awaiting a job in the north. He and Mrs Clifford had recently vacated a house which they had formerly rented with their late parents near Clifton, and which Mrs Clifford was saying had now been taken on by Captain Green. What really shook Pip, though, was a direct quote from the grieving Mrs Clifford saying that Captain Green had come home from the wars a changed man, and that he had bullied her brother into leaving the farm so that he could live close to his brother, the rector of Clifton. But Pip felt positively sick when she saw the words 'Mrs Clifford has been supported throughout by her friend, Miss Natalie Walker, who has been a stalwart comfort to her.'

Getting up, Pip had to go and throw some water onto her face in the ladies' loos before she could cope with reading any more. So this Natalie had come back. How odd that her behaviour sounded more and more like the Natalie Pip was seeking, because in the same article it had been reported that Mrs Clifford was going through a traumatic time as her brother had made Captain Green his executor; and also in his bequest, he was the man through whom Mrs Clifford would have to go for funds in the event of Mr Vaughan's death. Well that wasn't so surprising given that Gus had already been writing to Harry of how helpless Amy was. And the two of them were alert to the scheming of their Miss Natalie Walker, that was for certain. But was this Natalie at Amy's side every step of the way, haggling with the lawyers on her behalf while masquerading as the loyal friend?

Pip suddenly looked up and met her own gaze in the mirror over the washbasin. Hang on a minute! In Natalie's diary she'd written a date down – the date she was going back to! Or at least had been convinced she would go to. More prepared this time for the need to cross-reference, Pip already had the photocopies with her, and hurried back to the terminal where she was conducting her search. It didn't take long to find. Natalie had been intending to go back to 1823!

I have found a reference to the Vaughans taking lodgings in Hereford in the summer of 1824, she had written. *I checked for the season in Bath, and they were there the previous summer because Augustus Vaughan is briefly mentioned for some charitable donation whilst there, so why did they not go again in 1824? I must go through the portal to get to them in 1823! That way I can follow them back to Worcestershire and seduce this Augustus. He doesn't sound like the kind of man to put up much of a resistance. He only worked as some sort of pencil-pusher for the East India Company, after all. But he is wealthy! I wish I could get next to someone more affluent, but pulling that off might prove impossible unless I can contrive to create a believable introduction. So I shall have to make do with seizing a modest fortune at that time, and letting time and interest in a bank do the rest for me.*

"Then what the hell were you doing appearing in 18*11*?" Pip muttered softly as she began a frantic trawl back to that year in the newspaper. "Did you get the year wrong somehow?" More to the point, it occurred to her, how had Natalie thought she could pinpoint one specific year? Did she think it would happen by willpower alone? To her frustration, although the marriage of Amy Vaughan to Edward Clifford was mentioned in the paper in 1811, if Natalie had been there she certainly hadn't been of sufficient significance to be noted as being amongst the guests, although Harry's presence had been mentioned as best man. "So you knew Edward from school, eh?" Pip breathed. "That explains how you knew both him and Amy. You must have grown up together. I'd wondered what a man like you, Harry, was doing as friends with a wretch like Edward."

Another inspection of the photocopied diary provided Pip with the next clue. *I shall follow the spell I have to open the pathways to the beyond,* Natalie wrote, making Pip almost laugh out loud. Good grief, if the dozy woman had been thinking some piece of bad poetry by a New Age wiccan was going to do the job, then no wonder she'd come unstuck! *I've found some coins,* Natalie continued, although Pip thought 'nicked' was probably closer to the truth than 'found'. *Some gold ones from the seventeenth century and one from 1810. Not ideal, but gold is gold in any century! They'll get me by until I can get some man to look after me.*

The startling arrogance of Natalie's intentions still never failed to surprise Pip, but there at least lay the answer, and at last there was some logic to the matter too.

"You went to the time when the most recent thing you had could feasibly exist," Pip breathed, almost starting to believe in this now. "Never mind the spooky incantations! Time is time! As a person you could come from any time, but physical object would have a set period. Of course they would! That coin set the date!"

And it wouldn't surprise her if Natalie had gone through naked in order not to 'contaminate' the timeline. It was the sort of thing she could well have believed to be essential to her cockeyed rite anyway. So no modern clothing to hamper her progress, just the coins she was holding. Then another thought came to her. When had Paul's body turned up, then? She was going to have to make a guess that it was sometime within a decade or so. Maybe that portal had opened up approximately already by the time Natalie had found it, and then only had to be fixed, or rather fine tuned? Because the more Pip thought about it, an analogy with tuning a radio was the one which made most sense. Yet she was the first to acknowledge that her understanding of temporal science was non-existent. How this had worked would be something she would probably never understand.

Pip left her paperwork by the terminal to keep it for her, but took her bag and her mobile phone outside and rang Nick.

"Hi there! Any news on the dates from Arthur?" she asked, hoping she was sounding just naturally curious.

"Ah, yes!" Nick replied, sounding cheerful. "All of the timbers come back in line except for that one, and he's now saying that having looked at it again with you, he thinks it might be a section spliced in to make some kind of repair. He thinks it might even have been after something like a lightning strike."

"Does he, indeed! How come?"

"Well there's some of the same timber in the sealed off staircase patch of floor. Not all of the patch, but he took a small sample of the one piece, and in terms of colour and grain and all the other things he looks at, it's the same, even if the floorboard isn't thick enough to be able to date. So he can't prove it, but in his own mind Arthur says he thinks there must have been one hell of a storm and a strike. Maybe part of the old roof was already failing or had gone in the storm, we'll never know, but either the lightning struck right into the house, or on the roof, with the water damage coming in being severe enough to warrant those boards being replaced. He thinks lightning because it was just the one spot, you see. The roof generally failing would have probably resulted in more repairs in various places. Where that timber came from is another mystery. It shouldn't have survived that long at all in that good a condition, but Arthur's convinced his tests are right. However I can see his point when he says he won't be putting that in the official report. He's got his reputation to think of, and a random Roman piece of oak isn't worth wrecking your career over."

"No, not at all," agreed Pip. "I don't suppose there's anything in the records we have of the house of something like those repairs taking place? Some time like the early 1800s, for instance?" It was the most she could push him for information without him wanting to know why.

She heard Nick shuffling some papers, but then he came back on saying, "No, not a dickey bird, I'm afraid, but then it might have been the owners paying for it and the tenants doing the work. It's impossible to track down on an ordinary house like this."

Ordinary was the last thing Pip would have called Cold Hunger Farm, but she thanked Nick, accepted an invitation to dinner later on at the weekend, and then went back to her searching. She would give it one last go at finding out if a body had been found at Cold Hunger and then she would give up. Her enthusiasm was drained for today, and she was making only the most desultory of searches going back month by month from Amy and Edward's wedding when there it was on the page in front of her. A naked man's body had been found in early August 1810 near to Clifton by, of all people, Rector Green! That had to be the father, Pip guessed, but it had meant that as a man of the cloth he'd been believed when he'd hailed a passing carter to fetch help. Then her heart almost jumped out of her chest when she read that a trail of blood ran back into the then currently empty Cold Hunger Farm.

Shivering, she made herself go back to the start of the piece and read it properly. The Reverend Green had been alerted when he'd looked down the road to where the empty farm lay, only to see part of a human arm. He'd gone to investigate and had concluded that someone might have had a terrible accident, so had hailed the carter to fetch help and had hurried down to the farm. There he'd found the naked body of a young man outside the house. As Pip followed the story through a couple more entries, it transpired that no-one had ever seen the young man before, despite many enquiries. More shocking to the locals were the multiple stab wounds on the body done with a small knife. It caused considerable worry that a maniac might be on the loose, although the local magistrates had pronounced that foxes had dislocated the arm after death. To Pip, though, it sounded all too familiar. This was Paul's body post Natalie's ritual!

She printed off what she could from the file, suddenly energised again. What had Natalie done to him? And had it actually been Natalie who had thrown him out of some window after she too had gone through? Or had the poor soul still been alive when Natalie had abandoned him to his fate in the past, and had crawled out of the door but then died? It gave Pip the shudders whichever it was, but that body finally made her believe that however preposterous she might think it, Natalie had found a way into the past. She rubbed her sore eyes and went once more to the account of Harry Green's trial, and printed off what she could of that too, even though the last entry was horribly blurred and might not be readable even after closer scrutiny.

It was a relief to get out into the fresh air by the river and, although it wasn't so warm tonight, she took her time strolling back along the riverbank and over the footbridge. It was as she'd stopped on the bridge to watch a couple of swans gliding in to land on the river that she made another connection. Of course! In August 1810, when Paul's body had been found, the Vaughans had been still living in St John's, not at Cold Hunger! In her overworked brain she'd half wondered where the Vaughan's had been when a body had shown up on their doorstep, but of course then it hadn't been anyone's doorstep, much less theirs! But that in turn explained how Mr Vaughan had been able to rent the place for a song a couple of years later. Who would want to live in a place where a murder had been committed? No-one local that was certain, so the owners must have been delighted to find someone from as far afield as Worcester interested in the place. And had Horace Vaughan told his wife and daughter of the place's history, if he himself had known? Probably not, Pip thought.

But if the house was still vacant when the Vaughans had needed to move, then that was where Natalie had sprung from unnoticed too! When the dreadful woman had actually gone through in the months between the October of what was most likely 1810, and before Amy's wedding in June of 1811, was anyone's guess. And Pip had the strong feeling that Natalie would have arrived after Paul in the past, just as she'd exited the present some months after him. However much she didn't know about the mechanics of the passage through time, Pip believed that it wouldn't be so random as to deposit Natalie before Paul, thereby giving her time to murder him in the past. Because surely if Natalie had been lurking around Cold Hunger Farm for months, someone would have noticed? And that would have been mentioned in the old papers alongside the discovery of Paul's body.

It all made Pip pause and wonder seriously about timing, because given that Paul had appeared in August 1810, presumably it had been August when he'd left this time? Natalie had been strangely silent on the date of the actual ritual in the here and now – on dates in general, in fact – and Pip realised she'd assumed the whole thing had taken space in the course of a matter of days. But then if Natalie had been trying to get hold of animals to experiment with, then of course it had taken longer. She must look at that diary again when she got home!

And what a dreadful shock it must have been to Natalie, to find herself in 1811 instead of 1823, and Gus Vaughan not there but still out in India! That at least made Pip grin. Ever serve the bitch right! Why that had happened was something she could speculate on for years and never know the truth, and it might even have been Natalie not realising what she was seeing through the mirror in the first place. But it confirmed in Pip's mind what a fool Amy Vaughan must have been, because she could only have known Natalie a matter of a few months at most before the wedding. No wonder Harry had been shocked at seeing Natalie wearing Amy's ring!

Then as she was making herself a salad for her dinner, Pip made her last connections of another uncomfortable and unsettling day. If Natalie had been willing to murder both Paul and Dave to get what she wanted, then she was hardly going to stop there. What if she'd been forced to remake her plans in order to survive, but had never forgotten that Gus was her original target? Or maybe, despite her arrogance, Natalie had found nineteenth century men less easy to fleece of their money than she'd imagined? In which case it made so much more sense if Natalie had returned to fulfil her plans when the right time came around, only to find that Harry had warned Gus off.

"God, I bet you were pissed at that!" gasped Pip. "How furious would you be if you'd waited twelve years and then saw your plans all falling apart?" Furious enough to murder again, her own mind instantly supplied. And what if the amiable Gus had told his sister that if anything happened to him that Harry would still run her affairs for her? If that had got back to Natalie, then the only way she would get her hands on Gus' money would be to kill him and implicate Harry for the murder, so that he was removed as Amy's protector. A dim-witted woman like Amy would be putty in Natalie's hands, Pip was sure. In fact she had the nasty feeling that once Natalie had got full control of the money, and had moved it into an account she alone could access, Natalie would spread some rumour that poor Mrs Clifford couldn't face living at Cold Hunger anymore and was leaving, and then kill her too.

Indeed, if Pip's guess about the very nature of the portal was correct then all Natalie would have to do would be to bring Amy forwards with her, and all that would be left of Amy would be a pile of dust on Cold Hunger's bedroom floor. No, hang on a minute, Amy had died much later of old age, so something must have stopped Natalie from that part of her plan at least. Phew! One less body to worry about! And would the portal really work that way? Could it be that the mysterious beam which had been used to patch up the house had come through the portal? Not the mirror, obviously! But clearly the whole foundations of

Cold Hunger were prone to some kind of slippage in time. So was it some other event which had caused the timber to fall into another time? Had that been the initial activating event which Natalie had just stumbled upon despite all of her incantations and bloodletting? With that and a myriad other questions which she couldn't answer swirling in her head, Pip chose to watch some mindless TV in the hope of switching her brain off so that she'd sleep tonight. It didn't wholly work because her dreams were haunted by images of the man she now knew as Harry swinging from a hangman's gibbet as he reached towards her for help.

Waking early and all of a lather, as she sluiced herself under the shower to try and wash the ghastly images away, she realised she had come to a decision. Harry was as much her responsibility as Dave had been if it really was the same Natalie in the past, murdering there as well. And that meant that she couldn't rest easy until she'd done her best to save him. How she was going to do that she didn't know as yet. What she did know, based on the letters, was that to have Amy fingering him for Gus' murder would be a terrible knife in the back for Harry.

Chapter 12

Then and now

Harry ambled happily along the country lane, taking the long way round to get to Clifton. However grateful he was to Gus for paying for him to rent Cold Hunger Farm, there was something about the actual building which made him uncomfortable. A hint of a lurking presence which he couldn't shake off or dismiss as folly. In the month he'd been there he'd taken to knocking the garden back into shape as a kind of restorative exercise, every day going outside and doing something, however small. At first he'd been exhausted by doing little more than cutting a few trailing strands of the ramblings roses and honeysuckle back, but week by week he'd returned to something closer to his old strength. But even if he'd been worn out by a task in the garden in the morning, he found he couldn't face sitting in the house all through the afternoon and then the evening as well. At some point he had to get out and have a break from the oppressive atmosphere.

Today he was going into Clifton to buy some meat from the butcher and then call in to see Robert. He was expecting a letter from the army and had given the rectory as his contact address, so that although he tried not to impose his company on Robert more than a couple of times a week, today he felt he had a reason to call in without his brother wondering whether he was lonely. For some reason Robert had got it into his head that Harry would be pining for his army friends, and nothing Harry said seemed to dispel that. In truth, the officers Harry had set sail with hadn't been his friends at all. The ones he'd fought alongside while the regiment had been at war, and immediately after, had either died or decided to retire before the regiment went to India. Of the current men, only the two most senior men, Fearon and MacGregor were known to him, and they had long been above socialising at anything beyond simple officers' mess talk with a captain for whom further promotion seemed to have slipped by. And yet in his desperation after missing the ship to India, Harry had written to both of them in the hope that they could recommend some new post to him.

He was therefore deep in his own thoughts as he walked into Clifton-upon-Teme, taking no notice of his surroundings until he saw Robert actually running towards him, clerical garb flying like wings about him and pale-faced.

"Good God, Robert, what's wrong?" he called, suddenly aware that several people who were walking along the street had stopped and were watching in astonishment.

Robert tore up to him. "You've not heard?" he gasped.

"Heard what? What is it Robert? What's happened?"

"Gus," Robert panted. "Oh Lord, Harry! Poor Gus!"

Harry shook his head in confusion. "What's happened to Gus? Has the job fallen through? Have his investments fallen through in some way? What?"

Robert's face was agonised. "No Harry, he's dead."

"Dead? Gus? Oh no! How? His heart?"

Shaking his head, Robert reached out and gripped Harry's arm. "He's been murdered, Harry."

"Christ!" Harry couldn't imagine Gus having an enemy in the world. "Was it a mistake? Someone thinking he was someone else? An attack in the street at night?" Even that seemed a bit farfetched. Hereford was hardly a hotbed of vice like parts of London were, or some of the ports Harry had known in his time.

"No, he was killed in his rooms some time during the night. Amy called round to see him. She said he'd arranged to meet her and hadn't appeared. I'm told she was worried because he never let her down."

"Good Lord, she didn't find him, did she?" The thought of the hysterics which would have gone with that gave Harry the shivers all by itself. Amy would be playing that to the gallery for the rest of her life! Then he felt guilty for such a thought. Whatever else she was, Amy would have good cause to have hysterics if she'd found her brother's corpse. Then realised that Robert was saying,

"No. Luckily one of the other gentlemen rooming in the same house went upstairs." Robert seemed to struggle over how to say the next words. "The man who ...the man who came to tell me said ...said it was a terrible sight, Harry. He'd been hacked ...been stabbed many ...Oh Lord!" Robert passed his hands over his eyes as the people around them erupted into scandalised chatter. "Please come home, Harry."

"Yes, of course! Is there anything we can do for Amy and Little Eddie? Can I help in some way?"

Yet Robert was almost tugging him towards the rectory. Only when he'd opened the front door and all but bundled Harry through it, did Robert slam the door and say,

"They're saying *you* did it Harry!"

The room spun in a sudden, sickening lurch. "No!" Harry felt as though the ground was opening beneath him to hellish chasm. "Me? Why? Why would I ever harm one hair of Gus' head? We were friends! What possible reason..." Words failed him.

"Come into the parlour," Robert said more calmly. "We don't have long. Men came riding in from Hereford looking for you. The magistrates want to speak to you. Their men came here. I told them you weren't here, but that I thought you might have gone to meet the post coach as you'd mentioned coming into the village because of a letter. I'm sorry Harry, it was the best thing I could think of to say at the time. I was so shocked!"

"Not half as shocked as me!"

Robert half smiled but it fell apart into pity. "No. Not as shocked as you."

"You've not asked me outright."

"I don't need to. You always were an appalling liar as a child. Your face is an open book, Harry, and you couldn't fake that much shock. I didn't believe it when I was told, and I certainly don't believe it now I've seen you."

"Thank you."

"But I should warn you, there's even worse to come."

"Worse?" How could there be anything worse than being accused of a murder he hadn't committed?

"Oh it's worse," Robert sighed. "You see, they've come looking for you because Amy's the one who accused you." He watched Harry go white and sway, grabbing the back of the armchair for support. "I'm so sorry, Harry! Truly I am! I can't think what's got into the stupid woman to be making wild claims like that, but she says you and Gus had fallen out over money. That you forced them out of Cold Hunger Farm. Those men will no doubt have gone there by now, so there was no point in me not saying where you lived. They knew already."

"Why?" Harry gulped. "Why would she do that?"

Robert shrugged. "I can only guess, but I'd say she has a considerable grudge against you for stopping paying out left, right and centre for her, and for not paying for a house in Bath for the season this year."

"But murder? She can't believe I'd do that to Gus? Can she? I can see her trying to blacken my name in those circles she moves in, but *someone* has just killed her brother! Does she not want to know who that is? Who the real killer is?"

"Maybe she's not really thinking properly. In her shock maybe she sees this as a way of paying you back. Not thinking that you could end up by being actually accused. You know, like some silly schoolgirl accusation which later gets withdrawn and life goes on around it." Robert sighed deeply, then clasped his hands as if in desperate prayer. "I see no sense in this at all, Lord. All I can do is pray that this ridiculous accusation is proved false and the real killer is found."

However, Robert's prayers weren't answered. Harry was escorted off to Hereford and spent a wretched couple of days being questioned as to where he was at the time of the murder, and what his relationship with Gus Vaughan had been. Luckily for him, one of the magistrates was a former army officer who was prepared to listen to him, otherwise Harry dreaded to think what might have happened, and there was at least substantial and plausible doubt since no-one had seen him in Hereford at the time. If he couldn't bring witnesses forward to speak for him, at least he had the fact that they could find no-one who had rented him a horse for the day.

All he could hope was that no-one remembered what the Light Company's pace was like. If they did he might be in far deeper trouble, because although he'd been seen in Clifton the day before, they might just wonder whether he could have left in the night, got to Hereford, killed Gus, and then made it back again through the night. Given that it was over twenty miles to Hereford, and quite possibly nearer twenty-five, even taking the shorter route over the fields, Harry knew that had he been fit he couldn't have done it in the time, let alone as he was now. A single journey for his old self would certainly have been plausible, though, and therein lay the danger. With the exploits of Wellington's army still strong in people's memories, would a jury confuse what was possible for the outward journey and make it feasible for a return trip? That scared him silly, and there was also the shock that his word was no longer good enough – an awful thing for a man like Harry, who had always been known for his honesty and honour, even amongst the illustrious company of the regiment.

As it was, after that he was allowed to return to Cold Hunger Farm on the condition that he would stay within Worcestershire – for the actual trial, he'd been told, would be at Worcester Crown court. And he was bound over not to travel into Herefordshire to prevent him intimidating what the one magistrate had called 'these two vulnerable ladies'. Well Amy might be vulnerable at the moment, but Harry was damned sure her friend had never been that in her life. Then to pile on the final insult, Robert was having to standing surety for his good conduct.

"Bloody hell, Robert, I'm sorry to drag you into this," Harry said wearily as they opened the kitchen door to the farm and walked in.

For possibly the first time in their lives, Robert impulsively reached out and hugged Harry. "You're my brother! How could I not help you? And it's not as if you've even done anything!"

"You did get that letter written and sent to my bank in London after the wreck, didn't you?"

Robert nodded. "It went by the first coach, but even so I doubt we shall hear much yet."

"Yes, but even if they haven't sold much in the way of the gems and stuff yet, it will prove that I'm not the penniless wretch Amy has painted me to be. I know it's not much, but it's a start. I shall write again to them tonight, I think, and get them to write to the court detailing all that I paid out to the Vaughans over the years. Thank God I did so much through the bank because of being abroad! So there are records!"

Robert didn't want to say so, but he feared that his brother wasn't taking into account greed, and that the magistrates might think that even a man with adequate money might not be averse to having some more. He was more terrified than he'd ever thought he could be. Terrified that his honest and courageous brother was about to be convicted of a crime he was wholly innocent of on the testimony of two scheming women. And there were two of them, of that he was convinced, for wherever Amy Clifford went, there also went her companion.

As Harry poured them a large glass of wine each, Robert asked carefully, "What do you know of Amy Clifford's friend?"

"Ah, Miss Natalie Walker!"

"Miss? I thought I saw a wedding band on her finger?"

"You may well have done, but it was Miss Walker when I first met her. That's the young woman who followed Edward after he and Amy married."

By now Robert had heard everything about Edward's dreadful behaviour after the wedding, but his jaw dropped at the realisation that the woman he'd seen was one and the same. "That's her? Good God!"

"The very same!" Now Harry had a nasty thought. "And I believe that she tried to make advances to Gus not so very long ago. *She* really did have a grievance against me, because I told Gus just what sort of woman she was, and he wouldn't have anything more to do with her after that."

"Really?"

"Oh yes!"

"Then you'd be shocked to hear that she was introduced to the magistrates before you were brought in as the woman who'd had an unofficial understanding with Gus."

Harry could hardly believe what he was hearing. "Unofficial? It wasn't even that! There was *no* understanding! Not of *any* sort! Hell's teeth, how long was this fairy-tale of an engagement supposed to have been going on for? Did anyone else know?"

By now they'd walked upstairs to see what kind of mess had been made of the rooms upstairs as the men had searched for Harry.

"Well according to the clerk I managed to get talking," Robert said as they pulled the bed back into place, and rescued the sheets and blankets from off the floor, "they were supposedly keeping things very quiet because Mrs Parsons is a widow. She's told the magistrates that she's been very badly treated by her late husband's children by his first wife, who turned her out and left her all but destitute, but that her husband's will left her some of the money. She's been using her maiden name whilst here because of that – or at least that's her version! Apparently she didn't want to make it public that she was soon to wed Gus Vaughan, because she feared if she did she would never see a penny of her first husband's bequest."

"Christ!" Harry groaned. "What a load of crap! I bet her husband's family were appalled when he turned up with her! But she's a damned good actress, I have to give her that, so the horrid truth is that she'll likely be believed."

"But how do we disprove it?" Robert fretted.

Harry shook his head in despair and turned to half sit on the narrow window ledge as the room swam before him once again. Then he croaked in even greater shock,

"Fucking hell!"

"Harry!" Robert remonstrated, but then followed Harry's shaking finger as it stretched out and pointed. "God love us and save us!"

There in the dressing-room mirror was the figure of a woman – a woman who wasn't in the room, and whose surroundings were lit by a totally different light than that coming in through the window behind Harry.

* * *

Pip returned to the archives with renewed purpose. There had to be some way to scupper Natalie's plans, there just had to be! As she strode across the footbridge over the river towards the new library and archive complex, Pip was thinking furiously. Natalie might be mad as a box of frogs, but she wasn't stupid. That would mean that she'd done her homework regarding the money at least, and that got Pip thinking about banks. Back in the nineteenth century she was pretty sure there would have been a good many little banks dotted about the place, but they wouldn't all suit Natalie's purpose. It would have to be a bank which had existed pretty undisturbed throughout the intervening centuries, and there couldn't be that many of those about!

Once inside and able to do some searches Pip couldn't believe how easy it was to track down the only real candidate. Lloyds Bank had been set up in Dale End in Birmingham back in 1765, so it was definitely up and running in the nineteenth century, and it was the only provincial one still trading under its original name – and Lloyds was one of the big four British clearing banks these days. The other big Birmingham bank which had been the Midland Bank, and was now HSBC, hadn't come into existence until 1836. So that wouldn't have been any use to Natalie unless she'd wanted to hang around for another decade, and somehow Pip couldn't imagine that. No, it had to be Lloyds. However that wouldn't help her in the present – she was hardly in a position to wander into the local branch and ask them to check the company records going back to 1824! And of course it explained why the police had never come up with Natalie having loads of money when they'd been trying to find her in the here and now, because they would have only been looking for the modern woman's transactions.

But what to do with that knowledge? It was all very well knowing that Natalie would have targeted Lloyds, but how could Pip use that to help Harry? The one advantage she had over DCI Scathlock was that she was now pretty sure she knew Natalie better than him. So how would Natalie act? What would she do? Pip rested her head in her hands at the desk and cudgelled her brain. She knew next to nothing about banking in the here and now, let alone the past, so how could she hope to trace... That was it! The next link! Natalie was no better equipped to deal with the banking world than she was, so what was the betting that Natalie would have tried to get her claws into a banker? Yes, that made sense! But how would she do it? Bankers were pretty high up in the social strata of Georgian society as far as Pip knew. So would Natalie risk an affair? Pip pondered on that, and came to the conclusion that Natalie knew enough to know that a well-heeled Georgian banker wouldn't think twice about using, and then discarding, a woman he saw as little more than a whore.

"You'd marry him!" she breathed softly, as once again she returned to the indexes. "Dave might have said you'd never marry in this time, but then you don't see the time you went to as permanent for you, do you?" And that was the key. Natalie would risk marriage in the past if she knew she only had to stay long enough for her husband to set up the right kind of account which would last into the future. Pip began to smile with satisfaction as she realised that it might also have been sufficient for Natalie to have *thought* that was enough. Whether the damned thing really *could* stand the test of time wasn't really the point, as long as Natalie believed it would, and would act upon that assumption. And it would be an account rather than something like bonds, at least at first, Pip guessed, because Natalie would be wanting to keep adding to her fund, not sealing it after an initial deposit. Because the more she thought about it, the surer Pip was that even if Natalie did get her hooks into some banker, she was so greedy she wouldn't pass on the chance to fleece poor Gus Vaughan too.

Yes, Pip, thought, if she could somehow find a way to activate the portal and at least speak to Harry, then she could warn him. Tell him to ask about an account in Natalie's name at the nearest branch of Lloyds – probably still Birmingham at that stage. And it was at that point that she wondered if it might just have been Harry whose voice she'd heard at Cold Hunger Farm? He had been living there for a while, after all. It had been a strong voice, a military man's voice, the kind used to making itself heard. Somehow she didn't think the poor distraught Horace Vaughan would have spoken like that, and it didn't fit with the image she had of Gus Vaughan either. If she'd been rattled by the sudden voice from out of thin air then so must he have been, but there hadn't been any sense of panic in her ghostly man's voice. Understandable shock, yes, but not panic. Also, Harry had his brother living close by at the rectory, so had that been the other male voice she'd heard that day?

She looked at the records again, and at Natalie's diary. Gus hadn't come home until his father had been almost on his death bed, so there'd only been a short time when there'd been two men living at Cold Hunger. Yet the voices she'd heard had come through to the kitchen, implying a certain familiarity and casualness – how often in Georgian society did you invite a visitor of minor acquaintance into the kitchen? Almost never, Pip would have bet. So that meant that it was a fair chance she'd spoken to Harry already without knowing it.

"You're not getting away with this Natalie," Pip vowed quietly. If she couldn't find a record of Natalie marrying here in the archives, at least it was something else to tell Harry – if she could. Trace the banker and he'd have proof of Natalie's wicked intentions. But was there anything else she could trace? It occurred to her that maybe she could backtrack if she knew what evidence had been used during Harry's trial, and she turned to the court transcriptions.

Luckily he'd been tried here in Worcester, so she didn't have to travel to any other county to trawl the records, but even so it took her another day to find and then read through the transcripts. As she read her way through the old court records in their ferociously difficult legal handwriting, Pip couldn't believe how anyone could have been taken in by Amy and Natalie, but seemingly they had. In the first instance the court had heard how Harry and Edward had grown up together, which was fair enough, but Pip was appalled to read how Harry's generous settling of the Vaughans' debts to local traders was now being twisted into the machinations of a predatory man trying to worm his way into a grieving widow's affections. She was also surprised that the trial went ahead earlier than expected, when the lawyer representing Amy Clifford had asked for it to be heard in the space left by the collapse of another trial, scheduled to be heard much sooner.

That hurrying forward of the trial had meant that Harry had been able to present very little in his defence. Indeed, the more she read of the case, the more Pip felt that Harry had been so taken aback by the whole thing that his defence was hardly there at all. Where were the character references? The testimonies from men who knew Harry's character? Major MacGregor and Lieutenant Colonel Fearon hadn't gone out to India with the other survivors of the *Kent*, so why hadn't they been summoned? As Harry's superior officers they could have testified to both Harry's character and Edward Vaughan's. Not that Edward was himself of any great importance here, but Pip felt sure that if his feckless nature had come to light, then it would have been clear that Amy was near penniless, thus destroying any hint of Harry wanting her for her money. And it would have put Harry's actions in their proper light. And when had Gus put Harry in charge of his affairs in the event of his death? Had no-one asked that in the course of this unseemly rush to get Harry convicted? More and more, that leapt off the pages at Pip as being the big problem – that Harry had been so utterly unprepared to have to defend himself, and Natalie and Amy had made sure he never got the chance to find his feet in time to do so.

"Why the hurry?" Pip muttered furiously. "What's the rush, Natalie? You were going to get the money anyhow! Why were you pushing to have the trial done and dusted so fast? Did you fear someone would see through you?"

Then she found a clue in a mere aside in one of the newspaper articles towards the end of the trial. Mrs Clifford was due to travel abroad with her companion, the widow of Mr Horatio Parsons, to recuperate! Parsons! So she'd been right, the bitch had married – because who else would that be but Natalie? She made a note on her scribble pad to check up on the life and death of Horatio Parsons, banker and probably another victim of Natalie's. God bless the old conventions where a married woman was addressed by her husband's full name! Pip would hate to lose not only her surname but her given name as well in the process of marriage, but in formal circles that had been the convention. And it was soon confirmed, by her identification when she gave testimony in court, that Natalie Walker had indeed become Mrs Horatio Parsons.

That testimony was the best bit of acting Pip reckoned she'd missed seeing in a very long time. By the sound of it, Natalie had almost had the entire jury in tears with her tale of bereavement. In an Oscar-winning performance, Natalie had told them of how she had met Mr Parsons in Italy where he had been resting after a long illness. At Mr Parsons' family's insistence they had been all but physically forced to come back to London after the wedding, the clerk of the court here recording that Mrs Parsons had broken down as she related how her husband had died upon their return, and making Pip growl in disgust, "load of old bollocks!" under her breath.

Then there was the implication of avarice by Mr Parsons' children and Natalie's tearful testimony of using her maiden name to avoid their persecution. From the distance of the twenty-first century, Pip couldn't believe that no-one had thought to contact the Parsons family to see if this load of tripe had any basis in truth – but then Natalie wasn't the one on trial, she sadly realised. Even more outrageous was Natalie's claim of having been courted of late by Gus Vaughan, and her tearful eulogy to his kind and good nature. Gus had undoubtedly been every bit the good man Natalie said he was, as was also confirmed by other witnesses, but Pip was sure that someone who had managed to survive out in India for the best part of twenty years was unlikely to be such a complete twit as to not be able to see through Natalie.

Or had he been? Maybe he'd been sad and lonely and feeling left on the shelf? She gave herself a mental slap for forgetting just how easily Natalie had manipulated Phil. Dave had been a softie, but Phil was a sharper personality all round, yet he'd still become ensnared. What was it Dave had said about Natalie? That she was one of the sexiest women he'd ever met? Pip hadn't quite been able to get it out of him just what that meant, but maybe Natalie was one of those women who drew men to them like bees to honey? The few Pip had come across like that weren't necessarily the most pretty women, let alone beautiful, but they had an indefinable something which had men falling over themselves to get close to them. Had she underestimated Natalie as being one of those?

With Natalie's need for speed still niggling at the back of her mind, Pip returned to the local papers, hoping to find something which would shed further light on the trial and its aftermath, and all but missed a small advertisement low down on one page.

> The family of Mr Horatio Parsons of Holland Park, London, wish to know the whereabouts of a woman posing as his widow. A reward is offered for aid in apprehending this person, and also the valuables which went missing from the family home on the night of Mr Parsons' death. The woman may also be going under her maiden name, Miss Natalie Walker. She was last known of in Bath but is thought to have been journeying to

> Worcestershire. Anyone with information should write in the first instance to Mssrs Hodgkins and Barlow at Grey's Inn.

Pip gasped, "Fuck!" Had Natalie seen this before she went through the portal? Or had she just been feeling the net tightening around her? 'Posing as his widow' had an ominous ring about it. And how old had Horatio Parsons been? Pip logged on to the genealogical index, and began checking the London area for the years between 1820 and 1823 for the death of Horatio Parsons, and was rewarded to find the short entry for his passing in November of 1823. There wasn't a date of birth for him, and she didn't bother checking for a marriage to Natalie. If it was suspect enough for the family to be able to cast such aspersions on the ceremony, the chances were that it had never happened, or had maybe happened abroad in very dubious circumstances. What she did notice was that in her focused scrolling through she had already reached mid-October of 1824 for the issue with the advert. That was well after the dust had settled on the trial and no hint of what had happened to Harry.

She couldn't find a sentence being passed in the court records on him, either. That was very strange given that at the trial he was found guilty. The judge had adjourned the trial after the jury's verdict for him to decide Harry's fate, and the local papers seemed to have no doubts that Harry would be lucky to get away without being hung. Yet the follow up article wasn't there, as far as Pip could see. Then she went back to the newspapers and went dreadfully light-headed as she found that some things which she had read previously were still there, but were now completely illegible. All of a clammy sweat, she had to go to the ladies loos and splash some water on her face, because the terrifying thought was pounding in on her that history was changing. Was *she* changing history? God, that was a terrifying thought! What a dreadful responsibility!

Then she cupped some of the cold water in her hands and drank it to calm herself. No, the responsibility, if there was any, was to put right as best she could the wrong which Natalie had done. Could she save Gus' life? Probably not, because until Harry had taken over Cold Hunger Farm there would be no-one there who would listen to any warnings. In fact, if she tipped Natalie off by talking to Amy via the portal, things might get even worse – might Harry end up dead too, and accused of rape or something? And could she hope to manipulate the portal to shift the timing again? Unlikely, or worse, what if she inadvertently closed it and was then unable to warn Harry? It seemed to have flipped itself forward a decade from when Natalie went through, if she really had been talking to Harry in 1824. If it wasn't Harry and in 1824, then maybe she was talking to an earlier version of him? Or not him at all? For a second she felt horribly sick at the thought of all her efforts spiralling into chaos.

Then she forced herself to take some deep breaths and calm down. If she wasn't on the right trail, then why were some of the records for 1824 going hazy? She went back to the records and did a quick scan back to when Paul's body had been found. Phew! That was still there in solid black and white, not a hint of blurring at all! Never mind trying to understand the incomprehensible workings of the portal, her only window of opportunity was right where she was looking – at the trial. However, if change was possible, then she couldn't count on Natalie having seen the advert she herself had just read to make her panic and leave. So that must mean that any pressure on Natalie was in the past with her.

With rising urgency she began hunting for why or where Natalie and Amy were intending on going to out of the country, before she inadvertently did something and that account also disappeared. And now she was feeling pressure on herself to complete this before the portal shifted again too. Had it been that enormous thunder storm which had done it in some way? That was when she'd heard Harry for the first time. And if so, then she couldn't guarantee that this summer would go by without another massive storm. Damn it, time was everything both to her and Natalie!

"When? *When* are you going?" Pip hissed, frantically scrolling through the microfiche. There it was! Just a tiny entry announcing their imminent departure, only newsworthy because of Gus' murder, and still with no mention of what happened to Harry. Or nearly so, because the page was so blurred and faded that it was barely legible. The destination could have been Belgium, Berlin or Bologna for all the Pip could tell, but what stood out clearly was the 21st of September. What was the significance of that date? Pip rummaged her own diary out of her bag and flipped to the date to see what clue might be there. Ah, the autumn equinox! Pip did another quick online search and came up with eight key dates through the year. They were the old pagan Sabats she belatedly realised, remembering a fellow student who'd bored her silly with New Age rituals. Were they relevant to what Natalie was doing? She checked her papers again, glad she was at the end terminal, since by now she had papers all around her feet as well as on the computer desk. Yes! Paul had probably died on the first of August, otherwise known as Lughnasadh, and Natalie had surely disappeared at Halloween.

Was that it? Was the next time Natalie could pass through the 21st of September? Had she given that date so that no-one would notice if they weren't there after that? Or at least if *she* wasn't! She probably didn't give a damn about Amy's fate! And was the hurry because she was unwilling to hang on until Halloween? Her past, even in the nineteenth century, was catching up with her and she needed to cut her losses and run back to the present? Was that it?

Pip scrubbed her fingers through her hair, making her shock of brown curls stick up in all directions. It didn't matter whether she'd ever believed in such things in the past. Right now she was looking at possible evidence that somehow these dates were significant. As far as she could recall, the Roman pagan religions hadn't observed Sabats, but with all the nasty goings on with the cult of the Magna Mater at the spring, maybe the whole place had developed some kind of imprint for weirdness?

"You don't have to solve the 'how'," Pip told herself firmly as her head began to spin with all the implications. "Just accept that it happened regardless of how barmy it sounds. Come on girl, keep focused! If you can at least save Harry you've helped put some of Natalie's wrongs to right."

Forcing herself to write down just the salient points, Pip came up with some key questions she would try to get Harry to ask. If he could, he should object to the trial being brought forward, for a start. And then he must make the connection with the London lawyers seeking Natalie. That should throw her testimony into doubt. But what vexed her most was how he could reveal his true friendship with Gus Vaughan. Because Pip could see that if she told him to use the letters which she now had in her possession, the chances were that they would then not survive for her to find in the here and now.

And that frightened her. No, it more than frightened her, it terrified her! Because the danger then was, how would that impact on her own life now? Would she suddenly find herself doing something completely different? And would she even remember that there had been a strand of her life when she'd known about a man in the past called Harry Green? Would he be erased from her memory altogether?

Chapter 13

Modern day

Peddling her bike like a woman possessed, Pip tore down the country roads to Clifton and then round the twists and turns to Cold Hunger Farm. By her diary the full moon was tonight, and surely that had to count for something in this bizarre situation? Propping the bike out of sight in the old workshop, Pip hovered indecisively in the scullery. Should she try in the kitchen first? After all, that was where she'd first heard Harry's voice – and something purely at gut level still said it *was* Harry, however much her logical side was telling her there was no such certainty.

"Harry? ...Harry? ...Are you there?" she called out, feeling more than a little foolish speaking to thin air. There was no answer here in the kitchen, but had she been daft to even expect one? No, she had to try harder, her inner voice was urging her. Don't give up now!

"Think, girl, think!" she told herself furiously, as she pulled a can of Coke out of the shoulder bag she had slung across her body for ease while on the bike. Thirsty from the cycling she drank it quickly, then got hiccups. "Hic! Hic! ...Bugger!" she muttered, then hiccupped again. A right twit she was going to look trying to talk across time hiccupping like a mad thing! Then she caught sight of a faint reflection of herself in the window pane as she walked out of the kitchen, and winced. 'Mad thing' was right! Her unruly hair was all over the place, having been whipped by the breeze as she'd sped along. She really needed a mirror and the application of a good brush before she spoke to anyone!

Looking like that she'd put the frighteners even on a modern person if they came on her accidentally.

Of course! The mirror! How could she have missed that! That would be the place if anywhere where she would be able to make contact, and she hurried upstairs. The full-length mirror was still propped up in the bedroom, and Pip dragged her brush through her hair, calming the curls into something more presentable, thinking as she brushed. How had Natalie done it? The mirror had been on this bedroom side of the wall when they'd found it, and the wall to the other room sealed behind it. Yet after being here with Arthur and seeing the marks on the far wall, she was sure that originally it had been in the hidden room.

She went and looked harder at where the mirror had originally been located, and was gratified to see that once upon a time it must have rested on the board Arthur had taken a sample of. So the mirror had sat on a piece of that old Roman oak! That made a bit more sense. Then she looked up at the chimney breast to where the other mirror had been above the small mantelpiece. Of course! The forensic people had taken that away to look for proof of Dave's murder from blood traces, and maybe even some DNA from Natalie, but they hadn't bothered looking at the full-length mirror, because that hadn't been in the room at the time of the murder – or so they'd mistakenly thought! But it could have been right beside Dave when Natalie had actually done the deed!

"Was that how you did it?" Pip said out loud in her excitement. "Did you use Dave's blood to open the portal a second time? Is blood the thing that activates it?"

She turned round, looking at all of the lost room. It wasn't that big. But could Natalie have moved the mirror across it to the bedroom all by herself? Pip went out and tried to shift it. By dint of a bit of shoving she could move it more over the doorway from where she and Arthur had left it, but unless Natalie was a much bigger and stronger woman than she was, moving it across a room wouldn't be something she'd have done easily.

"How the bloody hell did you do it then?" Pip puzzled. Ah, but Natalie hadn't been alone! Dave had been with her. A still living Dave, and he'd been a pretty strong sort of bloke even if he'd not been obviously big and muscled. And Dave had been completely under Natalie's spell. Whatever she'd asked him to do he would have done almost without questioning, especially if she'd promised him something special afterwards as a reward – although Pip didn't want to dwell on what that might have been. The thought of what Dave and Natalie had done together had always made her feel a bit queasy.

So Natalie had no doubt made Dave help her manoeuvre the mirror so that it covered the doorway, but what then? Had she killed Dave, then sealed the room with her and him inside it and still managed to get through the portal?

"No you bloody fool of a girl!" Pip chastised herself. "How would she have plastered the wall if she'd done that, eh? When she sealed that room she, at least, had to be here in the bedroom."

It just wasn't possible any other way. Therefore that couldn't happen from behind, confirming that Natalie's exit from the modern age had happened in the bedroom, not the hidden room. So she, and maybe Dave, had at some point been here in the bedroom and facing the mirror out here. Yet all her own instincts said that the mirror had to be in contact with that bit of floor for the portal to be truly opened. In which case... Pip turned to stand in the doorway looking back and forth into the two rooms. How? How had Natalie done it?

She went and gave the mirror another shove, catching her finger on a splinter of wood on the doorway in the process.

"Ouch!"

She pulled the splinter out and her finger began to bleed, although not badly. Over the years Pip had suffered more than her share of thorn stabs from roses and other wickedly armoured plants, so she ignored it and grabbed hold of the mirror again only to get a shock. And it was a shock, as if she'd touched something electrical! A jolt which sent tingles up her left arm. She jumped backwards and looked at her hands. The splinter puncture was on her right hand which had been at the back of the mirror, but her left hand had been at the front, and looking at it now, she could see that her index finger and thumb had some of her blood on them from where she'd yanked the splinter out.

Almost fearfully she leaned round to look at the mirror's surface. It was still reflecting the window with the honeysuckle tendrils waving across the panes of glass, but there was a strange sparkling to it too.

"Bloody hell! That's it!" Pip gulped. Natalie must have done the initial activation while the mirror was still in its original place by using blood, then moved it. But whose blood? Okay, Dave had been a complete fool where Natalie was concerned, but Pip was sure he wasn't so besotted that he would have let her cut him up, then have helped her haul the mirror about. But what if Natalie had deliberately used her own blood? If just a smear of Pip's blood made the mirror go faintly sparkling, as if with the lightest dusting of glitter, then what would the effect have been like when it was in its proper place? And she mustn't forget poor Paul! He'd been cut so badly he died. So maybe Natalie regarded the mirror as already halfway to being open for herself by then?

Very carefully Pip squeezed her finger to get more blood out, and when she had a proper sized droplet, she smeared it down the edge of the mirror. The sparkling increased, but only down the side she'd smeared it on. Then she smelt it – tobacco! It hadn't been there before! So something was happening! But how to get the portal open more? Ideally she should get the mirror back to where it had been, but on her own that wasn't going to happen easily, and she was more than a bit worried that if she shifted it and then it fell, the mirror would smash and that would be the end of that. If only she could... that was it! If she couldn't get the mirror to the floor, why not lift the board and bring it to the mirror?

Racing down the stairs, she went to her bike's saddlebag where she'd put some tools, not knowing how securely the police might have shut up the house, and wanting to come prepared to force her way in through the rotten front door if necessary. The floorboard lifter was always a useful thing to have anyway – she'd even used it at the nursery to get some of the heavier plant pots unsealed from the ground when they'd bedded in too firmly. Now she took the stairs two at a time back to the bedroom with the short metal bar in her hand. In the hidden room she inserted the sharp, flat end under the end of the short stretch of ancient floor board and gently leaned on the curved end. To her relief it gave a little. She relaxed the pressure then heaved a little more firmly. The board shifted enough for her then to be able to get the claw end under the nail heads. In short order she had the two nails out of that end and was doing the same at the other end. From there it was an easy matter to lift the section of board out of where it sat.

"You're a troublesome little bastard!" Pip told it sternly. "Without you, Natalie would never have got anywhere and Dave might still be alive, not to mention what might still happen to poor Harry!"

She lugged it through to where the mirror sat and lined it up with the bottom of the frame. It wouldn't take much to lift the mirror up one end at a time until it sat on it again. Should she use the bar as a lever, or try to lift it without? Experimentally she slid the sharp end under the frame and managed to get the bar under the frame, lifting it by an inch at the corner. Quickly kicking the piece of floorboard under the corner, Pip half lifted and half levered until the bar was closer to midway along the length of the frame, and kicked the board more fully underneath. Now speed was of the essence before the strain of almost twisting the frame made the glass crack. Risking putting her back out, Pip heaved at the other end of the mirror and got it up enough to get the board completely under it. It wasn't central but it was stable, and she stood back and wiped the sweat from her face. Was it her imagination or was the room getting stiflingly hot?

She went to the window and put her hand on it. Although the sun was shining out there, a chill wind was blowing onto the farmhouse and the window was cold. Should she open the window and let some air in? Or was the heat she was feeling due to things beginning to work? She walked back to the mirror and tentatively touched its surface. "Wow!" The heat she felt made her gasp out loud. Not the kind of harsh heat from something like an electrical appliance, more like what she was used to feeling when working in the glasshouses at the nursery on a sunny day – diffused, but potent nonetheless.

Pip stepped back and thought. Was it worth trying to do more? She stepped forward to stand directly in front of the mirror. The smell of tobacco was still there, but clearer so that she could tell that it was more as if it was a smell which clung to someone's clothes rather than someone actually smoking. And there was another scent there too. Warm male! Not a repellent sweaty smell verging on acrid body odour, but the scent she associated with sharing digs with men who were working hard. A pleasant musky scent. Then she heard it – a man's voice! No, two men's voices! And if she wasn't mistaken it was the same two she had heard before!

That decided it. Pip had never had Dave's inclinations towards pain, but she grabbed her small pen knife and poked the splinter puncture hard with the point to make it bleed again. It was hardly a gushing flood, but squeezing her finger hard, she dragged it down the centre of the mirror and suddenly the whole thing shimmered. Nicking another finger in her desperation, Pip then dragged a bloody smear across the width of the mirror from the left to the centre, and then another from the right to the centre. Like clouds parting to let the sun through, the surface cleared and Pip found herself looking into the startled face of a tall, well-built man with sandy brown hair and green eyes, dressed in nineteenth century clothes. Beside him but looking out of the window was another man of about the same height but more of a dark blonde.

"Fucking hell" Pip heard the first man say, and the other respond,

"Harry!"

Hearing his name Pip almost cried with relief. She'd done it!

"Harry? Are you Captain Harry Green?" she called out, grabbing hold of the frame of the mirror in her excitement, then getting even more of a shock as her thumbs seemed to be pushing against a surface which felt more like stiff jelly than glass. It had a definite plasticity to it now, but there wasn't time to think about that now. "Arc you Harry?" she demanded more insistently.

The man stood up and Pip saw him swallowing reflectively, his face now white.

"Please don't go away!" she pleaded. "I have to tell you things! Have you just been accused of murder?"

She was aware that the second man now had his hands clasped in prayer and was reciting the Lord's Prayer. "And are you Robert Green? The rector? Because I'm not some demon or a ghost from the grave. I'm not going to hurt either of you!"

She was relieved that he paused in his praying, and the two of them were now watching her intently even if they both looked shaken beyond belief.

Taking a deep breath Pip began. "I'm a historian from a long time in the future. I know that sounds mad. It's a pretty crazy thing in my time too! But you must listen to me! There's a woman from my time who's come back to yours and she's dangerous. Very dangerous! Have you come across a Natalie Walker?" The way both of them jumped at the mention of the name was confirmation enough. "Well she's committed murder in my time." That really got their attention.

"Murder?" the man Pip presumed was Harry said, stepping forward.

"Yes, murder! She has some very odd ideas, and one of them was to come back to your time and get some money from someone, put it into a bank and then come back to my time to be a very rich woman on the interest. Whether that would ever work I don't know. But two men have been killed here in my world for her to get this portal thing I'm touching here to work." Then she forced herself to focus. "But that isn't the important thing."

Harry blinked. "It isn't?" It had suddenly dawned on him that this was the voice he'd heard before. The unknown and invisible woman who'd spoken to him in the kitchen on the night of the storm.

Pip was shaking her head, making her hair bounce around with unruly abandon. "No. Listen, there's some really important stuff I have to tell you, and I don't know how long this thing is going to be open for. So will you let me get those things out of the way, and then if there's any more time, I'll try to answer the questions you must be wanting to ask. Is that all right with you?"

"Errr... I suppose so," a baffled Harry replied, while Robert stood transfixed but hanging on to his silver crucifix like a drowning man.

Pip took a deep breath. "Right. Well the first thing is, I've seen a transcription of your trial, Harry, and they're going to try and bring it forwards. That's Amy Clifford's lawyers. I don't know who suggests it – whether it's Natalie and Amy, or whether it's the lawyer – but another trial gets thrown out and they bring your trial forward into the place the court has vacant. You *must not* let them do that!"

"Why not?" Robert asked, his voice shaky. "I'd have thought the sooner the better! Get it over with!"

"No!" Pip all but yelped. "No! Because if you think this is going to get thrown out as the farce it seems, you're so very wrong! Unless Harry gets chance to make a proper defence he's going to hang!" That was stretching it a bit given that she hadn't seen an actual sentence, but she had to make them take her seriously.

Poor Harry had gone white. "Hang? Truly? You mean the judge really believes I would do such a thing to Gus?"

Pip grimaced. "By the time Natalie and Amy have finished with their performances on the witness stand you'll be lucky to walk out of that court room without a mob baying for your blood! I'm not kidding ...errr, joking!" God, but she must remember to try and avoid modern jargon they wouldn't understand! "Those two could go on the stage with the complete story they're going to weave around you. So you mustn't let them start off with the upper hand! You *must* get yourself a good lawyer and make sure he stands his ground and keeps to the original trial date.

"Now when you've done that, there's some key evidence you *must* present. I don't know why, but in the version I've read, you never get to mention what your own financial situation is. Is there a good reason why you wouldn't?"

"No," Harry replied, puzzled. "In fact I've written to my bank in London already. Actually, I'm rather surprised that I haven't heard back from them yet."

Pip groaned. "Then you must go to London and see them in person!"

"I can't. If I leave the county then I'll be re-arrested and spend the remaining time until the trial in either Worcester or Hereford gaol."

"Shit!" Pip's language made both men blink, but she wasn't aware of their reaction because she was thinking furiously. "Then you must go, Robert!"

"Me?"

"Yes you! There's no restriction on you travelling is there?"

"Well none aside from my parish."

"And who's more important to you – your parish or your brother?"

That startled Robert. He looked from Harry to Pip and back again, then took a deep breath. "My brother!"

Pip gave a sigh of thanks. She'd feared this rector would be too in awe of his bishop or the rest of his church colleagues to take any risks. "Then tomorrow you travel with all haste to London and speak to Harry's bankers. You'll need sworn statements as to the true state of his finances and – and this is really important Robert, so take note – how long he's been in this state! Harry, I don't know if you're a pauper or a prince, but if you've been broke for years you have a case for saying nothing's changed, so why would you want Gus Vaughan's money now? And if you have cash and have had it for years, again you can argue why the sudden need now? If your financial situation has suddenly changed for the worse..."

"It hasn't."

"Thank God for that!"

Harry was quite touched by her obvious relief and the way that she'd not asked him to clarify how much money he did have. Maybe she did have his best interests at heart. He was even more convinced when she continued,

"And while you're there, Robert, you need to find these people." She dug in a pocket and produced a piece of paper which she pressed against the mirror. "The names are Hodgkins and Barlow at Grey's Inn. They're lawyers and they're trying to find Natalie. I found an advert in the local Worcester newspaper which appeared *after* your trial – that's the trial which gets brought forward – and these lawyers are acting for the family of the man Natalie is supposed to have married. He was a banker. A Mr Horatio Parsons."

"No!" Harry had gone even whiter and grabbed Robert as the room swam. "He's my banker!"

"Fuck me!" Pip swore, making both Harry and Robert exclaim,

"Pardon?" in surprise at a woman using such language.

She caught on to what they meant and waved their objections aside with an irritated hand. "Never mind my language! It's normal in my time! But wake up you two! This could be the missing link! If Natalie somehow knew who your banker was she's really tied you up in knots."

"Damn!" Harry gasped as understanding overtook him. "Amy! Amy would have known who I banked with because of the money I sent to her, via them, while I was abroad. And by chance it was the same bank Gus used. We never purposely set it up that way, or I don't think so. Maybe when Gus was getting his finances straight when he came back from India he chose my bank for simplicity. I don't know. We were both paying out for Amy and young Edward, you see."

"Oh and that brings me to another thing!" Pip added urgently. "You're in Gus' will, Harry. Apparently he left you in charge of his finances in the event of him dying first, because he trusted you to look after Amy."

"Did he? Good God!"

"Yes he did! And the prosecution are going to make a meal of that, because they're going to use it as a motive for you killing him. You get full control of all his money, you see."

Robert gasped. "That's what the magistrate's men meant when they said you'd fallen out with him over money! No wonder we couldn't work out what they meant! We were thinking of things like them assuming Harry was asking Gus for the money back which he'd spent over the years on the Vaughan family, but it wasn't that at all, was it?"

Pip shook her head. "No it wasn't. It's much bigger than that. It's all of Gus' inheritance and his estate, and I'm guessing that that's a much bigger amount of money."

Harry wiped a hand over his face. "Lord, I suppose it is! But do you know, I never asked him how much. It wasn't the sort of thing I felt I could ask. We just had this gentleman's understanding that we were spreading the costs of keeping Amy, and that if we both said we could afford to do it, then that was enough."

"Well it's not enough now!" Pip told him firmly. "Robert, you've *got* to get down to London and speak to whoever is running the bank now that Horatio Parsons is dead! Do whatever it takes to get them to swear to the courts up here as to the state of affairs with both Harry *and* Gus. But the other thing you *must* do is find out who Gus made his will with – the lawyer – and get a date for when he actually made Harry into the guardian of Amy and Edward. Because the longer ago that was, the less motive they can ascribe to you now, if you see what I mean."

Harry nodded, coming to stand right close to the mirror and look Pip in the eyes. "If it was ages ago, I had more financial need of that money then than ever I do now."

"Precisely! Why would you wait? And I have a strange feeling that he might have done that a lot longer ago than you suspect. I've read some of his letters to you, Harry – they were in an archive – and it's blindingly clear that he trusted you and always did. Maybe even enough to start using your bank in preference to another!"

Harry shook his head. "Poor old Parsons. He was a nice old chap. However did that damned Walker woman get her claws into him?"

Pip sighed. "I'm not sure exactly, but I suspect that he was ill, went abroad to recover, and she pounced on him. It might even have been that she worked her way into his household before that, but the people who will tell you that are his family. They're hot on the heels of her for stuff she stole from his house!"

"Good God! What a fool I've been!" Harry gasped. "When I came back here after the ship went down, Gus himself told me that while he and Amy were still in Bath, a lawyer's man came looking for Miss Walker, or whatever her name really is. He said that along with what I'd told him, it put him right off her!"

"Did he speak to that lawyer's man? In person? Face to face?"

"Yes. Yes he did."

Pip punched the air with one hand and the image in the mirror wobbled, making her grab it hard again before the triumphant "Yes!" had barely left her lips. "Then you get that man up here too! Get him to agree to testify to that. Offer to pay his expenses if necessary! He's the proof you need to show that Gus was already set against Natalie without you."

"Oh he was fully aware of what she was," Harry agreed. "That's what shocked me so much when I had the first hearing, and they told me that she was acting as though he'd proposed to her. I knew he hadn't and never would!"

"Then the more people you can find who can testify to that the better," Pip told him firmly. "The newspapers reporting on the trial are going to say – or at least the ones I read – that he was intending to work in the north. Could you write to his future employer and ask if he was intending to bring a wife with him?"

Harry's eyes had lost the glassy look of shock and were now sharp and alert. "Oh yes, I can do that! And I know that he was intending to stay in a room because he gave me the address. He actually said that it was a house for single gentlemen, because then he had the perfect excuse for not having Amy up to visit! I shall write to the owners of the house straight away!"

"Great! Oh and another thing! Natalie's intention has always been to put whatever money she can get her hands on into a bank which will survive into our own time. Now I can tell you that, unless she's got a whole lot better informed about banks in London, the one she will have chosen is Lloyds in Birmingham, and the more I've thought about it, the more I'm sure she will have used the head office, even if by now they have other branches. So once you've got yourself that lawyer, get him to start talking to Lloyds, because I'd bet a pound to a penny that Natalie will have opened an account with them, and she'll have been putting money into it as she's got hold of it. In fact, Robert, you might want to pass that fact on to the Parsons family. As bankers themselves they're ideally placed to get hold of the information both for you *and* them – because I'd bet some of old Mr Parsons' funds have ended up there too!"

Harry pulled himself upright, and suddenly Pip could see the gallant captain. Great! If her words had fired him up to fight this battle, all to the good!

"This knocked you sideways, didn't it?" she said sympathetically. "Of all the things to happen, you never expected Amy to make an accusation like this against you."

"No," Harry said, but with more of a hint of anger in his voice now. "No I damned well didn't – beg your pardon, miss!"

Pip grinned. "Don't worry. I'm more robust than that. I've spent many a summer digging in trenches with a bunch of lads. A bit of strong language is nothing."

"Digging? In trenches?" Robert spluttered, also coming forward into the dressing room. "Good Lord, what sort of woman are you?"

And suddenly Pip was very conscious of the way they were looking her up and down, and that a pair of battered combat trousers and a sleeveless summer T-shirt wasn't quite the kind of ladies' dress they would be used to seeing. "I'm a..." How to explain in a way they'd understand? "I'm an antiquarian," she said firmly, using the term by which anyone doing archaeological excavations at that time would have been known as. "That's how I got involved with this whole thing. Some Roman remains have come to light in this area, and I was working with some other antiquarians to try and see if there was any kind of Roman building here. Then we found a body," she found herself faltering at that.

"My dear lady, how awful for you!" Harry said with genuine sympathy.

Pip managed a watery attempt at a smile. "Yes it was awful, because you see, it was the body of a man whom I'd been previously engaged to."

"Heavens!" Robert gasped, quite unable to think of what else to say. However Harry was less easily shaken now,

"Ah, so that's why you took such an interest?" He was also somewhat in awe of the strength of character of this young woman if she could seemingly cope with such a revelation. For all that Robert regularly came into contact with death, he wasn't as used to what sudden death could mean the way Harry did, and murder was pretty sudden and often exceedingly messy. Quite how Amy would be at this moment in time, he didn't know and found he no longer cared to know, but he was absolutely certain that she would never stand as calmly as this young woman before him.

"Yes," Pip was saying sadly, leaning against the mirror so that her forehead was touching the slightly spongy surface. "It was all Natalie's doing. She'd known him before I did, and somehow she never really let go. Then she disappeared. Soon after that I saw Dave for the last time, and somehow I always thought he'd just left because he couldn't face me to tell me the truth – the truth being in my mind, at that time, that he still loved Natalie. So it was an awful shock to discover a body here in this room and then be told it was him."

"You didn't recognise him?" Harry's question was gently put, but he sounded a little surprised.

Pip wrinkled her nose. "Let's just say he was a bit ripe! He'd been walled up in here for four years. It was someone who knew us both who recognised a ring he wore and a very distinctive jacket."

"Good God!" Harry was even more surprised. She could speak of the realities of such a discovery with such calm, and yet he knew just what an old corpse would be like, and what she meant by ripe. "And you believe that Miss Walker actually killed him herself? With her own hands?"

Pip straightened up and looked him squarely in the eyes. "Yes I do. And I also have very good reason to believe that she killed another of her lovers, a young man by the name of Paul, and there's a connection between him and your family. Do you remember your father discovering a body out here in 1810?"

Harry shook his head, saying, "No, but by then I was already serving abroad."

But Robert's eyes went wide at the prompting. "Oh dear Lord! Yes! That poor soul! Father was quite distraught at finding him. When he went into the house with the squire, they found the trail of blood from where he'd dragged himself down the stairs." Then Robert went a strange colour, rushed to the bedroom's open window and gagged noisily.

Harry hurried to his side. "Robert? What is it?"

Robert straightened up and turned to sit on the sill where Harry had sat not so long ago. "In the dirt," he said, his voice a strained croak. "In the dirt beside the body was written 'Nat'. Everyone believed it was a last attempt to name his murderer, but it wasn't Nat as in Nathaniel, was it? It was Natalie!"

"Robert?" Pip called. "Was there ever an official transcription of this? A coroner's verdict, maybe?"

Robert looked blank for a second, then seemed to understand what Pip was asking. "Yes, of course there was. The coroner in Worcester had all the details written down, but with no suspect around it's probably just gathering dust in his office now."

"But how long after *that* did Natalie appear?" Pip pressed them. "You were surprised at seeing her at the wedding, weren't you, Harry! So what about other guests? People who are still alive and might remember the sudden and *unexplained* appearance of a young woman like her? You and Edward were only back from the fighting for a short while, but the majority of those who went to the wedding would have been locals, surely?"

Harry turned to her, his eyes bright and eager. "Yes they were!"

"And how was Natalie introduced to everyone? A young woman like that and on her own, how did she meet Amy? Mr and Mrs Vaughan were surely not such simple souls as to not want to know who their daughter was associating with?"

"No, not then they weren't," Harry agreed forcefully, "and Mrs Vaughan was always capable, even after the old man had fallen into despair. And do you know, I think I know the very man to ask!"

"Who?" Pip and Robert asked in unison.

"Our uncle. Uncle William! He might be an old man now, but I bet he still knows everyone who is of any consequence in Worcester! And he was there at the wedding, because in those days the Vaughans were still part of Worcester society. If anyone knows where Miss Walker came from, he will!"

"Excellent!" Pip enthused. "And when you find that she was known to no-one at all until she miraculously appeared by Amy's side, you have a case to put forward for her killing Paul on the basis that she didn't want anyone to know who she really was."

Harry frowned. "But how do we present this? You see, we have your word for this, and we can check the facts. But it's quite a leap from there to be able to convince a court that this wretched woman has murdered already."

Pip thought for a moment, then said, "I don't think you need to worry too much about making a watertight case against *her*. She's not the one on trial, after all, you are! So what you're aiming to do is make her testimony so suspect that the judge and jury start really questioning all of the evidence against *you*. And the murder you really want her to be brought to account for is Gus'! So your defence is a two-pronged attack. You need to prove that you had no motive and that she did, and then you also need to prove that you weren't able to be in Hereford at the time of the murder and she was. You see, I think what hangs you Harry is the fact that you don't defend yourself properly, and that there's no other suspect in sight. I don't even have to meet Amy to know that no-one in their right mind would think she could do it. But Natalie's a very different kind of woman, and you need to get the court to see that, and that she's perfectly capable of manipulating Amy.

"Oh, and you should check on something else too! In the paper – the newspaper I mean – they said that immediately after the trial, Natalie put it about that she and Amy were going travelling in Europe. I couldn't quite read the name of where they were going, but I'm pretty certain it began with a 'B'. Well you two will know better than me how easy it is for two women to pack their bags and go travelling in your time. Two women alone, remember!

Would you expect them to have made reservations fairly soon? Would they have to make some kind of special arrangements? In other words, is that real or just an excuse to get the trial moved?

"Because for all the public declarations of intent to travel, I don't think Natalie is going anywhere except here to this mirror, and back to my time! So anything you can think of which will prove to the court that this is merely her trying to manipulate *them* for her own ends will help. You see, I think Natalie will make some kind of case to the court about wanting to get Amy away from the town where she had suffered such a tragic loss, or some such guff. I'm convinced she does that so that Amy doesn't see that Natalie has taken over her finances so thoroughly that she's left with nothing!"

That made Harry and Robert gasp in shock.

"Oh yes! Natalie won't leave Amy a penny if she has her way! Also I'm positive this fairy-tale she wove to get the trial brought forward, when the chance presented itself, was to make sure you never found your feet and told the truth about her. She's worried by you, Harry! You actually frighten her, I think. She knows *you* know what she is – or at least in terms of how your society sees predatory women – and that she cannot let a hint of scandal creep into the court. So she has to keep the pressure on you so *you* never turn the tables on *her*, and like I said, you mustn't let her do that! Stand your ground, Harry, and argue that, with such serious accusations against you, you should have time to prepare a proper defence!"

"I will!" he said firmly, and by the look on his face Pip believed him. Then he suddenly smiled. "And you've made me think of something else!"

"What?" Pip and Robert demanded.

"Well, I would never have used this until now – would never have wanted to act so dishonourably, as I would have thought – but I think I can now bring up the matter of the Vaughan's finances. You see, old Mr Vaughan died near penniless, and for years I think most of Worcester society knew he was being supported by someone else. Until now, for Amy's sake and that of young Edward, I would have been awfully reticent to bring up in court just how poor they were – especially a court in Worcester! But you've made me see that in a very different light. Because the jury will be of local men of the city, won't it?"

Pip grinned and finished for him, "And they'll know about the Vaughans! You just have to remind them!"

Harry nodded purposefully. "Yes I do. I have to think of this in a very different way, don't I? I've been foolishly still thinking it would be wrong to drag Amy's name through the court. But she's my main accuser, so I have no choice, do I?"

Beside him Robert sighed. "No Harry, you don't. This young lady is right – if it's drag the Vaughans' history back up into the public gaze, or you being found guilty, then you have to do it to save yourself."

Pip watched as Harry walked back towards her and saw him sway slightly. "Harry? Are you not well?" she asked urgently.

"He's still not right after the shipwreck," Robert answered for him. "He won't admit it, but it's knocked him about something shocking. The magistrates were even saying he might have walked to Hereford, since they can't find evidence that he hired a horse. Walk to Hereford? He struggles to walk into Clifton!"

"Then bloody well tell them that!" Pip exclaimed in exasperation. "Christ, Harry! This is no time to stand on your pride! If you aren't well, then find a good doctor who'll examine you and testify that you couldn't have done that!"

"Our local doctor has been treating him," Robert said tentatively.

But Pip shook her head vehemently. "Not good enough! That gives them the opportunity to say that as the local professional men, you Robert, and him might be in league with one another to clear Harry. Friend of the family, and bollocks like that. Get someone important from Worcester to examine you and give evidence. Someone the court knows to be above reproach and who is unconnected to you."

She racked her brain for what other evidence might stand up in court. Years of watching *CSI* on TV had to count for something at this moment! Motive – she'd covered that. Opportunity – not brilliant, but if Robert got his finger out there might be a chance to scupper that properly. Shit! She'd forgotten M.O.!

"Crap, I nearly forgot! How was Gus killed? Precisely?"

Robert blanched at her language as Harry asked, "What does that matter?"

Pip rolled her eyes in exasperation, then remembered that she was talking to men who wouldn't know what a *modus operandi* was. "Sorry! I was thinking about stuff we know in my time. But seriously, it matters, because, you see, people who kill tend to use the same methods if they kill again. So, you're a soldier, Harry. How would you kill a man? I mean not in battle. Here. What weapon would you use? Could you kill with your bare hands?"

Harry shook his head. "Not like this I couldn't. At the moment I could just about scrag a chicken – no more!"

"But when you are well? And what about now? What would you use?"

Harry blinked but didn't have to think hard. "A carving knife, I suppose. I'd use it like a bayonet. I've had some experience of that when I was a lieutenant. We'd fire our rifles until the enemy got too close, and then fix a bayonet on the end of it and use that. But for preference I'd use a sword. I know what I'm doing with a sword."

"And how quickly could you kill with that?" Pip pressed him. "One cut? Several?"

"Oh, one! Especially a soft man like Gus who wouldn't fight back."

Robert went white. "Harry! For God's sake! How can you talk like that? He was your friend!"

But Pip wasn't going to let Robert upset the train of thought. "Don't be naïve, Robert!" she said sternly. "You and I know that Harry didn't kill Gus. But the twelve men who are going to try him are going to look at him and see a soldier, and to them that may well mean a killer too! So burying your heads in the sand and being precious over the specific way Gus was killed will get you nowhere. You have to put yourself in the place of people who don't know Harry's character and think of the questions they'll ask. So, Harry ...did Gus die from a single blow of the kind you would deliver?"

"No," Harry said sadly, "he died from many stab wounds."

"But could you have made that one killing cut even in your present condition?" Pip demanded.

Harry exhaled heavily. "Yes, I suppose if I'd wanted to I could."

Pip threw her hands in the air, "There you are then!" Then grabbed the mirror quickly again as Harry and Robert briefly blinked out of sight. "What you need to ask the judge and jury to consider is – why would you deliver multiple stab wounds when you could have finished the job in one go? Because if the first stab didn't kill Gus, then he must have been screaming like mad! Why would you risk that and have him potentially get help from one of the other men where he lived? He wasn't killed in some isolated country lane! He was in the middle of the bloody town in a shared house!"

"They said I must have knocked him out," Harry told her, his shoulders sagging dejectedly at the memory of his questioning.

Pip tossed her curls. "Oh rubbish! If you did that then there should be some bruising to show for it! A big man like you wouldn't just tap him! If you hit him hard enough to floor him it will be there on his body for all to see. And again, why would you stab him so many times if you'd already disabled him? You know the vulnerable spots. You could have despatched him with one thrust. And if they're making such a performance of you trekking all the way to Hereford and back, why wouldn't you kill the fastest way so that you had even more time to get back?"

Then she had another thought. "But if a woman did it, then maybe she wouldn't know where to put the knife for maximum effect? Or maybe she wouldn't have the strength? Think! If Natalie did this – and I for one don't doubt for a second that she is the killer – then how would she disable Gus? Did she whack him over the head with something from behind? Was he the kind of man who would stop thinking if she started to take her clothes off? Stop dithering and try to work out how she did it! Because if you know how the bitch killed him, then you can show that *you* wouldn't have done it *that way*, Harry. And on its own that's not much, but if you get the evidence from the bankers, and a doctor's report, and you can dig some dirt on Natalie and show that she had far more motive than you, then you're in with a far better chance of clearing your name."

Then the mirror wavered again and this time it didn't settle so easily. "Oh damn, I think we're running out of time!" Pip fretted.

"What's your name?" Harry asked urgently. "Who are you?"

"My name's Pip."

"Pip?"

"Yes, short for Philippa." Then a thought came to her. "In fact, if you want to really shake Natalie in court, tell her Philippa Devenish, the fiancée of David Marston, sends her regards. Remember our names!"

"Philippa Devenish and David Marston," Harry repeated, and Pip also saw Robert mouthing the names. "You think it will?"

"Oh yes!" Pip called as the image before her began to fade. "It will because it will tell her that someone is hunting her through the portal, and she's *never* expected *that*!"

Chapter 14

July 1824

As the woman in the mirror faded away, Harry called to her, "Will I hear from you again?" and got a faint,

"I don't know!" in return. "The first of August!" she seemed to be screaming at him, yet her voice was fading fast, and the 't' of 'August' was lost.

"Dear Lord Above!" Robert whispered hoarsely, looking from Harry to the mirror and back again. "Did we imagine that?" He went and tapped on the mirror and got the normal sound from the glass. "That defies all sanity!"

Harry drew in a deep breath. "Well for a ghost she was talking a lot of sense."

"You think so?"

"Well don't you?" Harry noticed how pale Robert was, and belatedly realised that this was testing his brother's already wavering faith to near breaking point. Female apparitions dressed in the most scandalous clothing were pretty far removed from his own experience too, but somehow he totally believed in her.

He took Robert by the arm, guided him to the bed and forced him to sit down, then went to the dressing table where he'd taken to keeping a small flask of brandy, and poured some into the glass which was upturned over the flask. Taking it to Robert, he thrust it into his brother's trembling hand.

"Drink that, Robert," he said gently, then sat down on the bed beside him. "Do you know what convinces me? It's the things she told us which we didn't know. No doubt we'd have eventually made the connection between Horatio Parsons and the fact that Natalie Walker has become Natalie Parsons. But Parsons is a common enough surname, and by the time we made the link it could have been far too late. Far too late for me at any rate. And how will you feel if we don't act on her suggestions and then it turns out that she was right? If you have to watch me walking to the gallows, knowing that if we'd listened I'd have been able to prove my innocence?"

Robert raised horrified eyes to meet Harry's. "You think she might be right about that?" He was surprised to see the steely gaze coming back at him.

"Let's just say I don't want to take the risk," Harry told him bitterly. "God damn Amy!"

"Oh Harry!"

"Don't 'oh Harry' me, Robert. It's how I feel, and I'm all the more angry for knowing that my kindly ghost was right about me too. I've still been trying to make excuses for Amy, even after what she's done. I've been trying to convince myself that she'll wake up and realise just how serious her accusations are. Can't you see? I've been pinning far too much of my hopes for getting off on her coming to her senses and telling the magistrates that she made a mistake. That she was distraught at Gus' death and lashed out without thinking." He scrubbed his fingers through his hair and sighed regretfully. "But she's not going to, Robert. If she was ever going to make such a move she would have done it by now, because surely *someone* is saying to her that I've been hauled up in front of the magistrates? She must know I stand accused! So if she cared a jot for what happens to me she would have done something to help by now."

"Oh Lord. Maybe she feels a fool?" Robert said hopefully, but Harry shook his head.

"To use Miss Pip's words, Robert, 'not good enough'. Amy can feel all the fools in creation, but that won't help me unless she acts. And if she won't act for fear of how she'll look to her neighbours, then it makes no more difference than her actively thinking me guilty. Her thoughts won't free me! She needs to speak up. So Miss Pip is right, I have to stop considering Amy and her bloody tender feelings, and start fighting this as if it was a battle. And I'll tell you something else Miss Pip was right about – why isn't Amy wanting to know who really killed her brother? Do you see what she meant, Robert? If it was me lying dead in that room in Hereford and you in Amy's position, if you had the slightest doubts that the person you'd fingered for the murder wasn't really the one, then wouldn't you be wanting to know who else was potentially guilty? Wouldn't you be making loud noises in public demanding further enquiries? And God knows Amy can be loud enough at complaining!"

"Oh Lord," Robert sighed as understanding crept in.

"Oh Lord, indeed," Harry said dryly. "You see now, don't you? Amy must really think me guilty, despite all the years of knowing me. It's the only way her actions make *any* kind of sense. And neither you nor I saw that, but Miss Pip did. So Miss Pip can't be a figment of our minds if she can argue for things we'd never even thought of."

"Oh Lord."

"Christ, Robert, can't you think of anything else to say? You're starting to sound like Captain Gibbon's pet parrot!"

Stung by that, Robert's head snapped up and turned to Harry to verbally tear into him for his blasphemous attitude. Yet the sun was on Harry's face and Robert realised how taut he looked, how very worried, and maybe a little scared too. Then Harry's next words made him feel ashamed.

"Will you go to London, Robert? Will you go to Horatio Parsons' family for me? Go and get the evidence which might clear my name? Because if you won't – if you're going to retreat into your faith and dismiss what we've heard here this afternoon – then I'm going to have to break my word and try to get there myself."

"Harry, no!"

Harry just raised his eyebrows.

"No, Harry, you can't be serious?"

"Can't I? What else am I to do? Sit here in this damned farmhouse and wait for the hangman to come and measure me for the drop?"

"Don't say that!"

"Why not? I've faced death a hundred times over on foreign battlefields, but I tell you, only that night on board the *Kent* comes near to scaring me as much as this prospect does. I don't know that I can walk to the scaffold with the calm that a captain of my experience ought to face certain death with. It would be bloody awful to face it knowing I'd done something stupid and earned the sentence. But I'm not sure I can go quietly knowing I'm completely innocent."

His words had tears flowing down Robert's cheeks unchecked. He'd not been able to fully face the ultimate consequence of Harry failing to clear his name until this moment, and now it shamed him to know that this must have been at the back of Harry's mind right from the time he'd first been arrested, even if he'd also hoped it might not happen. That his younger brother had never spoken of it until now only served to highlight his courage in such adversity.

"Of course I'll go," Robert sniffed, fishing a handkerchief out of his pocket to blow his nose. If Harry could face the prospect of the hangman without coming apart, then how could he not help him? "I'll send a letter to the bishop and ask for someone to come and take the services for me in my absence. Actually, I can take it as far as Worcester myself when I catch the London coach there tomorrow. I'll ask Tom Howie to take me to the city in his trap first thing."

Harry's face relaxed a little. "Thank you!" Then his nose wrinkled as Robert reached into a pocket and produced a cigar, which he lit and then drew on deeply.

"You don't like cigars?" Robert wondered. He'd thought all army officers smoked. That's what his friend Dr Morton had told him, but then he'd never seen Harry with one now that he thought about it.

"No, not particularly."

"Have you not tried them?" That seemed unlikely.

Harry gave him a watery smile. "Oh I tried them once or twice, but I didn't like them, and having to live on my wages rather than some allowance from a rich father, they were an expense I could do without. Then when we were hunting the French the one time, we found a small group of them because of the smell of the tobacco two of the officers were smoking. After that I decided I never wanted to be shot by some French skirmisher for the same reason!"

"Oh!"

"Now the smell of cigars reminds me of Gus – he always smoked even though I don't think he liked them much. I think he thought they made him look more manly."

Robert looked at the cigar he'd just taken out of his mouth and then knocked it out on the tin from his pocket. Suddenly it had lost all of its appeal.

They sat in silence for a few minutes, each deep in their own thoughts until Robert asked, "Do you really think this

Natalie woman could have killed him?"

Harry eased himself up off the bed and went to lean out of the window. The late summer sun was bathing the back of the farmhouse in soft golden light and the honeysuckle's scent was heady on the warm breeze. Instead of answering he asked a question of his own. "Do you think there's something about this house that brings misfortune on those who live here?" He was thinking of poor Mr and Mrs Vaughan, and then of Gus and himself, and so wasn't expecting to hear a howl of anguish from behind him.

"Robert?" He turned and just missed Robert lurching past him to heave up over the window sill again. "Christ, Robert, whatever's wrong?" he asked worriedly as he put a supporting arm under his brother's shoulders to stop him toppling over.

When Robert could straighten up he leaned weakly against the window frame croaking, "God forgive me. God forgive me for being such a fool!"

Harry went to the wash stand and brought the glass with some water in it for Robert to wash his mouth out with, then stood back with his arms folded, watching gravely.

"Oh Harry, I could have said something earlier if only I'd made the connection."

"Like what?"

Robert passed a shaky hand over his face. "What that woman in the mirror said about killers using the same methods? I should have noticed the similarity long ago! I should have said something when they first took you to Hereford. The young man she mentioned, the one Father found, he was stabbed to death."

Harry straightened up and met Robert's gaze keenly. "Stabbed? Yes, Miss Pip said that too. Go on!"

Robert had to blow his nose again and wipe his eyes in his distress before he could answer. "That's what shook Father so much. It wasn't just finding the poor man. I remember him saying to me that it was the way it looked like such a frenzied attack. The way someone had stabbed him over and over. 'Too many times to count' was the way Father put it. And yet they weren't deep enough to kill him outright. Father had nightmares even years afterwards, because he said he couldn't get it out of his mind that the poor soul had crawled in agony down the stairs to try and find help, only to die outside when he'd failed.

"I knew all of this Harry, and yet I never made the connection that Gus died in *exactly* the same way! I heard the magistrates talking before they brought you in. A frenzied attack is precisely what they called it, too. The act of someone who truly hated him, or wasn't in their right mind, is what they said. Poor Gus had over twenty stab wounds in him!"

Harry blanched. He'd not thought it would be that many. Over twenty was torture, not killing!

"If the same person committed both murders," Robert was continuing, "then that person can't be you, because you were far away fighting in Spain when the first man died. And there was the 'Nat' he wrote in the soil – I didn't see how that would help you with the killing of Gus when that woman said it, but I do now. The woman in the mirror was right – it helps you, because you weren't here the first time, and along with the number of stab wounds, it makes it look more like her than you! They were all shallow wounds. As though the person making them didn't quite have the strength to make them deeper. That's unbelievable for you, Harry. She was right, even weakened you wouldn't need to hack at the poor soul like that."

Harry felt the first glimmer of hope he'd had since this nightmare had begun. "Right, Robert, then before you go to London we need to find a lawyer in Worcester and you need to tell him this! He can then be getting the details of the old murder and of Gus' will while you're away. I think Miss Pip has given us a much needed kick in the breeches, don't you? I'm damned if I'm going down without a fight now! You go and speak to the Parsons, and I'll go to Uncle William and get him to start chasing his associates. Someone in Worcester must remember Amy and Edward's wedding and Amy's strange friend."

Robert managed a wan smile. He'd feared that Harry might become angry with him for not having made the link sooner – and he wouldn't have blamed him if he had. Thank God, he hadn't, though, and some of Harry's resolve was rubbing off on him too. "And one other thing."

"What?"

"I think maybe that woman was right about something else. When you're talking to Uncle William – if he'll see you, of course, and he may not – get him to recommend a good doctor! No, don't pull a face over that, Harry. You look terrible! Well if you can be reconciled to not protecting Amy, you can also resign yourself to admitting how ill you've been. There's no shame in it. Indeed, I thought that you were picking up until this happened, but since the news came you're looking more and more like the sick man of a month ago. So if Amy's accusations have made you ill again, and that can help you to overthrow this miscarriage of justice, then you must use it too, brother."

Harry winced, but then grudgingly nodded.

"So you *will* ask Uncle William for a doctor?"

"I suppose so."

"No, promise me you will!"

"Very well," Harry sighed, "I'll ask him."

"Will you stay here tonight?" Robert wondered. Even if the ungodly woman had been the strangest answer to his prayers he'd ever known – the means to helping Harry help himself – nothing on God's green earth would have made him spend the night here now. "You can have your old room at the rectory for as long as you want, you know that."

However, Harry shook his head with a smile. "Thank you, but no. I'm not worried by my friendly ghost. If the owners want me out, then I shall have to take up your offer, but luckily they're still down in Bath for the season at the moment and probably haven't heard the news, so I have a month's grace."

"But you won't sleep in this room, surely? Shall I help you move the bed through to one of the end bedrooms?"

"No thank you," Harry said cheerfully. "I shall be quite happy here." Robert's expression was comical to behold. Clearly he'd be anything but happy at the prospect, but Harry found himself wanting to be near the mirror just in case. He didn't think Pip would reappear again soon. The first of August was still a week away, yet there'd been something about her which had him already wanting to speak to her again. Being here in this room with the mirror just a few yards away in the dressing room made him feel somehow closer to her.

A very reluctant Robert finally left him with the promise that they would meet again first thing in the morning. By the time morning arrived the whole of the area was coated in soft drizzle, although to Harry it felt as though the sun should be blazing down on them to match his mood. This was the first morning he'd woken feeling optimistic that he might avoid the fate of the noose, and he could somehow face the prospect of a time in gaol as long as one day he would be free again – if such a lesser sentence was possible. To just be free of the label 'murderer' would be something, even if he was branded a predator to young women. If that happened he would pack his bags and leave on the next ship for India the moment he got a chance, but he had to have a measure of freedom for that to be an option. He'd left a message wedged into the frame of the mirror, the writing pressed to the glass just in case Pip appeared again, to say that he would be in Worcester for a couple of days, and now he was eager to be up and acting. Too much time had been wasted already, and he wasn't about to let more days slip by.

It was too early for Robert to call on the bishop when Tom the carter first dropped them off in Worcester, so they walked along the High Street looking for lawyer's offices. Harry was now insistent that they find someone who looked as though they were prospering through their trade, and they found two whom they thought might do, although they weren't open yet. He was also lingering because even more than the earliness of the hour for calling on family, he wanted to see his brother after he'd made the request to the bishop for time away from his parish. He didn't want to doubt Robert, but he feared that the bishop might talk his brother round to thinking there was little to be done, and that a trip to London would just be a waste of time.

It saddened him to realise that had it been his father he'd been relying on now, nothing at all would have happened. His father's world had condensed to such an extent that even the prospect of stepping outside of it would have distressed him to the point of paralysis, never mind that his son's life might depend on it. If his mother had been alive it would have been very different. For all that she'd looked the pretty, meek wife, she'd had the instincts of a mother tiger when it came to her sons. She would have gone to the very gates of Hell and beyond to save someone she loved, and these days, Harry realised if he was very much his mother's son, he also sadly recognised that Robert was getting more and more like their father.

Therefore he arranged to meet with Robert once more before he caught the London coach, and once he'd seen him heading in through the gates to the bishop's palace, Harry walked briskly round to the other side of the magnificent cathedral to the close where his uncle lived. No doubt the family would soon be moving to one of the grand new houses being built further out along the Tything, if the family factories were still doing well. Robert had told him that there were some spectacular villas going up on land close to the river out there, but mercifully they hadn't moved yet. If they had, it would have been too far for him to go and return in time to see Robert off.

Rapping on the door with gleaming brass knocker, Harry stood back and waited. A smartly dressed footman answered and ushered him into the hall to wait. That was the first surprise. Harry had been expecting to have to justify who he was and why he wanted to see his uncle just to get a foot in the door. The last time they had met face to face had been fifteen years ago, after all – hardly a close relationship. That his uncle came hurrying out still in his morning jacket and slippers to greet him was even more of a shock.

"Harry! My dear boy! Come in, come in!" the old man exclaimed, coming to pump his hand in welcome. "So glad you came at last!" That floored Harry. He'd not been anticipating anything like this warm a welcome.

He was chivvied through into a pleasant morning room where his cousin George stood to greet him.

"Harry! Of all the people!"

Harry wasn't sure that there was quite the same joy in George's voice, but at least he wasn't overtly hostile.

"How have you been?" Uncle William demanded, waving him to a comfortable armchair. "We read about you, you know! Kept all the entries in the papers about your regiment. Heard about that terrible night on the ship too! I sent a letter to Falmouth, but at first they couldn't find you, and then they said you'd left. We didn't know if you'd gone to India after all."

Harry was choked. Here was the pride in him he'd wished his father had shown, and he felt the most dreadful ingrate for not having come back and thanked Uncle William for purchasing him that first commission.

"So proud of you!" the old man was saying. "I used to see that old rogue Sir Roderick Clifford at the club, and hear him banging on about how much money he had to keep sending that wastrel of a son of his. Some of the fellows used to think he was just bragging about how much cash he had to throw around, but over the years I thought I began to detect a bit of desperation. I used to tell him, 'you shouldn't need to be sending him that much, Harry never asks me for a penny!' And you didn't! Stood on your own two feet like a man!"

Harry managed to clear his throat enough to speak. "Thank you, Uncle. I should have come sooner to thank you for what you did for me, but," he struggled with how to put this, "coming back here was not without its difficulties."

For the first time George's face cracked into a sympathetic smile. "Ah yes, your father. I told Father about that. I met Robert in town the one day, and he told me that Uncle had had a complete fit over you not writing often enough, and how he wouldn't have you or the war mentioned."

"Bloody disgraceful behaviour!" the old man growled. "You were his son! Not some damned hanger on from the wrong side of the family! And you did him proud. Did us all proud!"

"Well you're here now," George said soothingly, making Harry wonder if this had been a regular rant of Uncle William's over the years. It might explain George's slight coolness if he'd had Harry as the epitome of courage rammed down his throat at regular intervals. And had his uncle been angry that the rift between Harry and his father had kept him from visiting the rest of the family as well? It was something he'd not even thought about until now.

"I fear I'm actually here because I need your help," Harry said gingerly. "Not financially," he added hurriedly, "I'm comfortably set up these days. But I need your knowledge of the people here in Worcester. You see I'm in terrible trouble," and he carefully explained what had happened.

At the end he sat back and watched their faces. Uncle William was gradually going puce with anger, but George now had nothing but sympathy on his face.

"Good God, Harry! How utterly dreadful for you!" his cousin declared, with not a hint of doubt that he questioned the truth of what he'd been told. Then Uncle William exploded,

"Hang my sister's boy would they? Not while I have breath!"

Harry could damned near have broken down and cried with relief. Why on earth had he and Robert not come here sooner? But of course Robert never would, it belatedly occurred to him. Robert was as set against Uncle William as their father had been. It wouldn't have entered Robert's head that the old man might actually *want* to help. Even on the way into the city this morning, he'd been filling Harry's head with dire warnings of the likelihood of Harry being thrown off the doorstep by disdainful footmen, while his uncle turned his back. How stupid! How foolish! To carry a grudge like that for all these years, when all Uncle William had said was that he wouldn't finance Robert to go into the Church.

"What do you need first?" George was asking him.

"Well the very first thing is a good lawyer," Harry managed to decide, despite the whirlwind going on in his head. "Robert is to get on the London coach to go and find the Parsons, and we need his testimony over Father finding the other body to be taken down before he goes."

"Not a problem!" Uncle William said decisively. "Sir Arthur, next door but one, is a damned fine lawyer. Fletcher!" The last was a bellow which summoned the footman. "Go round to Sir Arthur's and tell him I have most urgent need of his services, then go to the bishop's palace and wait for a tall fair-haired man to come out. He's the Reverend Robert Green and he's to be brought here."

The footman repeated the name, gave a small bow of his head and disappeared.

"What else?" Uncle William demanded. In short order another message had been sent out, this time to a physician of note who Uncle William also dined with regularly, with a request for him to see Harry at his earliest convenience. Then they got down to the matter of tracing who might recall Natalie Walker at the wedding thirteen years ago.

"I remember the wedding, of course I do," George said thoughtfully, since he was two years older than Robert and had attended along with his parents, "but I was hardly taking much notice of a young woman of no consequence – at the time I was rather taken with a young woman called

Verity Clark who was there, you see!" And he and Harry exchanged smiles at the memory of such youthful passions. "It's a shame Mother's no longer alive, because she would no doubt have told you in an instant. That kind of social information she knew by heart. My wife, Flora, is upstairs seeing to the children's new governess, but there's no point in asking her because her family come from Warwick."

"Emma!" William said forcefully.

"Ah yes, Aunt Emma," George agreed at the mention of William's sister-in-law. "I don't think you ever met her, Harry. She's my mother's sister, so not really a relation of yours, but nothing gets past her! Sharp as a razor is Aunt Emma, even if she is seventy now! And she has the memory of a proverbial elephant when it comes to things like that. We'll get Robert's testimony written down and see him onto the London coach, and then you and I will go and pay her a visit this afternoon after you've seen Dr Gething."

Under other circumstances Harry would have laughed out loud at Robert's expression when he was led in by the footman. Daniel in the lion's den was nothing by comparison!

"Oh sit down, Robert, and stop dithering!" Uncle William said bluntly but without malice, as he rose to go and greet Sir Arthur, who had also just arrived.

"He's helping?" Robert whispered in awe to Harry as William's booming voice covered his soft aside.

Harry rolled his eyes at Robert. "Yes he is, and you've badly misjudged him over the years too! Just as you let Father's odd ideas colour your opinion of me until I came back, you've allowed Father to poison you against Uncle William. And if you can manage it, think on this, maybe Uncle saw that you were following Father blindly, and feared you might have just the crisis of faith you've confessed to me. He might actually have been trying to do what was right for you, Robert, albeit clumsily, and you cannot condemn him for failing to carry through his good intentions when neither you nor Father would listen to a word he said."

Robert sighed but said nothing, and Harry noticed he was still watching Uncle William warily as he and Sir Arthur joined them at the small table in the bay window of the morning room, looking over the garden. At Sir Arthur's request, Harry told his story over a second time, able this time to be rather more logical in his presentation as his nerves relaxed.

"Hmmm," Sir Arthur said thoughtfully at the end, and leaned back in his chair, steepling his fingers and looking at the ornate coving while he thought. After a moment he sat upright once more and looked earnestly at Harry. "I won't insult you by pretending that you aren't in awfully hot water. The evidence you can bring, even if you get it all, isn't particularly direct. None of it wholly convincing by itself. It's all rather circumstantial – but then the proof against you isn't exactly watertight either, so at least the two sides of the argument are balanced in that respect. The best chance you have is for Dr Gething to certify that there's no way you could have walked to Hereford, even as an infantryman. With no evidence that you acquired a horse, that makes it most unlikely that you could have got there and back, and that at least takes you out of the picture in terms of opportunity. Who is this other woman you've spoken of? Could we get her on the witness stand?"

Harry shook his head. "No, it's unlikely she would ...be able ...to stand. She's some way away, you see. Letters are one thing, but..." He left it hanging, desperate for Sir Arthur not to ask for more details about Pip.

Sir Arthur pursed his lips and made another note on

the paper he had before him, carefully lying the pen down again to avoid ink drips. "Maybe for the best. Another woman in the mixture might sound like she had a grudge against this Miss Walker, or whatever she turns out to be. The jilted bride, and all that stuff. I wholeheartedly approve of you getting in touch with the Parsons family, though. In fact I shall give you a letter of introduction to Hodgkins and Barlow, Reverend. That should facilitate your enquiries somewhat. No doubt they will be keen to hear of the woman they so determinedly seek, but a letter from me will ensure that they don't think you're another time-waster, and they must surely have had several of them by now if a reward is being offered.

"And I shall also mention Mr Vaughan's will. I can contact my fellow legal professionals here in Worcester to see if any of them wrote a will for him, but hc may well have chosen a London man and lodged the will with the bank for safe keeping. Since both he and you were clients of theirs, it would have made the potential execution of the will easier if they were involved right from the start. Hmmm. And I think I shall also check to see if Mr Vaughan amended his will with anyone in Hereford – just to be on the safe side, you understand. Don't want any surprises coming out when we get to court, do we?"

Within the hour, Harry and George were waving Robert off on the London coach, Sir Arthur's letter and an address for the Parsons family carefully tucked into an inside pocket. It was surprising what Sir Arthur knew, and the address had been found in minutes after his return home and consulting his files.

"Now for the doctor and then Aunt Emma," George said cheerfully, making Harry feel so much better. He loved Robert dearly, but if ever there was a pessimist in the family it was him, and just at the moment he welcomed George's calm and sunny nature as a blessed relief from Robert's ineffectual fretting. Dr Gething turned out to be a portly, round-faced man, ruddy of complexion and with owl-like spectacles, who looked more like an affluent farmer than a physician, but he certainly knew his business. In short order he had checked Harry over, made him try to run up the stairs to his surgery, and then told Harry and George with a smile as Harry clung wheezing on the banister half way up, that if Harry had been a horse he would declare him no longer fit for work and call for the knackers' man.

"That's a comforting prognosis," Harry replied weakly, not sure whether he liked the comparison even if it might save his neck.

"Quite so!" Dr Gething beamed at them. "You couldn't run to catch the next coach out of Worcester, let alone make a walk of over twenty miles. You'd be lucky to get there at all without fainting in a ditch!"

"And would you be willing to swear to that in court?" George asked pointedly.

"Oh absolutely! No problem at all, my dear fellow!" the physician replied. Then with a wink added, "And I know all of the judges on the circuit! Most of them come to me with their dyspepsia when they've been dining out whilst here and over done it. You're in safe hands with me, Captain Green, never fear."

As they were let out into the street Harry muttered worriedly, "I hope he doesn't over do it in court. A doctor who seems too much on my side might do me more harm than good."

But George shook his head reassuringly. "Oh don't fret over that. Old Gething might come across as a bumbling fool but he's as sharp as they come. You watch, he'll stand there with a perfectly straight face and say that he's never seen you before this day – which he hasn't – and not mention a word of Father sending you to him. So his testimony will seem completely unbiased – because why would he bother to protect or aid a stranger? Now then, let's have some lunch at the Talbot and then go and talk to Aunt Emma."

George's aunt lived a little way out of the city on the road towards Droitwich, in a former farmhouse which the city was already overtaking.

"It used to be quite peaceful out here," the old lady muttered darkly, as they were taken in to her parlour by a maid who looked even older than her mistress. However the ancient maid must have had help, because the house was spotless, the windows gleaming and the lace on the chairs pristine white. There was also a strong smell of mothballs about the place, reminding Harry of a visit to another old lady with his parents when he'd been a small boy. As children do, he'd commented on the smell and been given a long lecture by the old lady on the villainous nature of moths in linen cupboards. The memory made him smile, and he had to force himself to remember that this wasn't the same old lady, and to not look like a grinning idiot in her presence.

"Can't think why they want to build that great monstrosity!" she was declaring in offended tones, as she gestured through the window to the huge three storey mansion visibly rising within scaffold from over several fields away. "And there's more of them coming, too! There's going to be whole square, I'm told. It's going to be as fashionable as Bath or London, or so my neighbours tell me. Well why don't they go and live in Bath or London if they want that sort of thing?"

"Because they couldn't afford anything that grand in Bath or London, Aunt," George said soothingly as he went and kissed her withered cheek.

Emma sniffed disgustedly. "Well they're spoiling my view!" she snapped. "Confounded cheek of them, whoever they are! They haven't even had the decency to come and introduce themselves to me like civilised folk would. When I was younger such discourtesy would never have done. Your uncle would have had a thing to say on the matter, I can tell you!"

"Uncle never got a word in edgewise!" George whispered to Harry as his back was turned to her to come and sit beside him.

"What was that, young George?" she demanded.

"I was just saying we could do with uncle's help too, if he were here," George recovered neatly. "But in this instance we may have more need of your wonderful memory, Aunt." With great economy he outlined Harry's problem for her. "So we'd be incredibly grateful if you could think of who would have known who this young woman might have been, you see," he concluded and sat back.

The elderly lady pursed her lips and folded her arms under her considerable bosom, the hoisting of her bust releasing strong aromas of lavender water and mothballs into the room once more. "Who would have known? Hmff! *I* know!"

"You do?" Harry was so astonished he forgot his manners in questioning her like that.

"Oh yes, my dear captain, I remember that young baggage! And if your dear mother had lived to see the day she would too! It was quite the talk of the town for some weeks. Poor Mrs Vaughan. What a trial her life was. Such a silly husband, and her such a nice, sensible woman. And that fool of a daughter of hers, hmff! Silly little madam! All those hysterics and tantrums! Totally unnecessary. And I remember you at that wedding too, Captain. I recall saying to your dear mother, George, that if the young captain wasn't fond of the bride then my name wasn't Emma."

Christ, Harry thought, *was I so bloody obvious*? His face must have given his thoughts away even now, because Emma gave a satisfied smile.

"Ah, I was right! Not so fond of her now, though, are you?"

"No, ma'am," Harry replied wryly. "Not fond at all."

"Well consider yourself to have had a fortunate escape," Aunt Emma said with a wag of a gnarled finger in his direction.

"Yes and he needs a fortunate escape of another kind regarding the same young lady," George reminded his aunt and got a glare for his trouble.

"I know that, young George! I'm not decrepit yet, I was coming to that!" She hoisted her well-starched bosom again and the two men got another gagging waft of mothballs. "Now then, as I recall, the story the pert young miss wove was that she had been a governess in the home of a Mrs O'Gall of Connaught in Ireland while the family were in London and then Bath for the seasons. She then came to Mrs Holmes up at Ombersley when she advertised for a governess for her two girls." Aunt Emma gave a disapproving sniff. "We told Mrs Holmes that she would be better waiting and getting the references properly checked, but the poor thing was in such a state, she wouldn't wait. The previous governess had been got with child by her nephew Charles when he came to visit, you see. And Mrs Holmes had said the girl would have to go before word got out, and then the silly boy went and offered to marry her, and didn't even have the decency to go out of the county to do it! I know he was from the wrong side of her family, but really!"

George caught Harry's eye and winced. They were

clearly going to have to have the whole story or not at all, and trying to hurry the old lady up to get to the important bit wasn't going to help. She might just decide to start all over from the beginning to teach them a lesson in manners, as she saw it.

"And Emilia Holmes was so intent on having a governess in to make sure there was someone with her girls at all times – on account of young Charles having an even younger brother who also couldn't leave the girls alone – she took this woman, this Miss Walker, on on the assumption that the references would be good." She sighed. "Emilia Holmes is a dear soul but well... what do you expect, taking on a stranger like that? Your dear mother, young George, told her and so did I. 'Advertise again,' we said, 'just in case this woman isn't all she seems.' She didn't want to, but we sisters were of the same mind and pressed her, and a jolly good job we did, too! It turns out that Mrs Dionysius O'Gall doesn't exist! The address that Miss Walker gave Mrs Holmes was totally false – that never existed either!"

Aunt Emma sat back with a satisfied air, having leaned further and further forward in her seat with the excitement of recounting her tale, and gave a single nod for emphasis before hoisting her bosom again and resuming the account.

"Well all this took some time to work itself out. It didn't happen overnight, and dear Emilia was more than patient. When the first letter came back as 'addressee unknown' she wrote again with an expanded address given by that wicked miss. In the meantime, Miss Walker was living in the Holmes' house and eating their food as bold as brass! I'm told she did do a good job of teaching the girls in the six months she was there, but there's more to a good governess than just teaching facts – especially to girls! And Miss Walker had some decidedly odd ideas about what was right and proper for a girl to know and what wasn't. She told them they didn't need husbands, for heaven's sake! What kind of nonsense is that?"

"Baffling," George murmured, just to make out that they were interested in the education of Mrs Holmes' daughters.

"Yes, baffling, indeed young George! A woman needs a husband, and one of the steady kind, not a fly-by-night rascal like young Edward Clifford! One would never know if the roof over one's head was secure with a man like that! My dear late sister Martha and I knew why Mr and Mrs Vaughan allowed Amy to marry Edward. It was all that old goat Sir Roderick's doing. Horace Vaughan was always a dreamer. Very like your own father, Captain. Dear men, but complete innocents when it comes to the ways of the world. My own Jonas and Martha's William tried to warn poor Mr Vaughan. They told him that Clifford wasn't to be trusted, not even if you thought you had him all legally bound and put down in writing. The man's a weasel! Cunning and nasty! But poor Horace couldn't see it.

"I remember so well sitting in the parlour at the Vaughans' old house, over the bridge in St John's, discussing the wedding with Margaret Vaughan, and Martha and I saying that the danger with young Edward was that he was good looking and he knew it. Already, you know, there was talk that Sir Roderick shoved him into the army because he was in danger of causing a scandal here at home. Something to do with gambling and debts even at that tender age." She suddenly fixed Harry with a gimlet eye. "Did he get into trouble with debts in the army, Captain?"

Harry blinked a little at the directness of the question, then remembered that he must stop trying to protect these people. Edward was long gone and Amy had come close to wrecking his life. "Yes he did," he answered frankly. "I'm sorry to report, Mrs Griffiths, that even before he married he was in debt to several of the young gentlemen of our regiment, and some in other regiments too. And you were quite right, Edward knew the effect he had on women, but he also saw no reason to be faithful to his fiancée, let alone once she was his wife."

Emma Griffiths sat back with a smug smile, gratified to have been proven right. Harry felt wretched speaking about the dead like that, but realised that if he'd attempted to wash over Edward's misconduct, she would have thought less of him for doing so.

"I thought so!" she chortled. "I can spot a rogue like him a mile off! And young Miss Walker was very taken with him too, wasn't she?"

Harry could still wince at the memory of what he'd seen in the hotel room. "Oh yes, Mrs Griffiths, very taken."

"Well what you clearly don't know is that at the time of the wedding, Miss Walker had been out of Mrs Holmes' employ for over a week, nearly two! A niece of one of the coal merchants who regularly comes to deliver at the river wharfs applied when Emilia Holmes eventually re-advertised, and *her* references did stand up, even though she'd only been out of school herself a couple of years. So Mrs Holmes had told Miss Walker that unless she could provide *proper* references, she would have to go. Well she couldn't! No possibility of doing so either! But then as a result, poor Margaret Vaughan got bullied into taking the dreadful woman in when she left the Holmes'. Somehow Miss Walker had wormed her way into silly Amy Vaughan's company, and had wrapped her round her little finger. So then there were tears and tantrums on the eve of the wedding from Amy, insisting that her friend had to be given a guest room at the house, even though they would have a full house with family coming to stay, and as ever, she got her way. Horace Vaughan never could say no to her."

"And after the wedding?" George prompted her. "I don't remember much about afterwards."

"Well you wouldn't, would you dear? Not with you being so besotted with the Clark's girl!" George blushed again at the blunt reminder. "Oh after the wedding, that was when the fun and games really began! Within a day Mrs Holmes had spoken to the magistrates about certain items which had gone missing from her house. Pieces of jewellery belonging to the girls, I understand. Because they were still so young they didn't wear them on a regular basis, you see, but they'd noticed them gone when they came to wear them for the wedding. Well there was only one contender for the role of thief! Miss Walker! And then the pawnbroker on the High Street only went and had three of the bracelets in his window within the week! I tell you, if Albert Holmes had got his hands on Miss Walker I don't know what the consequences would have been! The shame of having to go and redeem his own daughters' goods from the pawnbroker! The poor man was outraged!"

"I'm not surprised!" George agreed, now fascinated. "I'd be furious in that position. What happened when he caught her?"

"He didn't," Harry supplied wearily, "because within the week she was with us – or rather with Edward – at the army's camp. Natalie Walker was Edward Clifford's mistress for at least three months to my certain knowledge."

Aunt Emma's eyes lit up like candles. "Was she? The minx!"

It clearly delighted the old lady to have some new scandal to add to her arsenal, but the supplying of another piece in the jigsaw of events had clearly endeared Harry to her, and he dared to ask,

"Are Mr and Mrs Holmes still alive? Still in the area?"

"Oh yes, dear! They're just down the road in town."

Now for the big question. "And would they be able to identify Miss Walker again if they saw her."

Aunt Emma bridled. "Remember her? I doubt they could forget her!"

"So they would be prepared to come into court and give testimony against her if they got the chance?" Harry dared to ask.

A beaming smile spread across Emma's wrinkled cheeks. "To give that woman her comeuppance? I should say so! Albert Holmes would be your friend for life if you gave him a chance like that!"

I've got her! Harry thought with a wave of relief. *I've got someone who can prove that Natalie spun a web of lies to get into Amy's company. That she's not what she says she is and never was!*

Chapter 15

Now and then

As the portal closed, Pip retreated and sank onto the window ledge, worn out by the emotional strain. Sitting there and looking at the mirror from across the room, she wondered once again just how Natalie had done it? Those multiple cuts bothered her. Even Natalie wasn't such a feeble thing as to not be able to deliver a good thrust of a sharp knife if she wanted – and Pip remembered Dave saying that Natalie was taller than Pip. Quite the goddess, was the term he had used. So although she probably wasn't some gym fanatic with pumped-up muscles, if the knife had any kind of an edge she could almost certainly do better than just small stabs.

Blood. The key had to be blood. Was it the quantity, or what? More cuts equalling more bleeding? She ruffled her hair in frustration. Would Dave have gone along with *both* of them making a cut on themselves? Sadly she realised he probably would. If Natalie had sold him crap of the kind you got in some teenage books, where friendship was sealed by making cuts and then supposedly mingling blood... Hmmm. Yes, Dave might just have been besotted enough to go willingly for that if nothing more harmful. Especially if at that point he'd thought he was going with her! So a cut on each of their hands, or maybe an arm or elsewhere, so that they wouldn't have slippery hands when moving the mirror? Then smearing it on the mirror to activate it while it was still in place, and cleaning their hands before moving it?

Yet Natalie had always intended to kill Dave and seal his body up. But was it necessarily to absolutely douse this mirror in his blood to keep it active, if not fully open? Natalie hadn't actually specified that in her diary. Nor had Pip ever asked DCI Scathlock for the details of how Dave had died. It had been too painful a subject. It was Pip herself who'd assumed there'd been multiple stab wounds for Dave's blood. But in truth killing him may have been more to do with Natalie not wanting him following her than any further need for blood. And if she already had a knife then she'd have used it, but it didn't mean Dave had died in exactly the same way as Paul had.

All Pip knew was that it would have been thought through in Natalie's twisted mind. The bloody murdering bitch wasn't an opportunist killer, it was premeditated every time! And she must have been worried when Paul's body had disappeared. Indeed, once she got into the past, if she'd heard of old Reverend Green finding the body, that must have given her a few sleepless nights. But before that in the present, Natalie's desire to kill Dave would create the overriding need to move the mirror. Not only to cover over the doorway and hide his body, but to allow Natalie to come back without having to hack her way out of the sealed room when she did so.

Pip felt a grim satisfaction at having worked that out. Yes, Natalie wouldn't want to have to break out of the room, because who knew who might be in the house by then? Even if it was only squatters, seeing a woman coming out of the wall would have them screaming blue murder! Whereas the old mirror might get moved around the house, but at least Natalie would potentially be able to see who was in the room. And like Pip, she would be able to hear voices too. Then Pip gave a gasp as another thought came to her.

"Oh my God! She didn't know that the mirror needs to be in contact with the old oak to fully open it!"

Of course! Because Natalie must have only moved it when it was already open! Her *only* reason for moving it had been to hide Dave's body, Pip realised with shock. She couldn't have tried to open it for the first time once it was moved to the doorway, or she'd have realised it wouldn't ...it *couldn't* open! And had Natalie tried to come back through the portal and found out already that it wouldn't open for her? Bloody hell, there was rough justice if she had! And immediately Pip went and levered the mirror back off the plank, and then tucked the plank out of sight inside the chimney of the bedroom. She'd be damned if she was going to leave Natalie an escape route and risk her coming through now, leaving a trail of destruction behind her in the past. No, Natalie wasn't going to reap the rewards of her villainous scheming in the here and now if Pip had anything to do with it!

But dare Pip get back in touch with DCI Scathlock and ask him to look for investments with Lloyds, in both the name of Natalie Walker or Natalie Parsons? Not really, because they would show up as being instigated so very long ago, and how on earth would she explain that to Scathlock? It was hard enough for her to believe all this, and she'd seen and spoken to Harry and Robert, so she could easily imagine Scathlock's derision at any such suggestion, not to mention the cynical DI Sawaski.

Then in horror she remembered that she was supposed to be having dinner with Nick and Richard tonight. Crap! She'd have to peddle like mad to get back, and she'd need a shower by then because if she'd been hot and bothered getting here, she'd be doubly so by the time she got back.

Should she try and put things back further? She cast about her and realised that there was no way she had time to replace the floorboard in its original spot – and she didn't want to be late at Nick and Richard's. If she was then she would have to think of some reason why, and for no reason she could put her finger on, she didn't want to tell Nick she'd got the portal to open. So she ran down the stairs, got her bike out of the workshop and set off for home, her iPod playing John Tams for her to sing along to on the way as she pedalled furiously. She shot through Lower Broadheath with a rousing chorus of the 'Spanish Bride', which felt very appropriate given that she'd just been talking to a soldier of the period the song related to, and made it home just in time to fall under a bracing shower.

Losing the fight with her hair for the second time that day, she arrived at Nick and Richard's flushed and tousled, clutching the bottle of wine she'd already bought for the occasion, and only twenty minutes late. Luckily, punctuality had never been her strongest suit, so they didn't remark upon it.

"My you look ...glowing!" Richard said suggestively. "Is that a man I see on the horizon?"

"Oh I wish!" Pip managed to quip back, hoping she didn't blush too furiously. Well Harry wasn't a 'man' in the sense Richard meant. Not a 'date' kind of man, although now that she thought of him she found herself wishing he was in her time. A man who could face that type of crisis, and not be the kind of blubbing wreck Dave would have been in the same circumstances, was suddenly more attractive than she'd anticipated.

"Oh go on, be secretive, then!" Richard teased so camply that Pip had to laugh.

"Actually I'm all of a flush because I went on a long bike ride and forgot the time," she told them. "Look at the state of my hair! Would I go to meet a man looking like the wild woman of Worcester?"

"Maybe not," agreed Nick, laughing with her.

However, once they'd eaten Richard's excellent lasagne, Nick's highly calorific limoncello cheesecake, and were curled up on the sofas with another glass of wine, the two seemed to brace themselves.

"What?" Pip asked. "Come on you two, cough it up, you're looking all secretive."

"We've got some news," Nick admitted. "Richard's got a new job."

"Woo-hoo! Good for you!" Pip hooted and raised her glass in a celebratory gesture. "I presume it's a move upwards?"

"Yes," admitted Nick, "but it's in Edinburgh." He seemed braced for Pip to burst into tears. Instead she just blinked.

"Gosh! A true move, then! What are you going to be doing?"

"I've got the chance to train up to be a full doctor," Richard said with understandable pride.

"I'll be going too," Nick said nervously, as if he was worried that she hadn't understood.

"Of course you, will! You're a couple. Heavens, Nick, I get that, but I also know that you two have only just been making ends meet ever since you moved into this place. This may have been your dream cottage, but you were unlucky enough to buy when property prices were at one of their peaks, and the last owners weren't exactly truthful about the amount of work the place needed, were they?" She smiled warmly at them. "You may love it, but it's become a bit of an albatross around your necks, hasn't it? So I can see that if you can sell it, then move into a place where the rents are fixed for students for a bit at first, you'll be able to get back on your feet financially again."

"Blimey! I thought you'd be distraught at us going," Nick said in disbelief. "I was expecting tears and pleading."

Pip got up and went over to hug them both. "Oh God, you two have been the most wonderful friends I could ever have wished for!" she declared from the heart, squeezing them both tight, then went and sat back on the other sofa. "But you see, this comes just when I'd been making a few decisions of my own."

"It has?" Nick wondered warily.

Pip smiled reassuringly. "Don't look so worried! It's just that this whole business with Dave rearing its ugly head again got me thinking," And she told them of her plans for moving on.

"I've been stuck," she concluded. "Stuck in this place, marking time, and going nowhere fast. I feel like I've been some bluebottle banging my head against one pane of glass trying to get through, when if I'd just moved a bit to one side there were all sorts of openings. In fact, I was dreading telling you that *I* was intending to move away from Worcester."

The two of them sat in stunned silence for a moment.

"For heaven's sake, say something!" Pip pleaded. "Don't just sit there staring at me!"

Nick blinked and took a swig of wine. "Wow! ...Big choices there Pip!"

"But I think she's right," Richard said more calmly. "Yes, you have been marking time, haven't you. But I wouldn't be too hard on yourself for that, Pip. I think it was part of the healing process. You'd had such a traumatic time of it, it would have been more wrong if you'd gone tearing off into the blue back then. If you'd done that, then I really would have been worried about you, because I'd have thought you were running away from everything and not facing up to how badly Dave – and Phil in his way – used you. But I think now you've naturally come out of the other side of it. In some ways, it seems like it's even been a good thing that Dave's body came to light, because it's given you the last piece of closure."

"That's exactly how I feel about it!" Pip exclaimed.

"Do you fancy coming up north with us?" Nick asked tentatively, but Pip immediately shook her head.

"No, although thank you so much for the offer. And it's not that I want to get away from you two in any way! It's more that I want to start standing on my own two feet again. I'll know where you are, and I promise I won't be stupid about not coming to you if I do need your help. But I want to do *something*. That's something with a capital 'S'! I can't go anywhere until the police have closed the case on Natalie, or have at least drawn a line under it as an open investigation, so I'm not going to disappear tomorrow. But I was even thinking about doing something like a short season as a chalet maid over in one of the ski resorts. Austria or northern Italy maybe. Something where I'll get my keep, and somewhere to stay, but a total change. It'd be a way to get right away from here and clear my head. To have time to think and at the same time have a roof over my head and earn some money while I'm at it."

She had no intention of scrubbing up après ski puke from the floor of any chalet, but it was plausible enough as an example to stop Nick and Richard from worrying.

"I might even then go on and find a summer job of a similar sort. You know, do the gap year I never did before, during or after uni'." She took a swig of wine herself to give her time to study their faces. They were buying it, thank God!

"Time to find yourself again," Richard mused, ever the

one to have picked up on the current psychological jargon.

"But what of your archaeology?" Nick fretted.

"Oh come on, Nick! Look around you! How many jobs are there in the field these days? You've got a good track record and it's still going to be a nightmare for you to shift jobs. For someone like me who's never had a full-time job at it, even with a university team, the chances of me getting the kind of job I can support myself on is nil. And I'm so very sick of 'making do'! Of doing crappy jobs just to keep a roof over my head. I wasn't joking when I said that earlier. I want to be at least reasonably content all year round, not living in anticipation for the few weeks on a dig in the summer, and being utterly miserable the rest of the time. That's fine for a year or two, but now I want to live a more adult lifestyle. To be able to make plans! Oh I know that even the best of plans can be overtaken by life, the universe, and everything; but if I'm not going to have the husband and the kids – and I didn't want to drag that up again, but Dave really killed the kids bit for me with his screwing around – then there has to be at least *something* else in my life to fill the void, and archaeology isn't going to do that anymore, because the opportunities just aren't there. Yes, I got my degrees, but not firsts. Not good enough to make me stand out from the herd, which each year is getting bigger as the next bunch of graduates come out."

Nick sighed and came over to top up her glass. "I hear you, and I know what you mean. It just saddens me, that's all, because you're good Pip. Really good, and it's a bloody waste for you not being able to use your talents."

She chinked the glass against the bottle in a mock toast. "Thanks for the compliment!"

"I meant it!"

"So did I. You've been amazing, Nick. You've supported me and pushed me forward at every chance. It's not your fault that the bigger economic climate has overtaken us. And... please don't be offended at this, ...but the way you're worrying over me and my job prospects is also part of this for me. You and Richard are a couple! You shouldn't be having me as a third party in the relationship all the time. And wonderful though your concern is, I'm not your responsibility! I'm mine! And all of a sudden I want that." Then to lighten the mood she playful pulled a face. "Bloody hell, guys! I'm talking about Austria, not the back end of Afghanistan! I'm unlikely to end up being kidnapped by the Taliban, or whisked away by pirates off the coast of Africa! There're few places more respectable than an Austrian ski resort!"

That seemed to do the trick, and the rest of the evening relaxed into more friendly banter. As she walked back along the Bromyard Road, though, Pip breathed a sigh of relief that she'd pulled the deception off. What would they have said if she'd told them she planned on going back to Cold Hunger Farm next week on the first? And she wanted to be able to go on the twenty-first of September too, because that might just be when Natalie reappeared. This year it was a full moon to boot, and Pip had a gut feeling that the portal could be energised enough for Natalie to push back into this time, even if the mirror on her side wasn't on the oak board. Richard might have been a good deal less happy with her state of mind if she'd told him that if she thought Natalie was coming back, then she was going to dial 999 and get DCI Scathlock out to make an arrest.

Much of course depended on what happened with Harry. If he really came up trumps, then Natalie might get incarcerated back in his time, and that would be a whole heap rougher than any twenty-first century women's prison! That would suit Pip even more – no parole, no clean cell, nor access to modern conveniences, was much more fitting.

But Pip would need to speak to him between now and then to find that out. So her first attempt would be at the old Sabat of Lughnasadh on the first of August, and then she'd see if the portal would work at least enough to talk on the sixth, when there was a new moon, and then on the twenty-first, when there was a full moon, before the big one in September came around. She had no idea if it would work, but she was determined to try.

In the meantime, she would go back to work at her current job and try to behave normally, although in truth, what she would do beyond September was by no means as clear as she'd made out to Nick and Richard. Backpacking had a certain allure for sheer unbridled freedom. Maybe Italy for the warmth, but the chance to go and see her grandparents' old farmstead up on the Scottish Borders was also pulling at her, along with the chance to walk the more northern Scottish glens. Bothies would give her somewhere to overnight on the longer walks, and her meagre savings would at least buy her food if she also stayed in hostels. You couldn't do digs as a student archaeologist and be afraid of roughing it for a while, and Pip found herself longing for the emptiness of the highlands. For space to think all this through once it was over.

When the evening of August the first came around, she cycled out to the farm, intending to spend the night there. If she wasn't at work the following day it was just tough. The lack of interest or concern when she'd returned and told them what had happened to Dave had ended any feelings of loyalty there. But Harry! God, she couldn't believe how much she wanted to talk to him again! What with being at work once more, she hadn't had chance to go back into the archives to see if any of the historical accounts were shifting, and so she had no idea whether he was being successful in defending himself. And it mattered to her terribly.

"Don't go falling in love with him," she kept telling herself firmly. "He's dead by now, remember! He's hardly going to come and walk you down the aisle in this life!"

Yet as the setting sun bathed the bedroom of the farm in tones of oranges and misty purples, her heart was beating just that bit faster. The mirror was up on its floor board again, and Pip had come better prepared with a slice of very bloody steak in a bag from the local butchers. She'd feigned a tummy bug to be off work today, so that she could go last thing to the shop and get the steak while the blood was still reasonably fresh. With any luck, that would do the job, because she didn't want to have to draw any of her own blood if there was any way around that.

Taking great care not to spill any, Pip opened the top of the bag, lifted the steak just enough to have a bloody piece showing, and wiped it on the mirror. For a ghastly moment nothing happened but a lonely dribble running down the glass. It wasn't working!

"Bollocks!" she swore bitterly, but then was rewarded by a distant voice saying,

"Language, Miss Pip!" in amused tones.

"Harry!" She clutched the steak and threw the blood from the bag at the top of the mirror and let it run down. Evidently cow's blood wasn't quite as potent as human, but it was good enough to work, especially in the quantity Pip had used.

His face swam into sight and they smiled at one another.

"Well?" Pip demanded. "What's happened? What have you done? Is it working?"

"My goodness, you're eager," Harry laughed, but even that laugh told Pip volumes. He'd not been anything like that relaxed that last time! Then as he told Pip of what he'd done, she found herself breathing several sighs of relief too. Thank heavens for that! It was working! However she was utterly unprepared to hear him saying,

"And she gave Mrs Holmes a reference for a woman in Ireland, a Mrs O'Gall of Connaught..."

"Woah! Hang on a minute! Not ...the five daughters of Mrs Dionysius O'Gall of Bitternutt Lodge, Connaught, Ireland?"

"Errr... Yes?"

Pip hooted with laughter.

"What's so funny about that?"

"Oh I'm sorry, Harry! Of course, you wouldn't get the reference because I don't think the book's been published yet for you."

"Book?" he asked suspiciously.

Pip grinned at him. "Oh yes! A book that will go on to be one of the greats of English literature! It's called *Jane Eyre*, and the young heroine of the story is a governess. Without going through the whole story, suffice it to say that at one of the crucial points in the book the hero, Mr Rochester, invents a lady with a vacancy for a governess to test Jane's reaction to leaving her post to see if she loves him."

"Oh God, not Mrs Dionysius O'Gall?"

"The very one! The book is so famous nowadays, pretty much every schoolgirl for generations will have read it at some point during her English lessons. I always had a bit of a soft spot for the book, which is why I immediately got the reference – I've read it many times since leaving school. Whether Natalie loves it too, or just had to remember that excerpt at some point for school and it stuck, I don't know, but no wonder your poor lady couldn't find the famous Mrs O'Gall!"

Harry was thinking furiously. "How far in the future? Can we use this as evidence?"

Now Pip had to cudgel her brain. "Well the writer, Charlotte Brontë, is alive by now in your time, although only a young girl I suspect, but the book doesn't appear until more like the middle of the century. Somewhere in the 1840s, I think."

"Damn!" Harry sighed. "That could have been useful!"

"Hell, yes! Proof that Natalie was telling a pack of lies from the start, and was so contemptuous of being caught that she'd use something which could be checked upon too! ...Oh heck!" The mirror had begun to wobble again, and Pip grabbed the steak this time and slapped it onto the mirror.

Without thinking she put her weight behind it as she streaked it across the glass, then found herself overbalancing, and the next thing – as she stumbled forwards – was finding herself being caught in a strong pair of arms.

"Harry?"

"Miss Pip?"

They stood clutching one another in shock. Harry was dressed in just a light summer shirt and breeches, and through the light cotton Pip's first sensation was of how warm he was. And there was strength in those biceps! No smell of modern after-shave either, just the faintest waft of lavender water from the laundering of the shirt – and that was going to need washing now that she'd planted her bloody hands over his arms and chest!

For his part Harry found his hands grasping her rib cage, then slipping around her back as she toppled into his arms. But she was solid! Not just solid as opposed to ghostly, but solid in comparison to other women he had known. He may have spent a long portion of his adult life besotted with Amy, but he wasn't a saint, and he'd spent enough nights with women to realise that there was some real muscle to this young woman. Her comment about digging wasn't just silly talk, then, the way Amy sometimes made ridiculous statements. Then he felt her stiffen in his grasp,

"Shit! Where are my clothes?" she all but shrieked, and suddenly he was blushing too as he realised she was completely naked.

Desperately forcing himself to avert his eyes, he turned and swept up the jacket from the dressing room chair where he'd dropped it, and swung it about her shoulders.

The way she grabbed it and pulled it about her, then stood in the middle of the floor looking frantically about her was reassuring in a strange way. For all of her sometimes outrageous statements, there was none of Natalie Walker's brazenness here. No shamelessness at being seen naked in a strange man's bedroom.

"Fuck!" Pip squeaked as she saw her clothes half in tatters on the other side of the mirror. "Oh crap! How am I going to get home now?"

"How are you going to get through the mirror?" Harry added, worriedly.

She turned away from him, wriggled into the jacket properly so that she had her arms through the sleeves, then smacked her hand hard against the glass. It didn't give an inch! She couldn't even reach the tatters of clothes to pull them through to her. Then it belatedly occurred to her that they would only disintegrate further if she did. But what the hell was she going to do now?

"I don't think I can get back," she said turning to Harry, suddenly feeling on the edge of tears.

He came and pressed hard on the mirror. "Oh dear. No I don't think you can." Not that he sounded in the least bit upset about that. "I'm afraid you'll have to stay here with me, at least for a while."

Harry felt his heart give little skip of excitement at that thought. Well at least he would be able repay his kind rescuer properly now!

He went out to the linen cupboard, found a large blanket and came back to wrap it around her. "There, that's a little more covering than my jacket, although you're welcome to keep that on too."

"Thank you," Pip replied weakly. "God, I'm sorry, I don't mean to sound ungrateful or anything. It's just that actually coming back to this time wasn't part of my plan." *Liar!* Her inner voice scolded her. *You bloody wanted to come back to meet him in person ever since you clapped eyes on him!* However, her sensible side was telling her that now it really mattered whether she came across as too forward or not. It was one thing to be the very modern woman from the safety of another century. It was quite a different matter to realise that you were very dependent on this man seeing you as the kind of decent woman he should treat with respect. Not that Pip thought that Harry was the kind to rape *any* woman, but she knew enough to know that the moral standards of her own time were very different from this one. And she would be very vulnerable out in wider society if Harry chose not to protect her at even the most fundamental level. How, for instance, was she to get clothes?

Harry, too, was thinking furiously, and it was uphill work when he was otherwise very aware that a pretty and vivacious woman was standing stark naked not three feet from him. "Clothes!" he said determinedly, as much to quell the rising temptation within as to comfort her. "Tomorrow we must get you proper clothes!"

Pip looked up into his face, brown eyes huge with worry, and doing all sorts of things to his inner equilibrium. "Err... Great! But how am I going to get them? I can hardly go shopping like this, can I? We're going to have to invent some reason as to why you have a woman without even her underwear in your house."

No underwear! God help him, he mustn't think too hard on that! It had taken him years to stop dreaming of seeing Natalie Walker astride Edward, and now he was likely to spend as many dreaming of Pip dropping that blanket and his jacket!

"Underwear. Yes. Hmmm." He turned and went out of the room, after which Pip heard sounds of frantic rummaging, and different doors being opened and closed.

"Damn!" he said returning, looking more than a little flushed. "Just wondered whether Amy left any clothing behind. Not that there's many wardrobes or anything still here."

"What about under the eaves?" Pip suggested. "Would they have forgotten about the odd trunk of unwanted things stored there?"

Glad to be talking about something practical, she pattered out on bare feet and round onto the landing, then into the old nursery space, Harry right behind her. In the anteroom she opened the cupboard doors under the windows, but nothing was there.

"Do you know which bedrooms the family used while they were here?" Pip asked Harry, desperately trying to keep the blanket around her lower body.

"Erm, the one I'm in was Amy's. The one you come to first beyond that in the far wing was Gus' on the occasions he lived here, and the one beyond it was Mr and Mrs Vaughan's. Eddie used this room."

"So what about the bedrooms to the left of us? The two in the oldest part of the house."

"Ah, I don't think they were ever used."

"Then they might be the place to store boxes?" Pip wondered.

"Possibly. I noticed some trunks of Gus' left for storage there when I moved in. I know the family rejected sleeping there because they were cold and damp, but you could be right." Harry turned and led the way to the door, then gallantly stood to one side to let Pip go through first.

"Oh!" Pip breathed, and smiled.

"What?" Harry said, perplexed and still rather bewildered by this turn of events.

Pip's smile got broader. "I'm just not used to such gentlemanly behaviour," she confessed, "but I could get used to it very easily!"

"Oh! ...Good." What kind of behaviour she had been used to Harry couldn't imagine. She was too well-spoken and educated to have come from amongst the truly poor, and even to his less than astute eye where woman were concerned, he could see that she was very different to the wives of the ordinary soldiers he'd met in the war against Napoleon. There must be some funny men in her world, that's all he could think.

In the two tatty bedrooms at the end there were a quantity of cobwebs, and the signs of several generations of mice setting up home, but also a good many large trunks.

"I think you should take your jacket back and leave me the blanket," Pip said considerately. "I'm going to get filthy going through this lot, and this jacket's nice wool. It would be a shame to spoil it."

"Well I was going to help you," Harry said pointedly, "and how would you secure that blanket?"

Pip thought for a moment. "Have you got a shirt already waiting to be washed? Preferably an old one? I could wear that instead."

Harry's eyes lit up. "Actually I have something better! When I was given all sorts of clothing after the wreck, one of the garments I came up here with was a farm-worker's smock. A long smock!" Thank God the blanket was there, because when she bent over the jacket was nowhere near long enough! Long smock, he thought desperately. Much safer! "It's good strong material and long enough for you to wear as a dress."

"Excellent!" Pip declared, blissfully unaware of Harry's inner chaos as he hurried off to fetch it, then gallantly stood outside the door while Pip changed.

Once she was clad in the long, thick, homespun garment, they began going through the trunks. The ones closest to them turned out to be filled with Gus' things, and Harry found his happiness fading fast as he saw the mementoes of Gus' travels spreading out before him.

"Wow! He had a good eye for fabrics!" Pip said in awe, carefully lifting a beautifully woven rug out of the way. "If he'd ever got round to decorating a house with all of this it would have been gorgeous!"

Suddenly it was too much for Harry and he sank onto one of the chests and buried his head in his hands. "And all he ever wanted was a little house on the edge of town with a wife and several children," he all but sobbed. "God! How cruel is it that he never got any of that? Poor Gus never had an enemy in the world 'til that bloody woman got her eye on his money." Then was startled as he felt Pip's arm come round his shoulders comfortingly. Her head then rested on the one shoulder as her hand came onto the other. All by itself that shocked Harry out of the worst of his depression – he'd never had a woman comfort him in that way before, but it was certainly a welcome change from Amy's constant taking.

"That's so sad!" Pip agreed. "He sounded such a nice man in the letters I read, and everything you've said of him confirms that. The worst of it is, if he'd been more of a complete bastard, Natalie would have found it so much harder to ensnare him. He might even have put up more of a fight at the last."

"I don't think I've ever hated anyone as much as I hate her," Harry confessed. "In the war we hated the French in general, but man to man I've never had anyone I would have described as an actual enemy. Even Sergeant Hobspawn! He was the sergeant who Edward served with. A truly evil man by anyone's standards. But *everyone* loathed him! I was no different in that, and I made sure he never got the chance to get his claws into me. But this woman I hate with a vengeance!"

"Me too!" Pip empathised. "All the rotten things which have happened to Dave and to me all seem to come back to her. The fucking bitch is toxic!"

She'd forgotten where she was for a moment, but at least her swearing brought Harry's head up to give her a slightly startled look, which was better than his misery.

"Come on," she said, clapping him on the shoulder. "Let's carry on and see if we can find me something halfway respectable for me to put on until I can get something better. Then we'll fight the fight together!"

That cheered Harry considerably, and the thought of what George MacDonald would make of his current fighting companion completed the lifting of the black thoughts which still threatened to overwhelm him every now and then, as just now. Once they got further back into the pile of chests they came to some of Amy's things, and here Pip got lucky. There were some quite serviceable bloomers and bodices which had been set aside and folded up in tissue paper.

"Put on a bit of weight, did she?" Pip asked mockingly.

"However did you guess that?" Harry wondered.

Pip showed him the seams on one of the bodices. "That stitching's been pulled very tight at some point! So I'm guessing she kept wearing it for as long as she could, but then had to get a bigger size."

She was pretty sharp if she could notice something like that, Harry thought. "Will they do for you, though? I mean..." He faltered, not sure of his ground in asking if she could get into the bodice.

"Oh I'll be pulling the string on the bloomers in pretty tight," Pip answered airily, "but the bodices might be a bit tight across the ti... across the bosom," checking herself just in time from being too blunt. That was going to be the big test for her. To not speak without thinking. She'd always had good manners thanks to her grandparents, and she was confident of coping with general politeness, but to have to remember to speak more formally in familiar company was going to be a hell of a challenge. "Ooh look! A dress!"

By the time they'd finished she had four pairs of bloomers and bodices, and a couple of night-dresses, all of which would do her for now. However the dresses were more of an issue. Pip was definitely fuller in the bust than Amy had ever been, and what had been a scooped empire neckline on Amy had Pip's breasts near climbing over the top. And the skirts were far too short on the two she could actually get into, coming too far up her shins for decorum in this age. But worst of all was the matter of shoes. Amy's feet were tiny in comparison to Pip's, and the only shoes she could get into were an old pair of Edward's, which were very obviously boyish.

"There's a haberdashers section in the general store in Clifton," Harry sighed, "but I don't think there's a dressmaker there. It's just not big enough for that kind of outfitter. But we're going to have to get you clothes from somewhere. I'm sorry, Miss Pip, but the only thing I can think of is to borrow a horse and trap and take you into Worcester to Uncle William's. George's wife, Flora, must know a reputable dressmaker over there."

"If you can get a horse each we could ride," Pip suggested. "I can ride moderately well, and we could go by night."

"Wearing what?"

Pip wrinkled her nose mischievously. "Got a spare pair of breeches I could borrow?"

The thought took Harry's breath away. Sweet God preserve him from that kind of temptation! Pip in close-fitting military breeches was the stuff of secret fantasies! And what Uncle William and George would say if they saw her like *that* didn't bear thinking about! "No!" he said more firmly than he'd intended, then was totally thrown by her throaty chuckle.

"Oh Harry! Your face just then was a picture!" Pure panic was what Pip would have called it. "But if you think that's too scandalous then the pony and trap it is. Where are they? The pony, I mean."

"In Clifton," Harry sighed. "So we still have to get you to Robert's before dawn."

"Clifton? I can walk that far!" Pip snorted. "Even in these boots! It's not that much of a hike, for heaven's sake. What is it? A couple of miles at the most, surely?"

"Probably double that unless we go over the fields, and the farmers will be up with the dawn harvesting at the moment."

"Okay, four miles down the lanes. I can still do that! It must be late now because it's got dark. If you can find your way by night, why don't we go now?"

The urge to sweep her into his arms was worrying Harry so much, he had to admit to himself that it would probably be safer to get her to Robert's as fast as possible. There temptation would be much easier to withstand, even though his other side wanted to keep her to himself for one night at least. So with Pip wearing one of his jackets over Amy's old dress and clomping along in Eddie's outgrown boots with a pair of home knitted socks underneath them, they set out on their midnight walk. It was the oddest night march Harry had ever undertaken, and bizarrely one of the happiest. Pip had slipped her hand under his arm as they set off, and then had surprised him by keeping pace with him, the two of them swinging along at a natural pace which suited them both. None of the snail's pace, aimless wandering he'd had to do in Bath here.

"Oh look, you can see Orion's belt!" Pip exclaimed in delight. "My God look at the stars! You can see the Milky Way! In my time there's so much light you never get to see the stars most of the time. The last time I really saw stars like this was my last visit to Nana and Grandpa's house on the Scottish Borders, years ago."

"You like looking at the stars?"

"Oh yes! I don't know as much as I'd like about the different constellations, but I do know the general stuff, like the fact that the star up in the top corner of Orion is Betelgeuse, and that it's a super-giant star which is why it looks red. And I always look for the Pleiades as the autumn comes on and they appear above the horizon again."

"I learned most of what I know of the constellations from having to learn Ovid and Homer," Harry admitted ruefully, "and as a schoolboy they had limited appeal!" He would have expected to feel some embarrassment at conversing with a woman better educated than himself, yet all he could think was how nice it was to talk about proper subjects. Not who was wearing this season's fashionable lace and who was not. *I could get used to this very easily*, he thought to himself happily.

They saw not another soul all the way into Clifton, not even up to the rectory. However rousing Robert without the whole of the village along with him, was somewhat harder.

"Lord, he sleeps the sleep of the righteous!" grumbled Harry darkly, as he shied more pebbles at Robert's bedroom window. "And why he bars the doors I can't imagine. There's nothing in there worth thieving!"

Then Robert's head appeared at the window, blinking sleepily. "Harry? Good God, what time is it?"

"Shhhh!" Harry hissed. "Come down and let us in, for the love of God, before we wake the whole village!"

"Ehh? Harry?"

"Robert, the bloody door!"

At least Harry had the fun of standing behind Pip, so that he got to see Robert's face as Pip walked in through the door. If Robert had been half asleep up until then, he certainly wasn't as Pip shrugged out of his jacket, straining the top of Amy's dress to near bursting point in the process.

"Jesus!" escaped from Robert's lips before he could stop himself, then managed to wrench his eyes from Pip's cleavage.

Suddenly Harry wanted very much to laugh out loud. Seeing his stuffy brother so disconcerted was a long waited for treat. Instead he managed to say, "You remember Miss Pip from the mirror, don't you Robert?" but somehow the laugh was still there in his voice. Then Pip turned round and winked conspiratorially at him and he lost the battle. As he collapsed on the hall seat in guffaws of laughter, Robert just stood blinking owlishly at them both.

"Harry? And ...Miss Pip? How? How did you get *here*? And at this hour? Harry? What's wrong? Why are you laughing? You've not got hysterics, have you?"

"It's very gallant of you both to keep calling me Miss Pip," she told them as Harry managed to get his laughter under control, "but in private just Pip will do fine. You don't need to stand on ceremony with me." Harry's sudden fit of the giggles she put down to the tension of the last few weeks, although she wasn't so naïve not to know that it was at seeing his prissy brother's reaction to her cleavage. She grinned herself, imagining what the reaction would have been to her costume which she'd worn when going to the occasional theatre performance of the *Rocky Horror Picture Show* with her old uni' friends. Six inch heels, fishnets and a black and red basque might just finish Robert for good!

However, to give Robert some credit, he recovered well and agreed to get the trap as early as possible, then they all got some much needed sleep, or at least that was the idea. Pip found she couldn't sleep, still having too much adrenaline rushing round her system after such a momentous night, and sat by the open window watching the dawn come up. Harry, too, couldn't sleep, but in his case it was fretting over his feelings for Pip, which seemed to be growing by the hour. Of all the times to find himself falling head over heels in love, to do it just as he was fighting to save his neck had to be one of the most perverse.

Chapter 16

August 1824

Harry had to admit that as a test of his family's willingness to help him, turning up first thing in the morning with a half-dressed strange woman was probably one of the tougher ones. Luckily Pip's own behaviour helped immensely. The way she immediately apologised for causing George and Flora any inconvenience softened the blow. That and the way she clutched the borrowed jacket around her modestly, clearly uncomfortable at the amount of flesh she was in danger of showing. She'd told Harry and Robert as they were setting off, that she thought the best story they could tell was one of her being another of the survivors of the *Kent*.

"I think we should say that to cover my poor state of dress," she said firmly. "If someone could give Harry a ploughman's smock to cover him up, then me having ill-fitting dresses will seem far less strange."

"But why would you have been onboard in the first place?" fretted Robert.

However Pip had thought of that too. "I'm going to stick as close to the truth as I can," she told him, "but my biggest hurdle will be that my behaviour isn't quite what you would expect of someone brought up in England now. So if we say I left England when a child and went to the Americas, that will be exotic enough to cover most eventualities. What I'm thinking we'll tell people is that I left with my parents and we went first to the West Indies, and then on to the mainland. I shall stick to the truth that my father died when I was ten and my mother remarried, and that I don't get on with her new husband. That's absolutely true! I left home as soon as I could! At sixteen I went to stop with my father's parents up on the Scottish Borders, but now I think I shall have to say it was with family in another part of the Americas. Perhaps my mother's parents – I hardly knew them in reality, so I'm unlikely to make a mistake between my own time and now.

"Where it will also change a bit is that I shall say I actually married Dave, although in truth we never got that far. He and I were living together from the time I was twenty-two," she continued blithely, oblivious to Robert's eyebrows nearly disappearing into his hairline at the concept of living in sin. "I know it's not anachronistic for a girl to marry at that age in this time, but I may bring it back to something like twenty or twenty-one to give us a bit more time to play with. You see, I think it would be a good thing to keep the fact that Dave has been dead for four years. If I do that, then it won't seem odd that I'm not mourning him more deeply at the moment.

"Now we know that Natalie was here in 1811, thirteen years ago, so in this time she's no longer the same age as me. Therefore, if asked, I shall have to come up with some other way for her to have met Dave other than at university. But once again, this is where I think it would be useful to have me meeting him, and us marrying, taking place in the Americas. It's usefully too far for anyone to check up on us! I shall then say I came back to this country with him. That sounds suitably respectable, doesn't it? Travelling back here with my husband? I'm trying to think of ways to keep me sounding respectable in case I have to meet any of your lawyers, Harry. I think we shall then say that Dave was working in Birmingham, and that was where he met Natalie. Do we know of her whereabouts four years ago which would contradict that?"

"Not at all," Harry confirmed. "In fact, you might not be so very far from the truth. Sir Arthur got some very quick results from his enquiries with the banks, especially once we mentioned that we were on the same trail as the Parsons in London. That bloody woman made a substantial deposit into the Lloyds bank in Birmingham around that time, and we have that on paper!"

"Brilliant!" Pip enthused. "So if she tries to say she wasn't in Birmingham at the time, we can actually prove her wrong. That's excellent! I think I can then keep fairly close to the truth by saying that I was distraught that Dave disappeared. God, I must remember to start calling him David, not Dave! That's not a common shortening of his name at the moment, is it?"

"Davey is a bit more used," Harry admitted, "but David isn't a popular name in England these days anyway. And round here Davey is more ....well it's more rural, more lower class."

"I'll stick to David!" Pip decided. "If he sounds too much the yokel someone might wonder what Natalie was doing with him. Now Harry, did she get much money from Edward?"

Harry laughed. "Money from Edward? Not a chance! He never had money in his purse for longer than it took to spend it! I think the attraction between those two was that they were both as scheming as one another. They were both after other people's money." Even knowing Pip's broad-mindedness he couldn't bring himself to add, 'that and sex'. Christ, Edward had hardly been out of the damned woman's bed unless his army duties forced him! Even in those days Harry had wondered where he got the stamina from, or had even that been more Natalie than him? Women in Pip's time seemed to be so much more forward than now.

However Pip was nodding thoughtfully. "Then I think if asked, I'll say that we had very little income, but that Dave ...David was pulled in by her promises of easy ways to make money. That makes him naïve but not malicious – which is true! He was always being taken in by people's tall tales. But now I need you two to come up with something for me. What would I have done as a young woman deserted by her husband? I can say that as far as the *Kent* goes, that I was travelling with one of the soldier's wives as a companion to get out to India. A purely temporary arrangement, and merely so that I could travel out to visit ...oh, let's say, ...a cousin of my father's ...who has offered me a place in his house for a while."

"But what would you have done out there?" Robert wondered. "Most women would be going out to *do* something."

"Like what?"

"Well if not to get married, to work as a governess. Or a companion. A nurse, maybe."

"Bloody hell, that's a grim selection!" Pip said with a frown. "I think governess is out. You said Natalie's modern views let her down, and they'd do the same to me, so I don't even want to get into a discussion of what I might have taught." She thought for some minutes as the pony clipped along the roads, with Harry, too, trying to think how on earth he could fit Pip into society.

"I know!" she said triumphantly. "This fictional cousin of my father's will have a very eccentric mother-in-law! The kind of lady who goes riding upcountry when they're in the hills during the summer. There really were ...sorry, *are* ...ladies like that out in India! I shall have been offered the job of becoming her companion because, having spent years out in the colonies, the cousin thinks I will be able to keep up with her since she's worn out my two predecessors in no time at all. She'll be a lady in her fifties, but I can't describe her since I've never met her. That will do nicely! So come on, what did I do between David disappearing in ...ooh, let's make it precisely which year, Harry? When was Natalie in Birmingham?"

"In the autumn of 1819. I think Sir Arthur said she made a deposit in mid September and then again at the beginning of November."

"Right, so if David disappears early in November 1819, that will fit. I then need to fill the gap right from the start of 1820 to the spring of this year. Four years! What would a widow do?"

"If you had a house of your own you would stay in it," Robert said immediately, but then got contradicted by Harry.

"No, Robert, only if she had money! If she was poor – and if Pip's husband had lost money she would be – she could only hope for some charity from the landlord for time to get her things together, then she would be forced to vacate the house unless she could pay the rent. And that means with what? Without a husband's money she would have to work at something. And if you don't mind me saying so, Pip, you won't pass for a lady's maid. You look far too tanned for most women." He cringed at his own next words. "Too used to working!" The last thing he wanted was to sound as though it was a criticism, but mercifully Pip didn't take offence.

"No, that's no bad thing!" Pip had just had another idea. "I think I shall have tried to hold things together for a while, seeking work in Birmingham. There's always been manufacturing of some sort going on there, so I shall have done basic housework for people, and have rented a room.

Not for anyone too wealthy, just people one step up from me – clerks in industry, sort of people. I think I shall have finally decided that I wanted to try and find the Scottish side of my family, and have gone north, but there's no-one left there anymore – that's actually true in my own time! But having got up there I shall have heard of work in the jute works which are being built just now in Dundee. I can tell you from my own knowledge of history, there will be strong links between those mills going up just now and the other side of the industry in India.

"That then makes sense if I say I wrote to my cousin saying I had fallen on hard times and was going to be working in the mill. This fictional cousin will be horrified – as well he should be! – because he knows what the work will be like, hence his offer of work for me in India. If your family should ask, I shall say I hope still to be going out there, but there's the matter of finding the fare again since the *Kent* went down, and it's still too early for letters to have come back to me to find out if he – the cousin – will pay again. Let's call him Michael Campbell since I have a real cousin called that. I've been living on the charity of the kind people of Falmouth since the wreck, until I heard about Harry's trial. Would you have been able to forward me the money to get here, Harry?"

"Oh yes!" Harry answered without hesitation. "Indeed, Sir Arthur told me last week that it would be a good idea if you were here!"

"Then here I am!"

"Yes, here you are," sighed Robert with a shiver, still not quite able to come to terms with Pip's physical presence.

Amazingly, the rest of the family had no such reservations.

"All the way from Cornwall on your own!" Flora

Colman exclaimed in awe. "My word you're braver than me! I should never dream of making such a trip!"

"In comparison to returning from the Americas, Cornwall to Worcestershire wasn't so very bad," Pip replied smoothly.

"But inside the coach with strange men!" gasped Flora.

Pip was tempted to mischievously say no, she'd travelled outside, but then that would make Harry look like a skinflint for not sending her enough to ride inside. Instead she just smiled and said, "I learned young how to take care of myself, Mrs Colman. I fear I may come across as rather rough for polite company, but the colonies are not so civilised as here."

"But you came when Harry asked you!" old William Colman declared vigorously. "That makes you a right thinking sort of woman, and I approve of that! If you're willing to add your voice to trying to clear his name, then you're welcome in this house!"

However, it was Flora whose help Pip really needed, and she was dreading being left alone in this woman's company. If Flora chose unwisely for Pip's clothing she could make her look a right sight in court and the subject of gossip, and Pip was praying silently that she wouldn't turn out to be too vacuous or petty-minded. It was a massive relief, then, to find that she and Flora rather liked one another from the start. If Flora was no great academic, she had the kind of sound common sense Pip found was of far more use in the realities of daily life.

"I'll send for my dressmaker to come here and see you," Flora told her calmly. "If we have to walk through the streets with you dressed like that people will wonder who on earth I have with me, and we don't want gossip about you just on the basis of what you aren't wearing. If you don't get seen until you're properly dressed, then we don't have to worry about what might be said."

Pip sighed with relief. "I think that's a really sensible thought. Thank you, Mrs Colman." However false it sounded to her to be calling people by their formal names, she knew instinctively that nothing would alienate her with Harry's family than a presumption of what they would see as unwarranted familiarity.

"Please, call me Flora," the lady of the house said kindly, to Pip's relief.

"And I've been Pip to everyone who truly knows me," Pip offered in return. Harry had introduced her as Mrs Philippa Marston, but Philippa wasn't a name Pip was comfortable with. "My mother only ever called me Philippa when I was in trouble!" she added with a smile.

Happily Flora returned her smile. "Oh I know what that's like! Even though Flora isn't a name which gets shortened, my mother could still add something to it when she wished to show her disapproval!" And they shared a smile at the individual memories.

After that it was much easier. The dressmaker came late that afternoon and brought samples with her, and Pip and Flora took over the morning room to spread the cloth samples out, and save the gentlemen's embarrassment over conversations about underwear. Miss Howes, the dressmaker, quickly began pulling samples of pretty cotton prints out as clearly her idea of what Pip ought to wear, but Pip was less than taken with them. She'd never planned to come through to this time, so she'd never given much thought to what a young woman of a certain social level would wear, and consequently it was yet another jolt to her equilibrium to be expected to be so girly. Even in her teens, Pip had never been one for floaty dresses. Now she was looking at a succession of pastel stripes and florals, all on delicate white backgrounds, making her feel as though she'd fallen into the wardrobe department on a BBC costume drama. This was *Pride and Prejudice* with a vengeance!

"Have you nothing a little more ...mature?" Pip asked with as much grace as she could muster.

"Don't you like them?" Flora enquired anxiously, while Miss Howes looked rather askance at her selection being so questioned.

Pip winced. "They're all exceedingly pretty," she said through gritted teeth. "It's rather that I feel they're a bit young for me."

"Young?" Miss Howes sniffed. "I don't think so!"

Wishing she could just go home and get into her old battered jeans instead, Pip forced herself into further negotiations. "I don't mean to question your expertise, Miss Howes," she said with what hopefully sounded like a degree of obsequiousness, "but how old do you think I am?"

"Miss..." spluttered Miss Howes, suddenly embarrassed at having forgotten Pip's name, but it gave Pip her opening.

"No, lovely compliment though it no doubt is for you to think me young enough to be a 'miss', I'm *Mrs* Marston, and I shall be thirty next birthday."

Miss Howes' jaw dropped. ""Thir... Good heavens! Well I never! You have the most exceptional complexion for a lady of that age," she said with more than a hint of doubt in her voice.

"I've been widowed for a good four years," Pip insisted firmly, "and was with David for a good many too. And I wasn't a child bride! Surely you must see that therefore I cannot be in my *early* twenties?"

"Oh dear," sighed Miss Howes. "Yes, if you really are that age, then these aren't quite so appropriate – although many of my more mature ladies still like to have these made into garments befitting their station."

However, Pip was shaking her head. "Well I would really love a little more colour, if possible, Miss Howes. Maybe *one* dress so pale, but not more than that!" Heaven help her, she'd be mucked up in no time in white! Even pale trousers were a disaster on her! Then as another set of samples were brought out a lovely raspberry pink with a light stripe appeared. "Oh now that's more like it!" she said with genuine enthusiasm. It was a far cry from the sugary pinks she hated, and just dark enough to be practical, but it also earned her her first smile from Miss Howes.

"Oh yes! With your dark curls that would look most fetching on you!" she agreed, and so the negotiations began again.

Yet the biggest problem in the end was one of time. Pip had never realised that it took so long to stitch a dress by hand, and she was faced with the awful prospect of many more days of barely daring to breathe in the tight dresses of Amy's youth. Please God the trial didn't come forward or she'd never be dressed in time! Only as Miss Howes was about to leave, promising she would do her very best to get at least one dress to Pip as soon as possible, Pip thought to ask,

"I don't suppose you have any cancelled orders do you? I mean dresses you've made, or part made, for ladies which they then decided they didn't want. Ones where you'd just be taking in or letting out, rather than starting from the very beginning."

"Would you accept such clothing?" the dressmaker asked worriedly, no doubt remembering Pip's protests over the fabrics.

"Oh Lord, yes!" Pip hurriedly assured her. "And to start with I'll even wear prints I don't particularly like if it means I'll get properly dressed that much quicker. Just to be respectable is a far more pressing need just at the moment than looking fashionable. If they're last season's, or the season before's, I'm hardly going to look any worse than I do in this outfit! And please don't worry about your reputation. If you don't want us to say you sold it to us *now*, if you see what I mean, we'll just say it was a dress I brought with me."

The sleekly dressed shop-owner was clearly thinking eagerly of offloading certain items of surplus stock as she said eagerly, "Please allow me to go and fetch some things for you to look at, ladies," and hurried away.

Within the hour she was back with two very harassed seamstresses and a huge bundle of cloth.

"There was a lady staying at Pitmaston House five summers ago," Miss Howes, said with clear irritation. "She said she was going to be staying with the family for longer than anticipated and would need more dresses. The lady of the house is a good client of mine, you understand, so I thought nothing of it when I was told that the bills should be sent to the house. Then I found out that the so-called guest had left under something of a cloud, and that the bills wouldn't be honoured."

"How terribly awkward for you!" sympathised Flora. "I do hope it didn't affect your further trade with the family?"

"It was a close thing," admitted Miss Howes. "The only way I could keep both the mistress and her daughters as clients was by smiling and letting the matter drop, but the dreadful woman hadn't chosen cheap materials. It cost me dearly, I don't mind admitting."

"People don't understand, do they?" Pip added. "They forget that you have to pay for the raw materials long before you get the money in for the finished goods. Many a good company has gone under because of cash-flow problems. And the banks have never been good at helping small businesses out with short-term problems."

"No! ...No, indeed!" a very startled Miss Howes agreed, shocked to find someone who understood business amongst ladies of this class.

"Right, let's have a look at this lot and see what we can do," Pip said firmly. "If what helps me, helps you, then we all win don't we?" Then belatedly realised that might be a bit of a modern concept, but Miss Howes was smiling in a slightly bemused manner even as she chivvied the seamstresses to open out the bundles of part-made dresses.

To Pip's amazement, the dresses seemed to have been made for someone very much of her kind of figure – rather broader across the shoulder than the women she was in the room with, who seemed to be typical of the better class of ladies she'd observed from the Colman's windows. As she selected a rather nice deep green and a rich burgundy, as well as a lighter-weight regency stripe in a delicate shade of blue, and another in a good quality cotton-lawn with a floral print, Pip couldn't help thinking that this woman had had rather modern tastes. As she expressed her opinion that they were lovely, she could see that these were materials which none of the others would have chosen.

"Am I making a mistake?" she asked anxiously. "Are these not appropriate?"

"I wouldn't say inappropriate," Flora said tactfully, "but they aren't the kind of materials a young woman of your age would normally pick."

Pip was surprised. "Really? Why?"

Miss Howes smiled faintly. "Well they're rather more the kind of materials the older ladies prefer. Erm, *very* much older ladies, if you understand me."

For a second Pip had thought it might have been Natalie who'd fleeced Miss Howes, but if she'd thought there was nothing anachronistic about that woman wanting older prints, then she too must have been older, so not Natalie after all. "Ah, not just older as in 'not young girls', I see. And are they cut for an older woman too?" Pip asked, worried that she might be seen as very much odder than she'd anticipated for admiring these gowns.

Again Miss Howes struggled to find a tactful response, given that this young woman was taking off her hands dresses she'd never expected to sell. "The cut is rather fuller in the skirts and bodice than a young woman might choose. And longer in the sleeve for the summer dresses."

"But isn't that easier for you?" Pip wondered. "You could take material out of the skirts to make them more ...appropriate, and shorten the sleeves? Surely that's far easier than letting them out? And they look like they aren't far off my size across the bosom, so it's minor adjustments, and you haven't begun to hem them, so that's alright, isn't it?"

The seamstresses were already brightening up and nodding their agreement, no doubt relieved that they would be spared late nights sewing by poor light to fulfil this urgent order. Miss Howes too, seemed to realise what Pip was saying, and how it could be to her benefit – less time on this commission meant more time on the work already in hand!

"Yes, indeed, we could take them in to fit you quite easily."

Pip hesitated to ask her next question, but felt she had to know. "So if these were tailored more to my age, would the matter of what material they were made out of matter less? Would they look less out of place? I'm sorry if I seem hopelessly ignorant, but I've travelled from the Americas, and then been too busy trying to survive after my husband died, to take much notice of fashion yet."

After the appropriate murmurs of sympathy over Dave's passing, the ladies all agreed that Pip would certainly pass without adverse comment in her new dresses, even if she drew few compliments.

"Good!" Pip breathed in relief. "I wouldn't want to disgrace Ha... Captain Green when we get to court and give Mrs Natalie Parsons her due desserts!"

"Parsons!" Miss Howes squealed in shock, losing her decorum in the process. "Mrs Natalie Parsons?"

Pip and Flora looked to one another, then Pip cagily answered, "Yes," but then suddenly realised who the lost client was. Shit, Natalie *had to be* that much older! Of course! "Did the scheming bi... madam cheat you too?"

Miss Howes could only nod in shock and it was one of the seamstresses who added,

" 'Er was a right one! Full of airs and graces, but I saw on 'er the marks when I measured 'er! Some man been at 'er the night afore or not long since, I tell 'ee! An' the word was 'er was settin' 'er sights on the master at Pitmaston. 'Im or 'is son, anyhow, the bisom! I told Miss Howes that. An' that's why 'er was chucked out so fast! The missus weren't havin' no loose woman in 'er house!"

Luckily Flora had recovered quickly, as had Pip, and now said smoothly, "Then you'll be glad to hear that Mrs Marston, here, has come to help clear my husband's cousin of a dreadful injustice brought on by the same lady."

It was still a shock to Pip to hear herself being called 'Mrs Marston'. It was something she'd long since forgotten about even in her dreams. Heavens, she mustn't forget that was the name she would be going by!

"Really?" Miss Howes was saying in shock, and the two seamstresses were all but prompting her to ask how, no doubt thrilled to be in on the gossip, and hoping to share it when they got home.

Flora was nodding emphatically. "Oh yes! My dear George's cousin, Captain Harry Green, has been accused by the same woman of murder."

"Murder!" the three women squeaked in shock.

"He didn't do it!" Pip told them firmly. "He'd been helping to provide for the widow of another local army man. The widow of Edward Clifford. Her father-in-law wouldn't give her a penny, I'm told."

"Oh 'e's a right old skinflint!" the other seamstress agreed. "Everyone knows Sir Roderick don't pay for nothin' unless 'e can't help it!"

Pip smile sweetly at her. "Well he wouldn't support his widowed daughter-in-law to help her bring up his grandson." That brought gasps of shock. "So her brother, Mr Gus Vaughan, was supporting her with Harry's help. Then just under a month ago Gus was murdered, and quite horribly. The ungrateful Mrs Clifford named Harry as the murderer, even though he was nowhere near the place at the time. She's a foolish woman from all I can gather, and the person really behind this is Mrs Parsons, because she wants to get her hands on Mr Vaughan's money through Mrs Clifford." It was giving her a headache remembering to call Amy 'Mrs Clifford', and to be formal over the man she thought of simply as Gus, but it had to be done to make her sound credible.

Now for the hard bit. "I was on the same ship as the captain, you see, in the same shipwreck, heading for my cousin in India. I too ended up in Falmouth in rags and with no money. Then when I heard of his misfortune I had to come to add my voice to his defence. I had to come because I hold her responsible for the death of my own husband."

Even Miss Howes clapped her hands to her mouth in horror. In a strangled voice she gasped, "*Your* husband?"

Pip grimaced. "Yes, four years ago we ran into Mrs Natalie Parsons in Birmingham. It must have been almost straight after she left here. She lured my husband off with talk of some scheme to make us all rich. For the first year or two I thought he'd just abandoned me for her. That was terribly hard." She didn't have to fake the catch in her voice at the memory. "But then I found out he'd died. Someone who knew us both found a body, and identified it as David from the distinctive jacket he wore and his ring. It was too late to be able to tell how he'd died, but in my mind I have no doubt that she stabbed him just as she stabbed poor Mr Vaughan."

The three dressmakers were staring wide-eyed at Pip, but in sympathy not in any negative way, while Flora, who had heard the story once already, was nonetheless shaking her head in dismay at Natalie's wickedness.

"I can't believe how brave you've been, Mrs Marston," she said sympathetically, but reminding Pip of how formal this society was – she might be 'Pip' to Flora in private, but in front of these women she would be 'Mrs Marston'. "And to think you were going to travel all the way to India to be a lady's companion after being left so destitute."

Pip sniffed, hoping it passed for grief rather than the bitterness she still felt over Natalie. "Hmpf! Made destitute by that woman's scheming! That's what makes me angry! When I thought it was my own foolishness for picking a poor husband it was different. But now it feels like she took him from me, then tossed him aside like an old shoe when he'd served her purpose. Whatever he was, he didn't deserve that, nor the horrible death she gave him. So you see, ladies, when I heard that she was trying to get Captain Green sent away for a murder he didn't do, just so that she could get control of Mrs Clifford's inheritance from her brother, I had to do something. I wrote to Captain Green's brother, Reverend Green, and via him Captain Green sent me the money to come here. And I shall tell my story to anyone in that court who will listen!"

"Well you won't actually go into court, of course," Flora added soothingly, "but you can certainly tell the lawyers and have your testimony read out."

Pip smiled weakly at her, but vowed that if she got her chance she'd be in that witness box in a heartbeat. These ladies might faint at the thought of being cross-examined by a sharp lawyer, but Pip was made of sterner stuff. *It can't be any worse than giving my first post-grad' paper at a conference*, she reassured herself. Three professors from her home uni', plus several eminent members of other universities, in the audience had made that a most harrowing experience, but in retrospect it had been good practise at surviving questioning.

However, it also must have motivated Miss Howes and her ladies into a fevered spate of sewing, because by the second day the two lighter-weight dresses had arrived. Coming downstairs in them and seeing Harry's face was worth the wait for Pip. She still didn't have any proper shoes and was having to make do with a rather tight pair of Flora's slippers, but he wasn't looking at her feet.

"My dear Pip!" he breathed in awe. "You look wonderful!"

"Why thank you kindly, sir!" Pip answered with a mischievous smile and a curtsey. "Do you think I shall be fit to be seen in public?"

"Oh yes!" was Harry's emphatic response. Thank God they were staying here and not at Robert's! And with bedrooms on different floors. The strain was beginning to tell on him, and it was getting worse with Pip looking more lovely every day. Never mind that she said that the garb he'd seen her in through the mirror had been practical, that dress did more for her than ever her own strange clothing had done. Once she also had shoes, he was most proud to be seen out walking with Pip on his arm. And the rest of the dresses were equally delightful as they arrived over the next couple of weeks, making Harry pay Miss Howes with an added bonus for her efforts. Pip had told him she had also been fleeced by Natalie, but this was on his account, not hers.

Then Sir Arthur appeared as September loomed, and told him that the trial would begin next week.

"It's still earlier than originally arranged," the lawyer told the assembled family, "but we have all the evidence to hand, so there's no reason now not to get it out of the way. I have the Parsons' lawyer's man put up in a hotel in Droitwich – just so that the prosecution don't get to hear of him too early! He'll testify, as will Mr Parsons' son-in-law. I've written to tell him when the trial will start and he'll be here too."

Yet there was a trial of another sort for Pip before then. As she tried on her completed new outfit in readiness for the court hearing, Flora dropped a bombshell.

"What are you planning on doing after the trial?" she asked Pip with an incredibly poor attempt at innocence. "You surely aren't thinking of going on to India now, are you? Robert's said nothing of any word coming from your cousin."

Bugger! Pip thought. She'd forgotten the story of the bloody cousin and the letter. "I really don't know, Flora," she said honestly.

"Oh good," Flora simpered, then came closer to Pip to almost whisper, "you see George has told me that Harry has said he intends to propose to you if his name is cleared! And we don't doubt that will happen now, do we?"

"Propose?" Pip echoed faintly.

"Oh, my dear! Don't you like him enough for that?" Flora asked worriedly. "Oh dear, oh dear! And George says he's most devoted to you!"

With her head in a whirl, Pip waved Flora to quiet. "No! No, it's not that! Good grief, after realising how loyal Harry was to Amy, I thought any woman would be incredibly lucky to have a man like that. And I certainly like him enormously! It's just that it's a bit of a shock, that's all. I know this probably sounds very silly to you, but I never thought of myself getting married ...again." Bloody hell, she was going to have to be careful how she put it all into words now! "It's more that the problem lies with me."

"With you? Oh, Pip, how could there be a problem with you?"

That made her smile. "That's very sweet of you to say so, Flora, but what I meant is this... That I thought I was very much in love with David, but once we were living together I realised he wasn't quite the man I'd thought he was."

"Oh dear!"

"Yes, that's about right actually, Flora. Oh dear. Nothing worse. Nothing terribly amiss with him." Well unless you counted the bondage gear, and she could hardly tell Flora about that! "He was just weak. I thought he would be looking after me. Or at least he would be once a family came along, since this was before I was told I'd never have children."

"No children? Oh Pip! How awful for you!"

Shit! She'd forgotten she'd not told Flora that bit!

"Is there no doubt?" Flora was asking with genuine concern. "No possibility of a mistake? Maybe if you were kept in bed for the duration of your confinement?"

"No, it's not like that," Pip said, trying to sound soothing. "I had a terrible infection. Inside. In my womb. I don't know whether I'd be able to carry a child, but that's rather beside the point. I can't conceive. I've seen several doctors. There's no doubt. And please don't cry on my behalf, Flora. I did a lot of crying when I first knew, but I've rather come to terms with it these days. But you see, because of that I never expected another man to want me." Well not in this day and age, anyway! In her own time being childless might have been less of an issue, and in truth her lack of a relationship was more to do with trust, but she couldn't say to Flora that she had been determined not to land herself with another useless prat like Dave. "But if Harry really wants me, then I certainly wouldn't object to Harry."

However, that night, Pip lay in bed fretting. Somehow she'd had it in the back of her mind that one way or another she would return home after this. But of course that might not be possible. All it would take would be someone moving the bloody mirror again and that was it, she'd be stuck here! And it had been over a month now already! In which case, she really had to think a lot more of what might happen. Part of her had already been feeling deep regret at the thought of saying goodbye to Harry. Hadn't wanted to go home, if she was honest with herself, however much she wanted to reassure Nick – who must be going crazy with worry by now. But marriage? Somehow that had always seemed such a big step to her. And having been so badly let down by Dave didn't make deciding any easier, either.

If he asked, would she say 'yes' to Harry? *Could* she say 'yes' to Harry? Was it any fairer to him – given what he'd been through already – to saddle him with a wife who would never fully belong in this world? At least she needn't worry about contaminating history by suddenly throwing in a whole batch of little Greens where there hadn't been any before. But what if Harry in another version of this time married someone else and had a family at last? *Oh God, you can't worry about that,* she told herself wearily as she slid towards sleep, *just decide what you want for once, girl!*

However, Flora had told George, and now George was having a manly heart to heart with Harry in the drawing room now that the rest of the household had gone to bed.

"So are you sure?" he asked his cousin. "Do you really want to marry a woman who can never give you children? And I don't think you should deceive yourself on this, Harry. Flora was quite adamant that there's no hope."

Yet Harry was quite calm. "I understand, George. And yet it doesn't make any difference to me."

"Really?"

"Yes. ...Look, I'd resigned myself to not having so much as a wife. That was how I was feeling this time last year. We'd had that bloody awful season in Bath with Amy whining all the time, and me thinking, 'Good God, how do married men stand this?' And so it wasn't such a terribly hard move to go back to the regiment and start preparing to go to India. I wasn't even sure if I'd ever see England again, George, let alone settle down with a family! If I thought of women, it was that I'd heard that many soldiers out in India have understandings with some of the native women. Enough to keep a man sane, but not marriage of the kind that you and Flora enjoy. Something comfortable enough, and I would have been prepared to make sure such a woman was well cared for and properly set up – I'm not like Edward was, able to use women and not think of the consequences. But to have the kind of companionship I find with Pip was something I never dreamed would come my way now. So yes, I will take her if she'll have me, and be very happy to do so."

"Then I hope all goes well at court and you have your chance at that life," George said resignedly, although Harry could see George wasn't happy at the prospect, even though he knew George liked and respected Pip. George could never have been happy without the full family, but Harry knew he was quite a different sort of man, and was content with what had been brought into his path – however strange that path might have been!

On the following morning, as she walked with Harry to the law court with the rest of the family, Pip couldn't help but feel butterflies of anxiety in her stomach. Please God, Sir Arthur knew his stuff! She couldn't help herself as they parted from him inside, putting her arms around him and hugging him tight.

"Take care, Harry!" she told him as she inhaled the scent of him through his army jacket. "I'm with you all the way!" Somehow the prospect of having him as her future husband had pushed her own feelings up a notch, and now she knew she would be distraught beyond measure if they lost this case.

"Thank you, Pip," he said softly, and she felt a kiss on the top of her head. That was all the affection either of them could show in such a public place and Pip knew, even so, she was lucky they were surrounded by family, so that the general public couldn't see her embracing him. Then she watched him march off in the company of two court officials, the upright military man, smart in his red coat and crisply laundered breeches, black boots polished to a near mirror finish. It had been a further expense to get Harry a replacement uniform in time, especially since he had no idea if he ever would rejoin his regiment, but he'd wanted very much to go into court with his head held high. Sir Arthur had said he thought it mattered little whether Harry went in in uniform or smart gentleman's dress, but to

Harry's mind it said that he was no down-on-his-luck captain, cast off by the army, but a proper officer just waiting to go back into service once the trial was over. And Pip agreed.

"You only get one chance to give the judge and jury a first impression," she'd told him, "so let them see you at your best. Make it a positive one! Show them what an honourable, upstanding man Captain Harry Green is!"

And with tears welling up in her eyes now, Pip thought that if they weren't impressed with what they were going to see, they bloody well ought to be! Somehow she would get Harry out of this alive even if she had to break every social convention to do it – and maybe organise a gaol break in the process! – but first they had to get through the next few days.

Chapter 17

September 1824

The first day of the trial was little more than each side setting out their cases in the broadest sense, and all of them went home feeling faintly deflated. Pip had no idea how much money William Colman had put up as surety for Harry – and it had possibly been a huge amount – but he was allowed home with them. Sir Arthur did tell them at the court, that in part this was due to the fact that the evidence against Harry was sufficiently weak for there to be some serious doubt as to whether he'd done the deed, making the judge give him some leeway. Yet it didn't feel like it somehow, and dinner was a very quiet affair.

On the second day, however, there was something different to catch Pip's interest, for Amy put in her first appearance. At first Pip couldn't work out who the two ladies were sitting behind the prosecution lawyer, hidden as they were behind the frills of the bonnets all women seemed to wear in public, often even indoors. But then something was said, Amy Clifford's name was mentioned, and she turned to look at the jury. No doubt once upon a time that little-girl-lost look had worked its appeal on people. Now, Pip thought it just looked ridiculous. Utterly incongruous on a rather stout lady of middle years.

And how old was Amy? Pip had to stop to work it out. If she'd been barely eighteen when she married Edward Clifford in 1811, then she had to be only around thirty-one, but she looked closer to forty if not even older. She certainly wasn't making any attempt to look after herself, that was for sure, but it shocked Pip to realise that Amy wasn't more than a couple of years older than her own age now. This whole business of transferring information back and forth between the two times had blurred things like that for her. But it was with real shock that she realised that the other woman had to be Natalie.

Where was Dave's goddess now? She was far more the old battle-axe! But then, of course, Natalie had been that bit older than him to start off with. As the prosecution lawyer droned on, making mountains out of molehills, Pip allowed her mind to wander. Although Dave had only been a year ahead of her at uni', he'd been the oldest in his year, while she'd been nearly the youngest. So in real terms there'd been closer to two years between them. And Natalie had been at least two years older than Dave, possibly closer to three, so when she'd gone through the portal she would have been something like thirty even then. And what with her going back to far earlier than she'd expected, she too had aged thirteen years just as Amy had done, not the mere four years Pip had. Heavens, that made Natalie forty-three, more or less! And the years hadn't been kind to her – but then her life since then had been more than a little precarious by the sound of it.

It amused Pip no end to realise that if Natalie ever made it back to her own time, she wouldn't be drawing any young men of the twenty-first century in anymore. Most of them would recoil in disgust at someone so haggard propositioning them, for Natalie was as thin as Amy was stout. No wonder she'd wanted her dresses cut full – they were to hide the bones and cover scrawny arms, not fat. No, Natalie would never be described so glowingly ever again! And in turn that quelled one of Pip's secret fears. She'd been dreading Natalie appearing in all her glory. She was already prepared for the fact that the jury in these times were all men, and if anyone was going to have an effect on them, then it would have been the younger Natalie, charismatic and seductive. Now, though, Pip could see that she would sway no-one with her charms, or at least certainly not from that kind of distance. Maybe, face to face she could still cast some allure over men, but not in this large court.

Coming out of her reverie, Pip realised that the court was about to recess for lunch, but it was only as she heard some of the other women around her talking that she got the germ of an idea. Even though the general structure of an English court was happily in existence by now and recognisable to Pip, it was still a surprise to her to see that there were nonetheless some major differences; not least being that the jury were out in the general press of people outside the court. Some of the men were even being joined for lunch by women who looked to be their wives, going by the body language and casual conversation.

"Do they not keep the jury separate?" she ventured to ask George as he led her and his father down the road to find somewhere to eat. Today Flora was otherwise occupied with domestic duties, although she would come to hear Harry's defence, and Harry would be eating in a cell.

"Separate?" Uncle William muttered in surprise. "Good Lord, my dear, why would they do that? There aren't *that* many men qualified to stand as jurors in Worcester and we all know one another. You could hardly hide Walter Ralph from anyone could you?" and he gestured towards a very portly member of the jury who was tipping his hat to a couple walking by. "Damned good butcher is Walter, everyone knows him."

Pip mouthed a silent 'oh' and said nothing more, but the incident made it clearer to her just how much it worked in Harry's favour having the trial here in Worcester. The prosecution must have tumbled to this at some point, because Sir Arthur had told them that his opponents had suddenly tried to get the trial moved to Hereford (once it had been clear that Harry intended to fight back), but to no avail, Sir Arthur had stood his ground. But she kept on the alert now, as they walked through the throng, and was rewarded with some overheard snippets.

"Did you see Amy Clifford?" she heard two ladies gossiping as they passed, and her friend saying,

"She looks very poor doesn't she! Such a pretty child all those years ago, but she's not making much of an effort nowadays."

"Well what do you expect, so spoiled..."

The rest was lost in the general din of passing carts, horses and people, but several times more Pip heard unfavourable comments about Amy and Natalie. So when she saw Miss Howes that evening as they walked home, Pip thought to ask her something. Leaving the men to walk on home, she made an excuse of ladies dress matters and hurried to speak to Miss Howes as she was locking up her shop.

"I'm sorry to bother you when you must be eager to get home," she began, "but that green dress you re-cut for me..."

"Yes," Miss Howes acknowledged tentatively.

"Oh don't worry!" Pip hurriedly reassured her. "I think it's lovely, and so does Harry! No, it's just that I was thinking that it's a very distinctive colour and textured print, and the lady who originally commissioned it from you was in court today."

"Was she?" Miss Howes exclaimed, suddenly all interest.

"She was! And I'm thinking that she might just remember that dress if I was to wear it."

"I'm sure *she* would," replied Miss Howes with a derisory sniff. "It's not exactly the kind of cloth I sell by the bolt every month – although I wish I could!"

"Then what do you think to this," and Pip outlined her plan.

On the fourth morning, Amy was called to give her evidence and sniffed tearfully throughout the whole proceedings. Pip couldn't help but feel satisfied at the way Amy kept wandering off into general complaints about how Harry had stopped paying for this trifle or that outing, despite her barrister's best efforts to focus her on blackening Harry's reputation. This was exactly what Pip had prayed for, but hardly dared hope for – that Amy would come across as a vacuous woman who scarcely knew what month it was, and whose testimony was bound to be questionable.

Much would hinge on this, Pip knew, given that Amy was Harry's main accuser. If she'd given a solid performance, eloquent, demure and credible as to the state of affairs between Harry and Gus, then Sir Arthur was going to have to earn his fee defending Harry. But with Amy failing at every turn to convince, the prosecution were now going to have to lean heavily on the other witness – Gus Vaughan's supposed fiancée. And Natalie might not be so alluring these days, but Pip knew she was no fool, and she at least would be lucid and very clear, and that Pip dreaded. Sympathy for a woman robbed of her intended might well sway those not yet convinced one way or the other.

Well Pip wasn't having that! As they all trooped back in after lunch, Pip made sure she'd changed her dress and was right at the front of the public gallery, well in view of the witness stand. The clerk of the court called Mrs Natalie

Parsons to come forward, and just as she turned and faced the rest of the court, Pip stood as if to adjust her skirt.

Suddenly oblivious to her surroundings, Natalie shrieked, "What's that woman doing wearing *my* dress?" There was a shocked gasp from around the court, but Natalie was taken off guard. "That's *mine*! How dare she! That's my dress, you thief!" And Pip stood stock still, as if taken by surprise, but allowing Natalie to see even more of the dress and that it was only minorly altered from the one she'd commissioned.

"Madam, be silent!" the judge bellowed, "I will not have such fripperies discus..."

But Natalie simply rode over the top of him with her more piercing voice. "That's *mine*!"

"No it is *not*," a calm voice came from the other end of the public gallery. Miss Howes stood up with dignified calm and said into the stunned silence. "*You* never paid for it! *You* tried to rob me of this garment by having it made with no intention of ever paying me for it. Therefore it is *not* yours and never was! It was left to me to get what compensation I could from the debts you left me, and therefore I sold it to someone who *could* pay. And by the way, my own solicitor will be seeking you after this court adjourns."

With perfect dignity Miss Howes then sat down again, after making an elegant curtsey to the judge and murmuring an apology to him. Since she'd told Pip that she had made the wedding dress for the daughter of the very same judge, there was little chance that she would be chastised for defending her reputation, and now he chose to ignore her and rebuke Natalie instead. However, for Pip the real payoff was that Natalie was now completely off balance. All the composure she had come in with was gone, and she struggled to answer the questions put to her with the kind of aplomb required to salvage the prosecution from Amy's debacle in the morning.

As they walked home that night Sir Arthur caught up with them. Doffing his hat to Pip, he smiled, and with a twinkle in his eye said,

"I shall be having to put you on retainer if you're going to part of my job for me."

Pip grinned at him. A grin which got broader when George exclaimed,

"Good heavens, do you mean you did that deliberately?"

Uncle William guffawed. "Don't be an ass, George! Of course she did! Clever lass!"

"It was Miss Howes who gave me the idea," Pip confessed.

"Really?" even the normally unflappable Sir Arthur seemed surprised at that. "Dear me, I must remember to settle my accounts with her rather more promptly!"

That made Pip laugh. "Well it might be nice, given what it costs Miss Howes every time she has to fill a commission and doesn't get paid until the final dress gets handed over, but that wasn't quite what I meant," and she explained about how distinctive the material was. "So you see I checked with Miss Howes and we both agreed that Mrs Parsons would certainly remember it, and particularly as the cut wasn't so different either." Of the dresses Pip had taken off Miss Howes' hands, the green had been altered the least. "From what I knew of Natalie of old, I guessed she would cope with being in the witness box, and with any questioning. I toyed with the idea of keeping the dress back for when you might question her, Sir Arthur, but then I thought that it might come a bit late at that point if she'd already made a favourable impression on the jury. Pulling that kind of trick then might also have seemed more obvious – you know, if people thought we were a bit desperate. So I reckoned it would be better to have her show herself in her true colours earlier rather than later."

Sir Arthur turned and bowed over her hand. "My dear lady, that's as clear a piece of reasoning as I've heard in a long while! I wish the young gentlemen studying under me could do as well," the last said with more than a little sarcasm, and Pip knew from Uncle William that Sir Arthur was despairing of the latest intake he had in his chambers.

"I was thinking of Gus too," Pip confessed, not wanting to say that she was also planning on there being some comments at the jurors' dinner tables tonight, with wives speaking up about what they thought of a woman who would cheat a respected dressmaker so – that might smack of jury rigging even in this era! "As much hangs on her being the kind of woman he would make a proposal to. I know you were going to call into question whether that arrangement really existed, Sir Arthur, but while she stood there in that court all calm and serene it wouldn't have seemed so farfetched."

"But now they've seen a screaming harridan!" George gasped in awe.

"And that engagement will look a lot less plausible, secret or otherwise," Sir Arthur concluded with a smug smile. "Excellent, my dear Mrs Marston! You've provided me with an opportunity I shall not squander!"

However Sir Arthur did far more the next day than rest on what Pip had begun, when he began the defence. With surgical precision he proceeded to dismember the prosecution. The first of his witnesses was Dr Gething, who gave an Oscar-winning performance as the disinterested professional man, but who left no-one in any doubt that at the time of the murder Harry would have been hard pressed to swat a fly, much less stab someone.

He was followed by the Worcester lawyer who had drawn up Gus' first will leaving Harry as the executor of his estate, and a long time ago it had been too.

Naïve about women Gus might have been, but where money was concerned he'd been razor sharp, acknowledging in the will that much as he loved his parents, he would not leave them money directly in case his father's former debtors got their hands on it. It had been made way back in 1817 when Gus had come home on leave from India. And having therefore seen for himself how incapable his father was now, he'd wanted to leave his mother and sister better provided for. Of itself it wasn't going to prove Harry's innocence, but it did force the question as to why he would have waited so long to act. He'd needed the money far more in 1817, but by the time he'd spent much time with Gus in recent years, his own fortunes had improved to such an extent as to not to be in need.

Then Horatio Parsons' son-in-law appeared in all his finery – the epitome of a reputable London banker – and confirmed that Harry and Gus had been working amicably to support Amy right from back as far as 1814. Ten years without so much as the slightest hiccup in their financial transactions was pretty convincing evidence that Harry had no designs on Gus' money. But he also testified as to the current healthy state of Harry's finances – no sudden withdrawals of cash which might indicate the paying of gambling debts or the like, no sudden expenses which couldn't be accounted for. Harry had been the perfect client and still was.

He also swore that his elderly father-in-law had been so ill he had hardly known what he was doing when Natalie – the very same woman who was a witness for the prosecution – had got her hands on him, although that was more of an aside than the main brunt of his testimony. What surprised everyone except Sir Arthur was the information that Natalie had tried to work her way into another banker's home before then, the testimony for which was provided by the Parsons' lawyer and read out. It certainly shifted the urgent need for cash away from Harry, and with it any motive for the killing, as well as undermining Natalie's testimony.

The lawyer's man who had spoken to Gus also came across well, giving his evidence clearly and without embellishment, so that by the time he'd finished no-one could doubt that Gus would never have proposed to Natalie unless he'd suddenly and irrevocably lost his mind. To Pip it was almost going too well. Why had this case been allowed to proceed if the evidence against Harry was so weak, she began wondering? But then, she had to remind herself, she and the family had known the Parsons would testify on Harry's behalf, as would the solicitor who had drawn up Gus' will – the prosecution hadn't. And the true state of affairs over that will were vital too. Yes, Gus had changed his will just lately, but only to insist that Harry be in charge of allowances for young Eddie as well, since the young man was showing an unfortunate inclination to follow his father where money was concerned.

Therefore everything Pip had said to Harry back the first time she'd seen him face to face was true. If he hadn't mounted a spirited defence then he would have been in real trouble. Had the facts all been taken at their face value, and not been set into the context of wider events and past histories, things could by now have been looking very gloomy. In fact, it could have been even worse, for if the case had been heard in Hereford there would have been no local knowledge of Amy and her family to remain unsaid, but lurking in the minds of the jurors. Here, no matter what directions the judge might make, those twelve local men would still remember that the Vaughans had been nigh on penniless for years, whereas Harry's family had remained respectable if not grand.

At those thoughts Pip permitted herself a figurative pat on the back. She'd done it! Saving some horrible unexpected turn of events, she'd saved Harry from the gallows! But Harry wasn't so easily placated.

"Gus was my friend!" he told her vehemently as they strolled along the riverside by the cathedral on the Sunday morning after church. "Someone killed him, and I want *them* to be brought to justice! It's not enough to clear my name if they go free."

"Could they bring a prosecution against Natalie immediately?" Pip wondered. "I think even the dimmest person in that court must be suspecting her by now."

Harry sighed. "The trouble is, Sir Arthur thinks they'll throw the case out on Monday – tomorrow – but if they do that then they won't get to the evidence of the body Father found. We haven't got there yet, nor to Mr Holmes' testimony, and that's the evidence which would throw the suspicion fully onto Natalie. I know Sir Arthur said it would be better to argue that the evidence against me is weak, rather than trying to show who else could have done it, but I really wanted that to come out in court."

"So did I," Pip agreed, turning to hug him tight. "In the meantime, we seem to very alone just here, so..." she put her arms around his neck and kissed him.

On the following morning the court had no sooner sat than the judge adjourned it again, and called the barristers to his chambers. After that, and with remarkable speed, the case was thrown out and Harry acquitted, with the judge insisting there would remain no stain upon his character.

In the consequent joyous celebrations within the court, it was only when Pip and Harry were walking out surrounded by the family, that Pip noticed Amy. She was sat alone on the steps, a small bundle of black huddled on the golden stone, sobbing. The worthies of Worcester were passing her by either unseen or with looks of disgust, leaving no doubt as to what they thought of a woman who could accuse a man who had so loyally supported her of such a heinous crime, and with so little evidence to do so. But what bothered Pip was, where was Natalie?

"Harry wait!" she said urgently. "Look!" and with a tilt of her head gestured towards Amy.

He turned, then saw Amy and sighed heavily. "Oh dear." His voice was flat and filled with a certain dread. "I did promise Gus..."

"No, not that!" Pip quickly corrected him. "She's alone! Where's Natalie? She wasn't in court today!"

That brought Harry's head up in shock from the dejected droop as his joy at going free had melted at the thought of resuming the burden of Amy. Behind them Miss Howes appeared with a gentleman in legal black, and they too were casting about them, looking at the crowd, then went to Amy. Neither Pip nor Harry needed to hear what was said to know that they were questioning her about Natalie. And equally Amy didn't know, going by the bemused shaking of her head. Indeed Amy seemed to be barely coherent or sensible of what was going on around her.

"We could see her back to where she's staying," Pip suggested softly to Harry. "That way you've looked after her enough to satisfy your conscience – and on the way we can ask her about Natalie!"

"We'll see you back at the house," Harry told Uncle William.

"But we have celebrations planned!" the old man protested.

"And we'll gladly join you in them," Pip confirmed, "but someone is missing today, the real villain of this dreadful case – Mrs Parsons! So in the interest of finding the real killer, we'll walk Amy to her lodgings – no more! She doesn't deserve more. In fact she doesn't deserve that! But she may know more than she realises, and Harry wants Gus' real killer brought to account, so we have to do this. It won't take long. There can't be many places in Worcester she could be staying at."

Uncle William wasn't best pleased, but he did understand that Harry wanted justice for his dead friend as well as himself, and so with a firm promise that they wouldn't be long, Harry and Pip approached Amy.

One look at Harry's face convinced Pip that she should deal with this.

"Amy, get up!" she said sternly.

A face red, blotchy and streaked with tears looked blankly up at her, then saw Harry and recoiled.

"Oh don't be stupid, girl!" Pip told her with ill-disguised impatience. "You've *never* had anything to fear from Harry, although God knows, just now he has good cause to want to spank you for the ridiculous little girl you are. Now get up from those steps!"

"Who are you?" Amy whimpered as she struggled to rise. After she'd fallen back the third time, Harry reluctantly went round to the back of her and hoisted her to her feet as Pip bluntly said,

"I'm Harry's fiancée."

Amy was so taken aback by that that she swayed precariously on the steps, forcing Pip to take one arm and Harry the other.

"Where are you staying?" Pip demanded. "Come on,

we'll walk you back. And where's your friend?" Amy looked up at her and the bottom lip began trembling again. "Oh for Christ's sake give the tears a rest!" Pip snapped. "God help me, Amy, but if you keep snivelling like that I shall give you such a slapping!" and the shock of being spoken to in such terms actually stopped the tears instantly. "You're just working yourself up into this state."

"I can't help it," Amy sniffled.

"Oh yes you bloody-well can!" Pip insisted, marching Amy along so fast the podgy woman was almost jogging to keep up, and unable to slow down when held on both sides. "Now where are you staying?"

"The Old Talbot," Amy supplied, but then had to concentrate on breathing as Pip strode along in time with Harry, skirts swirling and caught up in her other hand to avoid tripping on the hem.

However at the Talbot there was an unpleasant surprise.

"Well where's the money?" the man behind the bar demanded. "Your friend walked out of here without paying! She's packed your bags, and you've not paid for the last two days."

"But she had my purse!" wailed Amy in horror.

"Of course she did," growled Pip in disgust. "Holy crap, Amy, you're beyond useless! Well you'd better sell some of your jewellery to pay this good man, then, hadn't you?"

Yet once they investigated Amy's baggage, it was clear that she'd been left with not one thing of any value. Even a pair of beautiful kid gloves which had been a present from Gus had gone. So far Harry had said nothing directly to Amy, but now he glared at her and told her,

"For the memory of Gus which I hold dear, I shall settle this bill for you. You will then come to my cousin's and sleep in one of the servants' rooms until you can be taken back to Hereford. But you will not speak to anyone, you will have your meals in your room, and I will not see you while you are there, do I make myself clear? I will discharge my duty as Gus requested of me in his will, but from now on it will be done at a distance and through a lawyer. But before we go out into the street I'm going to ask you again, where is Mrs Parsons?"

Amy's lip began to tremble in earnest as she looked up into Harry's furious eyes, then got an even nastier shock as Pip added,

"And if you don't tell him, he's going to wait downstairs, and I shall show you what another woman who comes from the same place as Natalie can be like when roused! We both had to stand up for ourselves in some pretty rough places, so think again if you reckon the worst you'll get is a slap! Because right now I could rip your arms off and beat you senseless with the raggy stumps for what you've put Harry through!"

Over Amy's head Harry's expression turned in an instant from anger to amusement as he looked Pip in the eye, mouthing, "Raggy stumps?"

Pip shrugged as Amy wilted onto the bed. "Right, off you go then, darling!" she said brightly. "She's not going to tell us willingly so I shall just have to whack it out of her!"

"Noooo!" Amy wailed in panic, clutching at Harry's sleeve. "Oh please don't leave me alone with her!" and rolled terrified eyes Pip's way.

"Then tell us, where is Natalie?" Pip growled, earning her another amused glance from Harry, who knew that Pip could never carry out her threats.

"I don't know!" Amy hiccupped frantically. "Truly I don't! We walked to the court together, then just outside she said she wasn't feeling well and needed to find a privy.

She told me to go in and that she'd be with me before the judge came in – only she wasn't! Please believe me, I don't know where she is!"

Sadly, Pip and Harry had to agree that Amy seemed to be telling the truth. She really didn't know where Natalie had gone to. So they marched her back to Uncle William's house and up to the attic where the servants slept, and then went and joined in the celebrations. However, in a hurried discussion on the stairs, Pip convinced Harry that Amy should go first thing the next morning.

"We should take her as far as the Farm, not force your family to look at your accuser," she told him sympathetically, and he was glad she'd said that, because there was open horror from the rest of the family that Amy was under their roof.

"That ...that ...*hussy* is here?" exploded Uncle William at the news.

"She's destitute, Uncle," Harry said in disgust, "And God help me, I'm still the executor of Gus' will, so I fear I still have a duty of care towards her. Poor Gus could never in his wildest imaginings have foreseen as situation such as this."

Then Sir Arthur arrived to join in the celebrations, and upon being told of the unwelcome guest said thoughtfully,

"Then tomorrow I would go to the bank and enquire what has happened to the money in Mrs Clifford's account. The dreadful Mrs Parsons couldn't have touched the main money invested by Mr Vaughan, but there were regular amounts paid to Mrs Clifford for her household expenses via the bank on Broad Street – Mr Vaughan had been intending to move the matter to a Hereford bank, but hadn't done so at the time he died. If I were you, I would check whether that has been drained since Amy Vaughan had access to it. And you might need to check whether the rent has been paid on the house in Hereford, too, before you travel all the way over there."

He also told them that he would be speaking to his colleagues and the judges in Worcester to try to get a prosecution brought immediately against Natalie Parsons for Gus' death.

"Mr Homes, in particular, was most aggrieved not to have his day," Sir Arthur added, "and I think we have more than enough evidence to start proceedings, even if she's not present as yet."

However in one respect Pip didn't allow Amy to impinge on the celebrations at Harry's release. She'd promised herself that whether or not they were in his cousin's house come that day, he would be celebrating in a very private way with her that night. As soon as the household had settled for the night, she crept downstairs to Harry's and slipped in through the door without knocking, then snuggled into the bed beside him. Aside from a slightly surprised, "Pip?" he made no other protests, and found some of his wilder dreams becoming very real and physical.

At breakfast they were both barely able to suppress their smiles in front of the family.

"I think we've trespassed on your kindness for long enough," Harry told George and Uncle William as he held Pip's hand under the table. He desperately wanted to be alone with her tonight in a place where there wasn't the danger of the family hearing them! As it was, all he really wanted to do was take her back upstairs to the bedroom and carry on where they'd left off.

"But where will you stay until you're married?" asked George tactlessly.

"With Robert!" Pip answered brightly. Shit! Did George really expect them to be sitting around demurely doing nothing until then? "We can be looking for somewhere to rent while we're with him, and there's plenty of room at the rectory. More room than you have here with a growing family!" she smiled at Flora who was staring greenly with morning sickness at the bread on her plate.

"Would you consider continuing to rent the Farm?" George asked Harry, but before he could answer Pip had gulped,

"Oh my God, that's it!"

"What is?" Harry asked worriedly.

"Where Natalie's gone! Mrs Parsons! She's gone to the Farm!"

"But why would the damned woman go there?" demanded Uncle William. "She's no business there. Surely there's nothing for her there?"

"There are some of Gus' things," Pip told him, "some of which are very nice pieces which she could sell," then mouthed "mirror!" urgently at Harry.

"Oh God, yes!" Harry gasped, luckily not giving the game away in his shock. "Yes we should go as soon as we've seen the bank this morning."

Then as he and Pip were upstairs, and after briefly enjoying each other in another urgent but ecstatic coupling, Pip thought to ask today's date as she tried to straighten the bodice of her dress.

"I believe it must be ...yes it is, it's the twenty-first."

Pip pulled away as he began gently nibbling her ear. "Oh no! Harry, that's one of the dates when she was planning to come back. I mean go forwards! Forward to where she and I come from. It was in that diary of hers that I read! That's why she wasn't in court yesterday! She knew it would take time to get back to the mirror and she needed to be back there by tonight!"

That pulled Harry up sharply. "You mean she could get

away to your time? I thought the mirror didn't work going that way?"

"Not for me to go back on the day I came through." Pip admitted. "But I think Natalie believes that she'll be able to get back. She wrote that she tried to come back to this period the first time on the twenty-first – after she'd stabbed Paul but before she murdered Dave – but it didn't work. She wrote that she wasn't sure whether she hadn't used enough blood. But one of the other things she'd scribbled down was that you might only be able to go each way on certain dates. She'd sent poor Paul through to the past, in other words to now, on Lughnasadh – the same day I came through on four years later – and she came herself on Halloween, that's All Soul's Eve to you. There are two other dates. The first of February and the first of May, quartering the year up. Her theory being that at these quarters of the year you could go *backwards* in time. Then on the two solstices – midwinter and midsummer – and on the two equinoxes, you could travel *forwards*. I have no way of knowing if this is correct. It might just have been a fluke each time we fell through the portal and there really is no way back, but *Natalie* doesn't believe that!"

"We must hurry!" Harry gasped, grabbing his jacket and something else in a long bundle of waxed cloth from under the bed. "Come on!"

It turned out the Amy wasn't even out of bed yet, so with instructions to the Colman's two maids to get her up and dressed, and to meet them when they came out of the bank, Harry and Pip dashed off to consult with the local banker. He confirmed Sir Arthur's dire warnings. Letters had come asking where the money was for the rent on the house in Hereford, the landlord having been in contact with the bank already. And the account was utterly drained. Not a penny remained in it, and Natalie had even been in while she and Amy had been in Worcester, trying to get an advance on the next month's payment. Luckily she'd been bulked at that attempt.

"We don't operate like that," the banker told Harry disgustedly. "To a gentleman like yourself, with good credit elsewhere and with good references, it would be a different matter, but not in this instance. Oh no!"

Thanking the banker, but grieved at the thought that more money would have to be spent to sort Amy out, they hurried out of the bank to where George waited with a hired horse and trap, and a very disgruntled Amy bundled up in the back.

"Take care, Harry!" he warned as he got down and handed over the reins. For some reason he gestured to the long bundle which was under the driver's seat. "Be careful! We don't want you in trouble again so soon!"

"I will!" growled Harry, "But I'm not facing that woman unprepared!"

He all but threw Pip up onto the other side of the front seat, then nimbly jumped up and cracked the whip over the head of the horse. George had chosen well, and the spirited animal took off at a canter, forcing people to hurry out of their way as they shot out of the buildings along the waterside, and over the river.

At first Pip was too busy hanging on for dear life to question Harry as to what George had meant. Her only consolation was that Amy was wailing in terror in the back as she got bounced around with the luggage, Pip and Harry having already packed the night before with the intent of heading to the Farm anyway. However, once they were past Martley, Harry pulled over to give the horse a chance to breathe and pulled the package out. To Pip's shock, the first thing out was an officer's sword. Not the ceremonial sort with a beautiful pommel and an engraved blade. This one looked like it had seen real service.

"Not as good as my old one that went down with the *Kent*," Harry declared, making a few practise cuts and lunges, "but it'll do nicely! Good and sharp too!"

He buckled the sword belt around his waist over his coat, then pulled the other item out. It was a gun! A long one which Pip thought might be an early rifle. Certainly it didn't look like any musket she'd ever seen in museums, but armaments weren't a speciality of hers.

"A rifle?" she asked weakly.

"I am *not* letting that woman get away with murdering Gus!" Harry rapped out bitterly, giving Amy a black look as her wailing went up another notch at the sight of the sword and the gun.

"I didn't kill him!" Amy howled in panic. "I *didn't,* Harry! I could never! Not anyone!"

"Not you, you fool!" Harry snapped, but making Pip realise that Amy had never considered that it might have been Natalie who was the killer, and had utterly misunderstood who Harry meant by 'that woman'. She leaned over into the back and grabbed Amy's arm, giving it a shake to get her attention.

"He doesn't mean you, Amy! No-one could believe you'd do such a thing." That came out more derogatory than consoling. "He's talking about Natalie. We have good reason to think Natalie killed Gus. *She's* the killer! The real murderer!"

Amy went white. "No," she whispered. "Natalie? No! Why? Why would she murder Gus?"

"For his money, you silly wench," Pip sighed, grabbing the back of the seat as Harry flicked the horse into a brisk trot, then up into a canter again. "What did she tell you? That she'd look after you and Eddie? That she could manage your money for you?"

Amy was now so shocked she forgot to cry. "She said Gus was being silly saying I couldn't manage my own affairs. She said that she'd show me how to manage things. That as another woman she knew how important it is to have the niceties of life, like good linen, which Gus would never appreciate. She said he would be thinking of more manly things to do with his money, but that he would have to see things differently once he and she were married."

"You do understand that Gus never proposed to her, don't you?" Pip questioned, and was appalled to see Amy shaking her head. "Oh God, Amy, do you never open your eyes? Didn't you wonder that he was never openly affectionate to her? Gus, who was so kind to you? He wasn't just being shy. She just said that to fool you. He couldn't stand her! What she really wanted was control of Gus' money. She never was your friend, she was just using you."

Even irritated as she was with Amy's naivety, Pip couldn't help but feel a bit sorry for the other woman. It must be terrible to be so dim as to never have wondered about such things. Maybe once upon a time Amy had been capable of learning, but years of leaning on everyone and anyone had left her completely incapable of looking out for herself. Pip had never met anyone quite so helpless. No wonder Gus had been so anxious for Harry to be Amy's guardian.

"I need my laudanum," Amy weakly moaned from the back, and Pip wondered how often she'd fallen back on sedation as a means of coping.

They tore into Clifton in the mid-afternoon and paused at the rectory to try and find Robert, but no-one was at home. He hadn't been in court the day before to hear of Harry's acquittal because the trial had ended earlier than expected, but now Harry wanted to give him the good news even if it would be only the shortest of stops. However, a passing elderly lady said that Robert had gone to visit a sick farmer over the next ridge, and so they set off again.

On the rougher and less-used track Harry had to take the horse at a slower pace, but it still wasn't a long drive to Cold Hunger Farm. They took a slightly different route into the farm to the one Pip had used in modern times, going down into the dip and then taking a twisting track up the side of the hill to come at the house from the front rather than the side. This was the track Pip and Harry had walked down in the dark, and it explained to Pip why it had felt so unfamiliar – this track she'd never been on before because it had disappeared by her time. Yet as Harry drove the cart around the earth-mound which Pip knew contained the remains of the old chapel, she saw the side of the farmhouse in this era for the first time.

Pip had never been a screamer, but she screamed now.

"When did that appear?" she shrieked, as a startled Harry almost fell off the trap at her screaming practically down his ear.

"What?" he demanded.

"That!" she cried pointing with a shaking finger. There, embedded in the wall of the house was an old Roman shrine – a figure reclining, crowned with spikes and set into a niche in the wall. "That's not there in my time!"

"What? That old thing? It's been here as long as I've kno... Oh Christ!"

Now Harry looked shaken, for what shook him was not the shrine itself but the fact that the figure was smeared with blood. Fresh blood!

"That's a shrine to Cybele," gulped Pip, feeling very sick. "The Romans' Magna Mater – the Great Mother – but it's not a good cult." She swallowed hard and regained some focus and forced herself to look at it again. "Actually that figure's not Cybele, but Attis. Very androgynous! A pretty shepherd lad with terrible inclinations! And it's worse it's him and not Cybele herself. His cult wasn't encouraged even in a culture as bloodthirsty as the Romans'. Oh God, Harry, this is bad, very bad! I didn't know that there was a shrine actually as *part* of the house."

They both leapt down from the trap and, leaving a stunned Amy behind, hurried forward around a large lilac to look at the shrine. Then Harry gave a cry of anguish and pounced on something on the floor. As he turned and held it up, Pip could see it was a clergyman's surplice, and it was wet with blood.

"Robert?" Harry bellowed desperately, but all was silence.

Chapter 18

September 1824

"Christ!" Harry swore, "What the bloody hell is Robert doing here? He had no reason to come. He knew I wouldn't be here! Where is he? ...Robert? ...Robert, where are you?"

As he tried to shake the folds out of the garment, looking for rents which might suggest stab wounds, a small piece of paper floated to the ground, bloodstained but legible.

"What's that?" Pip exclaimed, pouncing on it before the breeze could blow it away. She picked it up and Harry leaned over her shoulder to read, grimly aware of the contrast between the soft scent of Pip's hair and the sharp yet cloying smell of drying blood.

> *Everything has gone wrong! I will be found guilty, there is no doubt now. I fear for my life and must flee the country. All others have deserted me, you are the only one I can turn to. Meet me at the farm as soon as you can! Tell no-one!*
>
> *Harry*

"Oh for God's sake!" Harry fumed bitterly. "Robert, why do you have to be such a fool? This isn't even like my writing!"

"It's hers," Pip groaned. "I'd know it anywhere after ploughing through that sodding diary for hours. But why did he believe it?"

"Because she played on his weaknesses," Harry answered bitterly. "He's never really believed that Uncle William and the family were helping me for anything other than an ulterior motive. Even after all they've done for us, he still thinks they want to pull me down. She must have realised that Robert wasn't in court, and guessed that he couldn't bear to watch me get sentenced. God curse her, but she's a clever, conniving bitch! It's just enough to get him out here, and not enough to risk getting a detail wrong which might make him question the note. But why did she want him here? Revenge on us?"

"No! Fuck!" Pip exploded. "Fuck, this is *my* fault! I should have known! She needs blood to activate the mirror! Oh crap, I shall never forgive myself if something happens to Robert because of this!"

"The damned portal, of course!"

"Yes, she's realised it's all gone wrong and needs to make certain she can get through to our time and safety."

"But why the statue?" Harry asked, forcing himself to a calm he was far from feeling. "Why besmirch that? No-one's seen that before – and I'm sure my father would have noticed something so pagan as a blood-soaked statue when he found Paul's body! So why now?"

"To get things started, I expect," Pip said regretfully, still shaking her head in frustration that she hadn't thought more carefully of how Natalie would get back. "She can't be sure that the mirror will activate in our time. I told you about the mirror having to be on the piece of old Roman wood, didn't I?"

"Yes."

"Well she doesn't know about that. So she must be thinking that on the previous times she's tried to return she wasn't doing enough of *something,* instead of knowing that the mirror must've been moved in our future time. After all, she thinks it's in an almost derelict house no-one knows about but her. So she must be thinking that she needs to empower the old link in some extra way, and if she's tried all the chants and loopy stuff – or worse, after all this time finds she can't remember them word for word – she'll be panicking and thinking sheer quantity of blood will do! And this is a shrine to a goddess' acolyte who liked his adherents to shed their blood for him and Cybele. This is definitely Attis' shrine, Harry. I saw one almost identical to it on a trip to Rome I did one February while I was still at university. And that fits with that fucking awful castration clamp we found on the dig here."

"Castration?" Harry had gone very pale. "Oh God, I forgot about that thing you mentioned. You weren't making it up that they did that to one another, were you? No chance you might be mistaken?"

"If you're hoping that might be something Robert is spared if Natalie has him somewhere inside, I'm so sorry, but it's all true. It's there in some of the Romans' own accounts which survive. The only hope is that the original priests used to do it to *themselves*, not to one another. So if Natalie wants to be absolutely authentic, then she has to persuade Robert to do it himself – and that might take some doing!"

"Lord, yes!" Harry breathed with only limited relief. Then grinned savagely. "Well just in case, we can put a stop to one thing!" and went and grabbed the rifle from the cart and began loading it. Only when he pointed it at the statute did Pip realise what he intended.

"No, Harry!" she cried grabbing his arm. "Not yet!"

"Why not?"

"Because if she does have Robert upstairs she might not know we're here yet. But if you start firing that thing then she'll know for sure! And you don't want her getting desperate, do you? What will she do if she panics?"

Harry immediately lowered the rifle. "Damn! You mean she might think she needs more blood all in one go?"

"Yes!"

"The whoring, double-damned bitch!"

"I agree! But let's stop her, shall we?" Pip said, strangely shocked by hearing Harry swearing. He was normally so polite it sounded strange to hear. She'd become uncomfortably aware that her own language was far from ladylike the longer she'd been in his company, and had been trying hard to moderate it, so she knew how disturbed he must be by this if he was swearing in front of her. "Let's go in by the front door if we can," she suggested as a way to try and divert him. "If we go in by the back and she's in the same bedroom as the mirror, she'll be able to see us if she looks out of the window."

Like thieves sneaking inside in the lengthening shadows of the coming evening, Pip and Harry crept silently in through the front door. If Pip had thought all soldiers of this time went in like bulls in so many china shops, she was surprised to see how easily Harry fell back into silent skirmishing mode. Of course, he'd told her he was in command of the Light Company, but she'd not thought of it in quite such practical terms until now. He had the long, heavy rifle held with practised ease and steady in his hands, bringing it to aim every time they turned a corner of the stairs.

At the top he made Pip stay back until he'd made sure all was clear, then allowed her to join him on the landing. Pressing their ears to the wall separating the landing from the dressing-room where the mirror was, and only a layer of lath and plaster from them, they suddenly found they could hear voices. One was definitely Natalie's, but was the other

Robert's? Or was it coming from the mirror? The voices were too indistinct to tell properly.

Soft as cats, the two of them crept along the small corridor which had created the dressing-room, and eased their way into the bedroom. It was empty. But then they heard movement from within the dressing-room.

"Get up!" Natalie's voice snapped. "Get closer to the mirror!"

"I can't," Robert answered feebly.

"Yes you can!" she spat furiously, then, "Ooooh!"

Pip tapped Harry on the arm, for he was just about to make a furtive glance around the door-frame and was in front of her.

She silently mouthed, "Let me see the mirror!" and ducked down low, so that he could still fire the rifle over her if needs be. Almost on her hands and knees, so that she wouldn't be silhouetted by her reflection from the bedroom window, Pip risked a glance round at the mirror. The portal had opened! Then she blinked and looked again. Someone in her time had moved the mirror! It was back in the dressing-room, and Pip could see that Natalie was thrown by that because she was standing starring at it. Robert lay forgotten on the floor, pale but very much alive and currently in no danger.

On an impulse, Pip stood up and stepped forward into the doorway making Natalie jump as she realised someone was behind her.

"Hello, Natalie, you don't know me, do you?" Pip said coldly.

"Who the devil are you?" Natalie screeched, even more off balance at the sudden appearance of someone she hadn't anticipated.

"I'm Pip, Dave Marston's fiancée." She let the words just hang there in the silence for a moment. "That's right. I came through too. Wondering why you couldn't see Dave's body rolled up in the carpet, were you? Well the police know about that now. You dropped your diary in your rush to get here. Remember what you wrote in that?"

Natalie had gone a strange shade of grey, and was looking into the mirror and then back to Pip in anguished indecision. It didn't take a genius to work out what she was thinking.

"Weighing up the odds, are you?" Pip sniggered without humour. "Wondering whether you can escape from me and get away in this time, or whether you dare go through and try to do your stuff in ours again?"

Then Harry stepped into her view. Pip didn't turn but stepped to one side away from the door, and from the corner of her eye saw the long barrel of the rifle come up. Strangely Natalie's face lost its fear and changed to a sneer.

"Oh that doesn't frighten me! The gallant Captain Green! You won't kill me! You wouldn't dare! You won't risk being dragged into court for yet another murder when you might only just escape the noose for that fool Gus'."

Harry's voice was like ice. "Oh I've been fully acquitted of Gus' murder," he told her, gratified at the way that surprised her. "And as for getting away with murder, Pip has told me all about this doorway into the future. I can shoot you now and then dump your body back in your own time. Who'll come looking for you there?"

Natalie screamed in temper and swung a clawed hand towards Pip's face. "You bitch! You spoil everything! You ruined Dave for me! You cunt..."

The click of the hammer being brought back on the rifle stopped her in mid flow, and her eyes flicked in sudden terror to the barrel which was now pointing straight at her.

"*Never* raise your filthy hand to my wife!" Harry

snapped, and there was a deafening crash as the rifle fired. But Harry hadn't fired to kill this time. If he was going to do that he wanted Natalie to suffer the anguish of not knowing which shot would be the killing one, just the way Gus could never have known which stab would be the last. This first bullet seared along her cheek taking the lobe of her ear off as it passed.

Natalie screamed in pain, and there was a croak of remonstration from Robert on the floor, "Harry, no!"

However, Harry wasn't taking any notice of his brother but was reloading with a speed which shook Natalie and Pip as well as Robert. The legendary speed with which nineteenth-century soldiers of the British army could reload muskets and rifles was one thing when you were reading about it in some text book, and quite something else when witnessed in person done by a very angry expert.

Clutching the bleeding side of her face Natalie backed towards the mirror.

"Oh no you don't!" Pip growled and lunged for her. "You're going back to Worcester with us and standing trial!"

She would have caught hold of Natalie had the dress not been wet with blood, but the slippery silk ran out of Pip's fingers as Natalie yanked it away, at the same time shoving Pip hard on the shoulder. Pip stumbled and fell forwards, but still managed to reach out and grab Natalie's ankle and haul back on it. The rifle barked again just as Natalie fell, creasing her scalp, but doing no more major damage. As Harry reloaded with frantic urgency, Natalie rose to her knees, bunched the long skirt up in her hands and plunged into the mirror. In her fury Pip lurched to her feet to follow, but was halted by a loud clatter and Harry's anguished, "Pip, no!" as he dropped the rifle and grabbed her, pulling her back into his arms.

"Don't leave me, please!" he gasped as he held her tight. "She's not worth that!"

He needn't have worried. As Natalie skidded onto the floor of the room in her own time, a figure appeared from beside the mirror where it had hidden out of view.

"Natalie Walker, I'm arresting you for the murder of Mr David Marston," DI Sawaski said with efficient calm. "Anything you say..."

But Pip didn't bother listening to the rest because through the bedroom doorway came DCI Scathlock and Nick.

"Christ, is that really Natalie?" Nick asked in awe.

"Oh yes!" Pip told him with a weak smile. "She's just aged about thirteen years to our four, that's all."

"The DNA tests will prove that for certain," Bill Scathlock reminded them calmly, stepping aside briefly to allow DI Sawaski to manhandle the squirming Natalie out and into the waiting arms of a very muscular female PC. As they disappeared out of sight, Nick came up to the portal.

"What are you waiting for, Pip? Come on, come home!"

He looked terrible, as though he hadn't had a decent night's sleep in weeks.

"Oh Nick! I'm so sorry to have caused you such grief!"

"You didn't say there was someone else waiting for you back in your time," Harry's voice said softly in Pip's ear. He was still holding her, but she felt his grip relax, and there was a sudden terrible sadness in his voice.

"Oh! ...No! ...No, Harry, meet Nick. Nick, this is Harry, the captain we found in the archives! Harry, Nick is my best friend – the best friend anyone could ever want! – but he's married to Richard."

Harry dropped his hands off Pip in shock. "Married to *Richard*? You mean another *man*?"

Pip turned and gave him a mischievous grin. "Yes, that's right. It's quite legal in our time."

From the floor Robert gave a howl of dismay. "Ungodly! Demons! All of you – even her! I knew it! Harry, for the sake of your immortal soul, let her go!"

Harry looked down at his brother in disbelief while Pip said,

"I think you've been in enough trouble for one day, Robert. I'd shut up if I were you!"

"Pip!" Nick's voice came urgently from the portal. "Come on! We don't know how long this thing will work for! We worked out about the mirror on the wood when we came looking for you and found the butcher's bag too, but we still don't know how long this bloody thing stays open for!"

But Pip turned and shook her head. "No, Nick, I'm sorry, I'm not coming back." Beside her she heard Harry's sigh of relief. "What have I got to come back for aside from you and Richard? Nothing. But here I've got Harry, and that's so much more."

Bill Scathlock stepped forwards now. "Pip, you have to realise that I can't stop this house from going on the open market much longer, don't you? The man who was to buy it doesn't want it anymore, so it's probably going to auction. I've managed to keep it closed up on the basis of the first investigation and then you disappearing. But I can't lie forever and say we don't know you're alive and well, even if I shall have to say that you eloped abroad or something. If this place gets snapped up – and it might, even with its gruesome history – then work could start very quickly."

Pip nodded. "I know, and I hear what you're trying to tell me."

"You've only known this man for a few months," Nick protested. "What happens if it doesn't work out? Where will you go? What will you do? The early nineteenth century isn't a place of equal opportunities for women, Pip! Be sensible, come home!"

Again Pip shook her head. "I know what you fear, Nick, and I love you dearly for being so concerned. I also hate the very idea of never seeing you and Richard again. But when we talked back in your cottage I told you I can't live as the spare part in your relationship, and I still feel that way. And here I have a real relationship. One of my own, and it means as much to me as yours with Richard does to you. And Harry isn't some random regency rake I've stumbled across. I know more about him than I do about anyone in our own time apart from you! I trust him. And more than that, I love him. Very much!"

Then she realised she had to give Nick something more. He deserved more. "Look. This portal should open on the winter solstice too. I don't know if I would be able to come forwards at that point, or whether I would have to wait until the first of February, but if you come here and open the portal at the pagan new year, we'll at least be able to see and speak to one another."

"Not Halloween?" Nick queried, proving that he must have read her own notes on the matter.

Pip smiled at him. "Come on, Nick, that's only six weeks away! I have to give Harry more of a chance than that! And DCI Scathlock, even if the house goes on the market now and gets sold, the paperwork will never go through that quickly! You can surely get access to the house one last time over the Christmas holiday season? No workmen will be beavering away on an old place like this in the worst of the winter weather. They won't risk the timber-frame getting wet by taking the roof off fully, for a start!"

Nick seemed on the verge of tears, but Bill Scathlock was nodding his head. "Yes, we can do that. One last time on December the twenty-first. Well I shall go and see what's going on downstairs. Join me when you're ready, Dr Robbins, there's no hurry."

As the burly detective padded out of sight, Nick turned to Pip again. "You're serious about this, aren't you?"

"Yes I am."

He wasn't happy, Pip could tell, but for the time that the portal remained open she managed to get Harry and Nick talking to one another, and when the mirror's surface wavered and then went back to normal, she hoped she'd assuaged the worst of Nick's fears. It hadn't been long enough to really make him stop worrying, she knew, but now she and Harry had to deal with Robert.

"What made you come?" Harry asked in disgust as he went and knelt down by his brother to examine his wounds.

"The message!" Robert replied indignantly.

"God, you're a fool!" Harry told him in disgust as he checked over the cuts to Robert's chest and arms. "Hmph! You'll live! Which is more than you deserve for such idiocy!"

"Harry! Don't be so ungrateful!"

Harry's expression darkened. "Ungrateful? Oh no, Robert, don't you dare accuse me of that! I told you that Uncle William would help, and what did he do? He put hundreds of pounds of his own money up as surety that I wouldn't run away! Hundreds, Robert! No business man does that lightly! He had to have real faith in me to part with that much of his money, albeit temporarily, so believe that if nothing else. He had true faith in me, not your kind. Faith that I had not – and would never – commit murder in cold blood, and especially not for something like my friend's inheritance. Never! He believed that of me without hesitation or questioning, Robert, which is clearly more than you did!"

Robert flinched away from Harry's anger. "No! I believed you!"

"Did you?" Harry growled. "No, Robert, in your heart of hearts I don't think you did. You see you never questioned that the rest of the family had deserted me when you got that note. Not for an instant! If you'd believed me as innocent as they did, you would have stopped and thought, 'wait a moment, that's not right!' But you didn't. And unlike them, you never were confident that the evidence against me was so slender that once Sir Arthur began questioning it in court, it would all fall apart. You were so bothered that I would inevitably be guilty that you couldn't even face coming into court with me to hear the evidence, much less the verdict."

"But I had my parish!"

"Your parish? Really? I cannot believe that if you'd actually asked the bishop, that someone couldn't have been found to cover for you while you supported a *brother* in his hour of need! Not some distant cousin who'd got into a bit of bother, but a *brother* who was being falsely accused of the most heinous crime."

Harry sat back on his heels and regarded Robert gravely. "Pip said Natalie had played on your own fears, but I see now just how much you were already halfway there. You were just waiting for the message to say that my defence had failed, weren't you? You had so little belief in my being in the right, it never entered your head that I might impress a jury. That via Uncle William, of all people, I might get a really good lawyer in the form of Sir Arthur on my side because he too *believed* I was innocent. He more than did his job, Robert! He went above and beyond what mere duty required him to do, and it wasn't just because of Uncle! If he'd thought I was guilty he would probably have taken Uncle William on one side and said he would do his best, but to expect the worst. But he didn't! He set about not only proving me innocent, but showing to the court just how dangerous one of my accusers was. And if you'd only come into Worcester a bit more often to watch, you'd have known all of this."

"You could have come and told me," Robert protested.

"What? And leave Pip, who'd risked life and limb to come and help me, all alone with a family she scarcely knew? Oh for heaven's sake, Robert! And you knew full well that we couldn't come out here together until Pip had something respectable to be seen out in – and that wasn't going to happen overnight!"

Robert's eyes flickered to Pip and there was no mistaking the dislike there. Harry saw that too, stiffened and stood up to step away from Robert and closer to Pip.

"Whether you like it or not, Robert, I'm going to marry Pip."

"No!" Robert gasped in anguish. "No, Harry, please think! She's not ...natural! Not normal! She'll disappear one night like the *sithe* that she is, leaving you with nothing! And how could you explain the disappearance of your *wife*? You'd never be able to marry again, not being able to explain where *she* went to! No man of the Church would marry you under such circumstances."

Pip felt Harry's arm go protectively around her, then him go rigid with anger as Robert babbled on.

"For heaven's sake," she interrupted him, desperate to stop him before he ruined Harry's affection for him forever, "I'm no *sithe*, Robert! A bloody *fairy*, for heaven's sake? I'm a bit too solid for that! Even for one of the fae courts, if you believe the legends of them riding in the Wild Hunt. You're not thinking straight."

"Oh I am! I know what you are!" was Robert's instant response. "Demon! Unnatural woman! Why did you not go back to Hell when you had the chance? Would you corrupt our whole family and condemn them to eternity in the fiery pit? Look on this cross if you dare," and he brandished the one on a chain round his neck like a weapon, "get thee gone, Satan!" His voice was getting higher in his distress, but got overridden by Harry's deeper growl of,

"By God, Robert, you're a sanctimonious fool! You're Father all over again, aren't you! I had intended to ask you to perform the marriage." Suddenly his anger was replaced by sadness. "I thought it would be so nice for me to get married from the rectory, with you performing the ceremony, as a way of replacing all the sad memories I have of Father, you and me rowing endlessly in that house in that couple of years after Mother died. To make things right again and for us to be a proper family. But that's never going to happen, is it? Not because I don't want it, but because every time there's a question, every time you don't see things quite the way I do, you'll fall back into doubting me. You'll be expecting me to follow your lead through the rest of my life on the basis that, although I've been to hell and back again in the wars, you know more than me of what you think of as real life. So I'm going to ask you one last time, Robert, and think carefully before you answer because much hangs on this. Will you marry Pip and me?"

Yet even as the words were coming out of Harry's mouth Robert was shaking his head, eyes wide and appalled and fixed on Pip. "No, in all conscience I cannot."

Harry sighed sadly. "Very well. I fear we shall see little of one another in the future, *brother*. Now on your feet! We have a horse and trap downstairs with Amy in it. We'll take you back to the rectory."

"I can't!" Robert whimpered pathetically. "Help me, Harry! I'm *bleeding*!"

"On your feet!" Harry snapped, grabbing Robert by the front of his clothing and hoisting him up with remarkable little effort. "Good God man, I've come through many a battle with wounds worse than that and thought I'd got off lightly! A few shallow cuts is what you have, that's all! They'll sting and probably bleed a bit for a few days, but nothing worse. Now be a man about it!"

The reproof made Robert blush, bringing him back to earth a little, and making Pip think his head had been turned by all of this. Looking into the future and seeing police with radios, women in uniform, and Pip expressing affection for a man who was part-Jamaican and quite dark-skinned, gay, and with a shock of red-tinted Dred-locks – quite possibly his idea of the very personification of a demon – terrified him. No doubt he'd recover by retreating deeper into his warped theology, which only worked when everyone was in their allotted place and behaving to type. But Pip could have cried for Harry, not Robert. He'd retreated into being the battle-toughened captain as the only way of dealing with what he saw as Robert's betrayal, and had shut down his feelings so that he didn't have to deal with them at this moment. She'd have to be very careful with him for a while over the subject of Robert, and he was right, it might be much better if they didn't see much of him from now on. Robert seemed to have a way of wounding Harry which no-one else did.

As Harry marched Robert downstairs he declared, "Uncle William wants to throw a big wedding for us in Worcester. I'd wanted a much smaller affair, and I think you probably did too, Pip."

Pip struggled to find a smile for him. "I'm not one for the big affairs," she admitted.

"Could you cope with it now?" Harry demanded more brusquely than he'd no doubt intended. "Only if this is the way people are going to look at you, I think we should have a wedding performed by someone more senior in the Church than Robert, here, just in case he starts protesting loudly in public!" It was said with considerable bitterness, and for that Pip could have slapped Robert very hard. Now when they married it would still be in the back of Harry's mind that his closest and dearest relative might make trouble for them, and Pip thought it beyond unfair that after all Harry had been through, that someone – let alone Robert – should take the shine off what should have been the happiest of days.

"Harry, I'll marry you whenever and wherever you want – even eloping to Gretna Green!" she quipped in an attempt to lift his mood. Luckily he got the reference. Pip had checked that tentatively in a previous conversation with Flora, and was relieved to know that already people were heading for the Scottish border for quick marriages.

"I don't think it'll come to that," he replied, but when he turned to her there was a softening of the expression in his eyes at least, even though the rest of his face remained stern.

Downstairs, Amy was still in the trap staring blankly about her.

"I have an idea," Pip said brightly. "Since you think me such an unnatural woman for this era, Robert. *You* can look after Amy for a few days until we can get her somewhere to stay!"

"Me?" Robert squeaked.

"Call it your penance for doubting Harry," Pip told him firmly. "She surely must fit in with your concept of the kind of vapid, useless wench you think a proper woman should be! You have a cleaning lady coming in already, so she can either help Amy with ...with whatever Amy needs help with, or she'll no doubt know another of the village women glad to earn a bit for a few days. It won't be for more than a week at most, so don't get your underwear in a twist over what this will do to your reputation. Anyway, one look at her and no-one will think you're having your dirty way with *her*! Even you can't think such a snivelling, stunned, bunny-in-the-headlights is sexy!" Privately she was wishing he'd had more time to know what a twenty-first century bunny-boiler was in the form of Natalie – he might not think herself so bad after that!

Harry had turned away and walked towards the statue once more, but it was only as Pip caught up with him that she realised that he was laughing.

"Harry?"

"Oh my dear, Pip!" he chuckled, "you have the most amusing way with words. 'Bunny-in-the-*headlights*'? What *is* that? And 'Get your underwear in a twist'? Is that an expression in your time? And only you would say outright that Robert might have his 'dirty way' with Amy," the mental image of which was enough to reduce him to another fit of laughter even as he hugged her to him. "You can cheer me up like no-one else! Now ...let's get rid of this damned thing once and for all."

He loaded the rifle once more and shot the head off the statue. Several more shots later and the androgynous figure of Attis was so many lumps of stone, the spikes of his crown now shards in the grass.

Pip nudged one of the pieces with her foot which had rolled closer than the others. "Under normal circumstances I'd be appalled at the destruction of a piece of ancient statuary – especially one as well executed as that one was.

Roman remains are so rare. But in this case I'm heartily glad to see the back of it. If we get rid of Robert and Amy to the rectory, shall we can come back here tonight? Then in the morning we can hack the rest of that damned thing out, then contact a local builder to come and make the wall decent before the owners notice anything's amiss."

The owners became more of a pressing issue when Pip and Harry returned, for on the kitchen table was a letter from their agent asking Harry to quit the place immediately.

"Leave that to Sir Arthur to deal with," Pip said soothingly. "A letter from his office explaining that you've been fully acquitted should smooth things over. I think I'll suggest he says that we only want the place until just into the New Year to give us time to find somewhere else to stay. And maybe, that if we stay until everyone has forgotten the trial, then they'll find it easier to let the place to the right kind of people – not those ghoulish enough to want to come because of its history. If the current owners or their family had trouble letting the place after Paul's murder they're sure to take us up on that offer."

"You're a clever and conniving woman and I love you for it!" Harry said kissing her. Once Robert and Amy had been got rid of, his mood had lightened considerably. "I think we'll go back into Worcester tomorrow, arrange for the continued hire of a pony and trap, see Sir Arthur, and tell Uncle William he can have his grand wedding. When would you like it?"

"I think as soon as possible to squash any gossip about us living out here together," Pip said with mock severity, even as she began unbuttoning Harry's shirt. "And it would be nice to wave a ring at Nick when I see him for the last time. I think, you see, that if we marry and it gets put into the local paper, he'll then be able to go and look in the archives in his time and see the announcement. And that will set his mind at rest that I wasn't just putting on a show for him."

"He'd think that of you?" Harry wondered.

Pip smiled. "Not in the negative way Robert thinks of you, no. It's just that in the last few years Nick's done a lot of looking after me – more so after Dave first vanished than recently. But he still thinks of me as vulnerable, and he worries about me. He's sort of become a mixture of the very best of friends and the big brother I never had. And he fears that finding Dave's body knocked me back, you see."

"Ah! Well in that case we shall do our best to set his mind at rest," Harry agreed happily, loosening the last of the laces on Pip's bodice.

The next few days were a whirlwind of activity, for no sooner were they back in Worcester then they had to head over to Hereford. The landlord from whom Gus had rented the house for Amy had sent a letter which Sir Arthur had passed on, declaring that even though the debts had been settled, he no longer wanted Mrs Clifford as a tenant. The house had to be cleared within the week or else the furniture would be sold off – and Harry said the house had been stuffed with every item Amy could squeeze in. He felt he owed it to Gus not to let his parent's furniture be despatched in that way, and Amy would need some of it anyway.

However once they got to the house, and Pip saw the furniture she declared,

"This is really nice stuff, Harry! I'd be delighted to have some of this for us!"

"You would?"

"Heavens, yes! And think of it in a practical way – we've spent an awful lot of your money in a very short space of time. Money well spent, even though I wish it hadn't been necessary. I know you're well set up financially, but we've been dipping into the capital amount a lot, and once that's gone we can't replace it easily. Especially since we don't know what, if anything, you'll be able to find in the way of work any time soon. So let's save ourselves the expense of having to purchase furniture and use this."

They managed to find someone with a good sized cart to remove the furniture, and with part of a barn to store it in until they could find a house to put it in.

"I hate putting stuff as good as this into somewhere as damp as a barn and with winter coming on," Pip sighed, "but we've got little choice."

Rather harder to decide was where to put Amy, and it was with this in mind that Pip undertook to sort through Amy's things and get rid of the clothing she would never wear again, as well as to empty drawers and wardrobes for the move. Without that there would be a ridiculous number of trunks to be shifted, and Pip began sorting while Harry went out to sort the business side of the removal. She began with the trunks which looked oldest, and soon had a pile of clothes which could be given away to the needy or sold off. A trip to the local church put her in touch with the vicar's wife, who gratefully agreed to have the clothes for the poor of the parish, and having cleared some space by getting the vicar's gardener to come round and take one trunk-load away in his barrow, Pip started on the next batch. So it was only as she got to the clothes which Amy clearly wore nowadays, and which she was packing into the returned empty trunk, that Pip found it.

"Harry!" she called downstairs urgently. "Come and look at this!"

He came upstairs still clutching a sheet of newspaper in which he'd been wrapping the china. "What is it?"

"Look at this dress! Is that what I think it is?"

Harry dropped the piece of newspaper and took the stained and stiff dress out of Pip's hands. "Oh my God, that's dried blood!"

"I thought it was. And look, the dress must have been drenched in it at the front! That's not just a cut finger. It's on the skirt and the bodice."

"Gus," Harry said in a voice filled with sadness.

"I fear so. I don't think that man from the house *was* the first person who found him. This looks terribly like it might have been Amy, and she clasped him to her. And that brings something else to mind. Something's been niggling at the back of my mind about Amy, and it's just come to me. It's her eyes."

"Her eyes?"

"Yes, those huge pupils. If I'd been in my own time I'd have said she was stoned," then hurriedly explained, "that means drugged. I'm kicking myself for being so naïve as to not have noticed."

"My love, you are many things, but naïve is something I would never describe you as," Harry said with a wry smile.

"But I have been," Pip insisted. "I completely forgot that laudanum is commonly used now."

"Yes, ...and?"

"Well laudanum is made from opium poppies, and in my time there are some very nasty street-drugs which get made from opium – heroin for one. Amy's a smack-head!"

"A what?"

Pip winced. "Sorry. Another street term. A smack-head is someone addicted to heroin in particular, although it tends to get used in a wider context to mean almost any kind of drug addict. But the thing is, Harry, when she said she needed her laudanum when we were bringing her to the Farm, I just thought she meant a nip to calm her shattered nerves after the last few days. But I think she meant it much stronger than that! I think she meant she needed her fix! ...That means her regular dose – the stuff she can no longer get through *any* day without!"

"But how does that relate to this dreadful thing?" Harry wondered, lifting the dress up and pulling a disgusted face.

"Because I think Natalie knew full well that Amy would be all over the place mentally at finding Gus, and doped her up! If Natalie drugged Amy sufficiently, then Amy may very well have no recollection of what happened that day. And she would have been very susceptible to Natalie suggesting to her that you did it!"

"Good God!"

"Yes indeed! But that means that Amy must have been on quite a high dose already, or a sudden and unaccustomed massive intake would have killed her. You see, enough just for a well-bred lady's headache wouldn't have her off with the fairies anything like enough. Hopefully Robert will have just given in to her demands and bought some, because otherwise he's going to know what hell on earth is really like as she starts to go cold turkey – I mean, starts to get withdrawal symptoms."

Harry's face broke into a wicked smile. "Really? Robert suffer? Hmmm!"

Pip had to laugh too. "Oh yes! She'll be screaming the place down and probably hallucinating too, as well as getting very sick. Somehow I never saw Robert ministering to the needy in quite that way. He's not one for the messy bits of life, is he?"

"Not at all! But what you say explains an awful lot. It's actually quite a relief to know that Amy wasn't in her proper mind when she made those accusations."

"I seriously doubt if she knew if it was Christmas or next week, so yes, it takes the personal aspect out of it. But

I'm afraid it raises another problem. You see she may never be fully right in the head again, even if we get her off the laudanum. Narcotics are notorious for inducing psychoses even after they've stopped being used, and everything I've heard of Amy makes me think she's a classic case for long-term mental health problems, because she was never that strong to start with. We're going to have to find her somewhere away from people and then employ a nurse for her. She's going to require someone with her every day for at least several months, and possibly permanently. In my time there are places where people can go to get help with such addictions, but now she's going to have to do this the hard way, and once she gets past the worst of the withdrawals we may find it's knocked her health about something rotten. Physically she wasn't a strong woman to start off with either, so we should assume the worst will happen and that she'll need constant care."

A hurried enquiry through the same vicar's wife revealed that there was a local widow who might well want the job, and then an agent in Worcester turned out to have a nice cottage out at Storridge which would suit.

"Perfect!" Pip declared. "Far enough from any town so that she can't walk in and try to get more laudanum, and quiet enough so that no-one will hear her screams."

The deal was settled within the week, and the furniture Pip had designated for Amy's use was brought over and installed.

"Please don't think I'm keeping the best for us and giving her the rougher stuff," Pip told Harry. "But there's not much point in putting good things in here. She may well smash some of it up before she's got through the worst, and it's undoubtedly better than anything Mrs Gorton has lived with in the past."

Mrs Gorton was the nurse – a large woman used to working in the city hospital and a good deal tougher than the kind of women Amy was used to associating with. Pip had explained what was needed, and Mrs Gorton's replies had reassured her that while Amy would be treated kindly, there would be no lack of firmness either.

"You leave young missus to me," she'd said matter-of-factly. "I'll see her through the worst and get her well again."

Robert, it seemed had known of another lady who liked her laudanum, and had supplied Amy with enough to keep her passably quiet until Pip and Harry had called in on the way back to Worcester with more. But it had driven another wedge between the brothers, Robert asking for the money for the laudanum quite bluntly, making Pip say,

"That's what being away with the fairies is like, Robert, not me!"

Yet one last thread remained loose. As the day of Pip and Harry's wedding drew closer, one thing vexed him.

"Where is that damned boy?" he said in despair as he read a letter at the family dinner table in Worcester.

"Is there a problem, dear?" Flora asked kindly as she passed Pip the vegetables.

"Harry wanted Amy's son, Eddie, to come to the wedding," Pip explained, "but we can't seem to trace him."

"I felt I should invite him," Harry added. "I am still his guardian, after all, and he was never here when all the fuss of the trial was taking place."

"How old is he now?" Flora asked.

"Oh, he's got to be twelve coming up thirteen," Harry replied distractedly as he read the letter again, "But he's not been at the school Gus and I sent him to for the best part of a year. I had a letter from the head last week saying he was glad I'd got in touch because we – or rather I, now –

am still paying fees for him, and they want to reimburse us. But I'm much vexed by the news that the school had been forced to discipline him harshly, only to have letters from Amy upbraiding them for doing so. What on earth was he doing running crying to his mother, and what was she thinking to interfere? He needs a firm hand, not spoiling – that was the ruination of his father, for heaven's sake. Then there's this letter today from the school where his former head thought he was transferring to at Amy's request, and they've never heard of Eddie."

"Oh dear, a little boy of that age out in the world on his own," gasped Flora, but Harry shook his head,

"No he's not little. That might be part of the problem! The last time I saw him over a year ago he was already shooting up. He was nearly as tall as Gus then, although Gus was always short for a grown man. Eddie only had an inch or two to go and he would match Gus for height, and unfortunately he's inherited the Vaughans' tendency to gain weight too. He was looking to be a match for his uncle in girth if he wasn't careful! And to be that portly at such a tender age as that didn't bode well for his size when he reaches twenty! So you see, he could pass for someone much older than his years, and Gus had written to me to say that he'd already had to pay off some gambling debts for Eddie. I fear the lad has Edward's feckless nature in that respect, so heaven alone knows what he's got drawn into if nowadays he looks sixteen or more."

"Well it's unlikely he'll make it for the wedding now," Pip said regretfully, "but afterwards we'll go back over to Hereford and look for him properly. That's where he's sure to be, because he'd need money off Amy whatever he was foolishly intending to do, and he'll think she's still there. Don't worry, Harry, he can't have gone far. We'll probably find him very scared and a lot thinner but in one piece."

As predicted, Eddie didn't appear in time for the wedding, but the rest of the family more than made up for it. The old church of St Helen's, just down the road from the cathedral, was packed to see Pip walk down the aisle in a shimmering gown of delicate ivory lawn, trimmed with lace, on Uncle William's arm. Harry stood resplendent in full uniform and Uncle William whispered to her as they approached the altar,

"I've never seen him look so happy! That's all down to you, my dear! And after what you've been through you deserve to be happy together," and that, Pip thought, was the final seal on her entrance into the kind of family she'd always wanted, not her distant and disinterested mother and half-siblings. And for Harry too, being surrounded by family soothed the hurt of not having Robert there. The last he'd heard, Robert had been considering taking orders and going into a monastery, his crisis of faith having been righted by his encounter with more of the world than he could stand.

"Maybe it's a good thing the rectory will have a new incumbent," Harry had said to Pip the night before the wedding. "Someone with a wife and loads of children to brush the bad memories away." Then had pulled her close for a goodnight kiss, very aware that the family were restless with excitement tonight. "And tomorrow I shall have a wife of my own – the very best I could have wished for!"

Chapter 19

1824 – 1825

With the wedding over, Pip and Harry briefly honeymooned at a hotel out towards Ross, but then needed to think about where they would live, Pip being determined to retrieve the Vaughans' better furniture from the barn before it got ruined. Yet before that could happen, Harry wanted to go to Hereford one more time and see if he could find any trace of Eddie, even though they'd already made one hurried trip before the wedding.

"I fear in my heart of hearts that I shall have to admit defeat," he told Pip after they'd spent a fruitless day searching the city.

In this era Hereford was somewhat smaller than Worcester, and neither were the size of the modern cities Pip had known so well – so there just weren't that many places for someone to hide. With only nine proper streets forming what Pip still thought of as just the city centre, and despite that older city being filled with over a thousand dwellings and six thousand people – as a local magistrate proudly informed Harry during their enquiries – it was still a small place to search. Eddie wouldn't be in any of the better houses, either as a resident or as a servant, and neither did they see any sign of him amongst the poorer people. A well-built boy of Eddie's background would stand out amongst the ragged urchins of the poorest alleyways, and facially he would never be mistaken for a grown man, whatever his stature.

Harry sighed sadly as they went down to eat at the inn they had taken a room in, "I'm afraid tomorrow we shall have to go to the workhouses."

"Is that so very bad?" Pip asked, concerned by his depressed state.

He squeezed her hand affectionately. "I forget you'll never have seen inside one of those places. Yes it is bad, very bad."

Come the following morning Pip came to realise just why Harry was dreading the visit as they went into the first of the three. The poor souls in them had sunk to the lowest level Georgian society could offer, and if there weren't as many people within them in comparison to the great edifices Pip knew were to come in Victorian England, it made them no less heart-wrenching to see. No wonder that even amongst her grandparent's generation there'd still been a spine chilling ring to the very word 'workhouse'. Right up to the turn of the twentieth century families must have lived in very real fear and trembling of this fate, Pip belatedly realised. Even for a toughened soldier like Harry, seeing women and children in such dire straits took its toll on him, and Pip found it harrowing.

"Can you face the final one?" he asked Pip as she had to pause after the second to have a tearful moment walking beside the river.

She dried her eyes resolutely. "If we can save just one person from that fate I'll do it, because even the son of a pair of hopeless cases like Amy and Edward doesn't deserve that," she declared. "But when we get our house, that scullery maid you keep saying I'll need will come from whichever workhouse is nearest to us, I want your word on that, Harry."

He smiled. "I wouldn't dream of arguing with you over domestic staff anyway, but as it happens I'd be delighted to do that."

So it was with a little more composure that they walked out to the workhouse of All Saints' parish and spoke to the superintendent.

"You're welcome to look around," he said genially, "but I can assure you we've had no lads of that sort coming in here. The last arrival we had was a much older man. A bit simple poor sod! Looks like he had a knock on the head somewhere. Found wandering around the cathedral, he was, but then that's nothing out of the ordinary. They all tend to go there looking for charity."

"And I bet they don't bloody find it!" muttered Pip disgustedly, as the superintendent went back to his office after summoning one of his men to show them around. "Bloody hell, no wonder your Robert fitted in with the bishop and his cronies in Worcester! Some Christians they are!"

"Hush, Pip!" Harry said urgently. "I know what you mean, but not all Churchmen are like that even now, but it's not seemly to criticise them in public, and especially not as a woman!"

"Oh joy!" Pip sighed grimly, pulling a face. "Women's liberation can't come a day too soon!"

"You're not regretting staying, are you?" Harry asked worriedly. It wasn't Christmas yet, and there was still the slight chance that Pip would leave if life here got too stressful. He couldn't take her love for granted or as a guarantee that she wouldn't want to go back to the security of her own time.

But Pip smiled and squeezed the arm she was holding. "No, not at all. Don't mind me, I'm just getting used to this, that's all. It's not all sweetness and light in my time either, you know. We still have children suffering shocking neglect and some awful poverty, even if it wears a different face to now."

By now they were walking at a slow amble through the building behind their guide, scanning the inhabitants whilst at the same time trying not to look too hard for fear of what they might see. Those incarcerated seemed to be mainly the old and the very young, and were either carding wool from the bits not good enough for garment making – which Harry and Pip were told would be used to stuff saddles with – or were spinning mop yarn, and the air was filled with tiny fibres from both. Under the pretext of needing her handkerchief to fend off the floating bits, Pip had to wipe her eyes of tears, but as she pause to do so she heard something.

"Harry!" a croaky voice called weakly. "Harry! Don't leave me here!"

Pip tugged on Harry's sleeve. "Harry, there's someone here who knows you!"

He stopped and looked about him. "No, I'm sorry, love, I don't think so. Tragic as it is, they're probably just desperate for a way out, and who can blame them."

"No, he used your name!" she insisted as the unidentified person called out again,

"Harry, please don't leave me here!"

Harry froze and began scrutinising the people.

"One of your old soldiers?" wondered Pip, imagining some elderly soldier thrown in here when he'd outlived his uses, then realise how pale Harry had gone.

"Harry! Over here!" and one of the pale figures raised a shaky hand.

In an instant Harry was nimbly negotiating the bales of raw wool pickings, striding his way over to the dark corner even as the warden was saying,

"Oye! Hold on sir, you can't do that!"

Pip saw Harry bend to look the man in the face, then stagger. When he looked back to her he was ghostly white. "This man is coming with me!" he snapped to the warden in his captain's voice which resisted any questioning.

"I can't just let you take him, sir," the warden said fearfully. "The superintendent would have me strung up!"

"Then get him down here and sort out whatever release papers are need! Now!" Harry barked, then turned to the man and with great care lifted him to his feet. With one arm around the smaller man's shoulders at the back, and the other supporting him at the front, Harry began walking him towards Pip. Clearly this was no time to stand on ceremony and Pip hoisted her cumbersome skirts to step over the trailing strands of mop yarn to get to them.

"Who is it?" she asked urgently as soon as she could without having to speak too loudly.

"It's Gus!" Harry said in a voice which shook badly.

"Fuck me, you're joking!" Pip gulped, only afterwards looking round to make sure no-one of importance had heard her. "*Gus*? Are you sure?" She peered hard at the small man who barely came up to Harry's armpit. He certainly had the look of someone who'd lost a huge amount of weight too quickly. His skin hung like bloodhound's dewlaps on his face, and there was a hideous scar running from the crown of his head down the right-hand side of his face. He looked as though someone had given him the beating of a lifetime, and without the aid of modern surgery to put him back together again. Yet through the wreckage of that face Harry had seen something familiar, and Pip couldn't question that since she'd never met Gus.

Looping her arm around him from the other side, she helped Harry walk Gus outside. It was a tense half hour with the superintendent, but Harry was so forceful and so adamant that the man clearly thought it wasn't worth the effort over one pauper, and Gus was released into their care. Then Harry insisted that a boy was sent to bring the trap to the workhouse to take them back to the inn, for Gus could never walk that far in his current state.

The landlord of the inn was equally aghast at their appearance, but again Harry would brook no argument and in a short time Pip was relegated to the public room so that Harry could help Gus have his first bath in months. That night was beyond strange. In theory they took another room for Gus, but he was in such a shaken state that Pip took the second room and left Harry to watch over Gus through the night. In the morning they paid the innkeeper handsomely for his trouble and set off in the trap for Worcester once more. And yet again Uncle William had a strange guest brought into his house.

"Upon my soul, life is never dull with you around, Harry!" the old man joked. "But you've excelled yourself this time by bringing home a ghost!"

Yet as Gus settled at the realisation that his rescue was no dream, and that he really was safe once more, they got more and more out of him which confirmed that he really was Gus Vaughan.

"But what happened to you?" Pip asked, after they'd told him all about the trial. "I mean it's clear you're not dead! But what happened that you couldn't come forward and tell everyone you were alive?"

Gus wiped his eyes, at the moment being moved to tears on a regular basis. His attempts to speak were also not helped by the fact that his injuries extended to his jaw, making his speech slow and hard to follow until you got used to it.

"Take your time," Pip added reassuringly. "I'm not

criticising. I'm just confused. Tell it as it happened."

Gus sighed, wiped his eyes again, then in his now very slow and deliberate speech began,

"I never knew Harry had been accused! I promise I didn't! I'd been out with Amy. She'd seen a bonnet she wanted. You know what she was like, Harry. You went out for one thing and came back with half a dozen! And she'd been so difficult since we'd been in Hereford." He paused and massaged his face. "So many times since I've wished I'd picked up my cane. The stout one with the horn handle." He wiped his eyes of sudden tears at the memory.

"But I knew I would run out of hands carryin' Amy's parcels. And as ever, I did. ...So we got back to my rooms. We went there because I'd heard from Eddie. He wouldn't go to his mother's house anymore, y'see. He said he had somethin' to tell us and was comin' to me. Didn't want to worry you, Harry, but I knew he'd skipped school already. Said he was stayin' with a friend nearby, but wouldn't say who. Think now it might have been *that woman*! So he knew about our move from the farm. I wasn't happy when I got the letter. He should have been in some kind of school, if not the one we'd picked! But I thought it better to hear what he had to say before callin' you in as reinforcements, so to speak."

He sighed and turned balefully to Harry. "How did we go so wrong with him? I never got to find out where he got money from. It wasn't from my allowance to him! He'd talked of an older friend before this, but I don't know who that was. Oh, Harry, he was like the worst of both his parents!" And Gus had to pause to collect himself again before continuing,

"Well Amy and I were openin' the door to my room when I heard it. But it was too late to stop Amy. She walked in and saw them."

Pip was on the edge of her seat, "Who? Who did you see?"

"Eddie and Natalie."

"Oh bloody hell!" Pip gulped, guessing what was coming even before Harry did.

Gus blinked. "Err, yes. It was a good thing it was daytime. No-one in the other rooms, you see. If it had been evenin', people would have come. People would have seen! Amy screamed. Well she would! Who wouldn't at a sight like that! Sharn't forget it myself, I know! There was Eddie, tied to the bed. Tied hand and foot to the bedstead! And that woman Natalie doin' things to him! But most disturbin', he was dressed in *my* clothes! Hadn't seen it until then. How big he'd grown. (Know I ain't the biggest chap, even when I was as I used to be, let alone now, but he was so *close* to my size.) So they were a bit loose around the shoulders and middle still, but not much. My best jacket and breeches, *and* my silk waistcoat from India! And there she was with her head at his..." He looked at Pip and went scarlet.

"Oh don't worry I can supply the image," Pip told him dryly, making him go even redder. "My late ...erm ...husband, Dave, gave me graphic descriptions of what Natalie would do, and I wouldn't. Did Eddie have something choking him too, in auto-erotic asphyxiation?" The two men looked blank. "Partial strangling? It enhances the man's experience, I'm told some men find, although I can't imagine why."

By now Gus had become puce, winced as Pip finished and whispered something to Harry, but Harry didn't quite get what he meant.

"What do you mean, she had something in her hand?"

Pip rolled her eyes. "What Gus is trying to say politely – except there's no polite way of doing it – is that she was giving Eddie a blow-job and stuffing a dildo up his arse at the same time. One of Dave's little fetishes which I wasn't about to indulge but got called a selfish bitch for refusing," she said blithely, only then realising that Harry had joined Gus in going red. "Oh heavens, Harry, what did you think I meant by strange? Not just the woman on top! Or doing it doggy fashion. I believe at one stage it even progressed to Dave having his nuts in some kind of strangle hold too, as a mock tourniquet for castration, but at that point I gave up trying to make sense of how that was pleasurable. ...Would you two like a brandy, perhaps?"

"Please," Harry croaked, drawing a hand over his perspiring brow.

When the restorative brandy had worked its effect on them, Gus recommenced his tale.

"Erm, well, I don't have to say more on what that woman was doin'!" he said hurriedly, then shook his head and bit what he could of his lip in distress. "But what was almost worse was that Eddie was enjoyin' it! He was beggin' her not to stop! I flew at her, Harry. I was incensed! To see her pervertin' a young boy like that. 'Twas more than I could bear! I grabbed hold of her and pulled her away, but she got hold of my cane which was by the bed. Struck me with it! Should have had it with me, then she'd never have got hold of it. The handle was bone, like I said. Came sharp, I can tell you! She struck again and again. And all of a sudden I realised she meant to kill me. I was terrified! I tried to fight back, but she was like a tigress! And strong! Try as I might I couldn't get the cane off her. Nor stop her from beatin' me with it. First blow sent me a bit dizzy, you see? Before I knew it I was backin' out of the room and down the stairs, and out into the back yard, and her at me every step."

He stopped and drew in breath having been nearly panting with the stress of the memory. "Outside she dropped the cane and took up a shovel. Before she hit me I heard Amy upstairs. 'You're not my Eddie,' I heard her scream. 'You look nothin' like him!' And Eddie cryin', 'Mother, no! Mother, stop!" over and over again. 'My Eddie is tall and handsome!' was the last thing I heard. Then that woman hit me with the shovel and I felt it cut." He fingered the ragged scar as another tear rolled down his cheek.

"Christ, she hit you with some force!" Harry said, appalled.

Gus tried to give a wobbly smile but it failed. " 'Twas sharp and ragged from shovellin' coal, y'see," he said shakily. "Cut me somethin' shockin'. Think I heard a terrible scream then. Not sure. Think she hit me again. Then she stopped. But I don't know what happened next. Think I went out into the back alley. Meant to get help. Really did, Harry! Can you forgive me? Not the man you are, y' see? Don't cope with getting wounded. Think I passed out somewhere. Next thing I can remember I'm in the hospital, but that fades in and out. First thing I truly remember is being in the workhouse. So sorry, Harry. So sorry."

Pip wanted to hug them both. Harry had his head in his hands, and although he had his face hidden she knew he was crying over the fact that Gus thought he needed to apologise. And poor Gus. What an awful thing to have happen! She went and gave Gus a quick hug first, then joined Harry on the small sofa which had been put in the Colmans' spare room for Gus' use.

"You have nothing to apologise for, Gus," she said firmly, but trying to sound kindly at the same time. "Never think that! We know just how awful Natalie could be. To my certain knowledge you're the third man she tried to kill and the only one to survive. This was no weak woman you took on but a cold killer, and I for one am very glad you chose to retreat so that you lived to be here now."

"Thank you kindly," Gus said with wobbling lips, "but what distresses me beyond any words I can find is Amy. How could she do that to her own son? Ever since you told me there was a body in my room in my clothes..." and he broke down. "What curse is on my family for that to happen?"

Now Harry looked up, damp-eyed, and shaken. "Christ on the Cross! Oh dear God I hadn't thought that through until now! Amy killed her own son. She killed Eddie! That's why I haven't been able to find him! He's in the grave with your name on! But why? Why do that? She *loved* little Eddie! *Adored* him!"

Pip sighed. "Now listen to me you two! Stop blaming yourselves! If there's anyone to blame it's Natalie!"

"No," Harry said, shaking his head. "No, Pip. Evil though she may be, for once this can't be blamed on her."

"Oh yes it bloody well can!" Pip said forcefully. "Listen! Even now Amy is half off her head on laudanum! Who did that? Not her! She wouldn't know where to go to get enough of it to get that addicted! Actually she probably wouldn't know where to get it, full-stop! Someone with a lot more cunning than her must have had a stock of the stuff before they got to Hereford, because the local men would surely question someone buying it in those quantities. If you could trace the road back to Bath with a description of Natalie, I bet every apothecary – or chemist, or whatever you call them now – will say they sold some to her. She wanted Amy as compliant and barely lucid as possible right from the start for her plan to work to get Gus' money. I think at the last she overplayed her hand, though. She went wrong because she couldn't resist the chance to pervert one more young man. She had to play the Magna Mater one more time!

"Well it came back and bit her! Poor Amy was so far out of her tree, so befuddled in her hallucinating, drugged state, that she didn't know who Eddie was. Remember what you said Gus? That he'd changed from when you last saw him? Was that the last time Amy would have seen him too?"

Gus sniffed but sat up a bit straighter in the wing chair. "I do believe so, yes."

"Right," Pip said firmly, "and was he much changed? I know you wouldn't have seen much in the short time between you getting into the room and Natalie attacking you, but in that short time what did you see?"

"He was taller and fatter," Gus said with a sniff, but the sniff was more reflex than decent into despair again.

"Was he like you in the face?"

Gus thought for a second but then gave a half shake of the head. "Not so very much. His hair was a bit darker than mine – too much sun in India for me, y' see. But he had Edward's sharper features comin'. Still too much the boy yet. But not my snub nose, and the start of Edward's stronger brow in the boy's round face."

He and Harry were now listening intently to Pip as she said, "Then can't you see that if you imagine you were drunk, really drunk so that everything is blurred, that Eddie might just look like someone pretending to be *Edward*? Do you see what I mean? I've only spoken to Amy in bits, but I know she refers to both her husband and her son as 'Eddie'. If she was so hazy as to barely know what day of the week it was, maybe she thought she was being haunted by some horrible travesty of Edward's ghost? Not her son but her *dead husband*! And in that wreck of her mind she might even have some knowledge that Edward was unfaithful to her back when he was alive. She might not ever admit it out loud, but maybe someone – even that awful Clifford sister-in-law you told me about, Harry – might have got a malicious joy out of telling Amy about that. But you have to allow for all of that being filtered through the haze of the massive amounts of laudanum Natalie was feeding her."

"She was all over the place, now you remind me," Gus said more calmly than he'd been since they'd found him. "Ever since we got back to Worcestershire it had been comin' on. And she was gettin' worse. I thought she was puttin' it on. Workin' herself up to some grand tantrum beyond any I'd seen before. I confess I was lookin' forward to leavin'! Hopin' I could get away before the storm broke. I never thought it was the poppy! Saw that in India, y' know, dear Pip. Most astute of you to spot it! There was a major's wife who got addicted and it addled her brain. Bless me, that was just how Amy was! I just never saw it!"

"Don't be hard on yourself, Gus," Pip consoled him. "With someone who had tantrums as regularly as Amy, you would've been hard-pressed to know the difference if it came on gradually."

Harry cleared his throat. "I think you might be the closest to the truth, Pip. Amy always worshipped Edward. She could see no wrong in him. It became an obsession. And she'd not spent enough time with the real Edward to actually know him – her husband was a man of her imagination, which probably even extended to how he looked after all those years. She'd made him into her own personal saint, and she was as devout as any nun. If she thought someone was desecrating his memory she would have been incensed. Furious beyond words."

"Exactly!" Pip said. "*That's* why the stab wounds were so many and so shallow! It was precisely what the coroner said it was – a frenzied attack by someone not in their right mind! Think of how Natalie was with Robert. He had several cuts, but they were done with calm purpose, all done to get plenty of bleeding. Controlled! And those on Robert were *cuts*, not stabs! And on Paul – he bled to death because he never got help and Natalie had wanted to get the maximum amount of bleeding from him, but it was controlled. She would never have gone at someone wildly like that. I should have seen that even if you didn't. But don't think for one minute that makes her innocent of this terrible crime. She wanted Amy compliant and never doubt, Gus, that she was planning to have you dead and the blame thrown at Harry's door. She was too pat with her story when it happened faster than she expected. Far too quick off the mark with her lies! Natalie had to have had that worked out already. All that happened was that she brought her plan forward.

"And Gus, don't blame yourself for not being stronger. Have you looked at that scar in the mirror yet? ...No? ...Well you should, because I can see two cuts there in that scar. I think the vicious bitch came after you and hit you again. She thought she *had* killed you! And what time did you say this all happened?"

Gus' face twitched into a lopsided grimace as he fought to remember. "About midday on the Wednesday."

"But the alarm wasn't raised until first thing on Thursday!" Harry exclaimed. "Amy said you'd failed to meet her the previous evening!"

Pip was nodding. "And that makes all the more sense of it! Don't you see? Natalie hits Gus a second time with what she thinks is the killer stroke, then realises that something's going terribly wrong up in the room. She tears back up the stairs and finds a blood-soaked Amy, and Eddie dead in the bed. Well she's planned on one corpse but not two! So something has to be done. She gets Eddie untied, then when it's dark gets Amy back to her house. I shudder to think how much laudanum she must have given Amy to keep her quiet for that long! My best guess at the rest is that she paid some rough men to cart your body away, Gus. There was no way she could get your body back up to the room on her own, so she was forced to leave Eddie there and get rid of you, because at least she could pretend you were just some beggar off the streets. She probably intended you to be thrown into the river. You were found in just your underclothes, so I suspect she cut you out of your clothes and they went onto a fire somewhere, so you wouldn't be identifiable.

"Meanwhile the men she used realised you were alive. They might even have taken her money and then decided they didn't want to be involved in something as illegal as murder. Whatever the true state of affairs were between her attacking you and you waking at the hospital we shall probably never know. Maybe they were even the ones who took you to the hospital saying they found you wandering by the cathedral. I don't think that's too far from what's possible. In the meantime Natalie gets Amy cleaned up, and she's had so much bloody laudanum she's forgotten the attack. That's become some bad dream in the night. But she's still hazy enough, and primed enough by Natalie, that when she's asked who might have killed 'Gus' she names you, Harry. And she's genuinely distraught over your death, Gus, because she doesn't associate the person whom she killed with you. In the chaos in her head they're two totally separate events. Eddie's death becomes the nightmare premonition, and yours becomes the unexpected reality."

It took the rest of the day for them to come to terms with the reconstruction, but the following day Harry had another thought.

"Gus should have control of his money back," he fretted. "I can't take it off him now!"

And so Sir Arthur was summoned once more and the strange facts presented to him.

"What do you wish to do about Mrs Clifford?" he said at the end.

"If you mean a prosecution," Pip answered for herself and Harry, "I don't think there's much point. She doesn't remember a thing. It's all gone, lost in a drug-fuelled haze. I'm not convinced we can even tell her what she did and that her son is dead by her own hand. Coming on top of the withdrawal from the drug, she might suffer a heart-attack or a stroke from the shock – because I fear it will be a shock. And she's safe where she is. Without Natalie Parsons around to create havoc, Amy on her own is no threat to anyone anymore."

Sir Arthur had made his own enquiries and had also concluded that Mrs Parsons had quit the country, although he could never have guessed quite how. "She'd said she had some relatives over towards the Welsh Borders," he told the family, "although we couldn't trace them. My guess is she's gone to Ireland as the quickest escape route, and from there she'll go either to the Americas or to Europe."

It was therefore agreed that Sir Arthur would have quiet words with those with the power to change things, and get control of Gus' money back into his own hands. Yet Gus was strangely unhappy about that.

"I don't feel safe alone anymore," he confessed to Harry. "Could I not come and live by you? Not in your house. You and Pip should have your privacy. But close! *Very* close, *please*."

Harry was rather worried about telling Pip that – it sounded a touch too much like volunteering her into a nursing role, and she'd not been keen on that even as a fictional role when they'd been creating her new life. However, Pip had instantly reassured him.

"No, that's fine!" she said with a warm smile. "I'd been thinking we should keep Gus close, myself. The poor man isn't right by a long way."

"But where should we live?" Harry fretted. "He seems worried in the towns, but I don't want to cut you off in the depths of the country, and Flora would be distraught if she couldn't see you regularly now she's become so fond of you. And I feel bad having promised you a trip to Scotland, because we won't be doing that for a while, either."

"Oh we'll get to Scotland eventually, don't worry," she responded airily. "But as to where we'll live, what about Malvern? There's going to be a major scientific discovery soon, and that will bring a whole new means of transport into being. They'll be steam powered and be called railways. Once that happens, Malvern will become really popular as a spa town. If we buy now we'll get a nice house which will only appreciate in value. And the town will gradually grow around us, so Gus can grow into the idea of more people around us."

"And it's only a short ride away," mused Harry. "Yes, I would like Malvern, and I don't think the family would be too upset by that. I think they were thinking of St John's, mind you."

Pip grinned, "Yes, but the houses there at the moment are too few for any decent selection to be on the market, and most are a bit grand for our budget! Until I saw it in the here and now I don't think I'd realised how much it will expand in the next fifty years or so. The Vaughans really came down in the world, didn't they?"

"Oh yes, and that gives me another excuse. If we're to have Gus living with us, then St John's is too painful for him. Too many memories."

In the end they found a pair of goodly sized semi-detached cottages in what Pip knew would one day be Malvern Link. One day they would be demolished to make way for other houses on Pickersleigh Road, but not yet, and Pip loved the view over the common. However her keenest pleasure came from the day when they moved Gus into his cottage. Pip had insisted on sorting him out furniture first, and decorating the place with some of the lovely things he'd brought back from India.

They led him in with his eyes closed then told him to open them.

"Oooh!" he gasped. "Oh this is so beautiful! Like a nabob's palace! Where did you get such things from? Dearest Pip you haven't spent all this on me, have you?"

She and Harry laughed with delight.

"No Gus," Harry said gently, "this was all yours already. You brought all this back in trunks."

"Did I? 'Pon my soul! Don't remember that at all!"

"Well you did," Pip assured him. "All I did was unpack it and put the things I thought would go together in the same rooms."

"You mean there's more?"

With childlike wonder Gus wandered through his new home giving gasps of delight at every room.

"And what's your house like?" he asked when they were sat in the cosy sitting room at last.

"Ah, that's not quite done yet," Pip admitted. "We shall be sleeping there from now on so that we'll be only a call away if you need us. But apart from the bedroom there's still decorating to be done."

However, Harry was more than pleased with what she achieved in their house. In truth he would have been uncomfortable with riot of colour which filled Gus' house. Their house was much more subtle, filled with softer shades and more restraint. And the first evening they spent in their parlour, watching the sun setting over the Malvern Hills, he thought life couldn't get much better than this, for in the midst of all of the arranging they had kept one important appointment.

On December the twenty-first they had travelled once more to Cold Hunger Farm, leaving Gus in George and Flora's care overnight. Once more Pip had come armed with a bag from the local butcher, and sloshed it against the glass of the mirror. This time the portal opened but not fully. She could make out Nick and hear his voice, but the image was fuzzy, and when she pressed her hand against the glass it was jelly-like but resisting the pressure.

"It's fine, Nick. I'm not coming back," she told him happily. "Look!" and she waved her wedding ring at him.

"I know," he said with more of a relaxed smile and held up a photocopy of an old paper. "I read about the wedding! Sounded like a big event!"

"It was!"

"What are you doing? Being the perfect housewife?"

Pip pulled a face. "I think it would take more than a shift of a couple of hundred years to achieve that! But before you ask me more, I don't know quite how this is all going to work because we still don't know what Harry's going to do in the long-term. Uncle William is dead set on setting Harry up in business, but we've no idea what sort! We've had a bit of an exciting time you see. Look in the court archives for Augustus Vaughan! There's more to his story than I can tell you now."

Nick looked quizzical. "Okay, Augustus Vaughan, I'll check before I go back up north."

"How's Richard doing?"

"Loving every minute!"

"And you?"

"I've got some teaching and I've got some work on an archaeology magazine – not perfect, but it's a start up there. We bought a kitten. Her name's Pip!"

Pip made mock gagging noises and pulled a funny face. "Oh please! That's too twee for words, Nick! Euw! Did you have to do that to the poor kitty?"

Nick laughed back. "No. Actually it's a male kitten, and he's called Grendel because the little shit has already shredded every curtain in the place!"

"Thank God for that!" Pip sighed, mockingly wiping her brow.

However Nick was also relieved. Her reaction reassured him the Pip was still the same girl at heart. He'd been fretting that the passage through the portal had maybe in some way befuddled Pip to the extent that she was currently simply going along with Harry – believing herself to be in love with him, but not quite herself. But if so there was a danger that in a year or so she might return to her senses and realise what an awful mistake she'd made in staying. Quite what he could have done in that case he wasn't sure – he could hardly go through and haul her back, and that made him more aware of the state of the portal itself.

"Pip, why is the portal not working properly now? We've done nothing different here from the last time."

Pip tilted her head towards Harry. "Someone shot the shit out of a shrine to Cybele and Attis which was in the actual wall of the place! Yes, Nick, an actual Roman shrine here in Herefordshire! If you go round to the south-side where the well was, and take the first layer of brick off at ground level beneath the workshop window, you'll find it. Harry and I had the shrine dismantled, but I've put some key bits into the wall for you to make the 'discovery' with."

"And to make sure the portal still worked?"

Pip laughed, "Well a bit of that as well. I didn't want to destroy it altogether and then find that if we'd done so good a job back in this time, that the portal would never work again. If that happened I might not ever have come back here, you see? We might have destroyed my chances of coming back here when I did, if you follow me – made my own trip back here impossible. No portal, no Harry, no falling through the mirror for me! And who knows what might have happened to me in that moment? I could have gone on as I was getting more and more miserable. We might even not have found Dave's body! Or if the portal only partly worked I might have disappeared, or fallen into a heap of dust in the worst-case scenario. Who knows? All *I* know about time travel is from watching a few episodes of *Dr Who*, and that's not exactly cutting edge science! That was the only argument which worked for Harry, I can tell you! He was all for grinding it into gravel!"

"I can't say I blame him."

Then Pip had another thought. "Have you had any spectacular thunderstorms lately, Nick? That might have shifted the portal a bit, too. I think that was the catalyst the first time I heard Harry's voice here."

He nodded. "As it happens we did have a very unseasonable one a few weeks back. A real cracker. Oh crap, this thing's fading!"

"Then off you go and make your reputation by finding the first full shrine to Attis in Britain!" Pip quipped.

Nick shook his head, smiling but still becoming upset at the thought of their permanent parting. "I shall miss you so much, Pip."

"Take care Nick. Watch for news in the old papers! Love you loads. Hugs to Richard."

"And you Pip. Love you too!"

The mirror turned back to silver, leaving only the reflection of Pip standing arm in arm with Harry. She turned to him with a happy smile.

"No regrets?" he asked, still just a touch wary of what the effect of saying goodbye might have on her.

However Pip shook her head firmly. "None! ...I know you've worried about how I'll feel cutting the last link with the world I grew up in. And yes, Nick and Richard were the closest thing I had to family, but I still might have lost contact with them if they'd decided to move to somewhere like Australia or Canada. No-one can predict the future that well, even in my time, but in a way I can now. I know what the greater future holds for people of this time, but most importantly, Harry, I have you. I had nothing to compare to that before. Never in a million years could I have imagined what I was getting into on the day I agreed to join Nick's dig, but I'm so glad I did!"

"Shall we go home, then?"

Pip turned and looked one last time at the old mirror. "Yes, time to go home!"

Historical Notes

There's no Cold Hunger Farm around Clifton-upon-Teme, but there is a Cold Hunger Plantation, from which I took the name. Also, the inhabitants of Clifton in this book are entirely fictional and based on no real people. However, there are several farmhouses in the immediate vicinity which are half-timbered with brick in-fill, and which are Listed Buildings, the details of which can be found online. None of them, though, have a Roman shrine built into the side!

The cult of Cybele and Attis is as murky as it is possible to get. Cybele was an eastern European fertility goddess, and anyone visiting the archaeological site of Ostia – the old port of ancient Rome – will find a huge open *campo* dedicated to the Magna Mater. So far that's not so unusual, and Cybele was equated with Juno and with Ceres and incorporated into the Roman pantheon. Rather stranger is the Sanctuary of Attis within the *campo* at Ostia, with its two forbidding representations of Pan standing guard on either side of the doorway. The book cover image of the shrine is taken from this place.

Attis was a shepherd god from Phrygia (or Frigia as it's sometimes spelt) which was the central part of Anatolia in modern day Turkey, and who – according to legend – having been unfaithful to Cybele, castrated himself in a fit of remorse. He then set the model for Cybele's most fanatical male adherents, who would self-castrate as an act of dedication! The description of the castration clamp I have used is of one actually found in the Thames, so Attis' cult certainly got as far as Roman Britain, and the rowdiness of the followers is attested in at least one contemporary source. If Cybele herself was acceptable to the Romans, those following Attis weren't! And as might be guessed, the early Christian writers were vocal in their disgust at such practices!

The story of the fire on board the *Kent* is all too true, and it went on to become hailed as a celebrated example of courage in desperate circumstances. All the names of those on board the *Kent* are real, although the otherwise anonymous Captain R T Green who is listed as being amongst the company, I have taken the liberty of renaming Harry and giving him a whole new life. (I hope that if anyone is a descendant of that Captain Green they will forgive me for rewriting history, and aren't too disappointed with the man I've created. And although Clifton-upon-Teme has a rectory, Harry's family as its rectors are completely fictitious.)

Of those who remained on board the *Kent* after the brig *Cambria* pulled away, some did die when it finally exploded, being too drunk to save themselves by climbing into the boats. However the vast majority of the *Kent*'s passengers were saved and the remarkable survival numbers are true. The last officers to leave the *Kent* were Colonel Fearon, Major MacGregor, Lieutenants Ruxton, Booth and Evans, and the ship's captain, Cobb; however I have taken the liberty of adding Harry Green to their number as a remaining army captain although the real Captain Green was no doubt already on board the *Cambria*. Anyone wanting to read more on the *Kent* should read *The Miracle of The Kent* by Nicholas Tracy.

I have tried to make the descriptions of the cities and towns of the early nineteenth century as accurate as possible – any mistakes are unintentional. St John's was already a suburb of Worcester and had been for many years as is attested by its lovely Norman church, but in the early nineteenth century it was still very rural, and populated with a few rather grand houses and some cottages. Pitmaston House now houses part of the local authority education service, and its grounds are a local park.

The development on the city side of the river, which soon would become the incredible elegant Britannia Square, was just starting to be built in the mid-1820s. However for the most part the city didn't extend into what is now the Tything at that time, with the focus of the city still up around the cathedral area.

Prior to the Poor Law of 1834, Hereford had three workhouses in each of three parishes – All Saints, St John's, and one in Quaker's Lane (now Friars Street) – but at the time of John Price writing his history of Hereford in 1796, the main one was All Saint's situated beyond Eign-gate, which is where I have Harry and Pip making their discovery. This was not the same building which now remains in the city, converted to a very different use, which was built in the late 1830s. As a whole Hereford had still not extended much beyond its medieval limits at the time of this story, although that would soon be changing.

And finally, if you get chance to volunteer on a local dig, go for it – you might not end up in another time, but it is great fun!

Thank you for taking the time to read this book.

I hope you would like to read other books like this, and the fastest way to do that is to sign up to my mailing list. I promise I won't bombard you with endless emails, but I would like to be able to let you know when any new books come out, or of any special offers I have on the existing ones.

Go to ljhutton.com to find the link

If you sign up, I will send the first in a fantasy series for free, but also other free goodies, some of which you won't get anywhere else!

Also, if you've enjoyed this book you personally (yes, *you*) can make a big difference to what happens next.

Reviews are one of the best ways to get other people to discover my books. I'm an independent author, so I don't have a publisher paying big bucks to spread the word or arrange huge promos in bookstore chains, there's just me and my computer.

But I have something that's actually better than all that corporate money – it's you, enthusiastic readers. Honest reviews help bring them to the attention of other readers (although if you think something needs fixing I would really like you to tell me first!). So if you've enjoyed this book, it would mean a great deal to me if you would spend a couple of minutes posting a review on the site where you purchased it.

Also by L. J. Hutton:

Time's Bloodied Gold

Standing stones built into an ancient church, a lost undercover detective and a dangerous gang trading treasures from the past. Can Bill Scathlock save his friend's life before his cover gets blown?

DI Bill Scathlock thought he'd seen the last of his troubled DS, Danny Sawaski, but he wasn't expecting him to disappear altogether! The Polish gang Danny was infiltrating are trafficking people to bring ancient artefacts to them, but those people aren't the usual victims, and neither is where they're coming from. With archaeologist friend Nick Robbins helping, Bill investigates, but why do people only appear at the old church, and who is the mad priest seen with the gang? With Danny's predicament getting ever more dangerous, the clock is ticking if Bill is to save him before he gets killed by the gang ...or arrested by his old colleagues!

The Rune House

A detective haunted by a past case, a house with a sinister secret, and a missing little girl! Can DI Ric Drake rescue her and find redemption along the way?

When DS Merlin 'Robbie' Roberts hears he's got a new colleague it's the last thing he wants, and especially when it's Ric Drake – infamous, recovering from a heart attack and refusing retirement. But when a modern missing child case links to one from Ric's past, and to a mysterious old house on the Welsh borders, they find a common cause. Do the ancient bodies discovered under a modern one hold the clue to both girls' fate, and does the house itself hold the key? As the links to the past keep getting stronger, Robbie and Drake must find a way to break the strange link before more children fall prey to Weord Manor's ancient lure.

Printed in Great Britain
by Amazon